PICTURE *Imperfect*

A SASSY SUSPENSE

"Cindy Procter-King presents readers with a suspenseful snapshot of a romantic comedy… loaded with humor, this is a must-read."

— NIGHT OWL REVIEWS ON PICTURE IMPERFECT

"Cindy Procter-King is a master storyteller. Not only do her characters invite the readers into the drama, the humor is non-stop. Comedy is a hard genre to write but Cindy Procter-King does it easily."

— THE ROAD TO ROMANCE ON HEAD OVER HEELS

"What a set-up for a comedy of errors! Everything that can go wrong in this scenario does go wrong, and the reader is well entertained by the comedic chaos."

— FALLEN ANGEL REVIEWS ON HEAD OVER HEELS

"I really enjoyed *Borrowing Alex*. It was smart and funny without being overdone. The characters do some pretty funny things in the name of love. I am definitely looking forward to reading the next book I find by Cindy Procter-King."

— JOYFULLY REVIEWED ON BORROWING ALEX

"I really like romantic comedy as a genre, but it takes some really good writing to make me laugh. This book made me laugh."

— FALLEN ANGEL REVIEWS ON BORROWING ALEX

Also by Cindy Procter-King

Love & Other Calamities
Steamy summer wedding romcoms

Deceiving Derek (Book 1)
Catching Claire (Book 2)
Before Brady (Book 3)
Just Janie (Book 4)
Trusting Trey (Book 5)

Love in the Pacific Northwest
Steamy romcoms

Head Over Heels (Book 1)
Borrowing Alex (Book 2)
Getting Over Brett (Book 3)

Destiny Falls
Steamy small town romance

Where She Belongs (Book 1)

For more books and news, please visit Cindy's website:
www.cindyprocter-king.com

PICTURE *Imperfect*

A SASSY SUSPENSE

CINDY PROCTER-KING

Blue Orchard Books

PICTURE IMPERFECT

Copyright © 2016 Cindy Procter-King

Picture Imperfect © 2016 by Cindy Procter-King

Published by Blue Orchard Books

Cover by The Killion Group

ISBN: 978-0-9936794-2-1

Digital: 978-0-9936794-3-8

For Steve, Ben, and A.J. I love you all.

And for Allie. Because every dog should have a book dedicated to her, and at "14 going on 15," she insists it be this one. (Actually, she's insisting on the next one, too. We'll see. I'm no pushover).

One

IF URSULA SCOTT had to look at one more naked man, she'd scream.

Loud and long.

Case in point, the cocky fifty-year-old adjusting his thong as he trundled toward the photography studio's tiny dressing room.

Shuddering, Ursula turned away. Okay, the guy wasn't *totally* nude but close enough. Their session was a memory she could live without. As were several appointments from this morning.

She lifted the camera strap over her head and carefully set her professional Nikon on the prop table. Behind her, the dressing room door clicked shut. Ursula narrowed her gaze.

Damn her boss, Victor McKenzie, hiding in his office. It didn't take a Mensa membership to figure out what he was up to—avoiding the questionable applicants responding to the model ad *he'd* placed in a Seattle print and online newspaper.

After the recent rash of vandalism the studio had experienced, Ursula really needed something in her life to run smoothly. Was it asking too much for that thing to be the test shots for her first magazine photo spread?

She spun her silver thumb ring. Six months from now, in May, she would buy Mackie's studio. Every assignment she completed in the interim would cement her chances of building a profitable business and assisting her parents with their massive debt. Her dad wouldn't accept her help any other way. Neither would her mom. Ursula needed to secure her future first, they said. No, insisted. And she was trying! With everything in her.

But sometimes working for Victor McKenzie, once a talented photographer whose industry contacts would transfer to her with the sale, tested her last nerve.

At a scuffing sound, she glanced toward the hall door. Stacy, the part-time receptionist, scurried in carrying the pumpkin-spiced latte Ursula had requested from the coffee shop next door. No foam, extra-hot.

Stacy handed over the latte, and Ursula's fingertips stung as she grasped the cardboard cup.

"Sorry I'm late." Stacy adjusted her black-rimmed glasses. "Eighteen more potential models are waiting to see you. I wrote their info on the appointment sheets, super-legible like you asked. It took a while."

"Thanks. I appreciate it." Ursula refused to treat the night-school student with Mackie's surly brand of disrespect. At twenty, Stacy was eager, organized, and a lifesaver on busy days.

"We're getting tons of calls about the test shots." Stacy pumped a fist. "It's only Wednesday, and we're booking into next week."

Ursula sighed. "We have to draw the line somewhere, Stace. I know *Seattle Lights* asked us to test everyone who responds to the ad, but at this rate we won't narrow the field in time." To accommodate the production window for the magazine's popular Valentine's issue, *Seattle Lights* required the "Real Men, Real Lives, Real Loves" photo spread completed by December. The rush job allowed Ursula two days to finish the preliminary shots and barely two weeks to photograph the eight men the editor would select from a shortlist.

Stacy's eyebrows bunched. "Should I talk to Mackie about it?"

"No. I will later." This morning's applicants weren't Stacy's concern. Leaning forward, Ursula whispered, "Tell me, are they all as sleazy-looking as...?" She nodded toward the changing room, where the thong monster had vanished.

Stacy shook her head, whispering back, "Some actually seem quite normal. And this one guy? I *so* want to take down his info."

"Go on."

"Tall. Six-two or -three," Stacy murmured. "Shoulders like a linebacker. Slim hips, trim waist. I'm thinking awesome abs." She crossed her fingers. "Masses of wavy dark hair. On his head. It's almost black, like yours, but with a rich chestnut brown mixed in. Great butt too. Hot, hot."

"Sounds promising." Ursula sipped her latte, and warmth curled in her tummy. "A variation in attitude is what I'm after. All this strutting around is growing tiresome." She wrinkled her nose.

Stacy giggled. "At least Mackie's letting you run the shoot, Urs. That's major."

Last week, when their boss had dangled the carrot, Ursula would have agreed. After what had felt like eons of toiling at small jobs to improve the studio's bottom line while he lazed around during the year of their agreement, finally the chance had arrived to showcase her skills to a significant client.

However, as she'd learned, Mackie's good deeds usually carried a downside. And *this* one was a doozy. A day after passing her the assignment, he'd let it slip that he'd skipped over obtaining her input on publicizing the call for models featuring the new Real Men angle, which he'd also failed to mention before, and now any dude and his doohickey could saunter in for the test shots.

So much for the *GQ* types Mackie had vowed would pose in front of her camera. Yeah, he was her employer, but how could he *not* pass on the correct information?

She wiped a palm on her jeans. The dressing room door opened, and the thong fellow emerged, wearing a sweater and baggy slacks.

The man shrugged into a jacket. "When will I learn if you're using me?"

"Calls will go out Monday, Mr. Hacklemire. Thanks for coming in." Ursula pasted on a smile until he left. Placing her latte on the table, she told Stacy, "Please send in the next guy. The sooner I complete this round, the sooner I can forget this day ever happened."

"Want the hottie first?" the girl asked, heading out.

"No, it's best to stick with the order of arrival. I wouldn't want to aggravate the mob." Ursula looped the Nikon around her neck. A minute later, as she adjusted lights and flash reflectors, the studio door opened and closed.

"Where do you want me, honey?" A sturdy man sporting a burgundy satin dressing robe stood inside the vast room. Sneakers shod his sock-less feet, and enough coarse black hair to outfit ten shaved monkeys forested his bare shins and partially exposed upper chest. "Name any position you like. I'm very limber." One of his eyebrows drooped in an obscene wink, and he curled his lips in what Ursula assumed he considered a sexy look.

Uh, *nope*.

"It's not just lounge-wear shots," she responded in a cool voice. This guy had shown up at her *place of business* not wearing pants? Unless he'd changed in the studio restroom near her boss's office, he must have.

She was two seconds from losing it!

The man stepped closer, hoisting a gym bag. "I brought my other gear along. Thought we'd start with my best look first."

Repressing the urge to roll her eyes, she accepted his information slip and scanned it. "Make yourself comfortable, Mr. Longfellow." She stacked the paper beneath the cat-shaped paperweight on the table. "I'll take your bag until you need to change for the shirts-on shots." She reached for his pack. *Big* mistake. He dropped the duffel and planted his hands on his hips.

His robe parted to reveal gold satin boxers with a gaping fly.

A gaping, *inhabited* fly.

She gulped, and some movement occurred.

Too much movement occurred.

The creep's creep was creeping out!

He winked again. "Mr. *Longfellow*."

"*What are you doing*?" Ursula flung up her hands, shielding her gaze for a merciful split-second.

"Just making an impact on ya', babe. There's a lot of competition out there."

"I don't care if the Sexiest Man Alive is out there! I'm not taking your picture today. Or ever!"

"I don't get my chance like everyone else?"

"You blew your chance when you perved yourself, buster. Get out of my studio!"

He lifted his hands, and the bathrobe fell closed. "Don't throw a chick-fit. I'm going."

"You bet your shortfellow you are." Ursula policed the dude to the reception area, her camera bumping her abdomen with every stride. Stacy's head popped up from the desk. Ursula escorted the creeper through the noisy throng and out onto the street. Chilly air swept in as she locked the glass door behind him. No way, no *how*, were more scumbags getting in.

She whirled to face the inappropriately dressed men milling around Stacy's desk. The scent of sweaty armpits permeated the air.

"Listen up!" Several heads snapped toward her. She pointed to the door. "If anyone else thinks this is a porno gig, they can leave. 'No-shirts shots' does not mean 'no-sense-of-common-decency shots.' If I see another piece of spandex or satin enter my studio, I'll hit the roof." She was up there already!

"I brought swim trunks. They're nylon," a Vin Diesel look-alike shouted. "That work?"

"Bermudas here!"

"Jeans."

"Sweats."

"Are mankinis made of spandex?"

Ursula clutched her thumping forehead. "I'm taking ten. Everyone clear your wardrobes through Stacy."

She stalked toward the main hall to the right of Reception. The male crowd parted as if she were an ovary-laden Moses commanding the Red Sea. She glimpsed linebacker shoulders and chestnut hair as she stormed past, but she wasn't in the mood for sightseeing. Right now, she didn't give a crap about anything but ripping off Mackie's head.

The heels of her shoes thundered on the worn linoleum. "Mackie!" She shoved his door. *Stuck.* She shoulder-rammed it. The old doorknob sprang loose, and she pushed inside the cluttered horror of Victor McKenzie's office.

Tinny music blared from a prehistoric transistor radio topping the bookshelf beneath the blind-drawn window. Mackie sat behind his gigantic desk, chomping a submarine sandwich.

Apparently, he wasn't the only one enjoying a snack. Red spiked pumps poked out from beneath the desk bottom. A female voice cooed, praising his proportions.

Ursula's stomach roiled. *Oh, God, not Jasmine?* His latest girlfriend.

She stepped back. "Sorry!" Really, really, *really* sorry.

The sandwich dropped to the desk. "Ursula? What the hell?" Mackie jumped up, hands scrambling for his zipper—and Ursula uttered a prayer of thanks that he wasn't a tall man.

A bonking sound echoed beneath the desk. "Ow, my head."

Ursula raced into the hall, camera bouncing. "Mackie, lock your door!" She slammed it shut.

"It was!" His gruff voice blasted through the partition.

"Then fix it. With a deadbolt."

"Don't be so judgmental! You never heard of Hump Day?"

Gabe McKenzie clenched his jaw against the dull ache from his injury gripping his ass. After seven years with the LAPD, rowdy crowds shouldn't rile him, but the scene in his low-life uncle's photography studio rivaled anything he'd experienced in California.

"Do you mind giving a guy some room?" Nudging a fellow in frayed jean shorts, Gabe signaled the girl at the reception desk. He'd returned to Seattle three days ago and had a physical therapy appointment this afternoon he couldn't miss. If his mom hadn't begged him to check out vandalism and threats at her brother-in-law's studio, Gabe wouldn't have ventured *near* Victor McKenzie Photography.

He signaled the girl again. Her attention remained riveted to the men clustered around her desk.

Gabe shook his head. Forget a polite request. He'd follow the raven-haired photographer who'd shouted his uncle's name as she'd charged down the main corridor moments ago, camera bobbing.

Moving slowly so he wouldn't strain his stiff right glute, Gabe passed around the corner and into a hall decorated with framed portraits. The photographer strode toward him now, her dark eyebrows furrowed. Behind her, an office door rattled on squeaking hinges.

Spotting him, she stopped dead in her tracks. "You shouldn't be back here."

"I need to see Vic."

She winced. "He's with someone."

"Then I'll wait. Here. But I won't return to that zoo." Gabe jabbed a thumb toward the waiting room.

"You don't have a choice, Mr.—"

"Gabe."

Her frown eased. In fact, for an instant, her full mouth tipped into an expression someone desperate for affection might mistake for a smile.

"I'm sorry, Gabe. Seeing Mr. McKenzie won't bump you to the head of the line. I'm in charge of the Real Men shoot, not him."

"I'm not here to have my picture taken." With a practiced eye honed by years on the job, Gabe catalogued her appearance in three heartbeats: around twenty-five, straight black hair hanging past her shoulders, white blouse tucked into jeans, chunky belt. Thick lashes framed dark blue eyes he wouldn't mind waking up to. Her left thumb sported a thick ring of hammered silver, the right pinky a slim gold band. What his salon-obsessed desk sergeant in Los Angeles would call a French manicure highlighted long fingernails that could easily emasculate a guy were he dumb enough to land on her bad side.

And this photographer no doubt *had* a bad side.

Man, even ticked off, she was stunning.

"Vic McKenzie is my uncle," he said.

Her gaze zipped over him. "You're kidding."

Gabe didn't require psychic abilities to read her mind—no family resemblance whatsoever. Vic stood maybe five-six, with a belly as round as a giant panda's. His hook nose, brown eyes, and olive skin bore traces of his Sicilian heritage.

"My dad was his brother," Gabe explained. "My grandparents adopted Vic as a toddler."

"Oh." Ursula looked confused.

"Vic isn't so bad. In small doses." Once a decade would suit this nephew. "I can't imagine it's a thrill working for him though."

She snorted. "Now you understand my problem." She lifted a hand. "Sorry. Gabe, I don't want to insult your uncle, but I'm having a horrible day. Someone screwed up the model ad for the magazine shoot, and I'm pretty sure it was Mackie. We wanted everyday Joes, so the state of their bodies isn't the issue. It's the state of their undress." She cringed.

"Undress?"

"The shorts. The tightie-whities. The thongs. The ad was supposed to read 'shirts off,' not 'leave your inhibitions at home.' Your uncle is lucky I'm not quitting here and now." She twirled her gold pinky ring. "But I *can't* quit, which he well knows."

"Look. I understand your frustration with my uncle, Ms.—"

"Scott. Ursula Scott."

"I really do need to see him. I promised my mom."

Her gaze lingered on the old T-shirt he wore beneath a battered leather jacket. She rested a hand on her large camera lens. "If you're Mackie's nephew, why haven't we met before?" she asked, looking him in the eyes. "I've worked here since May."

That deep, mesmerizing blue reached inside him. "Just moved back to town. Vic and I aren't close, but he's tight with my mom." Who kindly ignored the seedy aspects of her brother-in-law's life. The strip joints and endless women. Vic had placed Gabe's mom on a pedestal for as long as Gabe remembered. Vic remained on his best behavior around her, and she treated him like a younger brother. Her last link to Gabe's dad.

"Can you help me out?" he asked the photographer.

She chewed the inside of her cheek, mouth twisting. "The thing is, I'm not sure when he'll be free. Like I said, he's in a meeting."

The office door opened. A late-thirties blond woman in a neon-pink mini-skirt, orange jean jacket, spiked red heels, and layers of makeup pranced out. Ursula glanced over her shoulder as the new arrival sashayed toward them.

The woman dug into her purse. "He's all yours," she said to Ursula, juggling a lipstick and retrieving a small mirror. She opened the mirror, pushed out her bottom lip like a fish going for a lure, and smeared on bright pink lip color. She beamed at Gabe. "Hi. I'm Jasmine, Mackie's girlfriend."

"Hi. Gabe. Nephew."

"Cool."

"Sorry for barging in on you," Ursula muttered to Jasmine, avoiding the woman's gaze.

"That's okay. I was taking an early lunch." Jasmine returned her stuff to her purse. "Oh." Her long fingers danced on Ursula's upper arm. "Before I forget, Mackie says Brinley's Hardware sells the best deadbolts. He wants you to get that Stacy girl to buy him a new one."

Ursula's gaze flashed. "He can tell her himself. Unbelievable."

"He's a little busy right now."

"Oh, yeah?" Red flared high on Ursula's cheeks. "Well, I'm a whole lot *disgusted* right now. With him. You know, Jasmine, if you like being Mackie's carrier pigeon so much, feel free to tell him that I'm returning to the studio to finish today's test shots. It's not the fault of the men waiting in Reception if the ad got royally messed up. *Then* I'm heading home. For the rest of the day. And maybe the rest of the year." Her voice rose. "If Mackie wants me to finish this shoot, he needs to come up with some fantastic incentive. I want my name listed on the photo credits, not his. I want complete creative control."

Jasmine blinked. "How can I tell him all that? I don't understand half of what you said."

"Forget it. I don't expect you to remember anything." Ursula's eyes closed. "Jasmine, I apologize. It's my issue, not yours. I'll tell him."

"I'll mention the deadbolt," Gabe assured the woman.

"Great. I gotta go." Jasmine spun on her skyscraper heels and strutted toward a rear exit.

Clutching her camera, Ursula marched toward the waiting room at the front of the building.

"You're welcome," Gabe called after her.

She continued walking. "For what?"

"For thanking me for offering to speak to my uncle about the deadbolt."

She stopped. "I don't remember *asking* you to do anything." She strode on.

Gabe grinned. The way her ass wiggled... Had she guessed he liked its sexy curves and size? The perfect amount for his hands to—

Probably best if he kept that information to himself.

⚬

Knocking on the office door a second time, Gabe called, "Uncle Vic?"

No reply.

Opening the door, he peeked inside. Vic was asleep in his office chair. Stubby legs propped on the desktop, hairy arms dangling, head thrown back. His mouth gaped as he snored. His shoe nudged a half-eaten submarine sandwich, his lime-green sport shirt boasted hula dancers, and a scrawny ponytail scraped back his thinning salt-and-pepper hair.

Gabe shook his head. What did his mother see in the boor? After all these years, how could she still consider Vic her misguided, but harmless, brother-in-law?

Sore glute protesting, Gabe entered and closed the door. He stepped to the radio and flicked it off. "Uncle Vic?"

"Hunh?" Squinty eyes snapped open. "Whoozat? Doug?"

Gabe's father, dead over a decade.

Every time Gabe returned to Seattle, his mom said how much he and his dad looked alike at the same ages. Gabe spotted the similarities in old snapshots and memories. From the time Gabe was three, when Dad came home for lunch, he would let Gabe wear his police hat or sit in his cruiser. During Gabe's teen years, his buddies admired the tough-but-fair cop.

Gabe would never stop missing his dad. He'd grown up wanting to emulate him. Had followed in his footsteps when choosing a career. More than anything, he'd wanted to make his dad proud.

"It's Gabe, your nephew." He limped to the guest chair and sat.

Vic stretched, and his stocky legs slid off the desk. "Right." Then, as if realizing he hadn't sounded overjoyed, he added, "Good to see ya'. When'd you get in?"

"Sunday. My stuff is in storage until I find a place. I'm staying with Mom in the meantime."

Vic bit into the sub. "Finally had enough of LA, huh?" he asked around a full mouth.

"I think LA has had enough of me."

Vic guffawed, and a soggy bread chunk flew onto the floor. "Yeah, Evie said you caught a bullet in the keister." His expression sobered. "She was plenty broke up about it. Reminded her of Doug."

"I know." Gabe's chest tightened. "She doesn't need more heartache in her life, Uncle Vic. So I'm home for good."

His uncle sucked on the straw of a take-out cup. "How old are you now?"

"Thirty in a few months."

"Kind of young to be out of commission. Although I guess they gave you a huge chunk of change, huh?"

Gabe ignored the question about his medical pension. "I might not feel fast enough to work the streets, but that doesn't mean I'm leaving the life completely. I'm opening a private investigations firm."

"No more brown-nosing the brass. Sounds good," Vic said in his troll-munching-gravel voice. "I never understood how your dad tolerated that shit."

Gabe's shoulders stiffened. "First off, I don't suck up to my bosses. Second, I'd rather not talk about Dad." His father had died a decorated narcotics detective after twenty years with the Seattle City Police Department. His memory deserved Vic's respect.

Vic chucked the remainder of his sandwich in the trashcan. "Whatever." He dusted his hands above his desk. Bread crumbs littered the office files spread over the surface.

"Listen, Uncle Vic—"

"C'mon, kid, don't call me that. 'Uncle Vic' makes me feel like you're ten years old. Call me Mackie, like everyone else."

Gabe stretched his sore leg. "Okay…Mackie. Last night Mom said you've been having some trouble. She mentioned an inert grenade breaking the studio window a month ago?"

His uncle's beady eyes darted away. "Yeahhh."

"Did you report the incident to the police?"

"Of course. How was I to know the grenade was fake? Damn thing could've blown me up."

"The bomb squad came down?"

Vic waved a hand. "Show-offs. They couldn't tell if the grenade was fake by standing around and gawking at it, so they brought in the bomb dog and a bunch of experts. Caused a big brouhaha."

Gabe nodded. Many army surplus stores sold de-milled grenades as novelty items. While most of the units featured mangled or drilled bottoms, it was easy enough to reshape and camouflage the affected area with modeling clay and paint. Someone who knew what they were doing might even weld the holes and reactivate the units with explosive fillers and homemade fuses. No halfway competent bomb tech would rely on sight recognition to determine whether the grenade that had busted his uncle's studio window posed a threat.

"What did they find?" he asked.

His uncle—*Mackie*—frowned. "Why do you care?"

"Mom's worried."

"That Evie. So sweet." Mackie crossed his arms. "Some jerk-off stuck masking tape over the hole and painted it to make it look real enough. No fingerprints, no witnesses. Not even a security camera. The one next door went on the fritz, and the coffee shop farts wasted time 'researching options'"—he air-quoted—"before deciding to spring for an updated model. Won't get installed for three weeks. I relied on that camera. Pissed me off."

"You don't have your own security equipment?" Why was Gabe not surprised? His uncle was a tightwad from way back.

"I got lights in the alley," Mackie said. "No camera. No witnesses. Cops bellyached about both. Damn fools are useless. In the end, they said the fake grenade was probably kids getting their jollies. What do they know?"

Gabe ignored his uncle's cop rant. He was here because of his mom. "I saw a banger-type T-shirt shop next door." To the left of the studio. A coffee shop occupied the space to the right. "Do teens hang around there?"

"Yeah. Usually they ain't buying no T-shirts. They use the place as a pissing ground, the snot-nosed punks."

"What about on Halloween? Mom said you found hostile words and images painted on the waiting room display window the next morning. Something about your short and worthless life, she recalls."

Mackie rolled back his chair. "I shouldn't have worried Evie. I'll call and say I'm sorry I bothered her."

"It's too late, Uncle Vic. You told her. She knows."

"Yeah, but—"

Gabe peered at his uncle. "Tell me you reported the painted window."

"Like I'd give the cops the satisfaction! Dopes couldn't find their asses with both hands and a headlight. They found out squat about the grenade. Why would I ask them to look into some stupid graffiti that didn't hurt anyone?"

"Did you take pictures at least?" Without a witness or evidence, there was nothing the Seattle police could do.

Gabe's uncle stood. "*No.* I can see where you're going with this, kid, and it's not happening. No pictures and no calling the cops about those dumb paintings. Not then or now. I cleaned the window so my clients wouldn't see that crap. That's the last I want to hear about it."

Gabe shrugged. "It's your funeral."

Mackie grinned. "Not yet." He paused. "Your mother's really worried about me?"

"That's why I'm here."

"I guess I should have kept my mouth shut." He rubbed his palms together. "Well. Now you're home. That'll make her happy. I'm sure my troubles are over. You know, we should celebrate with a family dinner. I'll phone Evie—"

"Hold on. I met your photographer, Ursula." Gabe described the chaos in the front office. "She thinks there was some sort of problem with a model ad, and it's bringing in the wrong people."

"St. Peter on a pecker! Just when a guy thinks he can take it easy." Mackie stomped to the bookshelf and whisked a folded newspaper off a messy pile. "The ad's in the *Clarion*. Entertainment section. A big boxed ad. I shelled out for their website too, but a real paper shows class."

"Which client wants the pictures of the guys?" Gabe asked as his uncle cleared desk clutter and flattened the newspaper.

"*Seattle Lights* magazine. There's so much internet competition these days that the mag is trying a new direction with their annual pictorial. They didn't want to out themselves in the ad, so I placed it under the studio's name."

"Did you phone in the ad or fill out a website form?"

Mackie flipped pages. "Where is it?" He looked up. "Uh, no. I was gonna do it, but I had Stacy call them instead. She's the other girl. Part time." He turned more pages. "I don't believe this. It's not here. Crap almighty! I knew I should've done it myself."

"I'll look." Gabe stepped in front of his uncle and riffled through a local newspaper distributed three times a week.

Mackie paced the office, grabbing the take-out cup and slurping the contents before tossing the container into the garbage. The aromas of spicy deli meat and mustard drifted from the trashcan. "Find anything?" he asked.

"Not yet. Maybe Stacy put it in Classifieds." Gabe continued searching. "Why not advertise in the daily paper? You'd have greater circulation and exposure."

"Haven't you heard? Inflation, kid. I'm cutting back."

"Uh-huh." *Cheapskate.* "Plenty of online places are free."

"Class, kid, class. The magazine wanted a print paper. They didn't specify which."

A moment later, Gabe looked up. "Found it. In the Personals."

"What the f—?"

Gabe lifted the page. "See? A simple ad. No box, no bold print. Do you remember the wording?"

"Why?"

"Because this ad says…" Gabe read aloud, *"Looking for Real Men. Do you have what it takes to satisfy me? I want you in my spread."* He shook his head. Who would write this junk? *"Big, short, small. Long, skinny, tall. Photographs mandatory, clothing optional. Surprise me. Call Stacy at 555-0182. Victor McKenzie Photography. We'll make you famous."*

Mackie's bushy eyebrows pitched downward. He yanked open a drawer and flung a sheet of paper at Gabe. "Here's the *real* ad."

Gabe set down the newspaper and skimmed the ad copy, which called for everyday dudes to participate in a Valentine's Day pictorial. *"Models,"* he read, *"must feel comfortable posing without shirts for this tasteful series of photographs."*

"Comfortable, not freaking porn freaks!"

"Someone seriously screwed up." Gabe ran a thumb along his jaw. "Maybe on purpose."

"Not *someone*, you deadbeat. Stacy. She called in the ad." Mackie pawed a hand over his sparse hair. "Now I have to arrange a retraction. Damn it to hell." He snatched the office phone receiver. "I'm gonna ream her out something good."

Gabe punched the disconnect button. "Not so fast."

Two

"NOW WHAT?" his uncle barked.

"There's something else we need to discuss," Gabe replied calmly, placing the ad copy on the open newspaper. "Mom said she called you Friday about me coming home, and you mentioned receiving a dirty drawing in the mail. Something about porn lovers dying a slow death. It scared the hell out of her, Uncle Vic."

Swearing, Mackie hung up the phone. "Yeah. Evie pried that information out of me. I didn't want to burden her, but she could tell I was upset. *I* don't photograph porn. Stylish boudoir shots every now and then—"

"Where's the note?" Gabe interrupted.

"Shredded. I know, I know, it was a dumbhead move, but the thing made me nervous. Freaky penmanship. Like whoever wrote it was disturbed."

"Did you recognize the handwriting?"

"No, smart guy. If I had, I would've known who'd done it."

Gabe gazed at his uncle. "Careful with the insults, and consider what I'm saying. You had four incidents occurring in a month. You reported one and destroyed the evidence for two others." He tapped the newspaper. "This fourth incident reads like an audition for a skanky skin flick. We can't rule out a connection between it, the graffiti, or the shredded note. The broken window could be the link to all three."

Sweat beaded his uncle's upper lip. "Jesus."

"If you accuse Stacy of screwing with the ad, guilty or not, she'll deny involvement in *every* incident. Wouldn't you rather pin a suspect to the wall?"

His uncle swallowed. "Uh…"

"Mom would want us to nail this jerk, or she'll keep worrying." She had worried about Gabe's dad throughout his career, and she'd lost sleep over *Gabe's* choices all his life. Being the wife or mother of a cop challenged the strongest women.

Mackie scrubbed his hands over his face. "Damn it. I can't have her stressing out."

"Okay then. Did you hear Stacy call in the ad?"

His uncle shook his head.

"Maybe it *wasn't* Stacy." Gabe stepped toward the window. His sore leg ached. "Maybe Ursula called in the ad *for* Stacy, and neither of them told you." He turned and faced his uncle. "Or the snafu originated at the newspaper. Or another employee has it in for you."

"There's the janitor. He comes in late Tuesdays after we close. But he doesn't touch my office. I don't like the idea of strangers poking around in here."

Gabe nodded. "Did the magazine provide the ad copy?"

"Naw. Stacy wrote it last Wednesday, the day she was to call it in."

A week ago. "Is today the only time it runs?"

Another shake of the head. "It appeared Sunday too. The print editions and the website. Once the calls began rolling in, Stacy booked the appointments to start today. We had prior bookings Monday and Tuesday."

"Did you check the Sunday ad?"

Mackie's chin jutted. "Excuse me for having a personal life! I was busy."

"Doing?"

"You sound like the freaking cops. I took Jas to a late lunch at my place, all right?"

"Jasmine? I met her in the hall." Gabe hesitated. "Could she have done this?"

"Not a chance. She never knew about the ad, and we met at my crib. The deadline happened while we were there."

"Did you meet her outside your apartment or in it?" Gabe asked, then elaborated. "If someone saw you and Jasmine enter the building during the time the ad was placed, it will confirm her alibi." And also clear Mackie. Why his uncle would screw with his own business escaped Gabe, but he couldn't discount the possibility. "Victims" did bizarre things for oddball reasons every day.

"I caught Old Lady Chadwick staring at us. She's two doors down."

Good. Gabe would talk to the woman. "Chances are Jasmine has nothing to do with this."

"You really believe Ursula or Stacy do?"

"Stacy's a big question mark, but Ursula doesn't seem too fond of you. Granted, she's dealing with a lot of chaos out there, but maybe her frustration is for show."

"Huh. Like she's trying to throw me off her trail?"

"Perhaps. Another guilty person might act calm to deflect attention. You never know." The tingling of nerve damage shot down Gabe's bad leg. He rested a hand on the desk. "Maybe Ursula planned these incidents for ages, starting with vandalism then moving to threats. And now the ad, which might impact the magazine shoot."

"Why would Ursula or Stacy want to wreck the shoot?"

"Beats me. Ursula was pretty angry when I met her in the hall. She wasn't happy about walking in on you and Jasmine." Gabe let that sink in a moment. "She mentioned quitting."

"She won't quit. C'mon! She's buying me out in the spring."

Gabe straightened. "Oh? You're retiring at—what—fifty?"

"We'll see, we'll see. I might freelance." Mackie cleared his throat. "I don't need much. I'm a single guy, worked hard all these years..." He strolled around the desk and repositioned the chair. "The point is, Ursula and I got a deal. She helps me build up the business again then buys it for fair market value." He chortled. "The better my reputation come May, the more she pays."

"Whose idea was that?"

"Hers. She's so hot to have a studio of her own, no way would she mess with me."

"Hell, Uncle Vic, that might be true. On the other hand, maybe working with you hasn't lived up to her expectations." Given her comments in the hall, Gabe would stake his recovery on it. "Maybe she wants to scare you into selling earlier for below market value, so you won't have to keep dealing with vandalism and threats. As for the ad, did the magazine hire her or you?"

"Me. I used to handle gigs like this all the time, so when their regular guy eloped and they needed a freelancer on short notice, I fit the bill. I slipped the job to Ursula. Damn her whining. Always harping for more responsibility. I give it to her, and now this happens!" He hurled a pen at the bookcase.

"Okay...what if she wants you to look incompetent, so the magazine crosses you off their freelance list, damaging your reputation and lowering the value of your business before you sell? A variety of motives might apply. I don't know which. But I could find out."

His uncle squinted. "Would you have to tell the cops?"

"That depends on what I learn. I know Mom would rest a lot easier if I snooped around."

"I guess if it helps Evie feel better..." Mackie hiked up his pants. "Just so we're clear, I'm not paying you."

Gabe wouldn't expect anything else from his skinflint uncle. "I don't have my PI license yet. Mom asked me to wait until January. Enjoy Thanksgiving and Christmas with her." A small request considering her anxiety during the weeks following his shooting. "This is a freebie."

Mackie's cavernous nostrils twitched. "How will you look into this bullcrap without Ursula or Stacy catching on? I been getting more calls since Ursula came onboard. Unless she *is* screwing me, I can't have you doing anything to tick her off. I want to sell this place for the best possible price."

Gabe drummed his fingers on the desk. "You could play along with her for now. For all we know, she's not the culprit. Tell her you need her. Give her what she wants."

"I don't know what the frig she wants."

"Sure you do. She wants credit for her work. From what she said in the hall, you weren't planning to give her credit for the photo shoot."

"Meh. I meant to. Then I had second thoughts."

"There you go. Another reason she might be trying to sabotage your business. Give her the byline, keep her happy. Meanwhile, you'll have your eye on her."

"My eye? How?"

"Your *private* eye, Uncle Vic. I'm working for you now, so leave it up to me."

❦

Vic McKenzie tossed off his jacket and bee-lined for the fridge in his ground-floor apartment. Beer dangling between his fingers, he sank onto the plush recliner facing his new wide-screen TV. A couple of months ago, he wouldn't have risked indulging in any luxuries, but his sorry life was finally getting back on track. His blackmail swan song with a local politician would soon provide him with even more rewards.

Him *and* his future wife. Evie.

He'd pined for his pretty sister-in-law since before she'd married his dead narc brother. She'd shone a light into Doug's heart, encouraging him to see the good in a cruddy world. After she and Mackie were hitched, she would do the same for him. She had to, because the pressure of battling his compulsions was eating him from the inside out—the bimbos, the blackmail, the whole shebang.

With Evie by his side, he would conquer his demons once and for all. Now that her spineless boyfriend had screwed up, she felt vulnerable and out of sorts. Pair her susceptibility with her concern about the "vandalism" and the perfect time had arrived for Mackie to make his move.

He popped open the brew and chugged. *What a mother of a day.* While his plan to win Evie and his scheme with the philandering Seattle council president were proceeding smoothly, the mix-up with the models ad had knocked him on his keister. Now Evie's kid thought Ursula might be involved?

Mackie's assistant was a nag but hardworking and honest. Even before Ursula's offer to buy the business had sweetened his dreams of early retirement with Evie, he couldn't deny the photographer's integrity.

Someone in his outfit had to be hardworking and honest. Why should he deal with the pressure when Ursula thrived on the crap?

Had she buckled under the strain? *Was* she messing with him?

And Stacy? Needing every dime of her lousy salary for her night-school bookkeeping classes, why would she want to piss him off by botching the ad? She didn't strike him as the sort to punk her boss with a dumbass joke either.

Luckily, his nephew had come along. Ursula hadn't pestered him after Gabe's visit. Now, with Gabe humping to find out who'd trashed the ad, Mackie wouldn't have to deal with Ursula's attitude for the rest of the week. Gabe could.

Mackie chuckled. Apparently, Dougie's kid was as do-right as Dougie had been. Mackie had scammed his adoptive brother countless times, and now it looked like, if he wanted to, he could scam Dougie's son.

Ignoring the twinges of guilt concerning Doug, Mackie set aside his beer and thumbed the remote. The TV and shiny player sparked on. He dug through his favorite porno DVDs on the table.

Shuck a duck. None of them thickened his salami. He craved realistic footage tonight, not this phony Hollywood crud.

Leaving the beer, he ambled to a metal filing cabinet. Squatting, he skated open the bottom drawer holding assorted paperwork and his childhood stamp collection. A fake back existed in the drawer—a contraption he'd devised.

And people thought him stupid. *Good. Let 'em.*

He removed the contents of the drawer before slapping the false panel and tugging it out. From inside the space, the old videotapes beckoned.

His johnson grew puffy. There was nothing like VHS. The graininess, the scratchy sound, the authenticity. They reminded him of the unlit skin-flick theaters of his youth. Fun times.

Extracting the tapes one by one, he studied the labels until he located the tape marked LISA SANDERS. A clueless waitress when they'd met, Lisa had worked the magic for him many times, and she would again tonight. Jas hadn't finished her business this afternoon. Without the release, fantasies of Evie had hounded Mackie like a three-peckered billy goat.

An invisible ant crawled over his skin. *Don't think about Evie.*

Naked, on her knees, servicing him. *She's good, wholesome, not a slut gobbling meat for scraps of bogus affection.*

He returned to the TV and clicked off the DVD player. After starting the VCR he kept in mint condition for his special home-made tapes, he plopped onto the recliner and put up his feet.

Tits flickered on the screen. His dick jumped.

Oh, yeah, Lisa. Do it for me, baby.

Help me forget Evie.

❧

"I'm not taking it."

"*I'm* not taking it."

"Kim, you have to take the primary bedroom after Deni leaves." Ursula crossed her feet under her lawn chair and tucked her afghan around her hips. Thanks to her roommate suggesting they unload about their days while enjoying hot chocolate on the balcony of their apartment in Seattle's Lower Queen Anne neighborhood, she felt settled again. She'd even selected four possible models from the day's test shots. Mackie had stayed squirreled away in his office until closing, sparing her the humiliation of being arrested for his murder. "Historically, whichever roommate chooses the big corner room winds up engaged—"

"And, unless she grows some brains, married." Kim Perkins blew smoke rings into the chilly evening air. Her sleek blond hair brushed her jaw. "Poor Deni. Only five months until she's shackled to James for life."

Deni, their other roommate in the three-bedroom apartment, had met her fiancée at a corporate function last January. Two months later, James proposed.

"I don't think it bothers her," Ursula said. "She loves him."

"Yeah, *now* she loves him. Enough time has passed. Before, she suffered from a severe case of infatuation. Agreeing to the big M after eight weeks of dating is sheer lunacy. Can you imagine?" Kim blew another smoke ring. "Anyway, Deni can have love if it makes her bubble pop. It's not for me."

Ursula didn't buy Kim's cynicism. "Doesn't everyone want love sooner or later?" An image of Gabe McKenzie sprang to mind.

Moss-green eyes, engaging smile, and the backbone not to slink away when he caught her in mid-rant.

Too bad he attended family reunions with her hairball boss.

"I wouldn't mind a bit of love," she admitted, reaching for her mug on the wide wood railing. "Eventually. No rush. Just not, you know, right now."

When the time came, Ursula would follow her parents' example. Like Kim, the last thing she wanted was to bungee-jump into marriage only to rebound headlong to divorce court—the sad state of most of their group's folks. *Nope.* Ursula's mom and dad were best friends who relied on each other for everything. Their unwavering commitment and sensible approach to life had bolstered the family through several rough times. The fire, her grandmother's early onset Parkinson's disease, the debilitating stroke that sent Grandma Betty into a nursing home before the age of sixty, and Grandma B's death following a second stroke last year.

Heart squeezing, Ursula curled her hands around her warm mug. Her parents worked so hard. Her dad, a former cabinetmaker who'd lost his job to downsizing, cobbled together roofing and fencing work, whatever he could find. Her mom, a supermarket cashier with a painful case of carpal tunnel, placed every family member's needs ahead of her own.

Five years ago, her parents sold their home to upgrade Grandma B's care. Now they rented in an area that allowed Ursula's younger brother to save on accommodation costs while attending the University of Washington. Owen was on scholarship this year at U-Dub, a result of his fantastic grades.

Secure, stable, familiar. That was what Ursula wanted. For her family, as well as herself. Her days of dating slacker guys were long gone. Until she bought the studio, she would remain on relationship hiatus.

Kim flicked ash into an old tin camping plate on her lap. "Love doesn't come in bits, Urs. That's the problem. Love tackles you when you're not looking. At its worst, it consumes you."

"I can't say I've ever felt consumed. Tired of immature dudes only out for a good time? Yes." Her last two relationships imploded when she realized the guys were always late, always making excuses, and generally testing how far they could push her. At twenty-five, she was sick of all the BS.

"Well, I've seen the damage inflicted countless times on my sisters. So if you think I'm giving love or infatuation or whatever you want to call it *any* advantage by moving into *that* bedroom, forget it."

The sliding glass door opened. Deni Clarke stepped out, her lacy dress and ecru shrug showcasing her dark skin. Deni snatched Kim's cigarette and stubbed it in the ashtray.

"Hey." Kim's blue eyes snapped. "The sundeck is a no-cell zone, not a cig-free."

"I don't care. You said you'd quit by my wedding."

"That's in April. And they're low-tar."

"Kim, you have no willpower. You should start weaning yourself now." Deni sat in the chair to Ursula's right. "Brrr, it's chilly." She hugged her middle. "What are we talking about?"

Ursula sipped her hot chocolate. "Who gets your room when you move."

"Neither of us wants it." Kim jostled the camping plate on her knees. "No shared walls plus your own bathroom equals too much privacy. Which, as previous roommates would attest, results in excess sex." She eyed Deni. "And *that* too often leads to hasty engagements."

"It's a curse," Ursula said. She liked her small room. Decorated with flea-market finds and family photos, it was cozy.

Deni laughed. "If one of you doesn't move in, the new girl will get the largest space for the same rent. Is that fair?"

Ursula and Kim nodded.

The intercom buzzed inside. Deni bounced off her chair. "James!" She raced off without shutting the glass. Seconds later, her voice floated onto the balcony. "Urs, it's for you. He has pizza."

Ursula glanced at Kim. "Must be Owen." Her brother hadn't visited in a couple of weeks. They were due. She set down her mug, "Coming?" she asked, her grandmother's afghan nestling her shoulders as she rose.

"In a minute. Go see your baby brother." Kim tugged a new cigarette out of her sweater sleeve. "Meanwhile, mwahaha."

"You're impossible." Ursula went indoors.

Near the entry, she spied way more evidence of testosterone than nineteen-year-old Owen could hope to emit. Gabe McKenzie stood in the hall outside the open door. Five o'clock shadow covered his jaw. Not the overgrown evidence of hairy-back-gene variety, but the *oh-yes*-skid-your-stubbly-chin-down-my-body kind. Deni gazed up at him, hand resting on the knob and a star-struck expression glazing her features.

Ursula's mouth twitched. Yeah, the guy was hot, but why was he here?

"Gabe?" she asked, reaching them. "What's going on?"

"I thought you might be hungry." He extended a large pizza box, a sexy smile warming his face.

Wonderful. A gorgeous guy arrived bearing food, and *she* was draped in a fifteen-year-old, orange-and-brown crocheted blankie. That said, considering he'd changed into a raggedy fisherman's sweater, he didn't exactly qualify for the fashion police.

Except the oatmeal cable-knit molded his broad chest very nicely.

"How did you find me?" Even stalkers could be gorgeous. Also, there was that hiatus thing.

"Mackie. He wants me to butter you up. The pizza is a peace offering."

"Oh, you're the butter-up go-between," Deni teased.

Gabe chuckled. "Have you eaten?" he asked Ursula, and her pulse leapt. Most annoying.

"Not yet." She and Kim had been waiting until Deni left. Gabe towered over Deni and hovered a decent six inches above Ursula's respectable five-nine. "Deni, Gabe is Mackie's nephew. He recently moved back to Seattle from Los Angeles."

Deni smiled. "Welcome home."

"Thanks." Gabe looked at Ursula. "Can I come in? The pizza is yours either way."

"Urs, hint, hint," Deni murmured, nudging her.

Ursula stepped back, and Gabe moved into the apartment. He handed her the pizza. The aroma of freshly baked crust teased her nostrils. She placed the box on the kitchen counter, nearly colliding with Kim.

"Yikes, Kimmy, watch it." Ursula clutched her afghan before it slipped to the floor.

"Sorry. I smelled the pizza rumors. Ecstatic to see they're true." In the galley kitchen, Kim retrieved plates from a cupboard and stacked them on the box. She glanced at their guest. "Why, hello."

Ursula introduced them. The intercom buzzed, and James's voice transmitted from the lobby.

Deni arranged to meet her fiancé downstairs while Kim located forks and carted her load to the living room. "Urs, can you bring the Greek salad I made earlier?"

"Sure. Gabe, would you like a drink?" Crap, now she'd done it. She'd invited him to stay. So sue her, his comment about Mackie had sparked her curiosity.

"Beer, if you have it."

"Great. You can join Kim. I'll be there in a second." As he headed to the table, Ursula scoped out his tight butt and slight limp. He was obviously fit. So why was he limping? Had he suffered an injury?

She hadn't noticed a shamble to his gait this morning. But then, she'd been too miffed at Mackie.

Ducking into her bedroom, she lost her security afghan and ran a brush through her hair. No sense looking like a wildebeest. Back in the kitchen, she plucked two coolers and a light beer from the fridge. When she reached the small table pushed against a living room wall, Gabe and Kim had chosen seats across from each other, leaving her the end chair. Close enough to Gabe that their knees might graze. *Oh, joy.*

Gabe frowned at the beer label as if she'd asked him to swallow mosquito repellent.

"It's light beer or *no* beer." She offered a sugary smile. "Or I can bring you a wild-berry cooler."

He accepted the beer.

Kim asked, "The salad?"

Damn. Next she'd forget her brain around this guy.

Kim rose. "Don't worry, I'll get it." She sauntered into the kitchen.

Sitting, Ursula looked at him. "All right, why does Mackie want to butter me up?"

Three

Thirty minutes later, Gabe closed the empty pizza box in Ursula's tiny dining area and downed a mouthful of watery beer. Around the corner, Kim washed dishes and clattered utensils. Ursula remained at the table, fingernails rat-a-tapping the shiny surface. Her Greek salad sat unfinished in a bowl. In keeping with his cover as an amiable job-hopper come home, Gabe retrieved his fork and speared a fat black olive.

"You're a bottomless pit," Ursula said, her knee knocking his beneath the table before scooting away. "Planning on coming up for air soon? Or have we reached the point in the meal where you can eat *and* discuss your uncle?"

Gabe grinned and munched the olive. Ursula possessed a direct honesty he couldn't imagine her fabricating. Over dinner, he had purposely tried her patience, asking about changes to the city and fabricating a spotty employment history. Considering both she and Stacy were suspects in whatever was going on at the studio, he needed to appear harmless and not let on he was a former cop who intended to become a PI.

Postponing the conversation about Mackie also served as a stress test of sorts. If Ursula *was* responsible for the vandalism and threats, Gabe wanted her worrying that his uncle might be on to her and had wheedled Gabe into a visit to gauge her guilt—a classic Mackie move.

If remorse burdened Ursula Scott, she hid it well. So far nothing she'd said or done provided any hint she'd sabotaged Victor McKenzie Photography. But Gabe wouldn't stray off-course. During his years with the LAPD, he'd learned to cover his bases and check the alibis of every suspect. Especially one who stood to benefit if the value of the business plummeted under his uncle's ownership.

He stole another olive from her bowl. "I spoke to Mackie about the deadbolt. He's buying one tonight. I'm installing it for him tomorrow."

"That's nice of you."

"I'm a nice guy."

Smiling, she slid her salad toward him. "Have the rest. Waste not, want not, as my dad would say."

"Thanks." Hand on the rim of the bowl, Gabe swabbed a cucumber chunk in dressing. "I also said you wanted the byline for the magazine assignment. My uncle griped about it but agreed."

"What?" Ursula's hand clapped to her chest. "I *begged* Mackie for that byline. I offered my first-born. He went back on his word. Now you show up, and he's suddenly willing?"

Such passion. Did it shape every facet of her life?

Gabe leaned an elbow on the table. "I told him you threatened to quit."

Her mouth gaped. "*Why?*"

"You mentioned it. In the hall."

"I also said he realizes I *can't* quit. Gabe!"

"Threatening to leave worked with my old construction fore-man." One of the short-term jobs he'd fabricated for his cover. "He upped my pay and lengthened my lunch hours."

"Seriously, if I wanted to quit, I'd tell Mackie myself."

Kim's voice rang from the kitchen, "I told you to give him hell ages ago, Urs."

"Keep out of it, Kim. And stop eavesdropping."

"It's a small apartment. I'm not eavesdropping. You're talking too loud."

Gurgling sounds of the sink draining reached Gabe's ears as Kim entered the area off the kitchen normally reserved for dining. Instead, a communal desk inhabited the spot. A laptop, printer, and two tablets shared space with a shelf housing office supplies, knick-knacks, and a music dock.

Kim switched on the player, and Top 40 tracks flowed from the speakers. "That should help." She returned to the kitchen.

Looking at Gabe, Ursula shook her head. "Mackie's buttering me up by giving me credit for the shoot?"

"He hasn't always been an ass, you know."

"So I hear. The studio had a great reputation before he changed locations ten or twelve years ago. His name was mentioned in my art school classes. That's why I wanted to work with him. I don't know what happened to sour things"—

Gabe did. His father's murder. *Eleven* years ago. It had changed them all. Forever.

—"but when he hired me, he said the studio had lost money, forcing the move. There are a lot of beautiful old buildings in our area, but some businesses need sprucing up."

"I noticed." A bit of revitalization couldn't hurt that particular block. A tired-looking antique shop sat across the street, and a shabby souvenir store hulked nearby. In contrast, the coffeehouse on the right boasted recent renovations, as did an Italian bistro three doors down.

If Ursula's plans to buy the studio coincided with neighborhood improvements, the value of the business would skyrocket. Under *her* ownership.

She peeled the label off her vodka cooler. "My idea was if I came in while the business was recovering, I'd have a lot more opportunities like the Real Men shoot than if I worked for a photographer at the top of their game. I don't want to hang out my online shingle and compete with every other twenty-something who owns a camera and photo editing software. I want a solid opportunity with growth potential."

"Wouldn't a photographer with more work than he or she could handle make a better boss?"

"A commercial pro with an excellent reputation would have hired me as an assistant, nothing more. Mackie gave me first crack at buying him out. In six months, I'll own the place."

"He told me." That she readily admitted the same earned her a point in the innocence department.

On the other hand, she might have volunteered the information as a smokescreen.

"For someone who's not close to his uncle, you two seem to have discussed a lot," she said.

Gabe finished the salad. "He's a piss-ant, but my mother worries about him. He's our last living relative. If looking out for him keeps her happy, I'm all for it." Getting shot had a way of putting things in perspective.

"Where's your dad?"

"Dead."

"Oh." Her gaze shuttered. "Sorry. That sounds trite, but—"

"No worries. It happened a long time ago." The memories still hurt like hell during lonely nights. Losing a father at eighteen was rough, and certain circumstances surrounding his dad's death remained a mystery. The case had long since gone cold.

The music filling the dining area segued to a melancholy song. Shredding the cooler label, Ursula cleared her throat. "Did Mackie mention the ad?"

"That's partly why I'm here." Leaning back in his chair, Gabe dug into his front jeans pocket and retrieved a photocopy of the *Clarion* page. The movement placed pressure on his glute, spinning numbing pain through the injured area despite this afternoon's physical therapy appointment.

Jaw clenching, he passed her the folded copy. "You were right when you said there was a mix-up. For one thing, my uncle says *he* didn't phone in the ad." Smoothing his hand over the old fishing sweater that had belonged to his father, he waited for his beautiful suspect to bite.

"Well, I didn't place it. Stacy must have."

"My uncle said the same thing." Tomorrow, Gabe would attempt to corroborate the story by interviewing Stacy while he fixed his uncle's office door. He would also follow up with the newspaper as soon as possible, although Mackie's alibi that he and Jasmine were together during the time of ad placement held.

Before heading to his PT appointment, Gabe had checked with Mackie's elderly neighbor. He'd also examined the janitorial log in the studio bathroom and quizzed the custodian about his whereabouts last Wednesday. The man claimed he'd spent the morning on a first-grade field trip, a fact his son's school had verified.

It had been a busy afternoon.

Ursula unfolded the ad. Her eyes rounded. "What's *this*? No wonder I had a rotten day. And Mackie wants you to pacify me with pizza? Did this drivel run in the Sunday edition too?"

"My uncle didn't check the weekend paper. Did you?"

"No." She shoved a hand through her long hair. "I went to the Veterans Day parade in Auburn with my dad, or I would have. Stupid me, I thought Mackie would keep an eye on it. That'll teach me."

"He arranged a retraction for this Friday's edition. I was in his office when he called them."

Her shoulders sagged. "It doesn't matter. The damage is done."

Kim rushed into the living room, drying her hands on a dishtowel. "I can't stand it anymore. You guys keep talking above the music. Can I see this ad?"

Ursula blew out a breath. "Go ahead." She handed it over.

Slapping the dishtowel over a shoulder, Kim scanned the photocopy and snickered. "'I want you in my spread?' That's funny." She glanced at Ursula. "In a revolting way."

"It's not funny, Kim. It's weird. All this time I've worked for Mackie, yes, he's had run-ins with loitering teenagers but no vandalism until the broken window."

Gabe sipped his tasteless beer. "He mentioned graffiti at Halloween."

"That's right!" Kim punched the air as if she starred in a comic-book caper. "Mackie was furious about the graffiti when Urs went to work the next day. He asked her to clean it off, but she refused."

"He didn't *ask*," Ursula amended. "He commanded. I had a ton of work that day, and we were out late the night before. I was exhausted."

"Right, right." Kim placed the ad on the table. "We went to this fantastic costume party near U-Dub. Five of us packed into Urs's junky car. It stalled coming home. We had to call a tow truck."

"My credit card *didn't* appreciate it."

Gabe itched to ask the name of the towing company. If a receipt existed in their records, he would clear Ursula of another incident.

He remained quiet, hoping the talkative women would fill in the blanks.

Kim said, "But, Urs, you gotta admit, the guy from, um, what was the name of the towing company?"

"Andrews Towing."

"Yeah. The towing dude was *hot*, in a shaggy-haired way."

Thank you, Kim. Gabe would contact the company. The sooner he corroborated Ursula's Halloween alibi, the closer he would come to clearing her.

Or catching her.

Ursula gazed at the ad again. "I wonder if Mackie should go to the cops?"

"He did," Gabe said. "About the broken window. I guess he relies on the security camera next door for stuff like that."

"The coffeehouse camera isn't working right now," Ursula replied, substantiating his uncle's story. "I keep telling him the studio should buy its own security equipment instead of piggy-backing on someone else's. But he's—"

"Too cheap. I know." Gabe would visit the SCPD and peruse the police report for further confirmation about the out-of-order camera and other details of the broken window. The report was public record, available to anyone. He shouldn't encounter an issue. "It seems the cops blamed the window on kids."

Ursula shook her head. "What does Mackie plan to do about the ad then? Nothing?" Her tone evoked disdain.

Gabe placed the empty salad bowl on the closed pizza box. "You know, after meeting Jasmine and seeing the ad with my uncle, I wondered..."

"You don't think she had something to do with this?"

"He says no. They were at his apartment together when he thinks Stacy phoned in the ad." He snapped his fingers. "Hey, you weren't with Stacy when she called the paper, were you?"

"No. I was shooting family portraits in back. We're running a Christmas special."

Gabe would peek at the studio's scheduling software. If the customers for the pertinent time slots confirmed Ursula hadn't left the studio, he would score two out of four toward clearing her.

The situation appeared less favorable for Stacy.

"Just because I wasn't with Stacy doesn't mean she ruined the ad," Ursula said.

"Who else could it be?" Kim asked.

"I don't know. *Not* Stacy. She's a good kid."

Gabe skated a hand along the tabletop. "How long have you worked with her?"

"Two months. She started mid-September."

Kim chewed a thumbnail. "I need a cigarette," she muttered beneath the music. "Urs, don't discount Stacy. If it wasn't you—"

"What do you mean, *if* it wasn't me? I just said I was shooting portraits." Her gaze flew to Gabe. "Mackie doesn't think *I* did this?"

"Why would you?" her roommate countered. "Why would anyone?"

Gabe had to love Kim. She good-copped/bad-copped without realizing it.

Ursula jumped off her chair. "I can't believe he wasted one second thinking I'm responsible! I've toiled for that dick for months. If I didn't want the studio so badly, I *would* quit. Tonight."

Good God, the woman breathed fire. With her hands jammed on her hips and that sleek dark hair spilling over her shoulders, she looked like an Amazon warrior princess out to kick boss-ass. Her shining blue eyes and take-no-prisoners feistiness spurred fantasies of her long limbs tangling with his. On a bed, the couch. Hell, on a park bench.

"Now, Ursula, don't do something you'll regret," he said placidly. He needed her on his side. Until he cleared up this mess for his mother, he needed all the studio employees cooperative and clueless.

Who knew what he might uncover? If Ursula wasn't the suspect, he couldn't risk her interfering in his investigation and getting hurt.

"Why do you care?" she tossed back. "What do you get out of all this?"

He smiled. "My uncle knows I like to dabble. He promised I could dabble with you."

&

"*Dabble?*" Ursula stared at her handsome visitor askance. Gabe said the word like he wanted to have sex.

With her.

His husky voice should be outlawed.

"In photography." He shrugged. "Mackie said you'd teach me…if I asked real nice."

"Oh." Cheeks tingling, she massaged her aching forehead. As she wore a path in the living room carpet, Kim folded the dishtowel and placed it beside the salad bowl on the closed pizza box.

Gabe lounged in his chair.

"You want to be a photographer?" The idea didn't suit her impression of him in the *slightest*. "What about a new construction job? My dad might know a crew." A well-built guy like Gabe McKenzie stood a greater chance at obtaining regular work than a middle-aged fellow with a bad back.

His gaze never leaving her face, Gabe lifted one shoulder in another slow, sexy shrug. "I work at whatever catches my interest. Cameras other than the one on my cell phone qualify. Instead of doing the same old thing, why not learn something new?"

Wow, were *they* polar opposites. He flitted from job to job on a whim, with no sense of purpose or commitment. She plodded along, ceaselessly hammering at her goals.

She spun her grandmother's wedding ring on her left pinky. "But do you even like your uncle?" He had called Mackie a piss-ant. And an ass.

"Nope. I can put up with running into him every day if it means learning from you." He grinned, and her nipples tightened.

Do not *dive into the dumpster of regrets, Ursula.* "Why doesn't he teach you?"

"He says it'd be a pain in the butt." His eyebrows rose. "You know how he is. Why take on the hassle when you can do it for him? I'll help with the magazine job."

Kim's gaze brightened. "Urs, with an assistant, you'd finish the shoot in no time."

"An assistant I'd have to train." Added work. A distraction.

"So what?" Kim asked. "It's better than having Mackie decide to take over. Besides, you're not quitting. I won't allow it. You're too close to achieving your dreams." Her voice firmed. "Your dickhead boss obviously realizes you have talent. Why else would he tell Gabe to offer you the byline?"

"If Mackie believed I had worth as an employee, don't you think he might have mentioned it once or twice?"

"Oh-ho, don't be fooled." Kim crossed her arms. "Him *not* mentioning it is so Mackie. Right?"

Exhaling, Ursula nodded. Kim had nailed the turd. Mackie would never shower a lowly assistant with compliments. He reserved his fawning for the honeymoon phase of his revolving door of relationships. During the six months Ursula had worked for him, she'd met at least four girlfriends before Jasmine. The couple had been an item these last several weeks. Her stomach churned at the memory of walking in on them this morning.

She swiped a hand in the air. "I'm tired of his games. I'll put out the word for another photographer looking to retire."

"And have to start all over again?" Kim walked toward her. "Or sacrifice the Real Men shoot? If the studio doesn't meet the deadline, Mackie will blame you. Don't think he won't."

Ursula fisted her hands. "Shit!"

"*Six months*, Urs," Kim repeated. "Learn what you can from the experience and *then* do what you want."

Ursula's heart raced. Six short months of dealing with Mackie's bloated ego. It sounded more like an eternity right now, but she needed to consider her future.

Her plans.

With the *Seattle Lights* byline fattening her portfolio, she would look more qualified to prospective clients. The magazine might hire her again, possibly *before* she bought the studio. If they liked her work, they would hop over Mackie and ask directly for her.

"Scouring the city for additional mentoring opportunities only postpones everything," Kim murmured, brushing Ursula's hand.

Nodding, Ursula drew in calming breaths. Thank heaven for supportive friends and family who helped her retain focus. After she bought Mackie's studio, her parents could lean on *her* for once. With profits earned from *her own business*, she would help pay down the mountain of debt they'd incurred during her grandmother's experimental treatments for early onset Parkinson's as well as the expensive post-stroke nursing home care.

The financial double-whammy had turned her dad gray almost overnight. As much as her mom had willingly scrimped to help *her* mother, more than once Ursula had heard Mom crying over yet another bill.

Her father had promised he wouldn't say no to Ursula's offers of assistance once she owned the studio or worry about her chances of building a stable life, like he did now.

To be able to help her parents would feel incredible.

She pictured her dad's scarred laborer's hands, her mom's carpal tunnel wrist brace. Her mom deserved a gently-used car instead of riding the bus to work. A pair of comfy recliners would freshen the living room...

She looked at Gabe. "You start tomorrow. Bright and early. Don't let me down."

Four

Eve McKenzie dealt the last cards for her solitaire game onto the kitchen table. Two aces. *Excellent.* After this evening's losing streak, she craved a win.

As she positioned the aces above the seven card piles, the front door clicked open.

Her pulse quickened. Gabe was home. She released a breath.

"Mom?"

"In here." Ever since his injury, she'd lived like a mouse waiting for a hawk to swoop, tensing whenever the phone or doorbell rang, possibly bringing more bad news. Gabe's brush with death had been awful, but she didn't want her habitual worrying smothering her grown son.

Get a grip, Eve.

He entered the kitchen, and she lay down the cards, pretending with everything in her that she hadn't been praying for his safe arrival home, like she'd done for his father throughout the years of their marriage.

Remaining seated, she ran her hands over her pants legs. "Did you have a nice time?"

Nodding, he held up a bakery box. "Sorry I skipped dinner, but I brought dessert."

"You didn't have to do that, honey." But she smiled. "What sort?"

"Pumpkin pie. I thought we'd get an early start on Thanksgiving."

"Oh, Gabriel, I could have made pumpkin pie." She rose and squeezed his strong arms. *My son. Home. With me.* She kissed his cheek.

"I love your pie, Mom, but you're not my personal maid and cook while I'm staying here." He set the carton on the counter and flipped it open. The spicy scent of pumpkin wafted throughout her toasty kitchen.

Opening a drawer, she withdrew the antique pie-slicer her ex-boyfriend had given her last Christmas. She'd fooled herself into believing moving the reminder of Hal Henshaw out of its treasured spot in her dining room buffet to share space with everyday kitchen items would diminish its sentimental value.

She had been wrong.

"I'll slice," she said too cheerily, as if employing a tone of voice could banish thoughts of Hal. She'd barred contact when she'd rejected his proposal on the heels of Gabe's shooting. Who asked a woman to marry them out of the blue, while that woman's only child recovered from surgery?

Forget that Hal's timing lacked finesse, he'd made it sound like her wanting to fly alone to California to visit her son in the hospital reflected on *their* relationship somehow...and that her cherished memories of Doug lessened her feelings for *him*.

Her friends and brother-in-law agreed. Hal had come on too strong in August, pressuring her to look to the future when she'd needed to work through the heartache of nearly losing her son.

But their support couldn't eliminate her pangs of regret. Hal had disappeared from her life all at once, in some ways eerily similar to when she lost Doug.

Yet, in other ways, not the same.

Never the same.

Gabe took the pie-slicer. "You sit, Mom. I'll do this."

"Sorry. Hormones. I forgot my brain was attached for a minute." The old menopause excuse.

"That's okay. Want coffee?"

"Only if it's decaf. Too much caffeine in the evenings affects my sleep."

Gabe nodded, and Eve sat at the table. When had he become so confident and capable, her little boy who once ran through this house with his friends and his big chocolate lab Ruckus at his heels?

Before evil stole his father from them both.

She boxed the deck of cards as Gabe shuffled around the kitchen, filling the coffeemaker and doling pie onto plates. The rich scent of brewing dark roast tingled her taste buds, but every time he limped, her stomach knotted.

"I didn't expect you home from visiting your friend so early," she said.

"She's a new friend. I didn't want to overstay my welcome. Has Uncle Vic ever mentioned Ursula Scott?"

Eve shook her head.

"She's his assistant. I went to see her." He poured two steaming mugs of decaf. "You were right to send me to the studio this morning," He carried their plates to the table and returned to the counter for the mugs. "A big mix-up occurred with one of Uncle Vic's jobs while I was there. Who knows what else has happened that he hasn't told you."

Eve smacked the table. "I knew it. I had to drag that note out of him. What sort of sicko sends a businessman threats and dirty drawings?"

"I intend to find out."

"Good. Thank you."

Her son set down her mug. After fetching cream and sugar, he sat in the nearest chair. "He didn't ask for help paying for the broken window, did he?"

Face heating, Eve cupped her mug. "Honey, I know you think Vic lives to con me, but I promise he did not hound me for a loan. I offered, but he said his landlord's structure insurance covered the damage. We haven't spoken about it since."

"Sorry. I had to ask."

She sighed. How to make Gabe understand what Hal never could? "Son, other than you, Victor is all I have left to remind me of your father. He's come to mean a great deal to me since you moved out of state. If I want to lend him money, that's my right."

"Of course it is. Just don't expect me to like it."

"Fair enough."

He relaxed, and they ate their pie. Eve flaked off the doughy crust with her fork. "You haven't said why you visited his assistant."

"I needed to establish a reason for hanging around the studio. Only you and Uncle Vic know I'm snooping around."

A weight lifted from her shoulders. "Thank you again for doing this. It sounds silly, but I feel the need to watch out for him, like a big sister." A memory prodded her mind: the despair in Vic's eyes when she and Doug announced their engagement, then the inappropriate words he spoke to her in private the night before her wedding. Doug had gone to his grave without knowing how his younger brother had once felt about her.

But that was the past. Vic was family. Since that awkward moment following the rehearsal dinner, he had never failed to treat her with respect, and he needed her guidance and support.

Especially now with these strange occurrences at the studio.

"You're welcome," Gabe said, scooping pie onto his fork. "I can't work as a private investigator until I receive my state license. At this point, I can't even carry a firearm. Might as well help Vic."

Goosebumps speckled Eve's arms. "I would prefer it if you never carried a weapon again, Gabe. Do you really need a gun permit to operate your business?"

He gazed at her. "Mom."

The landline rang. "Finish your pie." She went to her vintage secretary desk in the living room. Glancing back at her son, she answered without checking the display. "Yes?"

"Eve." Hal's deep voice brushed her ear. "Hi."

"H-hello!" He must have read her mind.

"It's been awhile. I wasn't sure when to get in touch."

"I...I know. It's good to hear your voice, Hal. I..." *Need to see you. Need to screw my head back on right first. Need to figure out how everything went so wrong.* "Thank you for respecting my boundaries." She sounded like an automaton.

An awkward pause transmitted over the receiver. "Actually, I'm calling about my stuff, Eve. I want it back."

Stomach sinking, she rubbed the heart-shaped locket she'd

begun wearing following their breakup. The necklace was a long-ago gift from Victor to commemorate her years with Doug.

"I'll bring your things by tomorrow," she half-whispered, staring at the picture window so Gabe wouldn't witness her agony. "When will you be at the office?"

"Don't want to run into me, huh? Come on your lunch hour. I won't be there."

"That's not what I—"

Bzzzzz. The dial tone filled her ear.

Tears burned her eyes. Had she said the wrong thing? She wished she could change what she felt in her heart for Doug, but did Hal have to be so brusque? Gabe's shooting had scrambled her emotions. If Hal loved her, he would understand her confusion.

What does that tell you, Eve?

Hands shaking, she replaced the receiver.

"Everything okay with your boyfriend, Mom?" Gabe asked.

Here it came. Finally, she had to tell him.

"Hal isn't my boyfriend, son. Not anymore."

❧

Gabe strode toward the studio, estimating a dozen weirdly dressed men milling on the sidewalk in the chilly morning breeze, waiting for the door to open. He required food before he handled that motley crew—as good a reason as any for visiting the coffeehouse. While there, he'd ask the manager a few questions about their security camera and hours of operation Halloween night. Maybe a staff member had witnessed the pornographic window painting.

He entered the busy shop. As usual when visiting new surroundings, he surveyed the interior. Ursula stood at the condiment counter, shaking cinnamon onto a giant latte.

Never mind speaking to the staff this morning. He'd manage it another time. *Soon.* Connecting with his fake boss was more important.

Hands in jean pockets, he stepped toward her. "Hi."

She plunked down the shaker. "Okay, now you *are* stalking me."

"Nope, just wanted to grab a cup of joe before I impressed my new boss."

"Who, me?" she asked, the corners of her eyes crinkling.

Gabe smiled even while his thoughts drifted to his mom. He needed to find a way to connect with her as well, encourage her it was safe to unload her worries onto him. Last night, she'd bolted to bed shortly after Hal's phone call, and this morning she left the house before Gabe emerged from the basement suite. Her shift at the bank didn't start until ten. Clearly, she didn't want to discuss the breakup. She and Hal had dated for two years. Gabe had assumed a wedding waited around the corner.

Apparently not.

"Did you see the mob outside the studio?" he asked Ursula, focusing his mind on the job at hand.

She snapped a take-out lid onto her big cup. "Why do you think I ordered a jumbo-sized?"

"Point taken. I haven't had breakfast. Thought I'd buy muffins. Want one?"

"No, I ate at my place, thanks." She moved away from the counter, allowing a tall blonde access to the cream and sugar.

"Wait with me while I order?" he pressed, eager to poke into her motivations a bit more and return to the coffeehouse when she wasn't around.

Her teeth sunk into her bottom lip. "I should start today's test shots. Stacy doesn't work Tuesdays or Thursdays. Although, if I called, she might come down. She needs the money."

Gabe tucked away the scrap of information. He doubted it would lead anywhere. If Stacy wasn't snagging enough hours, why not apply for a second job? From what he could tell, it wasn't like Stacy had something to gain from Mackie's perceived incompetence.

Unlike the beautiful woman standing before him.

"Aw, those goons loitering outside the studio can wait a few minutes," he said. "Or have you already talked to them?"

"Egad, not before I've had"—Ursula downed a noisy slurp of latte—"at least a third of this." A half-smile curled her lips.

Gabe chuckled. "Then they have no idea you're the key to getting them out of the cold. Maybe my uncle will arrive before we leave here. He can deal with their crap."

Her smile broadened, reaching her thickly lashed eyes, and his lungs nearly collapsed from the impact. Man, what a change from her fight and spark yesterday. *This* spark felt completely different, the kind that tugged at a guy's soul as well as beneath his jeans.

"I'm buying the business in May," she said. "I need to take an active interest in its success."

In contrast to her earlier comment about leaving for the test shots, she moved ahead of him to the serving line. Her black leather blazer hung halfway down her rear, displaying curves enough to tease. The spiky boots peeking beneath the hem of her jeans sped his libido into overdrive.

He stepped beside her as the line moved forward. "It's great to see renovations in this area. If they continue, my uncle might jack up his price."

She sipped her latte. "Mackie owns the business, not the building. I'll gladly pay what a good business is worth, Gabe. I worked through the details with my bank. I have enough for the down payment." Excitement lit her eyes. "Sometimes I get so keyed up brainstorming ways to increase profits, I can't fall asleep at night. My contract with your uncle stipulates that I get first option. If for some reason I decide I don't want to buy the studio come May, he can't force the issue."

"Smart thinking." They reached the counter. Gabe ordered three muffins and a short cup of black Colombian.

"Deni's fiancé is an attorney." Ursula lifted her latte for another swig. "I'm taking their wedding pictures as a gift in the spring, so James prepared the contract as a favor. I needed your uncle's signature on something legal. Knowing he can't weasel out of this agreement is very important to me."

Nodding, Gabe paid the cashier. "You don't strike me as a woman who leaves her i's undotted."

"You don't strike me as an armchair psychologist. Which brings us back to the men waiting outside. They're responding to the trashy ad you showed me last night. Just because they look half-baked doesn't mean they won't suit the assignment. Let them learn our requirements. Appearances can be deceiving."

"Gotcha." Gabe retrieved his coffee and muffin bag. If he didn't watch himself, his clever fake boss would see through *his* deceptive appearance and blow his infant investigation to smithereens.

Thanking Gabe for holding open the coffeehouse door, Ursula stepped outside. The group waiting at the studio had proliferated since her arrival. Yesterday, Stacy booked time slots for anyone who'd called. Evidently, these early birds didn't understand the meaning of "appointment," or they'd responded to the seedy-sounding cattle call without phoning the studio in advance. Although Stacy had scheduled this morning's first test subject for twenty minutes after opening, complaints about the locked business rose into the crisp air.

She glanced at Gabe. "Today is a write-off for teaching you anything but crowd control," she said beneath her breath. "Could you call the names on the appointment list and explain what happened with the ad? That should cut down on the number of inappropriate applicants for today and tomorrow. While you're at it, if Stacy hasn't already done so, please reschedule any appointments accepted for next week. I need to fit them all in before this weekend."

Gabe nodded. "Crowds are no problem. My last job in California was as a Hollywood nightclub bouncer. If I can handle the tabloid darlings, these boneheads will be a breeze."

"Go for it. But remember, we might find a diamond in the rough. No matter how they react when they hear the wrong copy appeared in the *Clarion*, we treat them with respect." A lesson *she'd* required yesterday.

"Understood." Holding his coffee cup and muffin bag in one hand, he walked alongside her to the group. "You guys here for the Real Men shoot?" he asked.

Affirmative mumblings ensued.

"You too?" a fellow in front called.

"No, I'm assisting the photographer." Gabe's right palm settled on her back, and a shiver that had zippy to do with the cool temperature sailed through her. "Miss Scott."

"Open the doors then." This from a stout man in bike shorts. "My nuts are freezing."

Lovely. She mustered a polite smile.

"In a minute," Gabe informed the men in a don't-mess-with-me tone. "First, we need to inform everyone that there was a problem with the ad. We're looking for everyday dudes but not for anything distasteful."

"After I waxed my chest?" a bulky guy sporting a wife-beater asked.

A man in beachwear stomped a foot. "What kind of freak show is this?"

"I'm afraid that's outside my area of expertise." Gabe looked at her. "Boss?"

Ursula described the *Seattle Lights* spread. "Is anyone familiar with the February issue?"

A grunt flew from the rear of the crowd. "My wife buys it every year and compares me to the models."

Latte cup heating her fingers, she informed the group, "That's the cool thing about the article. The men featured *aren't* professional models. Previously, the magazine focused on businessmen, but this year they want to portray the lives and loves of a wide variety of Seattle residents. *Real* men, like all of you."

Gabe asked, "How many guys are we looking for, boss?"

"Eight."

Groans about the slim chances of being selected mushroomed.

Gabe scowled at the men. "Are you gonna gripe or listen to the woman?"

The complaints faded. Wincing, Ursula leaned into Gabe and whispered, "You call that respect?"

His coffee cup brushed hers. "It goes both ways. They need to respect you too."

The husky timbre of his low voice slid over her, and her tummy pitched in an extremely pleasant manner.

She glanced at the group. "The process is to shoot sample pictures of every man responding to the ad until two p.m. tomorrow. I don't want to cheat anyone out of that opportunity. My assistant and I will trim the pool to twenty applicants before sending their pictures to *Seattle Lights*. An editor at the magazine determines the final eight."

"*They* decide?" the man in beachwear demanded.

"Their publication, their choice," Ursula replied. "Next week, indoor and outdoor photo sessions for the eight begin. This project needs to wrap quickly, so if your individual schedules don't mesh with ours, unfortunately we can't use you. You'll also need to agree to a short interview with my assistant before your session today. If you're not willing to release information that will help us and the magazine determine our selections, we can't use you."

A curse shot from the crowd. "I don't wanna wait. What's wrong with the ad I read?"

"It was a mistake." She lifted her chin. "We'll hand out copies of the correct ad. Read it, and if you believe you fit the requirements, please stay."

Several men tromped off, grouching.

"Are the rules clear?" Gabe asked those remaining.

Group nod.

"Dude, my wife will be so impressed if I make the cut!"

"Yeah, it'll be like a Valentine's Day present for my wife. And my girlfriend!"

A wry smile tugged Ursula's mouth. She had grave misgivings her camera would love one-tenth of the present crowd, but she fully intended to proceed. According to what Gabe said last night, Mackie had asked the *Clarion* to fix the ad for tomorrow's newspaper and website listings. If she dismissed these men and more appropriate prospects failed to appear, she risked blowing the deadline for delivering her twenty to *Seattle Lights*.

And that *was not* going to happen.

The scissor blades glinted on the newspaper spread out on the table. A red circle outlined the ad. Several scrawled arrows pointed to the wording from all directions.

My words. My brilliance.

The asshole would pay.

It was impossible not to smile. Not to grin like a demented fool.

The paper had covered the wood surface over the last four days, but a victory like this was worth savoring.

First, Sunday, drawing the circle. Inhaling the sharp scent of felt ink squeaking on newsprint.

Since then, the scissors had sat. Waiting. Waiting, waiting. Anticipation building to an erotic level.

The scissors snipped a jagged square around the ad. The paper crinkled.

It doesn't get any better than this.

Except it would. A *lot* better.

Snip-snip-snip.

Ahhh.

$$\mathcal{F}ive$$

Seated at his desk, Mackie paged through the latest issue of his favorite girlie magazine. Noise from the front office carried down the hall—more idiots swarming the studio in response to the mangled ad. He'd entered the business from the alley and escaped into his boss cave as soon as he'd heard the commotion. If Ursula insisted on claiming the Real Men byline, let her handle the headaches that came with it.

"Damn it, Gabe, aren't you done?" he groused. The kid had called in Stacy for the day and then lent a hand interviewing the bozos waiting to pose for Ursula's camera. Fine and dandy. But now, all Gabe's grunting and shifting positions so he wouldn't strain his hurt ass while installing the deadbolt stirred memories of Doug's shooting, and guilt squiggled in Mackie's gut.

The useless emotion. Was it *his* fault he and his brother had happened upon the same warehouse that night? How was he to have known what Dougie had stuck his nose into? He wasn't a human police scanner!

His stupid guilt wouldn't help him win Evie. But cooperating with her son's dumbass "investigation" couldn't hurt.

"In a minute," Gabe muttered, gaze glued to his task. He fussed with the bolt some more before chucking the tools and old doorknob into a small metal chest. He grimaced as he wiped his hands on his jeans and stood. Closing the door, he turned the deadbolt back and forth.

Mackie squinted. "Whaddya doing?"

"Testing the lock for your next rendezvous with Jasmine. Is she the only woman in your life right now?"

"Why? You crying for some?"

Gabe massaged his hip. "I should talk to your ex-girlfriends."

"About the vandalism and shredded note? Hell, no. They might think I suspect them." Grilling his women would accomplish squat. A bunch of airheads, the whole lot. Insecure, eager to please, and easy to dupe. Besides, in preparation for committing to Evie, Mackie had restricted himself to Jasmine these last few weeks, and he definitely knew she had nothing to do with any "incidents." He flipped a magazine page with his thumb. "Look into Ursula and Stacy, like you said."

Gabe frowned. "There's the sabotaged ad to consider too, Uncle Vic."

"Oh, yeah." Mackie cleared his throat. He might have manufactured the note and the crap with the windows to keep Evie's attention on him and away from that pain-in-the-butt bean-counter, Hal Henshaw, but when it came to the ad, his fingers were clean. "I guess I can give you some names." Dead ends. "Weren't you gonna poke around at the *Clarion*?"

"Today, after I speak to Stacy." Gabe scratched his jaw. "Something's fishy with her. Ursula said Stacy needs the extra hours, but she sounded flustered when I called. Mentioned a family emergency. But when she got here, she pretended like she hadn't breathed a word."

"Maybe you caught her masturbating when you phoned."

"Excuse me?" Gabe glared. "You know, sometimes you're a real—"

"Hey! *You* wanted to look into this mess. I'm just brainstorming. Maybe she was embarrassed and made up an emergency on the fly."

Gabe turned for the door, then glanced back. "I need to ask about Mom."

"Now that's more like it." Mackie loved talking about Evie. He shoved his magazine into a drawer.

Gabe limped to the window and opened the dusty blinds. In flowed the goddamn sun.

"Hal called her last night," the kid said.

Fuck! "He did?"

"She said they broke up, but she wouldn't say why."

"Well, I shouldn't tell tales out of school, if you know what I mean." This was perfect! Evie had confided in him before notifying her own son.

"She's my mother, Mackie. I understand her reluctance to talk about an ex-boyfriend to a point. The thing is, I have a feeling their split is related to me somehow. That's why she won't discuss it."

"Why would you think that?" Like Gabe was the sis-boom-bah center of her universe! Like the kid abandoning his mother to play big city cop hadn't provided Mackie and Evie plenty of opportunities to grow close.

"Just a hunch," the tool-for-brains said.

Mackie conjured a smile. Gabe had surprised him with the news about Hal's phone call. Reconsidering the situation, he should allow Evie's son some credit. His future happiness rested on the timing of the breakup, and Gabe had unwittingly played a part in that. The kid's shooting had created the necessary groundwork for the split, but *Mackie* had manipulated a mushy snowball into a relentless avalanche.

Acting hesitant, he clasped the arms of his swivel chair. "Listen," he said in a buddy-buddy tone. "If I blab about what went down with Hal, your mother might feel she can't tell me other stuff she needs to get off her chest. Because that's how it is, you know. Unless she's seeing someone, she leans on me." None of the morons she'd dated since Doug died had impressed her like Hal Henshaw though. Mackie's bowels knotted. After developing his coping mechanism of screwing dozens of faceless women—the only reliable method for banishing raunchy fantasies of his lady love— that was the thanks he got?

The first man since Doug died to send Evie over the moon...and it hadn't been him.

Gabe's shooting had been like a sign from the universe for Mackie to step up his game. To win himself a wife *now* instead of waiting until he'd stowed enough cash from selling his business.

Between the sale and his final blackmail scheme, he and Evie would be golden.

Gabe persisted, "Uncle Vic, if you tell me about the split, Mom will understand it's because you care about her. She might get upset when she finds out, but in the long run she'll think more of you."

"All right," Mackie muttered, faking like Dougie's son had worn him down.

But no one tricked Victor McKenzie. *Ever.*

He ambled out from behind his desk. "It's about your shooting." He tidied file folders beside the computer. "Hal made it about him. When your mother flew down to see you, she didn't want him tagging along. Said she had to face the reality of nearly losing you on her lonesome."

Gabe rubbed his hip again. "Hal didn't like that she needed space?"

"It turned him into a freaking insecure mess. When she got back, he asked her to marry him. So she axed the bastard."

Gabe's gaze narrowed. "I thought they were good together."

"Well…" Mackie wanted a future with Evie more than anything, which meant making room in his life for Gabe. At least in the beginning. This was his chance to ease his nephew onto his good side. He couldn't mess up. "Maybe ol' Hal isn't as wonderful as Evie's led us to believe. Maybe she didn't want to admit that staying with him longer than any man since your dad died was a mistake."

"So she dated him until he proposed? That doesn't make sense."

The phone rang. Damn thing had been bouncing off the hook all morning. Halfway through the second ring, Stacy must have answered, because the shrill noise stopped.

"Hal pushed too hard," Mackie said. "Spouted crap like if they got married she wouldn't have to worry about someone dying on her again, him being the uptight sort who won't cross the street without looking both ways a dozen times. But she…" Mackie paused. He should get an Oscar! "Evie saw through his bullshit." With a bit of nudging. "Hal trying to put his needs before *yours* when you were down for the count in the hospital was the proverbial straw. All she could think about was *her baby* nearly biting the dust, and he thought the answer was to get engaged?"

"That doesn't sound like Hal."

Mackie spread his hands. "You haven't been around. Sure, he gave her a few days to think about it, but then he laid on the pressure, demanding a response." All right, technically, Hal had "asked" for a response. With Mackie's help, Evie had come around to thinking of it as demanding.

And, if someone wanted to get picky, Mackie might have hurried along the breakup by subtly pointing out ways Hal couldn't compare to Doug. So what? *He* wasn't the loser who'd proposed all of a sudden, before Evie was ready, like some randy sixteen-year-old spurting on his girlfriend's skirt.

Gabe stroked his chin. "Seems like she's still not over Dad."

"The way he died… That kind of trauma takes a lot of getting over."

"And I went into police work, which probably didn't help."

Mackie hesitated—for real this time. He couldn't turn the blame screw too much, or Gabe's ex-cop nose might smell a rat.

He strolled over and patted the kid's back. "Your mother has always respected your choices."

Gabe cast him a skeptical look.

Mackie lowered his hand. "I hate to cut short this bonding moment, but I got a location shoot. I have to grab my gear and some lunch first." While he was at it, he'd drop by City Hall and bluster a line of bullcrap outside Paul Bloomfield's office door. An earlier phone call had alerted him that the council president's schedule was booked solid, but terrorizing the pencil-neck's staff while Bloomfield cowered behind his desk would remind the politician *who* controlled the money drops.

"Thanks for telling me about Mom and Hal," Gabe said.

Mackie forced another smile. "Keep spying on Ursula and Stacy." *And stay away from my extracurricular activities.*

If Gabe followed his lead, in the end they would all get what they wanted.

Including Evie.

She just didn't know it yet.

"That's right, Mr. Withers," Gabe said into the desk phone in his uncle's office. "You can choose to keep this afternoon's appointment or would tomorrow morning work better?"

The man on the other end of the line hemmed and hawed. Like several other ad respondents Gabe had called, learning the test shots meant potential exposure in *Seattle Lights* magazine discouraged Withers.

Evidently, the fellow preferred the idea of posing for sleazy portraits.

"If you'd rather not come in after the changes I've explained, we understand." Whether Withers or anyone else dropped out didn't concern Gabe one way or the other. It might concern Ursula—if she was innocent of the studio sabotage and couldn't find suitable applicants to complete her assignment. For Gabe's part, in order to keep his new "boss" happy while maintaining his role as the studio gofer, he needed to put a stop to the day's pandemonium before he snooped around at the *Clarion*.

Withers blathered more. Gabe replied, "Yes, I'll cancel the appointment. Please accept my apologies for the misprinted ad."

Hanging up, he scanned the names left on his list. The last he knew, Stacy was chained to the waiting room desk dealing with the midday appointments while calling names on another list. Gabe had offered to call her portion, but she'd said she wanted to help. Nice of her, unless she'd intentionally overscheduled Ursula as part of a scheme to throw studio business into a turmoil.

At any rate, if Stacy remained as busy as Gabe had noticed earlier, now was a great opportunity to verify Ursula's alibi for placing the bungled ad. Last night Ursula had claimed she was with clients when Stacy called the paper.

Had his fake boss told the truth?

Leaving the desk, he strode to the door and opened it. The line of waiting men stretched from the reception area down into the main hall, nearly reaching his uncle's office. Stacy's frazzled voice echoed from the front of the building.

Closing the door, Gabe withdrew a folded notepaper from a pocket of his jeans. He walked back to the desk. During a hectic moment after Mackie left for his location shoot and Stacy disappeared into the staffroom, he'd peeked into the scheduling software for last Wednesday's client names and phone numbers. He'd discovered five appointments, two of which had occurred within the pertinent time frame for placing the ad. He'd scrawled the client details on the notepaper before Stacy returned.

Sitting at the desk, he glanced at the phone. The second line appeared free. In the event Stacy *was* his suspect and tried eavesdropping on his calls, he retrieved a burner phone from another pocket and punched in the first client phone number.

A woman answered. "Hello?"

Gabe affected a smile-saturated telephone solicitor's voice. "Hello, this is Matt Bennett with Quality Customer Satisfaction Surveys. I'm calling for Mrs. Straithern. Is she there?"

"This is she," the woman replied in a wary tone.

"Excellent. Mrs. Straithern, Victor McKenzie Photography hired QCSS to conduct a survey about their recent Christmas special. I understand your family visited the studio November seventh?"

"That's right. Why? We ordered several prints as well as the thumb drive. There isn't a problem getting delivery before Christmas, is there?"

"Not at all. On the contrary, Mr. McKenzie wants to ensure your appointment was trouble-free. Participation in the survey will qualify you for a coupon drawing for a *free* photography sitting eligible for use within six months. How does that sound?"

"Oh! Our niece is having a baby in January. If I win, can she use the coupon?"

"It's fully transferable." Easy to fabricate, considering a fictional client would win the freebie. "Mrs. Straithern, how was your family's experience at the studio November seventh? Did Mr. McKenzie live up to your expectations?"

"He didn't take our pictures. His assistant did. Such a pleasant young woman. Ursula was her name."

"My mistake. Let me check my records." Gabe waited a moment. "I see. You had Ursula Scott?"

"Yes, and she was wonderful. Really put my twins at ease. What a creative eye. She suggested cute, playful poses for the boys." A beat passed. "To be honest, I was skeptical about using the McKenzie studio. My neighbor booked the owner for her wedding two summers ago, and the pictures were a disappointment. But my cousin said Ursula was different, and was she ever. She created a lovely online gallery, and we chose our photos from there. Mr. McKenzie didn't offer galleries two years ago. I will say this, the price was a bargain. That's why we took the chance."

"Great. Did Ursula Scott provide your family with her undivided attention?"

"Definitely." A smile brimmed Mrs. Straithern's voice.

"Did she leave the studio at any time during your appointment?"

"No. May I ask why?"

"Mrs. Straithern, Mr. McKenzie wants to improve his business practices. He hired us to help determine if he requires additional staff. If Miss Scott used a phone or tablet or if she left the room for even one minute while you were there, he'd like to know."

"It's good he's looking to improve. No, Ursula remained with my family in the backroom the entire time. Another girl was up front. Stacy? Now that you mention it, she always seemed to be on the phone. I didn't notice Mr. McKenzie hanging around."

The woman's remarks further confirmed Mackie's alibi, which Jasmine and Mackie's elderly neighbor had verified. Score one for Ursula telling the truth about not placing the ad too.

Gabe asked, "Regarding the receptionist—"

The doorknob rattled. He tensed.

"Yes?" Mrs. Straithern asked.

Voices carried through the door, including Stacy's.

"Thank you for participating in the survey," Gabe finished. "If you win, your coupon will arrive via email next week." He slipped the disposable cell and the notepaper into a pocket. Grabbing the desk phone, he feigned studying his Real Men list.

Stacy blew into the room, slamming the door. "It's nuts today!" Her brown eyes were huge behind her glasses. "Have you finished your calls?"

He replaced the receiver. "Three to go. Then I'll help with yours."

"No need, I'm done. And starving. I forgot to pack a lunch."

Rising, he stepped around the desk. His hip ached. "Go out if you want. I'll man the front."

"Thanks, but I can't leave until I find my keys." Her gaze darted around the messy office. "Have you seen them? My house *and* studio keys. I lost the whole set!"

"Did you misplace them here or at home?"

"I don't know!" She gripped her skull. "I keep a spare key for my apartment under a flowerpot by my mailbox. I used the spare to lock my door this morning."

Gabe seized the opportunity to poke into the family emergency she'd mentioned earlier. "You sounded preoccupied when I phoned you to come in. Did you hang the keys in their usual spot last night?"

"I can't remember! But if I don't find them, Mackie will kill me. I left the studio keys at the coffee shop during my first week of work, and he was so pissed off I thought that vein in his temple was gonna burst. I hoped if I hung the keys on the same ring, I'd keep better track of them, but I've been so absentminded lately." She rifled through the sample photo albums on the bookshelf beneath the alley window.

Gabe searched Mackie's desktop. "Does your forgetfulness have anything to do with your family crisis?"

She remained turned away. "Uh, no, that wasn't a crisis. Just a spat with a loved one. Sorry if I made it sound like more."

"No sweat." He sounded like a cop interviewing a suspect. Luckily, Stacy's obsession with her keys consumed her.

Pushing aside the albums, she rustled through a stack of newspapers. "Not here!" She raced to an end table near the door opposite his uncle's desk. A huge half-body portrait of Mackie from at least five years ago hung on the wall.

"Did you have the keys yesterday?" Gabe asked in a helpful voice.

Stacy's hand swung up, knocking the picture. "Crap!" She straightened the fancy gilt frame. "Yes, I opened the studio with them."

"Were you in this office either then or today?"

"No. But maybe Mackie saw them lying around and hid them to teach me a lesson." She frowned, head tilting like a puppy's. "Wait!" She clapped her cheeks. Her glasses wobbled. "I'm a dummy. I remember where I left them now. Yikes, I didn't get much sleep last night."

"Out with a boyfriend, huh?"

"No." Her face reddened. "I had class, and then my mom called while I was streaming a series online. Everyone interrupts me!"

The phone rang. Gabe stepped back to the desk.

"Don't!" Stacy's hands flapped. "I'll answer out front. It's probably another salesperson, and this time I'm telling them off. We must be on a new list. They've been calling all day."

She flew out of the office, leaving the door open. Seconds later, the ringing stopped.

With an eye on the door, Gabe lifted the receiver and slowly pushed the button for Stacy's line.

Her voice pounded his eardrums. "No, Mr. McKenzie did not book a time to look at your stupid photocopiers on Monday!...Yes, I would know. Because I book the appointments....No, you *can't* confirm, because there's *no* appointment!" The phone crashed down.

Gabe disconnected. Stacy could definitely rip someone a new one. The question was, was Mackie on her shit list?

"Thank you for coming in, Mr. Dobson." Ursula smiled at the mid-forties man with a receding hairline, small paunch, and an incredible set of pearly whites. Accompanying him to the front office, she added, "If the magazine decides to use you, we'll be in contact Monday. Otherwise, depending on how busy we are, you might not hear until Tuesday."

"Monday, yes. Tuesday, no," Norm Dobson recapped. "Thanks."

"My pleasure."

Hopefully, the *Seattle Lights* editor would spot Norm's potential. He'd been a little nervous during the test shots, but Ursula possessed every confidence her camera would work wonders with his affable demeanor and sky-blue eyes. She couldn't wait to load her digital files onto the computer she shared with Stacy and determine her twenty recommendations. But first, she needed to plow through tomorrow's sittings.

She walked Norm to the door. Eight hours ago, she'd harbored major doubts she would survive today. Gabe had been a fantastic help, managing crowd control, the interviews, and assisting Stacy with rescheduling. So far their arrangement benefitted Ursula more than him. She needed to change that. After all, he was a volunteer.

Norm Dobson left. As the studio door closed, Ursula twisted her hammered-silver thumb ring. The reception area was blissfully empty, aside from Stacy and Gabe. He leaned on the counter-style desk chatting with the girl.

He was friendly, likeable, and far too sexy.

A lethal combination a wise woman would avoid.

Except she couldn't steer clear of him without breaking their agreement, and a Scott simply did not renege on their word.

"Thank God we're done for the day," she said, approaching the desk.

Gabe straightened as he faced her, and the tiny shiver she'd experienced outside the studio this morning launched another assault.

Stacy beamed. "You did great, Urs."

"Thanks. So did you. So did all of us. Handling the sheer number of applicants on my own would have been a nightmare." She glanced at Gabe. "I promise we'll get to the teaching. In the meantime, can I count on your help with tomorrow's interviews?" *So far, so good.* Maintaining eye contact without passing out was quite an achievement.

"You bet. By the way, my uncle asked me to double-check with the *Clarion* about the corrections for Friday's edition."

Ursula nodded. The community paper hit newsstands and home-delivery routes before seven a.m. "Good idea. We can't afford another mistake." Especially considering the paper only published three times a week and the *Seattle Lights* deadline for her shortlist loomed. "Did you find out what happened?"

"Some. My uncle was right when he said Stacy called in the ad—"

"But I didn't dictate *that* ad." Stacy's face screwed into a ball of anxiety. "Ursula, I'm sorry. I didn't use the wording they printed, I swear."

Ursula settled a hand on the girl's shoulder. "Did you read the copy to Tasha?" Their usual *Clarion* contact.

"Yes, but—"

"Don't worry then. It's not your fault."

"But *I* called. I'm responsible. Mackie—"

"Forget Mackie. He didn't place the ad, and he isn't dealing with the outcome. We are." The Real Men shoot was totally hers now. She planned to rely on her instincts. "I believe you, and that's what counts." Although if Stacy hadn't dictated the crude ad, who had?

"Ursula, *thank you*. Your faith in me is amazing. I'd love to talk more, but I need to hit the can. I would've gone already, but Gabe stopped by my desk." Pink tinted her cheeks.

Ursula suppressed a chuckle. *Crushing on the guy, are you, Stace?* "Go ahead."

The girl fled.

Crossing her arms, Ursula faced Gabe. "Told you it wasn't her."

"Uh-huh," he drawled, running three fingertips along his chin. "Believing she's innocent and having the facts to back you up are two different things."

"You must watch a lot of cop shows."

"Crime drama addict. How'd you guess?"

"Gee, I wonder." She retained a calm facade. Inside, her tummy fluttered. Gabe's sexy voice stroked her skin like a fine chamois cloth. "So, Detective, in your estimation, what are the facts?"

Leaning on the counter again, he beckoned her close. "Tasha Manning at the *Clarion* confirmed the studio's name appeared on the call display and that a young-sounding woman with a voice she recognized as Stacy's placed the ad. But...an hour later a man called from a local cell number and changed the copy."

The fine hairs on the back of Ursula's neck bristled. "*Mackie?*" she whispered.

"The fellow identified himself as Victor McKenzie. Tasha said he sounded strange, like he had a bad cold."

"Mackie didn't have a cold last week." What was going on?

"Maybe he wanted to disguise himself," Gabe said.

"But he gave his name."

"Or some other guy called pretending to be Mackie. Who knows?"

"Couldn't the paper track down the cell number using their call display logs?"

Gabe wobbled a hand. "Possibly, if they don't trash the info on a regular basis. Some of those logs expire after a couple of days."

"You're right. Our system only holds two hundred numbers before it overwrites." She sighed. "The *Clarion* must receive way more calls than we do."

"Not all is lost. You'll be glad to hear Tasha passed me to her manager, Todd Greenly. Todd is speaking to the production department. An old-timer retired last week, and there might have been alcohol involved."

"Some drunk pulled a fast one on Tasha at our expense? That blows."

Gabe smiled. "If no one steps forward, we might have to accept that we'll never learn what really happened. Unless we bring in the police to dig into phone company records…"

"Mackie wouldn't phone the cops over something like this." Fingers itching, Ursula grabbed a stapler, set it back down. "It shouldn't have happened, plain and simple."

"Todd agrees. He's printing a second retraction in the Sunday edition. That's on top of the retraction and corrections appearing tomorrow." Gabe glanced at the ceiling, eyes flicking back and forth. "I think I got that right." He looked at her again. "Also, he's not charging for the misprinted ads."

Ursula exhaled a gusty breath. "Thanks. You covered a lot. I have to say, you're efficient. I'm surprised you've had such difficulty keeping a job."

"I never said that. Maybe I like variety." His gaze swept her up and down, and pleasurable vibrations scattered along her skin.

Oh-oh. Romantic chemistry alert. Did Gabe consider *her* variety from the hordes of panting women he'd undoubtedly encountered in Los Angeles? Because she'd never met a more pant-worthy man.

Panty-*removing*-worthy. Heat burned between her legs, and her heart raced. From just a glance.

She stepped away from the desk, inserting necessary space between them. "I'm too exhausted from nonstop photo sessions to care about that ad anymore. As long as the magazine shoot succeeds, I'll be happy." It *needed* to succeed, for her future and her family's.

Gabe's eyebrows quirked. "Happy enough to go apartment-hunting with me Saturday?"

Stacy returned from the bathroom. "You're helping Gabe find an apartment?" Her brown eyes glowed.

Ursula's face warmed. "I said no such thing."

The girl bounced. "I'll go."

"Thanks, but one female opinion is enough," Gabe replied with a grin.

Ursula squirmed. Damn it, after all his help today, she felt bad turning him down.

Stacy nudged his shoulder. "Where are you living now?"

"With my mom."

The girl giggled. "Ursula, you have to save him from the loser existence of living with his mom."

Ursula's blood rushed. "It's the fifteenth. Any decent apartments becoming available for December will be taken."

"I'll move in January." His gaze zeroed in on her. "Come on, Ursula. The city has changed. I need a local's input."

"Yeah, Urs, what's the worst that could happen?" Stacy asked.

That she would enjoy herself. Gabe did too many crazy things to her body. She couldn't risk her heart becoming involved.

The last thing Ursula needed was to develop a soft side for a man like Gabe McKenzie. When it came down to it, he was another good-time guy, the sort with the emotional attention span of a gnat. During her early twenties, she'd endured enough romantic ADD to last three lifetimes. She wanted more from the man in her life. She deserved more.

And she would find it.

In a couple of years.

Six

Saturday morning, Ursula pulled on her jacket and fetched her purse in the entry hall of her apartment.

"Shouldn't your date be knocking on the door by now?" Kim asked, sipping coffee and tucking her legs sideways on her spot beside Deni on the living room couch. "You buzzed in Gabe three minutes ago." She gestured to her phone. "I'm timing him."

Yeah, to annoy her.

"He's not my date," Ursula reiterated for the umpteenth time. She should have told Gabe to meet her downstairs, but she'd needed to run back to her room for her cell and hadn't thought things through. Waiting at the elevator was a non-starter. Her friends would have hassled her for appearing too eager.

When they were on a roll, she couldn't win.

"Maybe that redhead in 208 accosted him in the lobby." Deni grinned over the top of her mug. "She's always lying in wait for James when he picks me up. 'Ooh, James, did you win your case?' 'Ooh, James, your coat brings out the color of your eyes.' Sometimes I think she *lives* in the lobby."

Ursula cast her friends the hairy eyeball. "No one has accosted Gabe."

"I might accost him…" Deni's eyebrows wiggled "…if I weren't engaged. He's cute."

Kim gaped. "You'll accost James, and no one else."

"I'm just teasing Urs."

"*I'm* in charge of the teasing around here."

"I can tease!"

"Only James!"

The pair twittered like a couple of teenagers.

"Shh, you two." Ursula tapped her foot. A knock sounded, and she practically ripped the door off the hinges opening it.

"Hi." Gabe stood in the hall, clasping several website printouts. "Ready to go?"

"Um…" Ursula's impatience with her roommates vanished. Now that opportunity presented itself, she took a moment to drink in the vision that was Gabe Hello-Hot-Fantasy-Man McKenzie. Nothing wrong with a little surreptitious looking. A day's growth of beard shadowed his jaw, and he wore his customary faded jeans. The guy could hold seminars on the Sexy Art of Casually Rumpled. Neither the rain flecks in his chestnut hair nor his damp black sweater detracted from the effect. "Want an umbrella?" she asked.

"They're for wimps." He uttered the standard Seattleite response. The wind could twist an umbrella into a giant pretzel around this town.

"Then count me *as* one." Ursula didn't mind a bearable daily mist, but when the forecast called for buckets of the wet stuff, she caved.

Saying goodbye to her friends, she retrieved a big umbrella from the closet and walked alongside Gabe to the elevator.

"You look nice," he said.

She hadn't worked at it. Nope. "Thanks."

"I didn't realize your roommates were home. I should have stepped in for a minute and said hi."

"No way. They've been hassling me all morning."

"About what?"

She slid him a glance. "You."

He punched the elevator button. "Why?"

"They think you're killer handsome and that I should go after you."

He laughed. "You're telling me this because…?"

"To see how you'd respond." He could handle the ribbing. The camaraderie that had existed between them since he'd showed up at her apartment bearing pizza had only developed further yesterday while they'd dealt with the last of the test subjects and selected twenty to submit to *Seattle Lights*. He infused a welcome sense of calm into hectic circumstances. Otherwise, she wouldn't have placed herself in temptation's way today.

"To see how I'd respond, huh?" he asked as the elevator arrived. They stepped inside the empty compartment. "*Are* you going after me?"

Ursula smiled. "No." The elevator chugged down the shaft. The outdoorsy scent of rain-soaked male enshrouded Gabe. The fresh fragrance of Irish Spring soap drifted from the V of his sweater.

She'd always liked the Irish.

"Because we work together?" he persevered.

"Because I'm your boss." A clichéd excuse, but she wasn't about to reveal that even if he weren't a temporary staff member, he possessed the earmarks of a Mr. Good Times.

"But if *I* were *your* boss…"

Like one of those billionaire movie characters? Her skin heated. "Dream on."

He produced a smug grin. "That's better than telling me to take a flying leap."

The elevator ground to a halt. Just in time. The attraction between them sparkled in close quarters.

Or was she the only one transfixed?

The doors slid apart. Ursula unsnapped the umbrella in preparation for the wet walk to the parking lot, and Gabe held open the lobby door as she exited the building.

Sidestepping a puddle on the walkway, she popped up the umbrella. Gabe ducked beneath the protective dome, took the handle, and lifted the umbrella above them both.

Rain pelted nylon. "I thought you said umbrellas were for wimps," Ursula murmured, eyeing him.

"Yours is so huge, I figured you'd look lonely under here without me." A gust of wind swept in, and he rubbed his hand gripping the umbrella. The computer pages jiggled.

"Oh, sure, big wimpy man." They turned toward the parking lot. "Did you drive here?"

He nodded. "I bought an old pickup before I left LA. It's parked down the street."

Hence his soggy appearance. "Let's take Reba. Um, my car. It'll be easier if I'm driving and you're reading addresses."

"Reba?" He closed one eye.

"It's short for Reba the Red Road Warrior, which she might have been in a previous life. You never know." Ursula led him to her old compact with dull red, oxidized paint. She unlocked the passenger door with her key. Reba's previous owner had lost the electronic fob, and the right door had long ago relinquished the ability to unlock from inside. Ursula didn't care. Reba was a survivor and she had heart, like all Scotts.

"You like being in control, don't you?"

"Losing all your worldly possessions can do that to a person," she replied without thinking. At his quizzical look, she explained, "Our house burned down when I was ten." Information she usually kept close until she really knew and felt comfortable with someone.

Odd that she felt at ease with Gabe after meeting him only three days ago.

His forehead furrowed. "Jeez, Ursula, that's terrible. Was your family okay?"

"The four of us made it out safely, thank God, but we lost everything. My parents' hard-earned possessions, my mom's few heirlooms, our photo albums and home movies. And my cat, Pierre." The poor little animal. He had always curled beside her while she slept. "The night of the fire, he ran under my bed when my mom started yelling for me and my brother."

"How old was your brother?"

"Four at the time. His name is Owen." With Owen safe in their mom's arms, Ursula had struggled to retrieve her frightened cat. "The smoke was overpowering. I stretched under the springs to reach Pierre, but he'd scoot back again, pressing into the corner. I was coughing so hard. My dad said he was sorry, but we had to leave." Dad had grabbed her around the waist, lifting her, holding her, murmuring his apologies that they couldn't rescue Pierre. As Ursula cried against his shoulder, Dad carried her out of the smoke and flames to join her mom and brother huddled on the neighbor's lawn. She would never forget the howling of the fire-engine sirens rending the cold midnight air.

Tears welled, and she wiped a hand across her eyes. "Sorry. I can't think of that helpless little animal without choking up."

"I don't blame you," Gabe murmured. "That's rough." He made no move to open the car door and get out of the rain. Gripping the umbrella handle, he wedged the printouts more firmly beneath his arm and cupped her cheek with his free hand. "What caused the fire?" he asked in a near-whisper.

"Faulty wiring," she responded through a tight throat. "The house was a few months old. My dad installed the kitchen cabinets himself. Insurance replaced what could be replaced, but you can't..."

"Replace a pet and personal mementos." Compassion reflected in Gabe's green eyes.

She nodded. "I cried for weeks over Pierre. For years, I had nightmares about trying to save him. He was an adorable black-and-white cat, a present for my fifth birthday." She stared across her car. The rain splashed the hood.

Gabe's thumb brushed her face, warm against her skin. "I had a dog. A galumphing chocolate lab named Ruckus. My mom said we created one whenever we were together."

Ursula's mouth curved, and she looked at him again. Somehow, while she relived the pain of her worst childhood memory, this man helped her smile.

"I can picture the two of you galumphing. Pierre used to purr against my arm when I sat on my bed and wrote in my little blue diary, which I also lost in the fire. Every day I would jot down one of his antics." After their house burned, she never kept a diary again. Her pre-teen mind equated recording her activities, hopes, and dreams as providing another opportunity for fate to rip them away.

"Did your parents rebuild?" he asked.

"Yes. But that was in Portland. A few months later, my dad was laid off. Eventually, he found another job here."

"And you lost out again. It must have been hard, moving away from your school and friends."

She nodded. "A lot of kids get uprooted because of job changes, death, divorce. I had my parents and my brother, and they were great." Why was she spilling her life story in the middle of a parking lot while the gray sky spit rain and a chilly breeze sliced against Gabe's damp clothes?

Why tell him any of this?

She tightened her grip on her purse strap. Something about Gabe McKenzie encouraged her to open up. The way he phrased questions. The caring tone of his voice.

Not only did he seem to understand her childhood trauma, he understood *her*.

"Is that why you became a photographer? To create new memories?"

"You could say that." He read her too well. Extending her reach beyond the shelter of the umbrella, she opened the car door. Cold drops splattered her bare hand. "My grandma gave me her old Instamatic film camera when I was twelve. It brought out the shutterbug in me." That first inexpensive Kodak had introduced her to a whole new world. The magic of containing life's mysteries within the lens. Capturing the joy and forgetting the pain.

Pictures had felt tangible to her. Worth a thousand sentences in a hundred diaries.

She still felt that way.

She angled her head toward her car. "Let's go before the rain starts falling *inside* Reba and the umbrella springs a leak."

Gabe slid into the car and placed the umbrella on the rear floor. Ursula climbed in behind the wheel, flipping through her keys while he shifted his legs in the cramped space Deni had last occupied.

His right hand shot to his hip, and he flinched.

"Sorry if it's uncomfortable," Ursula said. "There's a latch under the seat to move it back."

He adjusted the seat. "It's just this old injury."

"What happened?"

"I'll tell you sometime, but today"—he tapped the computer papers on his opposite thigh—"we have apartments to scout." He studied the listings.

"All right." She fired the engine. He encouraged her to spill her guts, then grew evasive. What was up with that? "Read out the addresses, and we'll decide on the most efficient route. But first, we find the nearest coffee hut."

Gabe faked interest in the ramshackle apartment building as the middle-aged landlady preceded him and Ursula along a second-floor hallway. In the four hours since he and his suspect had huddled beneath her umbrella outside Reba the Red Road Warrior, the rain had tapered to a drizzle. Thanks to Reba's heating vents, Gabe's clothing no longer chilled his skin, and they'd relinquished the umbrella. Everything was hunky-dory casual, but fooling Ursula with this charade of a day pricked his conscience. She'd shared the horrible childhood trauma of a house fire while he'd clammed up after one simple question. He hated keeping his past secret from a woman he easily imagined dating under different circumstances. Until he crossed her off his suspect list, he didn't have a choice.

They approached a door marked 2-D. "This building's in an excellent location," the landlady said in a cigarette-husky voice. "There's a gas station and convenience store around the corner."

"Sounds great, Mrs. Klein," Ursula said.

Gabe flexed his shoulders in a noncommittal shrug. Yep, he was a crud. With a capital C. Ursula didn't realize it, but 2-D was the last apartment they would view. He'd asked for her help today as a pretext for engineering an invitation back to her place. There, he would finagle a way to snoop around and, hopefully, clear her of more studio incidents. Then he could direct his focus more fully on Stacy.

Their visit to this building and others before it was more about maintaining his laid-back persona than finding a place, which he could accomplish alone. Surprisingly, the previous building had showed promise. That unit included a second bedroom he could use for his PI business, although the rent exceeded what Ursula expected a guy of his "limited resources" to pay—her wording when the manager left them in the kitchen to discuss his options.

The unit didn't vacate until February. Gabe would view it again alone next week. If another renter claimed the space first, he'd keep an eye peeled for similar openings in the same neighborhood.

The landlady for the current building unlocked 2-D. As Mrs. Klein and Ursula entered, Ursula glanced over her shoulder at Gabe. Her lips twitched. A second later, he realized why. The place was a throwback to hippie times. The thick scent of recently burned incense veiled a marijuana odor. Mrs. Klein's cigarette habit must have obliterated her olfactory senses, because she took no notice. An old couch bumped against a grimy kitchenette stove, and multi-colored beads hung in the bedroom doorway.

"It's real cozy." Mrs. Klein picked her thumbnail. "You two would love it here."

"The apartment is just for him," Ursula said.

Gabe jostled her arm. "I dunno, honey. I like this place a lot. Doncha wanna shack up?"

She smirked. "You do have charm."

Gabe informed Mrs. Klein, "She hasn't agreed to move in with me yet, but I'm hopeful."

The landlady chuckled. "Look at the bedroom. I'll stay here." She plucked a cell phone from the pocket of her baggy pants. "I need to check with hubby about dinner."

Ursula parted the beads and strolled into the bedroom. Gabe followed, the plastic streams clinking. In the living room, Mrs. Klein murmured on her cell.

"Why did you say that bit about me moving in?" Ursula whispered. "Landlords like reliable tenants. Now she'll think you're wishy-washy."

"*You're* wishy-washy, refusing to shack up. Don't sweat it, sweetheart. I'm not sleeping in this fleabag, so what does it matter?"

She leveled him an impatient look. "We just arrived, Gabe. Give the place a chance."

He scanned the bong collection on a desk. "I might have lived in LA several years, but I'm not this desperate." He wandered to the window overlooking a dumpster. "Nice view."

"Okay, what about the first apartment we looked at? Cleaned up, it wouldn't be so bad."

He nodded. "All right, I'll check out the first place again after the weekend. If it's still available, I'll pay the deposit." He had no intention of renting a hovel facing a fish plant.

"Why not return now? You can sign the agreement today."

She no longer whispered, so neither did he. "If it's the apartment for me, it'll be there Monday or Tuesday."

She shook her head. "We'll be busy with the Real Men shoot starting Tuesday, and Thursday is Thanksgiving. If you want the apartment, confirm it now."

Gabe plunged his hands into his jeans pockets. "I'm not stressing over a place to stash my few boxes of stuff."

She huffed out a breath. "Then why did you ask for my help this morning?"

"Because I like you."

"Gabe!" Blushing, she swatted his arm.

"It's true." Plus, he needed to stay close to her until he finished sniffing around. Before he drove to the studio yesterday morning, he'd called Andrews Towing under an assumed name and pretended he'd left his watch in Ursula Scott's car Halloween night. No luck getting his mythical watch returned, but his snooping corroborated her story about the towing company. His phone calls to Mrs. Straithern and another studio client Thursday confirmed Ursula hadn't abandoned her customers during the time the ad was placed or when the unknown man contacted the newspaper to change the wording.

The shredded drawings and threatening note remained a mystery. The suspect could have mailed them from anywhere.

As for the broken window, Gabe's uncle had reported it to the police as occurring late Tuesday, October sixteenth, after the janitor left.

Yesterday, during a late lunch, Gabe visited SCPD headquarters and examined the report, which included interviews with businesses surrounding the studio. While nothing in the public record indicated his uncle was lying, Gabe hadn't uncovered an alibi for Ursula for that night.

To cover his bases, he needed to clear her of four incidents. So far, he'd managed two.

Stepping closer, he touched her arm. Her summery perfume drifted to his nostrils, a welcome contrast to the funky scent of the apartment.

"Mad at me for dragging you around the city?" he asked.

"It's not that." She tossed up her hands. "If you like a girl, ask her to a movie, not to view apartments."

"Haven't we established that you don't date the help?"

She rolled her eyes. "You're impossible."

He pretended to backpedal. "Okay, you've convinced me. I'll consider the first building." Not a chance. "Want to visit Space Needle or Pike Place Market? I can't remember the last time I played Seattle tourist."

She glanced at her phone. "Sorry, it's past two, and I'm getting my brother from U-Dub at five. We're having dinner at our parents'."

"Doesn't he live with them?"

"He has a regular Saturday study group on-campus."

Good for Owen. "Let me buy you another latte before you drop me off. After all the time you've wasted on me—"

"No fighting in there unless you sign a lease!" Mrs. Klein hollered from the living room.

Ursula's lips curved. "I don't consider it time wasted. But we've been to Coffee-Quikky twice already. If I drink any more caffeine, I'll leap out of my skin."

He looked out the window. "It's raining harder again, and I'm cold."

Her smile broadened. "Serves you right for acting macho, arriving at my place without a jacket."

"What can I say? California sunshine fried my brain."

She laughed. "Deni will be on her date with her fiancé, but Kim might be home. She makes a mean hot chocolate."

"Doesn't chocolate contain caffeine?"

"We'll add extra milk."

Gabe plastered on a pleased grin, but his conscience chomped his gut.

If Ursula realized his real reasons for weaseling an invitation back to her place, her pretty smiles and infectious laughter would vanish.

Seven

Gabe fabricated stories about his life in LA while Ursula tackled congested weekend traffic. Remorse gnawed him throughout the drive to her place. Numerous times he reminded himself that a former cop on his way to becoming a PI couldn't allow a beautiful face and sparkling personality to dictate the course of an investigation. Otherwise, good luck developing a solid reputation.

He ambled into the living room. She remained in the entry hall, stowing her coat and umbrella in the closet. Kim, oblivious to their arrival, sat leaning forward on the couch, studying an open laptop on the coffee table. Smoke curled from a cigarette in a saucer. A phone and can of air freshener sat beside the laptop. The deck door gaped, allowing an influx of cold air.

He waved. "Hey, Kim."

"Shit!" She slapped shut the laptop. Jumping off the couch, she shouted toward the entry, "Ursula, couldn't you have texted you were bringing him home? I was concentrating."

The closet door clicked closed. A moment later, Ursula appeared in the living room, fanning her hand in front of her nose. "And smoking, I see." She chucked her purse onto the couch. "Kim, you *know* Deni and I hate cigarette smoke inside."

"Sorry." Kim stabbed the cigarette in the saucer. "Don't tell

Deni. She'll kill me." Grabbing the spray bomb, she zapped the air with a lemony scent.

"*I'll* kill you." Ursula marched to the glass door and whisked it shut. "If it's too cold to smoke outside, maybe it's time to take a hint that it's too cold to smoke, period." She walked back to the coffee table. "It's toxic for your health. And it stinks."

"I know." Kim pouted. "Ever try to break a bad habit?" She appealed to Gabe, "How about you?"

"No comment." No way was he venturing into a roommate nicotine war.

"Get the patch," Ursula instructed her friend. "Chew nicotine gum. There are a ton of options these days."

"I've tried them."

"Try again." Ursula lifted the laptop screen. "What were you so engrossed in that you didn't hear us?"

"Nothing." Kim smacked down the screen again, squashing Ursula's fingers.

"Ow!" Ursula yanked out her hand.

"Stop snooping."

"I'm showing interest in your life."

"Well, stop." Clutching her laptop and phone to her chest, Kim stomped down the hall toward the bedrooms.

Gabe peered after her, estimating the layout of the place. He needed to snoop inside Ursula's room without giving away his game.

But just then she gazed at him, and he ran a hand through his hair, acting casual.

A frown puckered her brow. "Kim's hiding something. I caught her like this last weekend too. Normally, she hears every whisper in this place, but something on that computer has her glued to it."

"Maybe she's seeking stop-smoking tips online."

"Like posting to a forum or support group?"

"Or she's online dating."

"Or it's none of your business," Kim said, returning.

Ursula asked her friend in a sweet voice, "Does this mean I can't charm you into making us hot chocolate?"

"Promise you'll keep your nose out of my stuff, and I'll make whatever you want."

"Ooh, a dilemma."

"I mean it, Urs. It was work. Can I help it if I'm behind?"

"In a word, yes."

Kim growled.

"What do you do?" Gabe asked her.

"I'm in HR at James's law firm. He's Deni's fiancé. She met him through me."

"It isn't only her Human Resources job our little Kimmy likes." Ursula grinned. "She's quite the matchmaker."

Kim groaned. "I didn't fix them up *on purpose*. Love," she added, as if the concept appalled her. "Who needs it?" She stared down Gabe.

He held up his hands. "I'm just here for the hot chocolate." Kim's body language clues weren't lost on him: arched eyebrows, widened gaze, unrelenting eye contact.

Either she didn't believe a word she'd said or she *was* hiding something. And trying to conceal the fact.

Ursula turned toward the kitchen. "Come on, sweetie. I'll help."

"In a second. I need to check something." Kim strode down the hall again.

Gabe accompanied Ursula past the tiny dining table. As she turned into the kitchen, he glanced at the communal desk. "I'm not sweetie...I don't think. But I can help."

She laughed. "That's okay. Sit down."

The *squeak-thump* of the fridge opening and closing echoed in the space between the desk and kitchen. Gabe tapped a finger on the desktop, feigning absorption in an assortment of printed pictures.

Would Ursula store a paper calendar in this desk or in her bedroom? Or did she use a phone app?

Entering his range of vision, she placed a milk carton on the counter. "Something caught your eye?"

"Yeah, these pictures. Is this your family?" Most of the scattered photographs featured a woman in various stages of her sixties, he guessed. The woman's face sagged on one side, indicating she suffered an ailment. A few prints were set in a flower-filled yard while others showed the woman with folks who were likely family members at several holiday and birthday celebrations, as if the photos had been taken over a span of years.

Some pictures included the woman in a residential care facility. In one photo, an attendant hugged the lady. Another shot portrayed Ursula and a black-haired young man—probably Owen, her brother —presenting the woman with a candle-topped birthday cake.

"Yes, mainly family," Ursula replied. Leaving the milk on the counter, she slipped in beside him. She pointed to a picture featuring the woman in a garden chair beneath a leaf-shedding maple tree. A walker stood beside the chair. "This was my Grandma Betty. Remember I said my grandma gave me my first camera? She's the grandmother I was talking about. She was young for a grandma, maybe forty-four when I was born. She had my mom when she was twenty."

"And you're, let me guess, twenty-five?"

"On the nose." She smiled. "Grandma B was into photography too. Sharing a common interest was fun. I loved hanging out with her. But life presented her with more than her share of challenges. She was only sixty-eight when she died of a stroke two weeks following last Thanksgiving."

Gabe's stomach tightened. The first anniversary of her grandmother's death loomed. He knew from losing his dad what that felt like.

Sheer hell.

"Ursula, I'm sorry."

"Don't be. She had the most amazing spirit. Nothing ever got her down. Her first stroke occurred several years earlier. That's why she has a crooked smile in the pictures." Her fingers skipped to an enlargement of a family at a turkey-laden table. "I took this one with a tripod and self-timer," she said, her sweater sleeve grazing Gabe's arm. "This is my mom, dad, and Owen, who is nineteen now. He was eighteen here."

In the photo, Ursula sat between her mom and grandma, an arm wrapped around both women. Her dad and brother stood behind the three ladies, bending down on either side of Ursula. Her dad's wide smile revealed a chipped front tooth. They looked like a typical, all-American, working-class family.

"You must've had to run to squeeze into the middle like that," he noted.

"When I want to be the center of attention, I'm like a gazelle."

He picked up the five-by-seven. "You look like your mom and grandma, who are both knockouts, by the way."

"Thanks. I've been choosing digital files and printing them over the last few weeks. My mom loves themed scrapbooks. I'm making one about Grandma Betty and will give it to her this Thursday."

Thanksgiving. He nodded. "Do you have cousins? Aunts and uncles?"

"My mother is an only child, but my dad has two brothers and a sister in Portland. They each have two kids. My mom's Thanksgivings are usually more crowded when she invites the Portland family, but last year was my aunt's turn to host her husband's side of the family and it was one of my uncle's sister-in-law's turn to host theirs."

When she explained it like that, his brain blocked. "Huh?"

"I know it sounds like a lot of people, but look at my roommate Deni and her fiancé. She has three sisters, and he has two brothers. Once their group has kids, imagine how jam-packed their Thanksgivings will be."

He'd rather think about Ursula. Her nearness stroked his veins. Her light perfume kicked butt all over Kim's smoke-and-lemon cloud, and her lips boasted a cherry-colored gloss she'd applied in the car after their last apartment-viewing.

One half-step closer and he could tug her into his arms and kiss those tempting lips. Skim his hands over her slim figure and zing their attraction to life.

But a professional wouldn't act on that impulse without a damn good reason. For now, at least, Ursula remained a potential suspect.

Gabe returned the picture to the desk. "I always wondered what it would be like to have a large family," he said, partly because it was true and partly because he needed to deflect the awareness humming between them before he sported a full-blown woody.

"Maybe someday you'll have a ton of kids and find out."

"Maybe I already *have* a ton of kids and don't know it."

She shrugged. "You don't seem like the sort of man women wouldn't want to tell."

"I believe I've mentioned my spotty job history?"

"Yeah, but you're nice and your jobs are a lifestyle choice. If you decided to settle down, who wouldn't want you as the father of their child?"

This was getting better and better. Except...

"At this stage, my family includes me, my mom, and Mackie. Sooner or later, my kids would have to meet him."

"Good point. Does he have kids?"

"Not that I know."

"Phew. The idea of that man reproducing gives me the shivvies." She stepped back to the counter and poured milk into a pot. "Are you spending Thanksgiving with him?"

"Probably. My mom invites him every year. I tried to attend when I lived in LA, but some years I missed." The timing of his shifts hadn't permitted annual Thanksgiving visits. If he'd booked off Turkey Day every year, his mom would have needed to spend some Christmases alone. Crime didn't take vacation.

Gabe hooked a hip on the desk. His sore glute clenched. Rubbing his lower back, he mulled over the imminent holiday. Considering his mother and Hal were no longer an item, Hal wouldn't join them. Gabe would miss the man.

He really should prod his mom to discuss the breakup. Her reluctance to revisit the matter made him wonder if she regretted her decision. He didn't want to rush her or make her feel uncomfortable, but talking it out might do her good. She had been alone too many years and grown accustomed to handling problems on her own.

But now Gabe was home and planned never to move away again.

"Here's an idea," Ursula said, interrupting his thoughts. "Buy your uncle a separate turkey and leave it on the counter for three or four nights while your mom is asleep. Maybe he'll get an advanced case of salmonella poisoning. Drop him at the dump instead of the hospital, and"—she flung out her hands—"poof. No more Mackie." Opening a cupboard, she retrieved a can of chocolate powder and placed it on the counter.

Gabe's neck hairs prickled. She'd joked about offing his pain-in-the-butt uncle a little too readily.

Kim rounded the counter. "Tut-tut, Urs. Powder affects the flavor. I use chocolate syrup."

Ursula moved aside. "I bow to your superior skills."

"Good." Kim pulled a wooden spoon from a pottery jug. "Vamoose."

Ursula smiled at Gabe. "We can sit at the table or on the couch."

"The sofa's fine. Mind if I use your bathroom?"

"First door on the left down the hall."

"The *left*," Kim emphasized, head dipping into the fridge. She fetched a bunny-shaped bottle. "The first door on the right is mine. And that's as private as my laptop."

"Got it." Leaving the kitchen, Gabe asked Ursula, "Do you share a room with Deni?"

Kim snickered. "Why? Are you imagining a Girls Gone Naked scenario?"

A light blush dusted Ursula's face. "Kim, you have a sick mind."

"Would I be a guy if I *wasn't* imagining it?" Gabe teased, and Kim laughed.

"They each have their own rooms," Kim replied. "And, no, I won't say which is Urs's."

Not a problem. He'd find out on his own.

❧

The bathroom door clacked shut behind Ursula's guest, the noise resounding down the hall to where she stood in the kitchen. A split-second later, the rickety fan whirred. *Excellent. Cover noise.* Because she had a bone to pick with her supposed friend.

She planted a hand on the counter. "Kim Perkins, Girls Gone Naked? *Really?* That was embarrassing. Why do you insist on razzing me around him?"

"Consider it a favor. If I left it up to you, he'd never realize you're interested. You always play it too safe with men, Urs."

"I'm not playing it safe. I'm on hiatus."

"Spin it however you want."

Ursula squinted daggers at her friend. Sometimes she hated how well Kim knew her. "I've spent a lot more time with him than you have," she said in a hushed voice. "He's no different from the last two guys I dated."

"Not true. He's way hotter."

"I'm not talking about looks." Ursula carried three mugs to

the coffee table, while her roommate stirred chocolate syrup into the milk heating on the stove. The old bathroom fan wheezed. To be safe, she switched on the music dock on her way back to the kitchen. A rock song with a heavy back beat filled the living space.

She adjusted the volume higher.

"I'll agree he's gorgeous," she said as the song blared. "But I have a hard time believing he'll stick with this assistant thing any longer than it takes to complete the shoot. *If* that."

Kim lifted her spoon. "And that's a problem? You're not looking for forever, Urs. You have to buy and build your business. That doesn't mean you can't enjoy Gabe *for now*. Try a different strategy for once, and go in with your eyes wide open. Inject some excitement into your life."

"By excitement, I gather you mean sleep with him."

"You're so smart. The milk is ready." Kim glanced at the counter. "Where are the mugs?"

Ursula's face burned. "Sorry, I took them to the living room."

Kim slapped her thigh, chortling. "Well, then, bring them back. Gabe definitely has you rattled. Since when do we *not* fill the mugs at the stove?"

Ursula stuck out her tongue. As she returned to the living room, a soft *snick* reached her ears.

She stopped.

Was that the bathroom door? If Gabe had heard them—

She grabbed the mugs. He didn't appear.

On tiptoe, she sneaked into the hall.

Empty. And quiet. Aside from the whirring fan and streaming music.

"*Spying* on the poor guy now?"

Ursula jumped about five inches. Kim stood right behind her.

"Cripes, Kimmy, you scared me," she hissed.

"You dropped my Daffy Duck mug," Kim whispered, gaze flicking to the carpet. "You're damn lucky you didn't break it."

"You're damn lucky you didn't give me a heart attack."

"Actually, in that case, *you're* damn lucky."

They giggled. Ursula snatched the mug. "Quick. Into the kitchen before he hears us."

They scurried to the stove, their boisterous laughter punctuating the music.

"What's taking him so long?" Kim asked, retrieving the saucepan as Ursula set the mugs on the counter.

"He's probably looking at the sports magazine James forgot here last week. I shoved it in a vanity drawer." Unlike Ursula, Kim hadn't grown up sharing one tiny bathroom with a brother and both parents. "I've never met a man who didn't read in the bathroom."

Kim's lips screwed downward. "Disgusting." She ladled hot chocolate into the mugs then pried the top off an aerosol can of whipped cream and squirted swirly fluff into all three cups.

Ursula patted the fuchsia mug. "Extra on mine."

"We're nearly out." Kim shook the can. "Want me to leave some you can use on him?"

"When we have sex?"

"You're catching on."

They giggled again. Picking up two mugs, Ursula adopted a stern look. "Kim, you know as well as I do that it's not going to happen."

"Because you refuse to date a guy who can't hold a decent job?" Kim carried her Daffy Duck mug to the living room. Ursula followed. "We're not talking marriage, Urs." Kim shuddered. "We're not talking a commitment. We're talking a change of pace, where *you're* in charge. Get Gabe, Get Laid, Get Out. It's the Three Gets Plan." Grinning, she sank onto the couch and elbowed aside Ursula's purse.

Ursula placed her mug and Gabe's on the coffee table. "I wouldn't mind an orgasm or two," she murmured beneath the music.

"Or three or twenty." Kim blew on her hot chocolate. "He certainly looks like he can deliver." She sipped from her mug. A whipped cream mustache decorated her upper lip. "Yum, tasty."

Ursula sat in the mismatched armchair, leaving couch space on the far side of Kim for Gabe. After hours spent apartment-hunting and now *this* conversation, she needed physical distance from the guy. She practically ran a fever just discussing the idea of sleeping with him.

"Don't forget he's Mackie's nephew," she said to combat the tingling between her thighs. "And that man is a bottom-feeder. I haven't known Gabe long enough to say he's not the same." She fiddled with the knee of her jeans, avoiding Kim's gaze—and evading the truth.

Gabe was nothing like his uncle. Gabe McKenzie was sexy, mysterious, a bit rough around the edges, but also funny and easy to talk to. From what she'd witnessed in the half-week she'd known him, he was also goodhearted. Within days of moving to town, he'd checked in on Mackie. Why? To make his mom happy.

How sweet was that? Most women would scramble over each other to date a guy who treated his mother like gold.

"A little slumming never hurt a girl," Kim said, lifting her mug for another sip. She licked off her whipped cream mustache. "With any luck, that's all he'll want in return."

"What do you mean? If Gabe wanted to sleep with me, *he* would be slumming too? Thanks a lot."

Kim chuckled. "No, no." The rock melody flowed into another. In the lull between songs, the distinct thudding of a closing door reverberated in the hallway. Kim whispered, "Shh, he's coming."

Ursula grasped her mug.

Gabe emerged around the corner.

"Hey, there," she said faux-casually. "Drink your cocoa. I have to leave for my parents' soon."

He eyed the seating arrangements. "Trying to get rid of me?"

"Never." Kim winked suggestively, and he smiled.

So, Ursula and her roommate thought having sex with him equaled slumming, huh?

Parked on the springy couch beside Kim while Ursula occupied the large, comfortable-looking armchair, Gabe sipped his hot chocolate and stared straight ahead. Building on overheard snippets of the women's conversation, he'd stiffened his posture until his spine felt constructed of rebar and hadn't uttered more than monosyllabic responses since Ursula had handed him his mug.

Truthfully, their trash-talking didn't insult him. It testified that they bought his cover, which he needed to maintain.

Between his eavesdropping and a discovery in Ursula's bedroom, he possessed enough information to quiz her about the broken window. He needed to get her alone for that. Maximizing the bruised-male-ego scenario might help.

"Did you put a deposit on an apartment?" Kim asked over the thumping music.

He shook his head. "I wasn't into any of the places."

"Except one." Ursula cradled her mug in her hands. "It's a studio with a small balcony. A few plants would do wonders for the place." She informed Kim, "Gabe might look at it again this week."

"I'm not much of a plant guy, and you said the magazine shoot will eat up all my time."

Her midnight-blue gaze assessed him. "You don't have to help me, Gabe. It was your idea."

That it had been. He inhaled through his nostrils. He couldn't care less about Mackie's headaches aside from how they affected his mother or might negatively impact Ursula's plans to buy the studio, should he, of course, prove her innocent of the vandalism and threats.

Then he cared. Very much. She worked hard. She deserved to achieve her dreams.

"You're right," he said. "Learning photography *was* my idea." He set down his mug. "Gotta go." More like he needed to guilt Ursula into doing the polite thing and escort him to the door for some creative questioning.

The roommates exchanged furtive looks.

"Was it something we said?" Ursula asked.

Gabe feigned a humorless laugh. Rising, he dusted his hands on his rear.

She plunked her mug on the coffee table. "I'll walk you out."

He'd counted on that.

Saying goodbye to Kim, he trailed his suspect out of the apartment and into the third-floor corridor. A man and woman in their thirties exited an apartment a few doors down. Holding hands and chatting, they strolled toward the elevator. The bell dinged, and the elevator whisked away the pair.

"Are you okay?" Ursula's fingertips grazed Gabe's arm.

"Overall," he drawled, "considering you think sleeping with a guy like me is slumming."

Red splotched her cheeks. "Gabe, I'm sorry. You weren't supposed to hear us, obviously."

"That's why the music's so loud?"

She nodded. "There's no excuse for what I said. It was the female version of locker-room talk, plain and simple."

"Oh, yeah?" He allowed his gaze to skim leisurely over her slim curves. "Guys like to believe the fairer sex wouldn't stoop so low."

She twisted the slim gold band on her left pinky, a habit he'd noted before. "Sometimes we do. Sometimes a girl will put down a guy to keep her friends from finding out how she really feels."

"Interesting." Rolling back on his heels, he slipped his fingers into his rear jeans pockets. "To be clear, you're saying you're *not* a fan of The Three Gets plan? Or that you *are*?"

Her blush deepened. "How much did you hear?"

"Enough. I turned on the bathroom fan by accident when I reached for the light switch," he fibbed. Along with the loud music, the whirring noise had concealed his footfalls—a calculated move on his part. "When I left, I forgot to turn it off." Another fib. "I heard you say something about sleeping with me. I didn't want to embarrass you, so I ducked into the nearest bedroom."

"Kim's room? After she warned you off?"

He shook his head. What was up with Kim and her laptop? "Yours, I quickly realized. The framed family photos were a dead giveaway. I looked at them to allow you and Kim time to finish talking. That's when I happened upon your wall calendar, which is open to October, by the way."

"So?"

"For one thing, it's November. For another, several dates were circled in red, including October fifteenth, sixteenth, and seventeenth." The grenade smashing the studio window had occurred on October sixteenth. "Who is Tom Haskell, Ursula?" Gabe forced a caveman tone. Although, undercover or not, he wanted to know.

Her gaze snapped. "A friend of my brother's. They met in chess club."

"Is Tom another candidate for the Three Gets Plan?"

Chin firming, she crossed her arms. "Insecure much?"

"Just trying to get a handle on my competition."

"Like I'd jump an eighteen-year-old boy. For your information, Tommy is having problems in first-year English. He had an exam that Thursday. I tutored him."

Perfect. An alibi to check.

"At his place or yours?"

"I don't believe this. You're jealous." Ursula poked his chest. "Here. We studied *here*, Gabe. Every night until midnight. Deni was home. Ask her."

"I'll take your word for it." He *would* ask Ursula's roommate, in a roundabout way, when he ran into the woman again. Now to "fix" things between him and his fake boss. "Sorry?" He showed his teeth.

"It's not funny." Her arms rammed across her chest again. "Kim is always after me to hook up with nameless dudes left and right. But that's not my style."

Hmm. So if she slept with a guy, did that mean she was serious about him?

"Maybe it's time you tried something new. How long has it been for you, Ursula?"

"None of your business."

"Because it's been three months for me." A truth riding on the coattails of his cover. He hadn't had sex since Tiffany Collingsworth dumped him for getting caught in the line of fire and spoiling her I-only-sleep-with-uniforms fetish. "I'm ready to murder my dry spell. How about you?"

"Oh, please. If I were planning on murdering anyone right now, it would be my overly sensitive, temporary assistant."

Gabe smiled. The lady protested too much. "Then you *are* interested."

"No. I want to kill you."

"That's unfortunate, because I want to kiss you." He doubted she would expect a guy of slumming caliber to wait for an invitation. Pressing his palms on the door on either side of her, he swept his gaze over her plump lips and fiery eyes. "You want it too, huh?"

"As much as I want to contract diphtheria." Her gaze cut away.

"Liar." Suddenly, the *real* Gabe needed to test the waters, damn his ethics.

Lowering his head, he placed two fingers on her jaw, coaxed her to look at him again, and bestowed a gentle kiss on her warm, soft lips. Her folded arms squashed against his chest, yet she didn't protest or struggle. Not even a little.

As he exuded more pressure, their tongues met.

He lifted his hands off the door, and she uncrossed her arms. He slid his palms beneath the long hair brushing her upper back. Her hands swept around his waist, and he moaned.

If they only ever shared one kiss, when his uncle's case ended he would take a fantastic memory with him.

The door opened behind Ursula. Kim grinned out at them, her expression evil incarnate. "Oops, the door banged. I thought someone was knocking. Seriously, Urs, you two should get a room. Your *bed*room."

Ursula scrambled out of his arms, raking her fingers through her hair. "Kim! Gabe and I work together. We—"

"Would rather get it on in the hall, where a neighbor could walk by and see you pawing each other?" Kim tittered. "Kinky, girlfriend. I didn't think you had it in you."

"Actually, a couple was just out here," Gabe contributed, and Kim tut-tutted.

Ursula plunged her head into her hands. "Oh, *crap*."

Hiding a smile, Gabe patted her shoulder. "No worries, boss. In the heat of the moment, I forgot myself. It won't happen again."

Eight

EVE SCOOPED a grocery bag out of the car trunk.

"Need help, Mom?" her son asked, exiting the house from the side door. The secondary entrance featured a small landing that descended to the basement and up a few stairs into the kitchen.

She nodded. "Thank you." A sweet ache tugged at her heart. Gabe's hair was mussed from sleep, and his sweatpants and T-shirt hung loosely on his big body. The similarities to his father at the same age were remarkable. "There are several bags. It's the last of my Thanksgiving shopping."

Yawning, he snagged five woven recycled bags by the handles and hefted them all at once. A breeze from the backyard chased a scattering of red maple leaves into the carport, and Eve flicked a glance to his bare feet on the chilly concrete.

"Why no socks, honey? You'll catch cold."

"That's an old wives' tale, Mom," he said as she retrieved the last bag and he nudged shut the trunk.

She shrugged. "I'm an old wife."

"Oh, yeah? Things back on track with Hal?"

"What gave you that idea?" Darn, probably the old wife comment. "Forget it. No, Hal and I never discussed marriage."

Her son's dubious glance pierced her.

"We didn't," she declared, feeling like a kid caught filching cookies, the evidence plastered on her face.

For a moment, they stood there while she pretended she hadn't lied and her son pretended to believe her.

Oh, Lord. She cleared her throat. Keeping details of the breakup from her adult son had become a badly ingrained habit. At first she hadn't wanted to risk the possibility of upsetting Gabe while he recovered from surgery. Now, exposing her knee-jerk reaction to Hal's spontaneous marriage proposal held the power to make their split more real.

More permanent.

As if it could *become* more permanent.

However, neither did she want Gabe guessing that his shooting had reawakened her grief for his father. She missed Hal, but her ex-boyfriend was *alive*. Once she got her act together, she could arrange to see Hal again. To possibly touch, hug, and kiss him.

But she could never kiss, caress, nor make love with her dead husband ever again.

If wallowing in that knowledge meant she was an emotionally stunted woman destined to live alone the rest of her days, so be it. She needed to mourn Doug again. To solidify his memory in her mind and heart every bit as much as she craved the reassurance that no more tragedies lurked in Gabe's future to rip him away from her too.

She couldn't bear another loss.

"We can talk about it if you want," Gabe said as they walked to the side door. "What happened with Hal?"

"I—I'm not ready." If she relayed the story, her son might consider her a fool. A middle-aged woman afraid to face the future. "I bought your favorite cereal," she said to redirect the conversation.

He glanced at the colorful box peeking from a bag. "Fruit-Zees? Thanks. But I'm not five anymore, Mom."

"I know. I've just been in a nostalgic mood." A major understatement.

He opened the door and braced his knee against it so she could enter the house first. She placed her bags and purse on the kitchen counter and turned toward him.

"Were you up late last night?" she asked. The wall clock read ten past one p.m., but the scent of fresh coffee filled the air and dark liquid brimmed the carafe.

Nodding, he deposited his bags on the table. "I was scouting information online about obtaining my private investigator license in the new year."

Hadn't he researched the subject while recovering in Los Angeles?

"In the middle of the night?" she pressed.

"My leg was bothering me. I couldn't sleep."

Oh, honey. Her chest pinched. She hated thinking of her child's discomfort, regardless that he was nearly thirty. In her mind, Gabe was still her baby.

"Isn't your criminology degree and your experience with the LAPD enough to satisfy the licensing board?"

"That's highly likely. But I still have to apply, and you and I decided I should wait."

Until after Christmas. Maternal culpability flooded her chest. "It pays to be thorough, I guess," she murmured.

The coffee aroma wafted from the pot. Gabe strode to the machine and lifted the carafe. "Want a cup?"

Shaking her head, Eve held her breath as her son retrieved his father's old Seattle City Police Department mug from a cupboard. She'd dug the mug out of storage yesterday during Gabe's absence from the house. Would he notice its return? The mug hadn't occupied her cupboard shelves for years.

Casting a cursory glance over the mug, Gabe reached for the coffee pot, and her nerves calmed.

"I'll talk to state licensing after I finish helping Uncle Vic," he said. "At the least, they'll fingerprint me, and I need a business license. The PI licensing process alone could take two months."

"Oh." Motherly guilt pervaded Eve's stomach. "Maybe you should start the procedure before January then. I didn't think it through when I asked you to wait. Um, give it until December? And thank you again for helping your uncle."

Gabe filled his mug with steaming coffee. "No problem."

"Of course you can live here as long as you need." Eve emptied grocery bags. A happy thought struck. "Honey, you can set up your business in the basement suite. The desktop computer is there.

You'll make better use of it than I ever have." She mainly depended on the wireless router for email on her laptop and tablet. "The place locks, so you'd have privacy. I need access to the washer and dryer, so you wouldn't be able to lock the door at the bottom of the stairs."

Her son lifted his cup for a slug of hot brew. "Thanks, but I need something larger than a studio. You should consider renting it out again, like when I was at U-Dub."

After his father died. "But you knew most of those boys." Gabe had stayed in his bedroom on the main floor while a parade of students bunked in the basement apartment. "Renting to college kids before you moved to California was fun, but now—remember the noise? The chemistry major with the nose piercings and that crazy motorcycle? I've felt uncomfortable renting to strangers since him." If she couldn't have Gabe with her, she preferred to live on her own.

An image of Hal's warm brown eyes popped to mind. She shook off the memories.

Gabe smiled. "It's your house. Let me drink my coffee. After, I'll put away the rest of the groceries and make us lunch." He ambled into the living room.

Shoot! Eve raced after him.

Fingers curled around his mug, Gabe stared at the fireplace mantel. "When did you bring out Dad's police memorabilia?" He glanced at his cup. "I've been home for days."

Okay, here it comes. If only in some small way, she needed to explain the situation.

Crossing to the mantel, she drifted her fingers down the portrait of Doug in uniform. Beside it rested his badge encased in clear plastic, the shadow box with his medal of valor, and the memorial plaque. The flag from his funeral lay folded in a triangular display case on a side table, and the memory album perched on the coffee table's lower shelf.

Last night, she and Gabe had played cribbage in the kitchen. After he went to bed, she'd pored over the album for a solid hour.

"Returning Hal's stuff on Thursday made me feel lonely," she admitted. "Why shouldn't I display your father's things? I only put them in storage because Kenneth insisted." The man she'd dated before Hal. "I told you I was feeling nostalgic."

Gabe studied the Department emblem on his mug. "Did you see Hal at his office?"

"No." She stroked the heart-shaped locket around her neck, cherishing the photo of her and Doug inside. "He arranged it so we wouldn't run into each other." Further proof they were through.

"I see."

No, he didn't. Which was how she wanted things.

At least for now.

She maintained a neutral expression, although inside her spirits withered. No matter how much she missed Hal, he hadn't been able to understand how she could love him and love Doug's memory at the same time. When he'd proposed, he'd asked for her entire heart, but it wasn't hers to offer.

Would it ever be?

The phone rang. Grateful for the reprieve, Eve hurried to the desk and answered.

"Evie?" Alarm tinged her brother-in-law's voice.

"Victor! What's wrong?"

"Put Gabe on the phone. I need to see him. Right away."

&.

Mackie paced the hall outside his office. When would Gabe show up? He needed the kid's cop-radar, damn it!

"Jas," he called toward the studio's closed bathroom door. "You *sewing* those clothes back on?"

Jas sauntered out of the can, her skirt and jacket neat again. "Is your nephew here yet?"

Mackie stopped pacing. "No. But, jeez, I'm freaking."

Snapping her gum, she stepped toward him. "I could continue where we left off," she murmured. "Pleasure you until he shows. That always helps you relax." She squeezed his limp johnson through his khakis, and he groaned.

"Baby, you know I *want* to." He pushed her hand off his pants. After hearing Evie's voice on the phone, he doubted his salami would cooperate.

Screw it! He really craved the stress relief Jas offered. He had waited and freaking *waited* to prove himself financially and emotionally worthy of Evie's love. It wasn't like his sister-in-law had crossed her legs to every man since Doug bit the dust. Just during those first few years, when Mackie couldn't mention her moving on without her crying enough tears to swamp a flood plain. Then his guilt would kick in, and he'd back off.

Evie must have slept with a couple of other assholes besides Hal under the guise of long-term relationships.

Long-term, ha! She would sleep with *him* for the rest of their lives.

Jas whined, "Awww."

"Sorry, babe," Mackie muttered. "Lousy timing." Any excuse to prevent his one and only bimbo from suspecting his sad physical condition, which was only temporary…

He hoped.

Stifling a wince, he turned his thoughts back to Evie. Precious Evie. When he finally confessed his love, his beautiful future wife would understand his sexual habits of the last several years—if she ever learned about them. No reason she should, but in case unsavory rumors drifted to her delicate ears, he possessed every confidence his serene, forgiving sister-in-law would realize the truth. He'd only dated slutty chicks like Jas to allow Evie time to accept that marrying him wouldn't disgrace Doug's memory. Would, instead, honor it in a roundabout way.

In the olden days, men married their brothers' widows all the time. It was a tradition.

Evie had saved Dougie.

Now she would save him.

A knock rapped on the alley door.

"Hi, Gabe," Jas greeted as Mackie's nephew blew indoors.

"Took you long enough," Mackie griped.

"I had to change, then drive here." The kid planted his hands on the hips of his jeans like a goddamned cocky gunslinger. "What's this about, Uncle Vic? More vandalism?"

Mackie thrust out his jaw. Not wanting to alarm Evie, he'd glossed over the details on the phone. Too late, it dawned on him that revealing more while she'd remained within earshot might have scored him major points toward gaining her sympathy and furthering their love.

Shuck a duck. The suction of Jasmine's hot mouth on him had rattled his brain. And once he'd smelled the fire—instant saggy cock!

No wonder he hadn't thought through the freaking phone call.

He spread his hands. "Someone tried to torch the place! I could've burned to a crisp."

The kid's ears pricked like frigging Lassie. "There was a fire? Where?"

"In the breakroom." A sour scent clouded the air. "Can't you smell the stench?"

Gabe inhaled. "With you, I never take anything for granted." He shoved open the door to the employee room, and the putrid odor of charred bean burritos swept out. "What the...?" Grimacing, he strode to the counter.

Mackie followed his nephew. Fire extinguisher foam slathered the outside top of the open microwave like slimy frosting on a gigantic cake. After Mackie had blasted the flames, he'd poked about inside with a fork and discovered his favorite post-sex snack melted to the plate. The memory of his flaccid pecker flapping as he'd grabbed the extinguisher and yelled at an equally nude Jasmine to help might have been funny under different circumstances. Like if *he* had set the fire.

Jasmine's high heels tapped the linoleum. "The microwave burst into flames."

"I see that." Gabe faced them. "Why are you here on a Sunday?"

Mackie's brain burped. "Uhhh."

"Just an extended nooner," Jas supplied.

Jesus. Mackie's throat clamped shut. The woman had no shame.

Gabe grunted. "You were having sex while using the microwave?"

"Mackie likes a bean burrito afterward. I decided to save time by putting it in the oven first."

"Jas, baby—" Mackie zipped her a pointed look. *Shut up!*

His nephew frowned at the ruined microwave. "Did you cover the plate with aluminum foil?"

Jasmine's head tipped. "Why would I do that?"

Bending down, Gabe examined the oven's destroyed interior and swiped at the extinguisher gunk coiling along the inside oven walls and top. "Did you tape foil in here for some reason?"

"No." Jas giggled. "I didn't even turn it on while we…you know. The burritos only take a minute or two."

Mackie glanced from Jas to his nephew as the kid gripped his bad leg and stood. "Whaddya thinking?" he asked Gabe.

"It looks like someone taped a square of aluminum foil to the ceiling of the microwave." Gabe fished a kitchen towel off the fridge handle and wiped his hands. "You can see shiny bits through the foam." He hooked a thumb toward the oven. "If that same person set the burritos to heat on high for, say, ten minutes instead of one or two, the combination of the sparks from the foil and the extended cooking time would have caused the fire."

Jasmine's giggles flat-lined. "Maybe I turned on the microwave and don't remember. Poop, maybe I screwed up the timer." She blinked at Mackie. "I don't think I did, but, *gawd*, I definitely didn't tape on no foil wrap." She chomped her gum. "Even I know that much."

"Someone did." Gabe tossed the dishtowel onto the counter.

"What the frig?" Mackie scowled. "Can we tell who?"

His nephew shrugged. "Beats me."

Mackie stroked his upper lip, willing the pounding of his heart to decelerate. Right, Gabe didn't want Jas clueing in about his cop background.

"Jas, you can leave," he mumbled. "Gabe and me need to discuss some stuff. He's my handyman, you know. And my, uh, new security guy."

"Aw, Mackie." She snuggled in against his stomach.

"I mean it, baby. Go." He patted her butt.

Tugging his ponytail, she kissed his cheek. "Catch you later, randy man." Hips swaying, she collected her purse and strutted into the hall. The alley door banged shut.

Mackie looked at his nephew. "Jasmine didn't do this. I let her in today, and we were in my office from the moment she put my meal in the oven until we smelled the fire."

Gabe strode toward the hall and peered both ways. Apparently satisfied Jasmine had left, he returned. "Were you with her—in here —when she prepped the burritos?"

"Nah, I was in my office. Organizing, if you get my drift." Bobbing his eyebrows, Mackie backtracked over the sequence of events. Setting up the ropes, choosing the tunes—

St. Pecker!

His fingers stiffened like petrified starfish. The ropes Jas used to bind him to the chair still dangled from the arms. In the commotion, he hadn't squirreled them away.

He'd have to fix that as soon as possible—without Gabe realizing something was amiss.

"Then how do you know she didn't sabotage the microwave?" the kid asked.

"She doesn't have the smarts," Mackie responded in a carefully monitored tone.

Gabe's right eyebrow hoisted. "She seemed pretty clear a second ago."

"Clear as cootie-caked candle wax! She's hooked on me. She'll do whatever I say." Including tying him to the chair and playing dominatrix. Nothing too raunchy, but sufficient to get him off. "We left the alley door unlocked. Someone could've snuck in, I guess."

The kid's smile dripped sarcasm. "There you go."

"Hah-hah. If you think Jasmine did this, why let her leave?"

"I'm not a certified PI yet. Unless you're willing to bring in the SCPD—"

"Screw that."

"*That's* why." Gabe glanced around the room. "I take it Jasmine's fingerprints are everywhere?"

Nodding, Mackie smothered a grin. Jasmine's fingerprints were the least of the bodily traces she'd left behind during their erotic games. "She's here most weekends. Wednesday in my office wasn't planned, but you know how it goes."

Gabe's eyes narrowed to slivers. "I could call Bill Cruikshank. Between the foam and Jasmine dropping by a lot, it's unlikely he'd find a pertinent print, but it's worth a shot."

"You're not calling Cruikshank." Mackie had hated Dougie's old partner before his brother took a bullet in the back, and he hated the guy now. Just another holier-than-thou, do-good asswipe who'd hogged Dougie's attention with their buddy-buddy-boys-in-blue bullshit.

"Bill could scan the room to eliminate specific prints," Gabe blathered. "The police would have to fingerprint Jasmine and your staff for comparison purposes. Processing could take awhile."

"Didn't you hear me? I said no. Jas would think I don't trust her. She'd get crabby. I don't need the grief."

Gabe stared at him. "Uncle Vic, have you considered somebody might have it in for you? First the broken window—"

Mackie laughed. How could someone be after him when *he'd* thrown the inert grenade, painted the new glass, and scribbled the crude drawings and threatening note himself?

Gabe scowled. "What's *wrong* with you?"

"Nothing. A man has pride. Do you think I want it getting out to Bill Cruikshank and his donut-munching cronies that some deadbeat's trying to scare the crap out of me with another stupid prank while I'm in the next room banging Jasmine?"

"Spare me the crude details, Uncle Vic."

"Don't you have to know everything? So you can do your job?" Mackie needed to keep the kid focused on his idiotic case *without bringing in the cops,* until he determined how best to manipulate Evie with these latest events.

Gabe grunted. "Where are your cameras?"

Perfect. No arguments.

"The DSLRs are in my van. I got an old Polaroid in my office. Kinda clunky, but it works. Why?"

"The instant camera is fine. We'll take pictures to record evidence."

"Use your cell phone." *What a dipshit.*

"I'll use both. The Polaroid provides immediate hard copy. When we're finished, you can clean up."

"You clean. You're the handyman."

Gabe snatched the dishtowel and chucked it at him. "*You* clean."

Mackie caught the rag. "Hey!"

"I don't have to be here, Uncle Vic. Tick me off too much, and I will leave. Get your camera. While I'm logging evidence, you can wrack your brain for that list of ex-girlfriends and anyone else who's sick of your attitude."

"All right, all right!" Mackie threw down the kitchen towel for dramatic effect. Baiting Gabe brought him no end of joy. Even better, his overreaction should prevent the kid from trailing him into his office. His nephew generally kept his distance for several minutes following a well-timed display.

Playing it up, Mackie stomped across the hall and slammed the boss-cave door. After switching off the radio, he hurried to his chair jammed against the front of the desk.

Finding the instant camera could wait. He needed to stash the proof of his afternoon plans with Jas before Gabe caught a glimpse of kink and decided to spill the news to Evie.

Matter of fact, he ought to tell Gabe not to let the cat out of the bag about him banging Jas in the studio at all. Even without the kink thrown in, Evie didn't need to hear that kind of crud from her son. It wasn't respectful.

Mackie's big hands stumbled on the first knot, thick and awkward on the chair arm, and he swore. Usually, Jasmine untied the ropes from both him and his chair. Her long fingers had certainly worked at mach speed to free him when he'd smelled the fire. Fear had pierced his gut, and his dick had withered on the spot. A frigging humiliating situation. In that moment, stashing the ropes had been the last thing on their minds.

Whisking the thick cord off the chair, he pondered his nephew's theory that someone might be messing with his head. Until this afternoon, he had taken it for granted Gabe's speculations were utter crock. Last Mackie knew, Gabe had yet to hear from the *Clarion* whether or not the botched newspaper ad was part of some retirement hijinks.

Regardless of whatever had gone down at the paper, the scare with the microwave proved his nephew might be on to something. A few of Mackie's former bump-bunnies had griped big time when he'd cut them off to restrict himself to Jasmine as part of his marriage-training regimen. Maybe one of his more high-spirited girls missed his monster eight-incher and was toying with him in a desperate ploy to capture his attention.

Could happen.

He coiled the ropes. *He* would toy with Gabe to protect the identities of the women most likely to have staged today's scenario.

Whoever it was, he gave her credit for showing a spark of imagination.

If she went too far, he'd revisit his decision. For now, he couldn't resist the idea of eventually figuring out who she was and taking her back for a final one-nighter of high-risk sex. An ideal farewell to his bachelor life before he married Evie.

Images of leather masks and floggers crowded his mind. His prick twitched, and he grinned. The big guy had recovered.

Bring on the party times, baby. Bring 'em on.

The camera rested on the table beside the pictures snapped this afternoon to test the expired packages of instant film. Trust that blowhard Vic McKenzie not to junk the ancient Polaroid. Well, he wasn't the only the one who hoarded souvenirs.

In this case, Vic's packrat tendencies had come in handy. The old-fashioned instant camera didn't contain any digital components to track a person or otherwise prove a pain in the ass. What a pleasure. Filching the camera from Vic's cluttered office before his arrival had been a snap. The boor rarely strayed from routine, often skulking around his office on Sundays, supposedly working.

Too bad Vic's latest blond 'ho had wandered into the viewfinder when Vic opened the studio's alley door to allow the skank entrance. The goal had been to capture *his* ugly mug on film as a token of today's triumph, not the big tits of his recent conquest. Maneuvering the bulky camera while hiding behind the dumpster had proven tricky.

Anger bubbled, threatening to drown the wild rush of excitement from this afternoon.

Forget the blonde.

Surveillance had occurred for several weeks, and Vic hadn't fooled around with another woman aside from Big Tits since the idiot vandalized his own business window on Halloween. It made sense he'd dip his humongous dick into the bitch whenever possible. Vic McKenzie got his rocks off by showering woman after woman with attention and gifts, hooking her on his sexual games and impressive sausage. Then, once a woman wised up to his despicable nature and refused to continue humping him on command like a horny lap dog, he employed whatever vile means necessary to ruin her life.

He'd finally gone too far when he'd stopped victimizing loser females and moved on to folks who deserved the best this crummy world had to offer.

Damn it, this afternoon could have gone better. Oh, to have been a fly on the wall when Vic smelled his precious burritos burning!

Or to have witnessed smoke and flames consuming the building, if he and Big Tits hadn't discovered the fire in time. Excitement leapt at the prospect.

But patience was a virtue, and today presented only a tiny preview of what was to come.

Remember that.

Time to ease up. Allow the creep to grow complacent. Sidetrack him with sloppy ploys. Lure him closer and closer until—*ka-boom!* The big send-off. What fun.

Because someone had to stop that douche bag Victor McKenzie from destroying another innocent life.

And, once every ounce of pleasure had been wrung from screwing with his misogynistic pea brain, someone would.

Nine

"STACY, WAIT." Ursula hurried to catch her coworker stepping off the sidewalk into the studio alley. Stacey's head was lowered and her hands shoved into jacket pockets. "Hey, Stace!"

The girl glanced back. "Hi, Urs." Voice hollow, Stacy tugged electronic buds out of her ears. "Sorry, I was listening to music on my phone."

"That's okay." Ursula bussed to work most days to save parking garage fees, but the rare treat of a clear blue November sky had prompted her to walk the last five blocks. "Stacy, are you okay? You look like the Monday doldrums have knocked you flat."

Stacy's brown eyes reflected dull as mud behind her glasses. "My sister thinks the craziness of this last week is affecting my studies, and I should quit. I guess I shouldn't complain about my job so much."

"You can vent to me all you want," Ursula said, and a faint smile tipped Stacy's mouth. "Honestly, do what you need to, but I'd miss you if you left."

The wind riffled the girl's light brown hair. "I'd feel like a loser quitting already. It wouldn't look good on my resume to work here only two months."

"Agreed," Ursula said as they entered the alley. "But maintaining your grades is important for those first resumes. You want to appear determined and reliable." Ironically, she'd offered Gabe similar advice on Saturday, while they'd viewed apartments. And where had traipsing through building after building gotten her? In the hall outside *her* door, her lips locked in his heavenly kiss, his large hands on her back, his touch rushing tingles up and down—

"Ursula?"

"Yes?" She returned her attention to Stacy. She had no business daydreaming about a guy like Gabe, no matter how wonderful his kisses had felt. She hadn't been kissed in over six months. On the heels of a long dry spell, Gabe's touch had felt incredible. Amazing. Luxurious, one might say.

Well, goose-down duvets felt luxurious. That didn't mean she should race to the nearest department store and buy one.

"Also, I need the money to pay for next semester," Stacy said, tucking her phone into a pocket and rubbing her hands in the chilly air.

"Is your sister older than you?" Ursula asked. They continued down the alley packed with a dumpster and a dozen cramped parking spots. The studio claimed two. One for customers and the other for Mackie's blue minivan.

Stacy nodded.

Ursula nudged her arm. "That explains it. We older sisters *think* we have all the answers."

Stacy's smile felt genuine this time. "Do you have a sister?"

"No, but my brother is nineteen. When he was five, I'd bribe him into letting me paint his fingernails before I'd push him on his swing. I was pretty convincing until he turned six."

Stacy laughed.

"To this day, he refuses to wear lavender, my favorite choice for his nails. Which sucks, because the color looks great on him. I bought him a lavender dress shirt last Christmas, and he exchanged it for a blue sweater within a week."

"Poor guy. You scarred him for life!"

"Stace, if you need money, I'll ask Mackie if you can work tomorrow to make up for Thanksgiving and Black Friday." The studio closed both days each November.

The girl's face lit up. "Would you?"

"Absolutely." Ursula opened the business's alley door. "I'll talk to him about bringing you in every day next week too. *Seattle Lights* is emailing the names for the Real Men shoot this morning. Gabe and I will be on location most days, so I'll need you in the office both weeks."

"Ursula, thanks!"

"You're welcome." She liked Stacy, and breaking in receptionist after receptionist sounded exhausting. In the last four months, two girls had quit because of Mackie's blustering. The receptionist before Stacy hadn't lasted a week. "When you're at your desk, if you could print out the editor's list as well as sending it to my personal email address, that would be great. Then I can access the info on my phone."

"No problem. Oh, Ursula, if Mackie agrees to more hours, I'll praise you to the skies."

Ursula chuckled. "Not necessary." She trailed the girl into the hall outside Mackie's office. Arguing voices carried from Reception. Most sounded male, a couple female. None belonged to Gabe, but Ursula identified an ornery baritone as Mackie's. "That's odd. Women didn't accompany any Real Men applicants last week, did they?"

"Not that I remember. I'll check it out. Today, I'm calling the guys who didn't make the cut."

"Thanks on both accounts. Feel free to put away your stuff and get a coffee before heading into whatever mess awaits. I'm betting you'll need the caffeine." Ursula did, at any rate.

They entered the breakroom. Gabe stood at the counter, slicing open a big box. A wide smile spread across his handsome face. "Hi," he said.

Ursula's lungs squeezed, and her heart actually pit-a-patted. Suddenly, she understood the phrase, *I forgot to breathe.* Last week Gabe had seemed comfortable with three-day-old beards. Not that she minded sexy stubble, but the clean-shaven smoothness of his jaw this morning reminded her, once again, of his expert kisses against her door.

Swoon.

Stacy stored her purse in a cupboard. "What's with the box?"

"Mackie bought a new microwave," Gabe responded. "He asked me to set it up."

A shiny fire extinguisher lay on the table. "Is this new too?"

Ursula asked. The ruckus from Reception receded, thank the universe and Mother Earth and Father Time.

"Yeah." Gabe dusted his hands on his jeans. "Mackie was working on the Windermere pamphlet yesterday and accidentally timed his lunch to cook too long. He had to use the fire extinguisher."

Ursula snorted. "Serves him right."

Gabe's green eyes pinned her in place. "You think that's funny?"

"Duh," Ursula replied, exchanging an amused glance with Stacy as the girl folded her coat on a chair. "He's burned his burritos before, but not enough to damage the microwave," she told Gabe. "He's lucky he didn't get hurt." She cast a glance over the dingy room. "I can't wait to slap a new coat of paint on these walls."

Gabe angled his head. "How did our discussion veer onto paint?"

"Sorry, don't mind me." She couldn't help planning. The space had potential.

"And how'd you know my uncle planned to eat burritos?"

What was this, an interrogation? "Because he doesn't heat up his pizzas and subs."

"He goes on binges," Stacy said as Gabe set aside the box cutter. "Right now, the freezer is stocked with burritos."

Ursula snickered. "With that diet, I'm surprised his arteries haven't clogged to the consistency of cement."

Stacy hid a grin behind her hand.

"Easy, ladies. He *is* my uncle."

Stacy flinched. "Sorry." The arguing drifted from the front office again. Stacy chewed her bottom lip. "I'll rescue him."

"Good idea." Gabe crossed his arms. "Sales reps keep arriving saying they scheduled meetings to push their products. Something about photocopiers and darkroom supplies. They're driving him crazy." He scratched his cheek.

Stacy's eyebrows leapt into her hairline. "You mean the calls that came in last week while we were swamped with the Real Men guys? I told those reps we weren't interested."

"What's this?" Ursula hadn't heard a peep about any reps.

"You were busy with the test shots." Stacy's lips firmed. "But Gabe knows. We talked about it."

As if only now recalling the conversation, he lifted a finger. "Oh, yeah. I guess they showed anyway."

Panic plastered Stacy's face. "All at once?"

"I'll deal with them," Ursula said. The girl deserved a break. She was frazzled.

"No, Ursula, it's *my* job. I told those clowns not to come, and they ignored me. I'm tired of being ignored!" She stormed out of the room, arms pumping at her sides.

"Go get 'em, tiger," Gabe said to her back. Glancing at Ursula, he flashed another dazzling smile. "Good morning."

"Morning." The small room shrank tinier than a closet. Was their kiss on his mind too?

He turned toward the box. Ursula's heart thumped like a bongo drum as he lifted out the Styrofoam-packed microwave. Her gaze glided over his broad shoulders to his trim waist...and very fine rear.

"Can you give me a hand?"

She snapped alert. "Be right there." She set her purse on the table before joining him at the counter. While he juggled the microwave, she tugged off the Styrofoam and plastic bag. Barely breathing through her nostrils, she savored the fresh, clean scent of his shaving cream. The man had good taste in grooming products, like his springtime soap on Saturday...

He positioned the appliance on the counter. Awareness hummed between them—well, she detected the exhilarating vibrations, at any rate—as he peeled off the protective plastic sealing the door and buttons. She retrieved the instruction booklet. Their fingers brushed, and her pulse sang a hallelujah chorus.

His eyes crinkled. "I thought about you yesterday."

"I thought of you last night." Argh, *why* had she said that? She stuffed the booklet between the microwave and fridge.

His low chuckle poured over her like rich, melted chocolate. "Did you now?"

Her mouth dried. The buttons of her leather blazer were undone, revealing her blouse. If he noticed her high beams, she'd die.

His gaze honed in on her lips.

Would he kiss her again?

Should she let him?

"Boss?" he asked in a husky tone.

Breathe, girl. "Yes?"

"I have a physical therapy appointment in an hour. I can't miss it." He massaged his thigh.

"Tell me how you hurt your leg, and you won't have to."

"Blackmail? Ursula, I'm surprised."

"Don't be. I'm evil through and through."

His eyes cut to an invisible spot above her shoulder. Her face prickled. Why wouldn't he share how he'd hurt his leg? Did her curiosity offend him?

She fiddled with her thumb ring. "Of course you can keep your appointment. You're my assistant for the magazine shoot, not my all-around lackey."

"Thanks." He plugged in the new microwave.

"I'll make coffee." High school graduation portraits began this morning. Not every secondary school utilized professional services this early in the year. At her prompting, Mackie had proposed an excellent package to the districts, and several schools had responded. Starting tomorrow, he would carry the student load while she managed the Real Men shoot. Today, she dealt with the teens. Facing all those overactive adolescent hormones required oceans of caffeine.

She stepped around Gabe. Then stared. "Where's the coffeemaker?"

He looked at her. "Huh?"

"It's not here." She gestured to the empty space beside the canisters. "Did Mackie destroy it too?"

Gabe's forehead furrowed. "I don't think so."

"Unless the coffeemaker grew legs, it couldn't have left on its own."

He ran a thumb along his chin. "It didn't. I spaced out for a second."

Ah. She knew how that felt.

"That coffeemaker was my mom's," he said, studying the empty spot. "She wanted it back so I could use it in the basement suite. My uncle knew that. He must have forgotten to buy another."

"Weird. I could have sworn the machine was here Friday before closing."

"Yeah, it was." He strode to the table, voice a bit distant. "I picked it up on my way to your place Saturday." Whistling, he spread out the fire extinguisher instructions.

"Oh." Why wouldn't he look at her? "I'll pop next door for coffee." She curled her hair behind one ear. "Want a cup?"

"A large Colombian." He studied the instructions. "Black. Thanks."

Okay, now he *was* avoiding her. Totally awkward.

She collected her purse and hurried to the reception area for Stacy's order. The sales reps had left, but Mackie's florid face and Stacy's tear-streaked cheeks indicated the trouble was far from over.

Voice booming, Mackie waggled his finger. "Another thing—"

Ursula stepped between boss and subordinate. "Mackie, stop yelling at her. You're not helping the situation."

His head whipped around, stubby ponytail flying. "I don't need a photocopier. The all-in-one works fine. And I haven't used the darkroom in ages. She should know that."

"I do!" Stacy cried.

"Then why did you book all those flipping meetings?" he roared.

"I didn't!"

"Mackie, listen to her," Ursula ordered. "Do you want her to quit? Stacy said she didn't book the appointments. Believe her. We have a dozen graduation portraits to shoot today, and the first teenager will walk through the door in fifteen minutes. Probably with a parent. Who will witness this bedlam you call a business and then tell their friends and relatives you're a loose cannon. Is that what you want?"

Oh, my God! She needed to help him build the business, not sit idly by while his coarse behavior tore it down. A thriving studio would cost her more come May but, in the long run, the investment would pay off. It was a simple concept.

His pig eyes flared. "I just need things to run smoothly for one GD day!"

"If you want things to calm down around here, offer Stacy more hours. She needs the work and you need the help, especially considering I'll be busy with *Seattle Lights*. It doesn't take a genius to add one and one."

His meaty hands fisted. "All right, *you* set her hours. But if this craziness don't stop, somebody's butt is gonna fry in a pan!" He stomped toward his office. If they were lucky, he wouldn't emerge until noon.

Stacy sniffled. "Ursula, thank you. I tried explaining, but he wouldn't listen."

"He's frustrated. That's no excuse, but mistakes are occurring more frequently since September, and he's having a hard time dealing with it."

"He hired *me* in September." Stacy howled. "I'm bad luck."

"No, you aren't," Ursula soothed. "We're taking on more clients, and Mackie is…" *a tightwad* "…hesitant to invest the profits into employee wages. Look at it this way. Because of the mix-up with the sales reps, you'll get those extra hours."

Stacy's shoulders heaved. "I suppose."

"It'll work out. Just don't quit. I need you." Ursula smiled. "I'm buying coffees. Want one? My treat."

"Chai tea sounds nice." Stacy wiped away her tears. "Ursula, wait." She dashed to her desk. "Mackie said he printed the email from *Seattle Lights* before the reps began arriving. Here it is." She handed over a paper. "I still need to send the email to your phone."

"Thanks. I'll check this out en route." Scanning the email, Ursula left the studio and turned toward the coffeehouse. Excellent, the *Seattle Lights* editor had chosen Norm Dobson as a model. She read the other names. Alan Cory, Deiter Reinhold—

"Watch out," a woman called.

Glancing up, Ursula walked straight into a tall blonde. The woman's coffee cup vaulted out of her hands. Like in a slow-motion movie, the top popped off and frothy cappuccino splashed onto the woman's winter-white coat, leaving brown tentacles dripping from the expensive-looking wool.

Ursula gaped. "Shit! I'm so sorry."

"It's not your fault." The woman retrieved the cup. "I wasn't paying attention."

"Please send me the dry-cleaning bill. I work right there." She pointed to the studio. "Victor McKenzie Photography. Here's my card." She fished her wallet out of her purse.

The woman protested, but Ursula insisted. First the microwave, then the coffeemaker, now creating havoc and swearing in the streets. The last thing she wanted was another business day shot to hell before it began because the bedlam that surrounded Mackie twenty-four/seven set her nerves on edge.

If she intended to buy the studio in six months, she needed to begin rectifying this endless stream of disasters ASAP.

❧

Gabe steered clear of Ursula throughout Monday, which wasn't difficult. The high school graduation portraits consumed her day, affording him and his uncle a chance to discuss the missing coffeemaker and coordinate their stories about requiring the appliance for the basement suite. Mackie claimed the absent coffeemaker was as much a mystery to him as it was to Gabe. They both recalled spotting it yesterday in the wake of the microwave fire.

Yet another glitch occurred Sunday, while they'd tidied the staffroom. Gabe's uncle had failed to locate the old Polaroid camera for cataloguing instant hard copy of the torched oven. Instead, Gabe printed photos from his smartphone on his mother's desktop computer back home. Mackie insisted he'd spied the Polaroid in his office a few days before the microwave incident, so it seemed both the camera and coffeemaker had vanished.

Monday evening, after an enjoyable dinner with his mom, Gabe had retreated to the basement to mull over the case. Yesterday Mackie made a stink about not contacting Bill Cruikshank or the Seattle police, but Gabe would be damned if he'd allow his uncle to dictate an investigation intended to bring his mother peace of mind.

He'd meant to check in with Bill anyway and let the man know he was back in town. Might as well bend the veteran Department member's ear and perhaps gain some insight on the case.

Walking back and forth near the bed, he dialed Bill's home number on his personal cell. Bill's wife answered, and they chewed the fat before Bill came on the line.

"Hey, pal," the older man said, a smile in his voice. "How are you? Heard about your shooting. Horrible thing to happen, for you and your mom. She's dealt with so much heartache." Bill cleared his throat. "Ah, hell. Listen, Gabe, it's good to hear from you."

"Thanks, Bill. It's great to hear your voice." Sinking onto a kitchenette chair, Gabe asked, "How are you doing? You sound well."

"I am. Still fighting the good fight for a few more years. Darlene keeps me busy on days off helping with her gardening projects. And you know what? I don't mind all that much. It's not as much fun as fishing with your dad and you boys, but... Hey, I overheard her tell you Ross's wife is pregnant?"

"She did. Congrats, Bill. You're going to be a grandpa." A knot formed in Gabe's chest. His dad would never enjoy grandchildren. The piece of scum who'd killed Doug McKenzie had made sure of that. "How does it feel?" he asked, forcing a hearty tone.

"Truth be told, damn good. Boy or girl, I'm buying our first grandbaby a little fishing pole. Darlene will have my hide for tearing her away from her fruit and vegetables, but as soon as that wee one can walk, it'll be camping and fishing time again for Granny and me. The grandtikes can tag along."

"They'll love it. I always did." Gabe fetched a bottle of water from the narrow fridge and uncapped it. For the next several minutes, he leaned back in the kitchenette chair, sipping water while he and Bill reminisced about annual father-son fishing trips to Oregon and joint family camping trips to the Olympic Peninsula. Gabe had ridden bikes, swam his arms off, and burnt marshmallows in the campfire with Bill's sons.

Eventually, the conversation shifted to Gabe's plans for his PI business and his snooping around at the studio. Yesterday, while Mackie scoured his office for the instant camera, Gabe had retrieved a handheld ultraviolet light from his jacket pocket and checked the area around the charred microwave for identifiable prints.

"I didn't want to bother the police with smudges," he told Bill, getting up and strolling back and forth by the bed again, water bottle in hand. "The studio is overrun with the magazine job. It's pretty wild, and prints are everywhere. Just nothing clear."

"The smears make sense, seeing as it's a place of business.

You're an excellent cop, buddy. Like father, like son. If there were usable prints, you'd have spotted them."

"*Was* a cop," Gabe amended.

"Who will make an excellent PI. It's in your blood, pal. I trust your instincts."

"Thanks." Bill's confidence in his abilities meant a lot. Growing up, the man had felt almost like a second father, especially during those first difficult years after Gabe's dad died. Gabe had never felt comfortable sharing his grief with Mackie.

"I offered to cart away the microwave for my uncle," Gabe spoke into his cell. "The idea was to store it in Mom's shed, in case I decided to take a second look. But Uncle Vic said he would dispose of it. I think he was half-afraid I would show it to you, and you might, I don't know, judge him."

Vic came off like a blowhard, but childhood insecurities stemming from his time in foster care ran deep. After the adoption, Gabe's grandparents raised Victor as their own. Regardless of their efforts, Victor developed a weird hero-worship/sibling-rivalry relationship with Gabe's father. It was like some hollow place inside Mackie could never be filled, although Gabe's mom had done her best since Dad died to include him in their small family.

Bill's heavy sigh transmitted loud and clear. "Your uncle never cared for how close your dad and I were."

Wasn't that the truth? Favoring his bad leg, Gabe finished his water. He recalled his parents discussing Mackie's issues with Bill and other members of the SCPD, when they thought Gabe was out of earshot. Mackie had griped about Dad's few friends outside the force too—as if he'd wanted Gabe's father all to himself. To not only be Dad's younger brother, but his only friend and confidant, despite their six-year age difference.

Setting the empty bottle on the kitchenette table, he directed their conversation back to the case. "Do you know of other businesses that have been hit with small fires or microwaves blowing up?" he asked Bill.

"None that come to mind. I'll check with the uniforms who were in the vicinity, but there hasn't been a pyro on the loose or anyone released who likes fires."

"Okay. How about anything going on around one p.m. in the area that might have taken the police away from that street?"

"Negative again." Bill paused. "I'm not much help."

"All information is useful."

"You sound like your dad. Tell you what, if I hear of anything unusual happening in the neighborhood, I'll let you know. And if you want to run anything else by me, give me a shout."

"Will do." Gabe sat on the bed. Earlier today, his physical therapist had instructed him to rest his leg, but his feet twitched with the urge to move. He got up again. "Have a great Thanksgiving, Bill."

"You too. And be patient with your mom. She's had it rough. Not only because of what happened to your dad. Your injury…" A gruff note edge Bill's voice. "Emotional trauma can trigger painful memories."

"And cause her to relive them. I know." Gabe shoved a hand through his hair. *Damn it.* "She's worried about me carrying again once I have my PI license."

"Your weapon is your protection, but fear isn't always rational. That might be part of what's happening with your mom. Even why she let go of Hal."

Hand on the back of his neck, Gabe dragged in a breath. "I think you're right." Getting her to *talk* about Hal was hard. Gabe's dad had handled the birds-and-bees discussions, and Mom hadn't dated until Gabe's senior year at U-Dub. Shortly after graduating, he'd moved to California. They'd spoken weekly on the phone, had emailed, texted, and video-chatted, but the ups and downs of her romantic relationships had never made it onto the agenda.

In his early twenties, Gabe had been okay with that. Other than sheltering her from the dangers of his job, he hadn't *really* considered how placing a state between them might have affected her or her relationships. All this time, he'd assumed he was doing her a favor.

Bill said, "With your injury occurring a few months back and the holidays around the corner, your mother might be feeling vulnerable."

"I'll keep that in mind." He wouldn't fail her again.

"It's definitely something to watch out for. Speaking of the holidays, why don't you two come over one evening around Christmas, when Dale and Ross visit with their wives?"

"Good idea. It's been too long."

They said goodbye, and Gabe tossed his phone onto the nightstand with a frown. Reclining on the double bed, he folded his hands behind his head on the pillow. Bill had made valid points about Mom. Gabe hated the possibility that his own shooting had reawakened her agony over losing Dad. Or that his injury might have inadvertently placed undue pressure on her relationship with Hal. But the timing was clear, and that hurt like a knife slashing skin.

His mom deserved some happiness. A son who helped with yardwork, cleaned the gutters, and shoveled the driveway clear of the odd snowfall. Dinners out, laughter and smiles. Another great love of her life. Ultimately, a daughter-in-law and grandkids.

A well-rounded family, like Bill's. His mom deserved it all.

A full home and a full heart.

Thoughts meandering to Ursula, Gabe crossed his ankles on the bedspread. He felt crappy about how things were going with her too. The lying about his past, pretending to be someone he wasn't. But he was undercover. Secrets were part of the job.

Yeah, yeah.

He studied the dotted ceiling tiles. He needed to find a way to speak to Deni Clarke about Ursula's movements the night of the broken window. Alternatively, he could locate Tom Haskell, the student Ursula mentioned tutoring during the same time frame. Which was the better option?

It seemed every day another incident of potential studio sabotage occurred, piling onto the events previous to his return. Like yesterday...

Had the person responsible for the microwave fire returned to the scene and filched the ancient Mr. Coffee after Mackie and Gabe left the building? For that matter, had the suspect swiped the Polaroid camera *before* Mackie and Jasmine arrived for their rendezvous? The missing camera and coffeemaker were small potatoes compared to attempted arson, vandalism, and threats. Was the suspect mocking his uncle?

"Why?" Gabe speculated aloud. Who would do such a thing?

Someone familiar with Mackie's background might know exactly which buttons to push. Mackie had provided a list of ex-girlfriend names today. Gabe would begin there.

"This is getting weirder and weirder," he mused. But his mind thrived on solving the puzzles of this outwardly bizarre situation. For example, the set-up for the microwave fire could have occurred prior to Jasmine's appearance at the studio, while Mackie waited for her in his office. In which case, when Jasmine slid the plate of burritos into the oven, she might have failed to notice the aluminum foil taped to the microwave ceiling. Or the suspect might have had the balls to creep into the building via the unlocked alley door *after* Jasmine prepped the burritos. In other words, during the very time Mackie and his girlfriend were getting it on in his office.

Despite whatever might have occurred with the microwave—

"Whoever stole the coffeemaker and possibly the camera would have required a building key," Gabe mumbled, following the logic trail. No signs of forced entry existed for the front or back doors or for his uncle's office window. Gabe had checked while Mackie cleaned up extinguisher foam.

Pushing off the bed, he paced the room. Last week Stacy Thompson freaked out about misplacing her keys. Was he supposed to believe someone had stolen them, cut copies, then returned them?

This morning Stacy mentioned locating her set, but when Gabe asked where, she busied herself escorting a high school student to the studio proper, where Ursula snapped portraits. Gabe had needed to leave shortly afterward for his physical therapy appointment. Now, massaging his leg, he wondered if Stacy's anxiety about her supposedly misplaced keys had been for real…or a side effect of her guilt.

Bang!

Gabe jumped as a sharp gunshot noise ricocheted through the house.

"Mom!" He bolted upstairs.

Ten

"Mom, where are you?" Gabe raced into the living room. She stood at the front window, peeking through the blinds. Her fingers shook on the slats.

"A car backfired." Her voice quavered.

He swooped an arm around her shoulders. "I'll step outside and take a look."

Tears brimmed her eyes. "No, honey. Please don't leave."

"Aw, Mom." He hugged her close.

"Sorry I'm a wimp." She sobbed against his shoulder. "I was watching TV, and the noise ripped right through me."

He squeezed her tighter. "You're far from a wimp. The sound startled me too." And, as a former cop, he knew better. But a gunshot had killed his father, and a bullet had ended his career. Both events had carved away precious pieces of his mother's heart and soul.

Tears moistened his shirt as she wept against his chest, voice quiet. "The worst night of my life was receiving the phone call that you'd been shot and…and were in surgery. Worse than hearing about your father." She released a ragged breath. "Gabe, don't get me wrong. I loved your dad deeply. The night he died was terrible. I felt like I was being torn in two. But nothing, *nothing* prepares a mother for the possibility of losing her child. I don't know how I would have survived if I'd lost you."

"Hey," he murmured, rubbing her back. "PI work is nowhere as dangerous as being a cop. Most of my cases will involve cheating spouses."

She glanced up. "That doesn't stop me from worrying."

"I don't need to become an investigator, Mom." He placed a tender kiss on her forehead. "I can apply to law school. I had good grades." Becoming an attorney had never appealed. He'd considered the career while obtaining his criminology degree. Perhaps he could revisit the idea. He wasn't twenty-two anymore, chomping at the bit to patrol the streets.

His mom shook her head. "Honey, no. It's bad enough you felt you had to move to Los Angeles to protect me from your natural desire to follow in your dad's footsteps. From who you *are*." She patted his cheek. "I'm your mother. I'd worry if you drove an ice cream truck. You are home, and I'm grateful. But I will not stand in your way." Retrieving a tissue from her pants pocket, she dabbed her eyes.

"Mom..."

"I will not hear of it," she said in her do-not-track-mud-into-the-house tone. "I love you. I am so proud of you, son. Of the boy you were and the man you've become. When you have children, you will understand."

Gabe squeezed her hand. "I love you, Mom. You are an incredibly strong and supportive woman. You've stood by me my whole life. Now it's my turn to support you."

"You do. You're a wonderful son."

"Hear me out." He looked into her eyes. "The other day you said I should get the ball rolling toward applying for my PI license."

"In December, instead of waiting for January." Her gaze flickered. "Yes."

"I've been thinking about it, and I don't want to rush things." He didn't want to rush *her*. She needed time, and they had so much to discuss. His dad's death. His move to California. Hal. Maybe not tonight, when she'd just experienced a scare. But as soon as he wrapped up his uncle's case—an important step toward allowing her to quit worrying about Mackie—they would sit down and tackle those tough subjects. In the meantime, Gabe would follow her lead and provide the support *she* needed. What she indicated she could handle.

"What do you mean by not rushing things?" she asked, hand twitching in his, as if she realized the hard questions were inevitable. And she dreaded them.

"I'll apply for my license in January, like we originally planned. I found an apartment that comes available February first. I signed the agreement today." He waited a beat. "Is February too soon?"

She pressed a hand to her heart. "Oh, Gabriel, that's wonderful news. February allows me breathing room. And January for your license? Do not give it another thought. I *will* adjust." She took his arm. "Enough of my blathering. It's Thanksgiving in three days, and my son is home. Let's watch an old movie, and you can tell me about your new place. I'll only dole out decorating advice during the slow parts."

Gabe chuckled. "You got it, Mom." They strolled to the couch and sat on the plump cushions.

Man, it felt good to be home.

The next morning, the crisp scent of falling leaves tinged the air as Gabe dug Ursula's camera bags out of the studio van in a recreation center parking lot. Maples, ashes, and oaks bordered the asphalt, the tree branches heavy with multi-hued foliage. He surveyed the clouds streaking across the sky, and his chest expanded as he drank in the fresh Pacific Northwest air. He'd missed Washington autumns. The bright, if infrequent, sunshine and thick, green grass. The Space Needle piercing the downtown skyline while Mt. Rainier hovered, a protective guardian, in the distance. Elliott Bay and Lake Union close. He'd even missed the damn rain.

The forecast called for showers in an hour or two, and this time, sporting a hooded jacket, he was prepared. But for now the hood remained down. The sky presented large patches of blue amid its cloudy dome. The scene reminded him of one of those snow globes his mom collected when he was a kid. Except, instead of wintry flakes within, autumn leaves, harvest vegetables, and frosty berries swirled.

The reality that he was back—for good—burrowed into his bones.

Ursula accepted the camera bags, gripping the handles. "How do you like the job so far? Is a photography career as glamorous as you imagined?" The cool breeze rustled her long hair. Like him, she wore a hooded jacket over jeans. The sexy boots he'd noticed at the coffeehouse last week peeked out from below the denim hems.

"I said it sounded glamorous? Funny, I don't recall." Gabe reached for the location-kit duffel bag containing a load of equipment.

"Actually, I think you said something more along the lines of working at whatever catches your interest."

"Ah, yes. My dabbling. Now *that* seems right." He closed up the van. "Did I forget anything?"

"No. You're a great assistant."

"I try." He hooked the large equipment tote over his shoulder. Yesterday he'd spooled out a line about the new microwave and missing coffeemaker in an attempt to trap Ursula into revealing a clue which might peg her as his suspect. Her comment about painting the staffroom could be taken one of two ways. Either she was intent on devaluing the business and the possibility of scorching the counters or cupboards would facilitate her goal or she was excited about moving forward with her plans.

He had a hard time believing someone who'd suffered their house burning down would employ similar means to sabotage the studio. Yet, a childhood trauma might inspire a fire bug.

"Earth to Gabe?"

"Sorry. Zoned out again." Dimwitted Gabe dovetailed nicely with his cover. Lucky thing, because this was the second time he'd waved the space-cadet flag.

"I asked if you're sure you want to keep helping me. You'll be so busy you won't have time to search for a paying job." She turned toward the recreation center, where she would snap shirts-off pictures of their first Real Men model, Alan Cory, a lanky accountant in his early thirties with spiky brown hair and rimless glasses. A half-hour ago, Gabe adjusted lights and handed Ursula various lenses while she photographed Alan in his office wearing a sports jacket and tie, then again in khakis and a polo shirt, holding a golf trophy. Afterward, Alan drove to the rec center in his own vehicle and now spoke to a muscle-bound dude near the double doors.

"Who wants to work over the holidays?" Gabe replied with a wink intended to disguise his wandering thoughts. "January will be here before we know it." Last night he'd brainstormed Stacy Thompson's obsession with misplacing her keys. But where in Ursula's apartment did she store *her* studio keys? In her purse? Or on the communal desk where a roommate could have plucked them up?

Did Kim Perkins or Deni Clarke harbor a secret vendetta against Mackie?

"If you say so." Ursula smiled. "Did you like the shots in Alan's office?" she asked as they walked toward a footbridge arcing over a stream between the parking lot and rec center.

Gabe nodded. "But we can't shoot every model at a desk. Wouldn't that defeat the magazine's idea not to focus on business suits?"

"Great, you picked up on that. The editor selected Alan because of his sports background and money management website. It's an interesting contrast, so in his case the desk pictures work."

Gabe shrugged. "Not all athletes are meatheads." They lugged gear over the bridge.

Her soft laugh drifted to his ears. "True. I scoured Alan's blog archives last night. He's compiled a lot of useful information. If the magazine mentions the site and his social media profiles, more readers will find him, and we will have played a part in gaining him greater visibility."

"Good point."

During their drive from the studio to Alan's office, she'd explained the "Real Men, Real Lives, Real Loves" photo spread in greater detail. The article featured both married and unmarried men. The editor wanted her to snap some guys with their significant others, thereby fulfilling the "Real Loves" angle. Interviews with other fellows would include home photos with their partners, allowing the article to double as Valentine's gifts.

Alan fell into the second camp. His wife had no clue he'd tested for the shoot.

They neared Alan and the muscular fellow. The latter man wore a hoodie and sweats emblazoned with the rec center logo. Gabe placed Ursula's photography gear on the concrete as Alan commenced introductions.

"Ursula Scott and Gabe McKenzie, this is Lance Resnick. He plays in my basketball league and manages the community rec center." Alan glanced at Resnick. "Promise you'll keep quiet about the pictures around Donna."

"What? You think I'd ruin wifey's Valentine surprise?"

Gabe looked Lance up and down. Something in the dude's tone of voice bugged him.

Lance shook Ursula's hand, his gaze traveling hungrily over her slim body. When his eyes lifted, his smile dripped wolf slobber.

If Ursula noticed, she didn't let on. "Thank you for permitting us to shoot in your gym, Lance," she said politely.

"My pleasure."

Gabe glared at the guy. Lance wore a wedding band, but that didn't stop him from holding Ursula's hand longer than necessary. So much for athletes *not* being meatheads. This bum carried a slab of chuck atop his corded neck.

Lance opened the rec center door, signaling Ursula to enter first. Lance followed, and Gabe and Alan brought up the rear.

Signs pointed out an auditorium on the right. The left produced an information counter and pool access. A woman corralling three young kids queried the clerk about swimming lessons. Her voice echoed off walls painted in bright colors, and the sharp scent of chlorine swamped the lobby.

Alan gestured to the pool doors. "I'll change in there."

"Doesn't the gym have changing rooms?" Gabe asked.

Lance shook his head. "We use the space to host kids' programs and birthday parties. The basketball league rents a regulation-sized court in a newer center."

"I see," Gabe said as Alan disappeared through the pool doors. Lance jogged into the kiddie gym and unlatched a sports equipment cupboard. Hanging back, Gabe whispered to Ursula, "Why such a tiny gym?"

Leaning close, she said, "Commercial photography is about creating illusions. Lance offered us free use of this space. We don't need to shoot a full court, just the area in front of the net."

Gabe eyed the baskets. "Those are pretty short hoops."

"Alan is tall but thin. If I angle the shots properly, the camera will portray him to his best advantage. He'll look like he's slam-dunking the ball, and his physique will appear more filled out."

Clever. "You mean like Steroid Boy's?"

Her lips tilted. "Stop it."

He quirked an eyebrow. "Just sayin'." He unzipped the location kit. "Where would you like the lights?"

Draping her jacket over a chair, she directed the set-up. Lance loped over with basketballs stuffed under his arms. Moments later, Alan arrived, baggy team shorts low on his hips and court sneakers squeaking on the shiny hardwood. A scattering of brown hair dusted his naked chest. The guy wasn't cut, but appeared fit.

Alan scooped a basketball off the floor. "What do you want me to do?" he asked Ursula.

"Just start playing. Pretend we're not here." She fastened a massive zoom lens to the larger of two cameras and looped both camera straps around her neck.

Nodding, Alan dribbled down the court and slam-dunked the ball. Lance cheered, and Alan glanced back. "Get that?"

Gabe looked at Ursula, who was busy adjusting camera settings. "Not yet," she answered Alan. "Carry on."

Alan resumed shooting baskets. Gabe shadowed Ursula around the gym, repositioning the lights whenever she asked while Alan played. She'd nailed the rationale behind the short hoops. Alan couldn't miss. Every time he slam-dunked, Lance clapped and whis-tled. Ursula snapped dozens of pictures. She was a real pro.

Lance trotted over, gaze locked on her breasts. "We should get Alan playing some one-on-one."

"Nice idea." She lowered her camera. "Care to join him?"

Lance whipped off his hoodie and T-shirt, revealing Popeye arms and freshly waxed, bulging pecs. Spicy body spray wafted off him in suffocating waves.

"Alan," Ursula called across the court. She coughed. "Lance will play with you. I'll crop him out of the pictures. Maybe leave a body part here and there."

"A body part?" Lance flexed each pec in a peacock display of dancing muscles.

"An arm or hip or leg," she said without looking at him. "I can't include your face in the pictures. Only Alan's. Sorry."

Grumbling, Lance jogged toward Alan. Gabe swallowed a smile.

Ursula lifted the smaller camera off her neck. "Here," she said, passing him the digital. "You shoot some."

Her nearness filled his senses. "Any tips?"

"The best way to learn is to jump in." Her soft voice caressed him. "Experiment if you'd like, but I've set the shutter speed. If the pictures are poor, we'll delete them." Her finger grazed his hand as she indicated the shutter release button. "Point and shoot. Hold down for continuous shooting. The way I've set it up, it's no harder than a phone camera. Use the viewfinder, not the screen. It might feel strange at first, but for our purposes today, it's more precise."

His skin perked up where she'd touched him. "Thanks."

Pink colored her cheeks. "You're welcome."

She glanced toward the men playing one-on-one, and a lopsided grin spread across Gabe's face. She was pretty when she blushed.

Hell, she was pretty all the time.

Following her directions, he raised the camera and composed pictures. Damn it, Alan and Lance were motoring. Every time Gabe thought he caught a decent shot, Alan dribbled out of view and he snapped an empty net. The continuous shutter made him feel fumble-fingered. He removed his jacket and began again.

Lance retrieved a third basketball and dribbled it into Gabe's personal space. "Put down the camera, man." Lance bounced the ball between his legs. "Play with us." He kicked a second ball near a folding chair. The ball smacked Gabe's shoe.

"Can't. Bum leg."

Puffing and stinking of sweat, Lance nodded toward Ursula, crouched behind the net. "A chick on her knees. Just how I like them."

Gabe eyeballed the jerk's wedding ring. "Screw you, juice monkey. Aren't you married?"

"For a piece like that, maybe not." Resnick grinned, the basketball whack-whack-whacking the floor. "How'd you wreck your leg?"

"Motorcycle accident." A version of the truth. The tumble from his old bike occurred three years before his shooting. "Spun out running over a dirt bag."

Resnick sneered. "Well, tough guy. Want to impress her? I do."

Gabe gritted his teeth. "Shut your face."

Lance continued dribbling. "Grab the ball. First one to sink a basket wins her heart—or whatever else is on offer." His tongue lolled.

That did it. "You piece of shit." Gabe thumped the camera onto the chair and slammed the guy against the wall. The ball bounded onto the court as Gabe planted a foot on hardwood and jammed his arm across Resnick's throat. Injured glute screaming, Gabe muttered, "Insult her again, and I'll rip you apart."

"Fuck you." But Lance's eyes widened, breath rancid. No trace of his overpowering body spray remained. His pores oozed fear.

"Gabe!" Ursula's boots echoed on the court floor. Alan shouted Resnick's name.

Gabe's leg buckled, pain piercing the muscle. He released Resnick.

The coward darted to his outerwear, bunched the clothes into a ball, and raced out of the gym. "Catch you later, Al! I have a meeting."

Yeah, with Losers United.

Gabe's thigh throbbed. Bending over and massaging the spasm, he clenched his jaw. "Damn it." He'd allowed a moron with a shrunken-testicles complex to goad him. Resnick probably baited every male within ten feet to compensate for his puny hoops.

"Oh, no!" Ursula called again, reaching him. "Your leg!" She grasped his shoulder. "Are you okay? What were you doing?"

Steeling himself against the pain, he grinned up at her. "Being an idiot or defending your honor. Take your pick."

Ursula had met more than her share of ego-driven asshats while testing Real Men subjects at the studio last week, but Lance Resnick occupied a category all his own. Talk about smarmy. What was the rec center manager thinking, taunting Gabe and slipping her oily looks throughout the basketball session? Did women really fall for his lines?

When she'd reached Gabe, worry twisting her stomach, he'd

insisted he was okay. Recognizing male pride when she saw it, she didn't grill him. Her dad needed space when he was hurting too.

A red-faced Alan apologized for his teammate's behavior, and Lance fled the gym faster than a mouse scuttling from a famished cat. Ursula finished Alan's session, and the trio left the recreation center as a group. Gabe limped while hefting the location kit to the van but declined her help or Alan's carrying the gear.

Wincing at the thought of Gabe's discomfort, she stood back as he stored the bags on the rear seat. While they drove toward the first location for another model, he adjusted the passenger seat as far back as possible. Leaning against the window, he stretched his injured leg along the floorboard. His open jacket revealed the moss-green V-necked sweater molding his muscular torso. Even hurt, he radiated masculinity.

Hands on the wheel, she glanced at him. "How's your leg?"

His mouth tightened. "Fine."

"Gabe, you're hurt." Defending *her* from Lance somehow. From the creep's lewd looks and come-ons. She hadn't heard the specifics, but Lance's infantile behavior throughout the session spoke volumes. The guy must have put down her or Gabe to instigate Gabe's wrath like that. "You should see a doctor."

"I'll ice my leg later. Besides, it's feeling better." He swung his knee. "See?"

"I'm serious. Check nearby clinics on my phone." She nodded toward her purse on the van floor behind her seat. "Or I can drive you home. You should ice your leg now."

He looked out his window. The right-lane traffic motored alongside them. "Home is too far. You'll miss your appointment with Norm Dobson, and I won't be around to help."

"But you're in pain." She slowed the van for a yellow light and stopped behind a white SUV. "Either you agree to see a doctor, or I'll take you home. We can buy ice at a grocery store on the way, some sandwich bags, a dishtowel. I can fashion a little ice pack."

An attractive gleam lit his eyes. "You're cute in nurse-mode. Got one of those old-fashioned white caps and a uniform hiding in your closet?" His sexy grin pumped up her heart rate. "What was your Halloween costume anyway?"

"One of the three witches from *Macbeth*. Kim and a friend of hers were the other two. And don't change the subject." The light flashed red.

"Believe it or not, I'm thinking." Gabe tapped his skull. "It's Tuesday. Thanksgiving is Thursday, and we're not working Friday. How many business days remain until your deadline?"

"With the magazine?" Eyes on the cross-traffic, she estimated her schedule. "Six, if I average two men a day. Four more sittings this week and the remainder next will work."

He shook his head. "What if something happens to disrupt your plans?" Swinging his knee again, he ground the base of his palm against his hip. "I won't risk this assignment. It's too important to you."

She stared at him. "Your *health* is important." He'd hurt his leg while working with her. While dealing with a slime like Lance. She had yearned to whack the dolt herself!

"Like I said, cute when worried." Gabe's eyebrows waggled. "You'll make a good mom."

"Thanks, but—" She sucked in a breath. They were getting nowhere. Distracting her with compliments? *Not gonna work.*

The light turned green. After driving through the intersection, she maneuvered the van into the right lane and took a corner into a quiet neighborhood.

"There's a food vendor." She pointed to a variety of small businesses flanking a park. "We have time. Let's get a snack before heading to the doggy day care." The business Norm Dobson operated with his wife. "If you won't let me take you to a doctor, at least check with your physical therapist before we eat. If she wants you to ice your leg right away, we'll buy supplies from the convenience store I happen to know is around the next corner." She grinned.

"Don't tell me you scouted Norm's locations in advance."

"I might have taken Reba for a drive last night. What can I say?" Preparing her route had saved them time already. Much easier than wrestling with Mackie's outdated GPS or continually consulting her phone. "There's a Walgreens nearby. They might carry instant cold packs."

"I am not stripping off my jeans in this van."

An image of his naked body flashed through her mind. Unclothed, what would his broad chest and flat stomach look like?

Powerful, she'd bet. With the perfect balance of sculpted muscle. An *ordinarily* easygoing guy like Gabe wouldn't lift weights for hours on end to develop shiny, Lance-Resnick-like man-titty.

Pretending to remain focused on the road, she slid Gabe a glance. The V of his sweater displayed hints of dark chest hair, and she had admired his broad shoulders and tight butt since day one. She imagined him running in early mornings, before he'd hurt his leg. Strong limbs pumping, lungs drawing in and expelling air. His mind pinpointing the coming workday, considering potential problems and solutions. A routine.

But wait. According to everything he'd told her, he was not addicted to routine.

"No cold packs," she conceded, parking the van along the grassy square. "We'll do the ice thing *over* your jeans." *Argue that.* He couldn't. She made too much sense. "First, the food and calling your physical therapist." She'd witnessed Gabe consuming large quantities of pizza. The shirts-on sitting for Norm Dobson occurred just before noon. Gabe would be hungry, and their timetable didn't permit a proper lunch break.

As if on cue, his stomach growled.

"One mention of food..." She smiled. "You have a cell, right? Call your PT." She cut the engine.

Grumbling about nurturing females, he retrieved a smartphone from his jacket pocket and tossed his wallet onto the console between their seats. "I'm buying."

"It's on the studio. Meet you at the park bench."

Eleven

Ursula placed an order with the food vendor. As the man set down two steaming cups of apple cider with cinnamon sticks for stirring, she caught sight of Gabe wandering toward the cart, tucking his phone into his coat.

He picked up the cups. "Smells good. Thanks."

"You're welcome. I hope you like hot cider. It's locally made."

"Any warm beverage on a fall day is ideal."

Nodding, Ursula gazed at the gray clouds obliterating the earlier patches of blue sky. "Looks like rain's coming."

Gabe pointed to the hood hanging down the back of his jacket. "I have an instant umbrella this time."

"I noticed. See, you can learn."

"You're a good role model."

Another compliment. A girl could grow accustomed to his gallantry.

She collected the bag of warm, soft pretzels and, side by side, they strolled in companionable silence to the slatted bench. Gabe's limp had improved since he'd walloped Lance, thank goodness.

They sat, Gabe on her right, his hurt leg extended in front of him, heel balanced on the grass. Preschoolers played on a jungle gym while moms and nannies chatted and supervised. A couple of seagulls squawked at the base of a trashcan.

"Here you go." Gabe passed her a hot cup of cider.

She set down the drink with a quick thanks before opening the vendor bag. She'd ordered two varieties of homemade pretzels, and the contrasting scents of cinnamon-sugared dough and spicy mustard glaze drifted from the sack. Her mouth watered.

"What did your physical therapist say?" she asked Gabe.

"Like I figured, I'm to ice the muscle tonight and take ibuprofen. I just saw her yesterday. Because I was so touched by your concern, she's also fitting me in late this afternoon."

He was only teasing, but butterflies scattered inside her tummy. "That's a relief. I'm glad you checked."

His shoulder bumped hers. "Anything for you, boss."

Tingles shot *everywhere*. He was so sexy. So incredibly tempting.

"Salty or sweet?" She held up the pretzel bag. "I bought two of each. It's not much, but we can stop again after Norm's session, if you're hungry."

"I'll be okay. Lemme see." Peering into the bag, he lifted out paper napkins and arranged one on her thigh. Her skin sizzled. "You're sweet, so I must be salty," he said, selecting a giant pretzel with chunky sea salt topping the beer-mustard glaze. "Smells incredible." He ripped off a big piece, chewed, and swallowed. "Tastes amazing." Eyes crinkling, he sipped his cider.

Ursula's butterflies fluttered and soared. She bit into her cinnamon-sugar-sprinkled pretzel. "How's your leg?"

His eyebrows hoisted. "Hello, dog. Meet bone."

"Excuse me? I'm a canine?"

"Hardly. But determined? Yep."

"Indulge me." The folded pretzel bag rested on her lap, her snack on top. She picked up her cider and stirred the hot liquid. The cinnamon stick accentuated the cozy autumn notes of the aromatic drink.

"Still hurts a bit," Gabe admitted.

Interpreting his alpha-speak, the incident in the gym had damaged his injured leg more than he wanted her to know.

Not a surprise. He'd planted his leg hard on the court floor.

"I'm sorry." She sipped her cider. "Lance deliberately tried to rile you, dribbling his dumb basketball between his legs like he wanted to challenge you to a wrestling match or something."

Gabe ate his pretzel. "*You* don't have to be sorry."

"I was in charge. I should have told him to check his ego at the door." She nibbled her tasty snack, the cinnamon spicy on her tongue. "Aren't you concerned he'll press charges?"

"He wouldn't dare. His wife might learn why I shoved him. He's a jackass. I couldn't twiddle my thumbs while he disrespected you."

"What did he say?"

"Nothing I care to repeat. Verbal leers."

"Well, I'm not interested." In married men like Lance. Against her better judgment, Gabe was increasingly becoming another matter. Would he have responded to Lance's taunts if *he* weren't interested in her? "Thank you for defending my honor, as you put it."

"So I'm not an idiot?"

Laughing, she raised her cider for another sip. *Being an idiot or defending your honor*, he had said at the gym. *Take your pick.*

"You're one of the nicest guys I've ever met." A *thousand* butterflies tumbled around inside her.

"I bet you say that—"

"To all the boys? Nope." And she shouldn't have confessed the same to Gabe. She possessed minimal self-control around this man. Was it any wonder? He might be a good-time guy, but he'd stood up to Lance without her asking. He'd volunteered for the magazine shoot to learn photography, and she was benefiting in countless ways. Without his help, her schedule over the next several days would be insane. He tolerated Mackie's eccentricities with more patience than she could possibly wrangle.

Like her, Gabe had suffered loss. While discussing the *Clarion* ad at her apartment last Wednesday, she'd bluntly inquired about his father only to discover the man had passed away "a long time ago."

When Gabe was a little boy? A teenager?

Upon blurting the question, she'd realized her rudeness. But he hadn't called her on it. As if wanting to spare her embarrassment, he'd stated the facts and moved forward.

She set her cup beside her hip again. Gabe genuinely cared about people. Whatever he chose to do, she couldn't picture him *not* helping others.

"You're a mystery," she murmured. "More complex than I thought at first."

"Is that a good thing?"

She lowered her gaze. "It is." She plucked her pretzel off the bag. *Easy, Ursula. He's only human. A man with faults like any other.*

That wasn't how she felt though. It wasn't how *he* made her feel deep inside.

"Did you leave anyone behind in LA?" she asked. "A girlfriend?"

His gaze shifted to the playing kids before returning to meet hers again. "No."

Ursula studied his classically handsome jaw line. "I don't know. I think you might have."

His mouth hiked up at one corner. "You can ask that after our kiss outside your door?"

On Saturday. Her heart skipped a beat. He'd mentioned his dry spell. Three months.

"But there was someone in the summer." She would show him how this puppy treated her bones.

He finished his pretzel, and she passed him a cinnamon-sugar one.

"Okay, there was someone." He shrugged. "A fling. There have been a lot of 'someones' over the years. I mean, hey"—he flourished a hand over his jacket—"who wouldn't want this?"

She laughed.

"But no one's ever stuck," he added, voice reflective. "Guess I never found the right woman."

"Maybe you weren't ready."

"I didn't think to search. I was twenty-two when I left Seattle. Settling down was the last thing on my mind. And that's all I'm gonna say on the subject...boss." Winking, he munched his second pretzel.

He couldn't fool her, referencing her declaration on Saturday that she didn't date coworkers. Whenever he called her boss, their conversation in her apartment's rainy parking lot sprang to mind— as did thoughts of their amazing kiss that same afternoon.

So what if Gabe had bedded dozens of women while sowing youthful oats in California? That didn't change who he was today. He might be a good-time guy, but he was also a *good man*. His hot glances and sexy smiles were just icing on a tasty Gabe cake. The *real* man—the kindhearted person who cared about his mom and helped his grouchy uncle—lived within a hunky exterior.

How had he managed to remain single? She couldn't be the first girl to glimpse his possibilities. What sort of women had he dated before moving home? Had he left a trail of broken hearts in California? Was he friends with any of his exes? Had he remained in contact with one or two?

Dare she ask those sorts of personal questions?

The cool wind flicked her hair in her face. Gabe brushed away the strands, his thumb grazing her cheek, his tender touch churning her emotions.

Overhead, seagulls squawked.

He glanced skyward. "Don't look now."

"Rain?"

Plop.

"Omigod, seagull poop!" Sticky and slippery, smack dab on her scalp.

The slime oozed onto her part. Tossing aside the pretzel bag, she whipped up her hand.

Gabe chuckled. "I've got it." Grasping her upper arm, he moistened his napkin with his tongue and dabbed at her hair. "None hit your coat, but your hair needs reinforcements." He dipped the napkin into his cider and swiped the soggy tissue over her part.

"I've been bombed!" A full-on belly laugh rumbled through her as she hunched on the bench, hugging her arms and rocking back and forth.

"Hold still," Gabe instructed, cleaning her hair.

"I can't." Her cup toppled over. Cider streamed through the bench slats onto the lawn at her feet. "What a mess." What was it with her and hot liquids? She was lucky the cider hadn't soaked her jeans or scalded Gabe. "What will Norm think? I need perfume. Or hairspray. Or mousse. Or something!"

"There's that Walgreen's."

"Yes, we'll stop there." Then speed to the doggy day care. Well, not speed. She couldn't risk a ticket. But she would punch some freaking metal.

"I dunno," Gabe said as if he dealt with seagull stink every day.

"I like the cider scent. Reminds me of an orchard." He got up. "The vendor will have a decent cloth. Be right back."

He strode off, a shuffle to his gait. Gabe McKenzie—great guy, hotter than a heat wave—ignoring *his* discomfort and looking out for her again.

Seagull poop and all.

How had he managed to remain single?

"Nice place," Gabe said as Norm and Melissa Dobson toured him and Ursula around their urban dog-care business. He'd heard about such places in LA but had never stepped inside one. Hands in jeans pockets, he scanned the Pooch Lounge, where several dogs napped on sofas.

Unreal. He appreciated the service the Dobsons offered, but on the job he'd encountered toddlers barely subsisting in drug houses, sometimes locked up for days in soiled pajamas with only a scraggy teddy bear for comfort while Mommy and Daddy smoked a little crystal. These Seattle canines led better lives. The big, scared eyes of those mistreated children would haunt Gabe forever.

Melissa beamed. "Thank you. We love it, especially because we can bring our darling Juno to work each day." She tugged Norm close. "Thanks again for choosing my husband for the article. I've been so excited since we learned why you need models, I can hardly stand it. Isn't that right, honey?"

Norm stared at the rubber floor, shifting his feet. In Gabe's amateur opinion, unless the man relaxed he would make a lousy Real Men subject.

He exchanged a quick glance with Ursula. Voice kind, she asked Norm, "Are you sure you want to do the shoot today? We can postpone until Monday."

Damn, she was cute. Her scalp shone with a thick coating of the scented hairspray she'd purchased at the drugstore. She needn't have worried about the seagull bomb. Disinfectant tinged every room and hallway of the Dobsons' business. Hairspray or not, the couple wouldn't have smelled the bird goop—or Gabe's cider fix.

"I don't want to wreck your schedule," Norm responded in a lackluster tone.

Melissa chimed, "And I'm leaving Sunday to visit my sister. I wanted to take Juno."

The plan had been for Norm to pose with the couple's Siberian Husky for the shirts-on photos before Ursula shot a few more pictures including Melissa and their business. Gabe had arranged the location kit and portable backdrop within a barricaded section near the Pooch Lounge.

He suggested, "How about we snap pictures of Norm with Melissa and the dog today then do the ones of Norm in his hot tub while Melissa is out of town? Evening shots might make a nice change." And wouldn't impact Ursula's schedule.

His beautiful pretend-boss smiled. "Excellent idea. Melissa? Norm? How does seven p.m. Monday sound?"

Melissa grinned. "I'll find our girl." She strode toward the grooming station.

Norm released a world-weary sigh. "Sorry for being difficult. It feels like a lot is at stake. *Seattle Lights* is a big deal."

"Try not to think about the magazine," Ursula reassured the man. "Just play with your dog. We'll do the rest."

"What if the readers don't like me?"

"The editor wouldn't have selected you if she was afraid of that," Gabe said.

"Gabe's right. Norm, it's natural to feel nervous, but don't worry. We'll ease into the formal poses. I'll use a tripod and remote shutter release so I don't spook Juno. Then it won't feel like I'm in your face."

Norm's jaw worked back and forth. "All right."

"Great. I need to pop out to the van. Gabe, can you help with the equipment?"

Nodding, Gabe followed her outside. Rain drizzled from the pewter sky. They each lifted their jacket hoods and strode onto the wet sidewalk.

At the van, she faced him. Her forehead wrinkled. "This is unexpected. Norm seemed so comfortable during the test shots. Today he won't look me in the eyes."

"He didn't have anything to lose last week." During the day-care tour, Gabe and Ursula learned Melissa had teased her husband into responding to the porno-sounding ad. Norm didn't seem the type, but who was Gabe to judge? Plenty of placid-looking individuals enjoyed kinky sex lives behind the privacy of closed bedroom doors. "Melissa wasn't hanging around then. Even after I told him about the magazine, he was convinced the editor wouldn't select him."

"He said that?" Ursula unlocked the van, and Gabe retrieved the tripod.

"Yep. We talked while Melissa gabbed your ear off out back. Norm thought participating in the test shots would satisfy his wife. Now he's worried his stomach will look chubby in the shirts-off pictures, that their clients will think less of him, and so on."

"Poor guy. He barely has a paunch." Her gaze skipped down Gabe's raincoat.

"You checking out *my* paunch?"

Her eyes twinkled. "Your lack of one."

"I don't lack in other areas."

"Oh?" Her head tilted. "Really?"

A jolt of lust booted him in the gut. Damn it, he was flirting with her again instead of cementing his cover as her assistant. But she was so damn flirtable. So damn likeable. Poles apart from Tiff Collingsworth, who'd just wanted an uncomplicated lay—all Gabe thought *he'd* wanted for years.

What was it about Ursula that made him itch for more? What would it feel like to have a woman with her abundance of positive qualities in his life? Caring, determined, family-oriented. Someone he could visualize introducing to his mom.

His chest tightened. There was a first. His mother had met a couple of his girlfriends during his college years, but not a single woman since he'd moved to California. Whenever she'd visited, he hadn't happened to be dating mother-meeting material. His life had revolved around the job.

He gripped the tripod. "Come on. Norm and Melissa are waiting."

Ursula grinned as they hurried back to the building. Under the eaves, they swept off their hoods. He opened the door, and she entered the business, her summery scent mingling with the fresh smell of the rain.

She glanced over her shoulder. "You know, Gabe, you have excellent people skills. If you decide against photography, you should look into a career that takes advantage of them."

"I will." She had him pegged. "Melissa alert," he whispered. "Three, two..."

Ursula turned. Melissa walked her freshly bathed and dried dog toward Norm on a lead. Norm greeted the dog, and the couple approached Gabe and Ursula.

"Melissa, she's beautiful." Ursula stroked the husky's thick fur. "Her eyes are the same blue as Norm's."

Melissa chuckled. "She takes after her father."

They headed for the barricaded area, away from the client dogs. Ursula and Gabe doffed their wet coats, and Ursula set up the tripod.

"Norm, play with Juno on the sheet," she directed. "Scratch her ears and rub her tummy. However you would play with her at home. That's it."

A few feet away, Gabe watched as Ursula snapped pictures with the aid of the remote shutter release. Norm's features remained stiff at first. Then Gabe selected two dog toys while Melissa retreated to her office for a phone call. Soon, Norm and Juno inter-acted like fun-loving dog and owner.

Ursula changed the camera settings several times before detaching the camera from the tripod and approaching the pair from different angles.

"Thanks," she said when Gabe ambled over. "Getting the squeak toys was the key."

"Juno's not looking at the camera half the time."

"It's more natural if the dog doesn't. If I shoot enough pictures and the editor wants Juno facing the lens, I can swap one dog head for another with computer software."

"Isn't that cheating?"

"Photographers switch animal heads all the time. It eliminates stress during sessions for both dog and owner."

"The things I'm learning," Gabe murmured as she clicked more photos. As a cop, he'd dealt with criminal aspects of photo manipu-lation, but Gabe the laid-back assistant was a total newb. "We should return to the rec center. You could work your magic on Lance Resnick. Swap his head for one with more brains."

She glanced up. "We're back to dissing Lance?"

"He's a dick."

"Who wouldn't cross my mind if you didn't keep mentioning him."

Gabe couldn't help himself. His Neanderthal side wanted to bash in Resnick's skull, toss Ursula over his shoulder, and stomp toward the nearest cave. Make her his.

"You're right," he said. "I'll forget the jerk."

"Good. Because I have." She lifted her camera again.

Norm had noticed she'd stopped taking pictures. Clutching a dog toy, he asked, "We done?"

"Not yet, Norm," Ursula called. "Sorry."

Gabe dipped his head to her ear. Heat spearing him, he whispered, "Neither are we."

Ursula finished the shots of dog and owner and progressed to poses of Norm sitting on the white sheet. When Melissa returned, she focused her attention on couple portraits to round out the "Real Loves" angle of the magazine spread. Only the photos of Norm alone in his hot tub remained, and Monday would work fine. She'd rather Norm relax and enjoy himself than force the man to continue the shoot as previously scheduled. Overall, between completing Alan Cory's photos and coaxing Norm through his shirts-on session, it had been a productive day.

She and Gabe returned to the studio, and she parked in the alley. In the breakroom, she removed her jacket and stored her purse. "Darn it. Mackie hasn't replaced the coffeemaker yet." She gestured at the counter. She craved a caffeine pick-me-up.

"I'll head next door. They sell coffeemakers."

"Those brands are expensive."

"That's what my uncle gets for not replacing the old one when he said he would." Gabe grinned. "I'll be thirty minutes. I have something to do."

"Your physical therapy appointment?"

"No, that's later on." He took off.

Ursula stared at the empty doorway. What errand could he possibly need to run in this neighborhood? Pawning an item down the street? Flirting with the clerk in the T-shirt shop—like he'd flirted with *her* at the doggy day care? Why even enter the studio if he'd planned to leave right away?

It's none of my business.

Gabe was a charmer. Free to flirt with whomever he pleased or run a simple errand, if that was all it was.

Shaking off a weird sensation, she headed to the front office. Two teenage boys and their mothers sat waiting for graduation appointments. One mother paged through a magazine and double-checked her watch. Ursula greeted the kids and moms on her way to the desk.

Stacy looked up from the computer. "You're back early."

"Long story. How are the grad sittings going?"

"We're a little behind," the girl whispered behind a hand.

"How did that happen?" Ursula whispered back. "We booked plenty of time per student."

Stacy hunched over her keyboard. "Mackie hates this sort of thing," she responded in hushed tones. "He says he's rusty."

Oh, brother. "Until we sign more commercial clients, he can't afford to limit his jobs," Ursula whispered.

"Tell that to him."

"I have." Numerous times. The man would drive her up the wall —if she let him. She rapped her fingernails on the desk. "Do you need a break?" she asked Stacy.

"Like you wouldn't believe. Check with boss-man first?"

Ursula gave an efficient nod before trekking down the left corridor to the studio proper and knocking.

Mackie opened the door, scowling. "*What?*" he barked. Sickly-sweet men's wafted from his thick neck. If she wasn't mistaken, the same brand as Resnick's.

Her stomach curdled. "Gabe and I are back for the day. Would you like some help?"

He glanced back at a teenage girl positioned against a backdrop of ivory columns and green vines. The mother, a busty brunette in her early forties, fussed with the teen's extravagant gown.

"You can take the boys out front." Mackie's gaze gobbled the mother's voluptuous figure. "I'd like to do—uh, wrap Mrs. Jackson's session with her kid." He sucked his lips. "They upgraded to Package D at the last minute. The girl might get nervous if we switch photographers now." His eyes remained riveted on the mother's jiggling boobs.

"Uh-huh." Ursula pivoted on her heels. "I'll be in Reception." *Throwing up.*

She relieved Stacy, and the girl left for the breakroom. A minute later, the desk phone rang.

"Victor McKenzie Photography," Ursula spoke into the receiver. "We'll make you famous."

"Hello," a pleasant female voice said. "This is Eve McKenzie, Victor's sister-in-law. Is my son Gabe available? I tried his cell phone but reached voicemail."

"Hi, Mrs. McKenzie. This is Ursula Scott. I work with Gabe."

"Oh, yes, Ursula. He's mentioned you."

Ursula smiled. "I'm sorry, Mrs. McKenzie, Gabe is out. Would you like to leave a message?" She reached for a pen.

"I'll try his cell again. I'm not a fan of texting. So impersonal."

"That's okay. He won't be long."

"All right. Well, then, please let him know I'm having dinner with my girlfriends from the bank tomorrow but not to worry about tonight. I'm making pork chops in mushroom sauce. He loves that dish."

"Sounds delicious." Ursula jotted the message. Gabe had lived on his own since twenty-two and appeared fully capable of feeding himself. After several years of her son residing in a different state, his mom must love having him around.

"Once he moves into that nice apartment, I won't have as many opportunities to spoil him, so I'm doing it now," his mother said warmly.

Ursula stopped midway through writing the last sentence. "He rented an apartment?" He hadn't said boo to *her* about that, and they'd been together all day.

"Yes, dear," his mom replied. "He viewed a lovely apartment Saturday. Near where you live, he mentioned."

The place with the second bedroom he'd said he couldn't afford?

Stomach rocking like a boat on a stormy lake, Ursula said goodbye and hung up.

She twisted her rings. Could Gabe not meet his expenses? Was his mom lending a hand with the rent? Why hadn't he just said something?

Whatever. She scribbled the remainder of the message. She'd tack the note onto the studio fridge for ease of reading later.

"I'll be a minute," she told the waiting mothers.

Message in hand, she headed toward the breakroom. Gabe's low voice drifted into the hall, and snippets of his conversation with Stacy reached Ursula's ears.

She frowned. He'd returned already? That was fast. And why was he quizzing Stacy about the keys the receptionist had misplaced for one piddly day? It was bad enough Mackie harangued the girl left and right. Why on earth would Gabe—

Ursula rushed into the room. A cheerful-looking Stacy paused in the process of plugging in a shiny new coffeemaker. Gabe, clutching the coffee bag, glanced over his shoulder, his gaze hot and smoldering.

The yummy scent of banana-nut muffins wafted from the counter.

"Fresh java's on the way." He smiled. "Want a muffin?"

She shook her head. "I'm confused. Didn't you have errands?"

"Changed my mind. I thought you might be hungry."

That was right, they hadn't eaten lunch. And he wasn't hassling Stacy. They were engaged in small talk, passing time like any other amiable coworkers.

Grow up, Ursula. Before she began coming across like Neurotic Girl, she needed to stop reading between the lines of situations that didn't exist. Forget about butting into *Gabe's* choices for *his* apartment and pass on the message from his mom.

She had enough to obsess about, and paranoia did not become her.

Twelve

PAUL BLOOMFIELD STRUGGLED to knot his bowtie. Christine's antique French telephone rang on the white provincial desk in their sumptuous bedroom, and he fumbled with the slippery black silk. If his wife would permit him to wear elasticized ties, he would have been ready to leave for her handpicked charity event five minutes ago. But no, in the old-money world of Christine Eleanor Rasmussen Bloomfield, Paul the Seattle Council President, future mayoral candidate, and eventual Washington state governor couldn't be caught dead wearing a strap-on bowtie.

The phone rang again, and Christine's melodious voice floated through the closed door of the adjoining bathroom. "Darling, can you pick up? I'm applying my face."

"Yes, sweetheart." Tie dangling off his collar, Paul grasped the porcelain receiver. "Bloomfield residence," he spoke into the elongated mouthpiece.

"Hello, Paul," a smug baritone grated in his ear.

Paul stiffened. "McKenzie, I distinctly specified you are not to call me at home," he hissed. He'd purchased a disposable cell phone for the purpose of their unsavory business transactions. Only he and McKenzie knew the number.

Victor McKenzie snorted. "Get it straight, Paulie-boy. You don't specify anything. *I* do the specifying."

Perspiration dotted Paul's upper lip. "Yes, of course. Forgive me." His heart raced beneath the starched fabric of his dress shirt. *Don't blow it, Paul.* "I'm just a little frustrated."

"So am I," McKenzie growled. "You disappoint me, Bloomfield. We had a deal, you pansy-assed dipshit."

Mouth dry, Paul shot a glance to the bathroom door. "We still do," he whispered into the phone. If Christine learned McKenzie was blackmailing him—

"Then why are you screwing with me?" the lowlife growled.

"I'm not!" *Damn it.* Modulating his tone, Paul repeated smoothly, "I'm not."

The bathroom door opened. Christine looked out, one eyebrow filled in, the other partially done. Her conservative navy blue gown sheathed her slim body, and her blond hair curled on top of her head like an exquisite crown.

"Who is it?" she asked, an inquisitive glint in her eyes.

"My brother," Paul lied with a straight face. "He's wishing us good luck raising money for the homeless shelters tonight." Ostensibly, he and Christine attended fundraisers for charitable purposes. In reality, the gatherings provided opportunities to garner financial and political support for next year's mayoral race.

Thanks to his wife's forgiveness following Paul's error in judgment with a prostitute four years ago, Paul would declare his candidacy in the spring. Christine's efforts toward improving his public persona since the unfortunate incident had saved his political hide. The media frenzy had nearly ended their marriage. Paul couldn't risk another scandal—a fact McKenzie banked on.

"Is your she-cat there?" the boor snarled in his ear.

Paul clenched his jaw. "Christine is present." Gambling on his wife's long-established behavior patterns, he said into the phone, "Does Julia wish to speak with her?"

Christine mouthed, "I don't have time." She pointed at her diamond-encrusted Rolex, a please-don't-leave-me-I'll-never-stray-again gift.

A bit of a fib, that straying part, as it had turned out.

However, at the time, Paul had meant it.

McKenzie cackled. "I'd love to chat up the twat."

Paul's cheek twitched. *How dare he!*

"Sorry, my mistake," he said with a glance to his wife. "She left the room to speak to Rosa."

"Who's Rosa?" McKenzie asked.

Paul remained quiet while Christine disappeared into the bathroom. Her insistence on dressing him aside, she was the prize of his life and he didn't want to lose her. Her family's political connections were as strong as her ambition.

"*Who the fuck is Rosa?*"

Skull thumping, Paul mumbled, "The housekeeper."

"Oh, yeah? Does she spread 'em for you, Paulie-boy?"

"Don't be vulgar. The woman is sixty."

"Right, you like your beaver hot and juicy, don't you?"

Paul squeezed shut his eyes. He *detested* Victor McKenzie. Five years ago, on the heels of Paul's first election, an advertising flyer featuring McKenzie's photography studio circulated City Hall. Eager to please Christine, Paul hired the loser for a wedding anniversary portrait. The next year, feeling invincible following numerous political successes, Paul stupidly solicited a hooker for oral sex. He chickened out before unzipping, but the streetwalker blabbed the story to the media. Unbeknownst to Paul, McKenzie had taken note.

An incensed Christine threatened to leave Paul. To the Rasmussen family, private indiscretions were possibly forgivable, but public humiliation simply was not tolerated.

When the hooker's story slammed the papers, the TV, and internet, Paul couldn't understand the community outcry. It wasn't like he'd followed through with the deed. Actors and a former president had survived worse PR nightmares, the latter emerging with his marriage intact.

With an eye to that tidbit of political history, Christine had come around to envisioning herself and Paul in the "intact" camp. A public apology and increased charitable work resurrected Paul's career and repaired the damage to his marriage.

"Answer me," McKenzie bellowed.

"Yes," Paul grated through gritted teeth. "What man in the prime of his life likes it dry?"

McKenzie cackled, and Paul rolled his eyes. Must they share these crude conversations? Why couldn't McKenzie state his business and hang up? Paul couldn't alienate the man. Late this August, a week before Paul attended a municipal conference in California, a news story about the symposium mentioned his name, piquing McKenzie's interest. The photographer recalled the hooker scandal and quickly conjured a blackmail scheme—with Paul as his unsuspecting prey.

After the conference, Paul learned McKenzie had traveled to California on the sly and hired a bimbo to ply Paul with booze with the intention to lure Paul onto the beach at midnight. Paul hadn't taken her bait...beyond a conversation and some innocent flirtation in the bar...but McKenzie's doctored photos of the woman with another man who appeared to *be* Paul told a different story. One he couldn't afford getting out, especially taking into account that he *had* strayed, albeit here at home.

If McKenzie stumbled upon Paul's real indiscretion, his political aspirations would go up in smoke.

If *Christine* discovered either slip-up, so would his marriage.

Paul had learned his lesson. Never again would he sleep with or even compliment another woman. He just wanted to pay off the blackmailer and move on with his life.

He scrubbed a hand over his face. "What do you want?" he asked McKenzie.

"For you to stay in line!"

"I made the first pay drop," he whispered. "The second isn't due for days."

"What about this Sunday? Someone broke into my studio and left a nasty surprise."

"I don't know what you're talking about."

"You sure as hell better not! Because if I find out you or some thug on your payroll set my microwave on fire, not only will I hand-deliver the pictures of you dogging around in California to your ball-breaker wife, I will personally see to it Chrissie has plenty of male comfort after she kicks you out. You get my drift? I like my beaver hot and juicy too."

Visions of McKenzie having sex with Paul's virtuous Christine filled his mind.

Shuddering, he clenched the phone. "You wouldn't."

"Try me," McKenzie threatened. "Don't cross me, Bloomfield.

You have plans. I have plans. We can help each other. But not if you cross me."

The brute disconnected. Hands shaking, Paul hung up and paced the room. How odd that someone had set fire to an appliance in McKenzie's derelict photography studio. And the swine thought *Paul* possessed the courage to have done so? That would be the day. If Paul owned one ounce of fortitude, he wouldn't mess around with a pathetic fire. He'd break into McKenzie's apartment and slice open the cretin's carotid artery with piano wire. He'd relish the power surging in his veins as life drained from McKenzie's disgusting body.

The bathroom door opened again. Christine swept out, both eyebrows filled in and red lipstick brightening her mouth.

Gaze widening, she scanned him up and down. "Darling, where are your shoes and tuxedo jacket? Oh, Paul, your bowtie."

He grasped the black silk slipping off his collar. "Sorry, I was preoccupied."

"With tonight?"

Among other things. He nodded.

"That's my darling." Stepping toward him, she knotted the tie then pecked him on the mouth. "Am I showing?" She glanced down.

Paul patted her flat stomach. "Not yet."

"I suppose, for seven weeks, I can't expect much. But my baby bump will be huge when it counts."

Paul offered an appropriate smile. Christine had timed the pregnancy of the one child she'd agreed to bear for him so her protruding belly would coincide with his spring announcement to run for mayor.

"You'll look beautiful no matter how much weight you gain. You always do."

Lips curving, she clasped his hand and assumed a waltz position. Humming "Hail to the Chief," she directed them around the bedroom.

Paul hated it when she led. "Christine, we have to leave."

"Shh. I'm imagining dancing at the inaugural balls after we take the White House. Won't it be divine?"

"If we get that far."

"Paul, you ninny, we most certainly will. Council president, mayor, governor, president of the United States of America. It's a perfect progression." Demeanor regal, she inhaled a breath. "Then we'll *both* have everything we've ever wanted."

Chest tight, Paul deciphered her meaning. As long as he never betrayed her trust again.

❧

"You were a great help today," Ursula said with a glance to Gabe as she barreled Mackie's van north toward Seattle on the Valley Freeway. Traffic was moderate for the afternoon before Thanksgiving, but heavy winds had whipped up. While she appreciated Mackie allowing her use of the van to increase exposure for studio advertising painted on the side, if rocks chipped the windshield he'd probably dock her pay. "I couldn't have taken those wonderful shots of Gavin or Darrell without you. The way you kept them talking took their minds off the shoot." As a result, she'd now accomplished three out of eight Real Men sessions. Norm Dobson's contribution remained half-finished.

Gabe lounged in the passenger seat. "Not a problem. I figured middle-aged men might find it difficult removing their shirts for a beautiful woman, even if they applied for the job." His broad shoulders shifted in his insanely sexy, battered bomber jacket.

Ursula grinned. "How about Gavin removing his shirt in front of you?" Not every model was straight, including Gavin. "And the guys who responded to the botched ad didn't have a problem stripping to their underwear."

"You weeded out the worst. The rest seem like regular Joes, exactly what you wanted."

"That's it, pour on the flattery." An Audi passed them, and Ursula checked her speedometer, reminding herself to focus on traffic.

"Okay," Gabe said. "You're talented and fun to hang out with. Should I continue?"

"How about brilliant, witty, intelligent?"

"Modest and unassuming."

She laughed. "Hunger makes me blunt."

"Want to take the next exit and stop for hamburgers?"

"I'd love to. I'm famished." She read the roadside signs. The exit wasn't for several miles.

Relaxing, she concentrated on driving while Gabe scanned messages on his phone. Over the last few days, especially at night as she lay in bed, tossing and turning, fantasizing about her handsome assistant, she'd thought a lot about her conversation with Kim last Saturday while they'd fixed hot chocolate. Her friend hadn't outright stated that Ursula was out of touch about relationships, but Kim might as well have. Ursula only had to reflect on her reaction to Gabe's mom's phone call yesterday to realize that. She'd responded to the news that he'd rented an apartment as if he required her permission to decide where he wanted to live or how he might pay for it, when he had the perfect right to choose a place or not discuss the injury to his leg or make any other life decisions without her nosy intrusion.

She gnawed the inside of her cheek. Had she scared off other guys because she took dating too seriously? Should she follow Kim's advice and reconsider her hiatus?

As her friend had pointed out, once she owned the studio, she would be swamped with building the business and helping her parents. Why not go for the gusto now while she had the chance? While opportunity, so to speak, sat right beside her. Live a little with a man who didn't expect—or desire—a future.

With a man like Gabe.

No, *with* Gabe. She wasn't interested in anyone else.

A honking car overtook the van, and she snapped her gaze to the speedometer again. While she'd been daydreaming, they'd lost speed and the right rear tire felt funny.

Gabe pocketed his phone. "Everything okay?"

A crossover flew past them. "I'm not sure. We might have a flat."

He cocked an ear. "You're right. Slow down. It's getting worse." He indicated a dirt patch spreading off the shoulder. "There's a good spot to stop and see what's going on."

Checking her mirrors, she switched on the blinkers. Several cars changed into the left lane to accommodate their decreasing speed.

She eased the van to a crawl and parked on the pull-out. The vehicle sagged to the right.

"We definitely have a flat," she said. Mackie would be steamed.

"It'll be dark soon." Gabe slid out of the van. "Hit the hazards and watch the traffic when you get out. I'll come around and help."

She shook her head. "I can manage. Meet you at the back." She shut off the ignition and pressed the dashboard button to illuminate the hazard lights. Traffic whizzed past as she climbed out of the van. The wind plastering her short wool skirt against her tights, she trudged to the rear of the vehicle.

Gabe crouched, examining the right back tire. Ursula fought the wind in her hair. She should have dug in her purse for a rubber band and fashioned a quick ponytail.

She scoped out their surroundings. Warehouses and loading trucks peeked through the trees on the far side of the freeway. To their right, more trees and green space suggested they'd need to endure a long walk before they reached a subdivision or retail area.

"It's deflating, all right," Gabe murmured. "And I found the culprit." He tapped a small gray disc in the tire treads. "We took in a nail."

"At Darrell's house?" Ursula bent to study the disc. Her jacket sleeve brushed Gabe's shoulder. The scent of old, comfy leather and the masculine energy emanating off him rushed tingles through her body.

"Hard to tell. It could have been leaking a day or two." Rising with a wince, he wiped his hands on his jeans. "I'll see what my uncle has for a spare. You sit inside and stay warm."

Ursula gazed at him. His leg probably ached. But she wouldn't mention it. *Nuh-uh.* "Gabe, sitting in the van while you come to my rescue is so last century. If we're changing the tire, I'm helping."

"Whatever you want." He smiled. "Can you apply the parking brake and pop open the back door?"

She did as requested then returned to find him sorting through Mackie's cluttered cargo hold, an area she avoided unless absolutely necessary. She and Gabe had been storing her photography equipment within easy access of the sliding door behind the driver's seat.

"What are you looking for?" She curved her messy hair behind one ear.

"Wheel chocks to lodge against the left front tire. It will make the van more secure." He searched again. "Looks like he doesn't have any."

"Actually, now that you mention it, he does. He left a new box open on the passenger seat a couple of weeks ago, so I asked him what they were." As part of their deal that she purchase the studio, Mackie had agreed to maintain the van. She might decide to buy it along with the business and transfer ownership of Reba to her brother. "He stuffed the chocks back here." She pointed to a Mexican blanket covering some lumps.

Gabe sorted through odds and ends. "Nothing."

"That's weird. Your uncle must have removed them for some reason." Ursula explored the grassy area beside the dirt patch. "Will these work?" She lifted one large rock and toed another with her shoe.

"Perfect. I located a tire-changing kit. We're in business." Gabe set a jack and the toolkit on the ground. After positioning the rocks, he crouched and retrieved a tool.

"What now?" Ursula asked. Yes, she was a *phenomenal* help.

He gestured toward the cargo hold. "Don't ask me why my uncle keeps a bald trailer tire in there. It's useless for a spare."

"A bald tire? Where?"

"Beneath the second blanket."

"That makes no sense. When he bought the chocks, he sprung for a spare. I saw it. Brand new. He planned to swap it for the tire under the carriage thingie."

"The chassis," Gabe corrected. "Maybe he decided to store the new spare at his place until he had time to make the swap."

"Yeah, but why toss a trailer wheel into the mix?"

"I dunno." Gabe tugged an earlobe. "I peeked at the old spare. It's not in good enough shape to drive back to the studio, but it will do until we reach a tire shop. I know a guy who can patch the flat."

"Great." Mackie might be as useful as a fried camera card, but Gabe was very handy. A result of his assortment of temporary jobs, she presumed. "What can I do?"

"Resist the urge to climb back in and bounce up and down. I don't want the damn heap collapsing on me."

She chuckled. Dragging hair out of her face, she watched while he inched himself on his back beneath the van, released the spare, and shoved the tire toward her shoes. She dragged the wheel to the flat.

Grunting, he maneuvered out from under the vehicle again. Dirt covered his very fine rear. Standing, he swatted the denim clean. "Now we need a pry bar."

She retrieved a metal tool bent at one end. "Show me what to do." The less strain on his leg, the better.

"*You* want to change the tire?"

"Damn straight," she said in a tough-trucker tone. She smacked the pry bar against her palm, dinging her grandmother's wedding band on her left pinkie.

She hunched in front of the flat. Gabe knelt beside her with a grin. Their legs brushed, and a thrill chased ripples along her limbs. She would have *good* dreams tonight featuring a hot mechanic who looked, smelled, and smiled like Gabe McKenzie.

Heart beating in rhythm with the blinking hazard lights, she slipped him a glance. His lashes were thick and dark, his eyes so mossy green, it was criminal. The way his gaze zeroed in on hers...

If he chose tonight for their second kiss, she wouldn't object.

He said, "You want to insert the pry bar under the edge of the hubcap and carefully lift it up."

Insert the what into who? "Like this?" She followed his instructions.

"Exactly like that," he said in a soft, low, utterly erotic voice.

Her nipples pointed under her knit top and jacket as the heavy wind fluttered her hair and chapped her cold hands. *Ursula, Ursula.* What sort of woman got off on a guy's voice while he taught her how to change a tire?

Well, she knew the answer. The sex-deprived type.

"Keep lifting the pry bar along the cap to loosen it," he murmured. "Then we'll pop it off."

He would have *her* popping in a minute.

She concentrated on the task. He yanked off the wheel cover and set it aside.

"Team work," she said, feeling ridiculously triumphant.

He attached a tool of some kind to a dealy from the tire kit. "Turn the wrench until the lug nut loosens." He demonstrated.

She almost broke an arm accomplishing the feat, but the nut thingie finally cracked.

"You're doing great." He removed the gizmo and set it by the cover. "I'll loosen the other lug nuts, or we'll be here until midnight."

"I thought you said I was doing great." But she saw his point. She passed him the wrench.

The loosening accomplished, he positioned the jack. "Now the fun part." He pumped the jack, elevating the van until the flat grazed the ground. Grimacing, he removed the nuts and hoisted the van further. After tugging off the flat, he positioned the spare and jiggled the wheel while twisting on the lug nuts by hand. The wheel in place, he lowered the vehicle with the jack.

"Do you want to try the wrench again?" Rubbing his thigh, he held out the tool.

His leg must be killing him. "Okay." She tightened the nuts before he took over and tightened them again. He lowered the van completely and tightened the nuts a final time.

Attention to detail. She was impressed.

"You're sure that'll hold?" she teased.

"We can't be too careful. In fact, this last nut is giving me trouble. Can you stomp on the end of the wrench? Rest a hand on my shoulder so you don't lose your balance."

Gripping his shoulder—*ah, physical contact*—she raised her right shoe and stepped hard on the wrench. The nut tightened.

"Excellent." His hand curled around her left calf, warming her skin through her patterned tights.

Was he eager to touch her too?

"Feels good to me." She glanced down at his face, and her pulse leapt. *He's staring at me.*

Her thighs heated, and desire swished in her veins. But Gabe didn't caress her leg or move to stand, just continued gazing intently at her.

Lowering her foot to the ground, she sighed.

"What?" The wrench dropped off the wheel as he rose.

"You're never going to kiss me again, are you?" Her hiatus would never end. If Gabe didn't want her, there was no point.

She wanted him—and him alone.

He eyed her. "Last time your reaction was something like 'Oh, crap.'"

"That doesn't mean I didn't enjoy it."

"I have low self-esteem. You wounded me." His sparkling gaze refuted the words.

"I'm sorry." She placed a hand on his jacket. "The thing is, I've changed my mind."

"So kiss *me*." He spread out his arms.

Oh, sure, make me work for it. Not that she didn't deserve the torture. She definitely did. In her mind, she'd lumped him in with the slacker guys of her past. Players who'd manipulated, cajoled, and outright lied to avoid accountability in relationships. Who hadn't respected her as a woman with plans, dreams, and responsibilities.

Gabe wasn't like that. He wasn't like his crabby uncle, and he wasn't like any other guy she'd ever met. He was *Gabe*. Honest about who he was and what he wanted. Reliable. Forthcoming. Incredibly sexy.

She moistened her lips. It was decided. If *he* wanted *her*, she was all in. There was something comforting, not to mention *exciting*, about realizing in advance that what she saw in Gabe McKenzie was exactly what she would get—an amazing time with an engaging hottie of a man. No surprises and no future.

If she anticipated an end point, how could she get hurt?

She curved her arms around his waist, her cold hands meeting leather and denim. "I'll kiss you, all right," she murmured, stretching to press her mouth to his.

He squeezed her in a snug embrace. The kiss began soft and gentle. Ursula groaned, needing more. He delivered, slipping his tongue into her mouth and his hands beneath her jacket while the passing cars honked and her hair fluttered around their heads like a flag.

She lost herself in his heat, his touch.

Inches away, a horn blared. They broke apart.

A sedan stopped behind them on the shoulder. The door opened, and a man leaned out. "I saw the hazards. You folks need help?"

Gabe waved. "Thanks. We have everything under control."

Ursula straightened her coat. *Speak for yourself. Her* internal hazards blinked ten million miles a minute. That had been one heck of a potent kiss.

Was she wrong to want him? Would she get hurt?

She swallowed. There was only one way to find out.

Thirteen

SETTING down the tray in the fast food restaurant near Ray's Tires, Gabe slid onto the bench opposite Ursula and divided their meals. They'd cleaned up in the restrooms, Ursula emerging with her wind-mussed hair tidied into a ponytail that draped the front of her top.

She pulled out her wallet. "Thanks for getting the food. What do I owe you?"

"Nothing. My treat."

"Come on, Gabe. Knowing Mackie, he's paying you a pittance."

More like zilch. Maintaining his easygoing cover, Gabe lifted one shoulder in an unapologetic shrug. "I'm a guy." He inserted straws into cups. "Let me pretend I can afford to take you out for hamburgers."

She studied him. "Okay. *If* we agree I'm buying your lunch next Monday and Tuesday. Meals are an expense when we're on location, no different than the pretzels yesterday."

"You can buy Monday. I'm getting Tuesday," Gabe bargained. Would she feel as generous if she learned he wasn't the man she assumed? That he was investigating her, even though, more and more, the evidence pointed to her innocence?

If he told her the truth before completing the case, not only would he act against his training but risk placing her in danger.

What sort of danger, he didn't know yet. And that was the point. *He didn't know.*

Until he connected the dots, he needed to protect her while continuing to clear her. At least he'd made progress toward the latter.

Last night he'd initiated contact with Tom Haskell, Ursula's alibi for the night of the broken window. Using a bogus social media profile, Gabe located Tom on a group for University of Washington students and messaged the guy about possible English Lit tutors. Haskell hadn't responded so far, but when he did, Gabe would quiz him about Ursula's credentials and attempt to corroborate her whereabouts for October sixteenth.

"Gabe." She placed her wallet on the table. "You're frowning."

Because I really like you, and you have no clue who I am.

"Hunger makes me grumpy." He mirrored their conversation in the van, before she'd noticed the flat.

A smile tipped her lips. "Well, Mr. Grump, I'll accept your counteroffer to buy lunch Tuesday, but the studio is picking up our snacks and coffees throughout the remainder of the assignment. No arguments."

"Deal." He unwrapped the hamburgers. Once Ursula sank her teeth into something, she found it damn near impossible to let go. He knew her well enough to realize that much, and it solidified his decision to stay his course.

Even if he cleared her entirely, telling her what he was up to—and what impact, if any, his findings might have on her plans to buy the studio—would mess with her head and possibly screw with her ability to meet her deadline. The holiday weekend complicated her commitment to pass her files to the magazine editor next Friday. For his mother's peace of mind, he needed to find out who was threatening his uncle's business and *then* decide what to tell Ursula. He didn't want his actions and choices hurting or affecting anyone else the way his shooting had affected his mom. If Ursula never wanted to see him again after learning the truth, he could retreat from her life knowing he'd done everything within his power to protect her from harm.

"Let's eat," he said, squirting ketchup onto his french fries. "I'm hungry as a bear."

"Me too." She returned her wallet to her purse. "You know, you're stubborn."

"Spoken like the proverbial kettle." He had chosen a table in the emptiest corner of the family-packed restaurant. As Ursula dug into her burger, five kids and one harried-looking man swarmed the next table. The booths shared a half-spine, and a boy around four or five clasped the partition. The child's huge brown eyes zoomed in on Ursula's meal.

"Want to find another table or switch sides?" Gabe asked, leaning forward so Ursula could hear him despite the children's chatter and the man's attempts to curb the noise. "I count four banana splits and ten grubby little hands."

"I don't mind." As the boy plopped onto his seat, she licked mustard off her upper lip. "Yummy."

Gabe chuckled. He really liked her. He wished they could start again or had met under different circumstances. Normal ones, like in a bar or club or through a mutual friend.

"Where do you put the food?" he asked. "You're skinny as a rail, but you eat like a horse."

She munched a french fry. "I hate to break it to you, but compliments aren't your strong suit."

"What about those nice comments driving back from Darrell's?" *Pour on the flattery*, she'd said, and he had. She worked hard and deserved recognition.

"That was business. This is personal." Grinning, she picked up her milkshake.

"I think we can agree I don't have a problem with your figure." When he'd held her leg by the van, and then later while they'd kissed, he'd mentally hogtied his hands to restrain himself from exploring her curves. "I appreciate a woman who doesn't nibble her food. They're a rare breed in LA." Tiff had weighed every morsel she'd permitted in her mouth.

A light blush colored Ursula's face. "If I scrimp on lunch, I need to make up the lost calories later. When I was a teenager, the popular girls called me Bone Rack, and I hated it. I take after my mom. She could eat whatever she wanted until she turned forty. She's forty-eight now and still slim compared to other women her age."

"You have fast metabolisms."

She nodded. "Kim says I'm lucky, but sometimes I wouldn't mind gaining a few pounds."

Why would she say that? "Where would you put them?"

"My chest."

He shook his head. "You're perfect."

"Maybe I'm wearing a padded pushup."

"If you need someone to confirm that to the brauditors…"

"Like bra auditors?" She chuckled. "So, tell me, Gabe, we made it to Ray's Tires thirty minutes after closing. It was pretty nice of him to stay open just for us, and he seemed friendly, glad to see you." She sipped her shake through the straw. "How do you know him?"

Stalling, Gabe chewed a bite of cheeseburger. He'd called Ray Hillson from his personal cell after Ursula returned to the van in the wake of their Good Samaritan's departure. "Customer satisfaction is Ray's number one priority," he hedged.

"You know that how?"

"I got a lot of flats as a kid."

"And *how* did you know to visit Ray's to get them fixed?"

Typical Ursula. She wouldn't let go.

"Ray was a friend of my dad's." Gabe placed the remainder of his burger on the wrapper. Ray had been with the Seattle City Police for thirteen years. He'd burned out dealing with the ugly aspects of the job and his marriage took a hit, ending in divorce. Opening the tire shop had allowed the man to rebuild his life. "He helped out my mom and me after my father died." Similar to Bill and Darlene Cruikshank, except Ray didn't have kids.

Ursula's gaze softened. "What was your dad like?"

Gabe shifted his milkshake from hand to hand. See, *this* was why he'd dated mainly badge bunnies like Tiff Collingsworth in Los Angeles. Fun, beautiful, uncomplicated women. He'd still expected fidelity from Tiff, and their breakup during his recovery in the hospital had hurt. She'd dumped him for another Department member a little too readily but not before accusing Gabe of erecting walls. Even at his most vulnerable, following surgery, he wouldn't open up, she'd said.

Hell, until then, he hadn't realized she'd *wanted* him to. Other exes had lodged similar complaints. Was he really so reluctant to let someone in?

He drank his shake. Maybe Tiff had been onto something. He'd moved home at least in part to settle down. How would he ever find someone to spend the rest of his life with if he remained closed off?

He coughed. "My father was a cop."

"Mackie's *brother* worked in law enforcement?" Ursula's eyes widened.

"Yep. Dad was a fine, upstanding citizen. Hard to believe he fathered a guy like me, huh?"

"Don't say that. It just took a second for my mind to make the leap." She fiddled with her napkin. "Were you living in Seattle when he died?"

He nodded. "Born and raised. Dad was with the Seattle police, and he made a dumb mistake." Like father, like son. Except Gabe's misstep hadn't cost him his life, although it easily could have, leaving his mom widowed *and* childless.

A lump swelled in his throat. "Late one night, a CI—short for confidential informant—called Dad with a tip about a case. Dad arranged to meet the guy near an abandoned warehouse. The building isn't there anymore." Thank God. A headstone in the graveyard provided enough reminders for Gabe and his mom without the physical site of his father's killing continually stirring bad memories. "It's a long story, but Dad decided to meet the guy without his partner, Bill."

Ursula's forehead creased. "His partner was okay with that?"

"No." Gabe bounced his good leg beneath the table. "Later, Mom and I learned the informant was fairly new. The guy didn't trust Bill yet, but he trusted Dad. Partners work together, but it's not unheard of to meet an informant solo." An invisible band squeezed his chest as memories of his father filled his mind. The last time he and Dad were together, they'd been watching a game in the living room while gabbing about sports, Gabe's high school grades, and girls. His mom went to bed early with a headache. Not long after, one of Gabe's buddies called with an invite to a movie, and Gabe didn't return until it was time to crash. He woke in the middle of the night to his mother's cries of anguish. Hands down, the worst day of his life.

If he hadn't split to hang with his group, would his dad have met the CI?

"Oh, no," Ursula said, voice tender. "Gabe..."

Forcing a swallow, he sucked back more milkshake. "The informant's statement said my dad wasn't there yet when the guy arrived at the meet spot. The dude found the streetlight busted, glass all over the place." He swallowed again. "When the CI realized a drug deal was going down inside the warehouse, he left to alert Dad. But he couldn't reach him. The informant's archaic cell had died, and he couldn't find a pay phone." Pausing, Gabe released a heavy breath. "My father was in the wrong place at the wrong time." Similar to how *he* had been in the wrong place in August.

"He was caught off guard," Ursula half-whispered.

"Yeah." The backs of Gabe's eyes stung. He gripped his cup. "Details are fuzzy, and there were no witnesses. All we know for certain is Dad arrived at the warehouse after the informant left." He spoke almost in a monotone. He would *not* lose it in front of Ursula or those five little kids. "Dad entered the building, and there was an exchange of gunfire. My father and the druggie bled out before the ambulance arrived."

"They *shot* each other?"

He nodded, neck hairs prickling. The circumstances of his father's death had never sat right with him. The SCPD investigated all leads, but Gabe's heart couldn't accept the results. As a teen, he'd honored his mom's request not to fixate on facts they couldn't change. As an adult recovering from his own mistakes on the job, he needed closure.

Once he opened his PI firm, he intended to look into his father's case. Too many questions remained unresolved, like where the bodies were found—the suspect's in the warehouse loft, his father's on the ground. The suspect took a bullet in the chest. Forensics matched the slug, plus two others lodged in the loft wall, to Gabe's dad's gun. The pattern created by undisturbed footprints suggested Doug McKenzie likely spotted his suspect before the guy got off a shot. So why had Dad not checked to make sure the guy was dead? Why had he turned away?

It didn't fit.

His dad had been an exemplary cop. He knew the ropes, and

this rotten perp had nailed him in the back. To worsen matters, most of the footprints were spoiled when the ambulance arrived.

Gabe wondered to this day whether a third party might have entered the warehouse. The CI supplied a solid alibi proving he hadn't returned to the scene after running to find a phone, so that element of the case got sidetracked.

Shoulders stiff, he swept his hands beneath the table and stilled his knee. "The good news is the informant's tip led to the Seattle police solving the case my dad was working on," he said gruffly. "The scumbag who killed him left behind an evidence trail a mile long. His bosses wound up behind bars."

"The *good* news?" Ursula pressed fingertips to her mouth. "Gabe, your father was murdered. Without a witness, you'll never know what really happened. That must be hard to live with." Tears brimmed her eyes.

"It is." His throat felt packed with sand.

She reached across the table. He placed his hands on top of her smaller ones. Gently, she rubbed the skin between his thumb and forefinger.

Damn it, if she continued those light, stroking movements, he *would* shatter.

"I can't imagine losing my dad until he's ancient," she whispered. "Losing my grandmother was difficult enough. Gabe, I'm so sorry."

Inhaling, he firmed his jaw. He'd relayed the story of his father's death to a handful of women in LA, and none of their responses had sucker-punched him like this. He hadn't only opened up to Ursula, he'd spilled his guts.

What was different now? Was it living in Seattle again? Guilt over his numerous half-truths. That they had each lost a loved one? Or *her?*

Of all the women over the years, why could Ursula Scott dig under his skin?

Headlights gleaming in the dark, Ursula pulled the repaired van into Mackie's space behind the studio. Gabe's pickup no longer occupied the second spot, as it had this morning. Uncle and nephew had swapped keys in case Mackie needed to leave before Gabe returned.

"After we put away the gear, would you mind driving me home?" she asked, cutting the engine. "I'd rather not take the bus this late, and it looks like Mackie and Stacy are both gone." Like her, Stacy usually bussed to work, and the girl never stayed past five.

The alley light illuminated Gabe's handsome face. "No problem. I can't believe I finally get to drive this thing."

"Well, I *am* the senior employee." Ursula flipped the van keys in her hand, and he grabbed the electronic fob, flashing a sexy grin.

"Also, you're my boss." He winked.

"I don't think of myself as your boss anymore." Especially not after he'd relayed the tragic story of his father's death. When he'd spilled the truth at the fast food place, her heart had ached for him —for the teenager and the grown man. It had been poignantly obvious from the pain in Gabe's voice and on his face that he'd loved his dad a lot. That he still missed him and always would, like Ursula would always miss Grandma B.

As horrible as it had felt losing her grandmother last year, Gabe's father had been *murdered*. The poor man had *bled out*. He had died alone on a rough warehouse floor, not surrounded by family in a residential care facility.

Back at the restaurant, it had felt like the most natural thing in the world to reach across the table and clasp Gabe's hand. Shortly thereafter, he'd changed topics, as if he'd felt uncomfortable revealing something so personal. They'd finished their meals and walked back to Ray's Tires to fetch the van. As they'd driven to the studio, Gabe reverted to his regular charming demeanor, and Ursula took the hint to lighten up.

"We're more like temporary coworkers," she said, opening the driver's door.

"Who make out?" he asked with a hopeful look.

Pulse racing, she nodded. *You can do this, Ursula.* No more obsessing about their two kisses and where they might lead. No worrying that his jack-of-all-trades lifestyle didn't suit her need to plan. She would borrow a page from his playbook and enjoy the excitement she felt around him instead of freaking out about his rightness or wrongness as a life partner.

He cracked another grin. "This job has perks." He climbed out of the van and opened the side door to retrieve the equipment.

Meeting him, she hefted a smaller bag. Inside the building, they strode down the hall past Mackie's office to the waiting room and then up the second corridor to the studio proper. While it was a hassle lugging equipment the length of two halls for each location shoot, Mackie felt the seclusion of the backroom presented fewer opportunities for thieves.

A good point, but Ursula often wondered if the old building was up to code—an item for her checklist when she bought the business.

Gabe stored the photography gear in the big room's equipment closet. Backdrops, lighting systems, and props filled the vast space.

"I had fun today," he said. "Flat tire and all."

"Me too." The man exuded enough pheromones to intoxicate a nun, and their kiss on the side of the freeway had been spectacular. She wasn't ready to say goodbye for the night. "You have a keen eye. Want to learn a few techniques?" She placed her purse on the prop table.

"Techniques?" Sensuality resonated in his deep voice.

"*Photography* techniques. We never have time when we're on location. You act as my gofer. I hate it when Mackie treats me like one."

"I don't mind being your gofer. I go for you."

She laughed. Gabe had a great sense of humor and a quick mind. An ultra-sexy combination.

She dug a rarely used camera case out of the equipment closet. "Part of the deal was to teach you photography." Her voice echoed in the high-ceilinged room. "We need a subject." Slinging the case strap over a shoulder, she went to the prop corner and selected a three-foot-tall doll she sometimes posed with little kids. "Curly will do." She ruffled the doll's red wool mop-top. Curly wore a yellow T-shirt with denim suspenders and possessed flexible limbs which allowed him to stand.

Gabe wandered over. "Did you find that thing in your childhood toy box or at a *Chucky* revival?"

"Neither. I didn't have time to grab so much as a stuffie when my dad carried me out of the flames." All her efforts had centered on saving her cat, at which she'd been an abject failure.

A ruddy hue suffused his face. "Sorry. Your house burnt down, and I'm making jokes."

"Gabe, your dad was killed. The two experiences don't compare."

"I was eighteen, not ten. I also have pictures and videos of the good times."

"I miss not having reminders," Ursula agreed, putting the camera case on the floor. She posed Curly beside a child-sized table and rested the doll's hand on the surface. "My parents made copies of my grandmother's photos, but it's not the same as having my original baby book or other mementos." She perched the doll's left hand on its hip. "That's one of the reasons I became a photographer. I can't do anything about the memories I lost. I can create new memories though."

In a way, being a photographer placed her in control. But had her lifelong need for structure influenced how she approached romantic relationships?

Did she crave *too much* control?

Gabe shucked off his jacket and folded it near the cat paperweight on the prop table. Ursula followed suit.

"You mentioned creating memories in the rain last Saturday," he said. "I like your philosophy." His buttoned shirt was a shade lighter than yesterday's moss-green sweater, and the color highlighted the dark specks in his eyes. She held her breath a moment. Sheesh, he was handsome. "If you want to create memories, why not specialize in family pictures instead of commercial work?" he asked.

He had touched on her favorite subject. "Commercial photography is more lucrative. If the Real Men shoot goes well, it makes sense to continue on that path, at least to start. There are a ton of professional portrait studios in the city, not to mention folks all over the internet trying to stake a claim. If I want to reach my goals, I need to stand out."

"Ah, ambition. What are your goals?"

She arranged a tripod and maneuvered the lights. "Someday I'd love to specialize in creative baby and toddler portraits, like little girls dressed as fairy princesses in elaborate settings or a dad cradling a newborn against his naked chest. Photographers can get imaginative with wedding pictures too. A bride in an extravagant gown playing in the sand or mud with a child from a previous marriage. Or both bride and groom jumping in a pool for underwater photos. Frolicking in the ocean or rain. The list goes on and on. A bride playing paintball would be fun."

Gabe's eyebrows arched. "Women really pay to have their wedding dresses destroyed?"

"Wealthy ones do. They consider it along the lines of a post-wedding fashion shoot. These brides pay thousands of dollars for a gown they only wear a few hours. Depending on the photographer's approach, trash-the-dress pictures can become pieces of art."

"You don't seem like a money-oriented person," he said as he helped with the lights.

"I'm not. It's the creativity. The money has benefits, I'll admit."

"Such as?"

She paused in her work. Gabe had told her how his father died. She wouldn't feel right not sharing more about herself in return.

"My parents are in debt." Her heart pinched. "It's pretty bad, Gabe. My grandmother not only suffered two strokes, she developed early onset Parkinson's disease at thirty-five." Poor Grandma B. Life had tossed her challenges at every turn. It didn't seem fair that one person should experience so much suffering, but her grandmother hadn't grown bitter or angry. She had advocated for change but remained positive.

Gabe rubbed his jaw. "I'm sorry, Ursula. Isn't the early onset variety the disease Michael J. Fox brought to national attention?"

She nodded. "My mom was an only child. My grandfather died in a car crash when Grandma Betty was fifty." Gabe's mom would understand the difficulties Grandma B had faced, the emotional devastation of suddenly losing a husband.

Releasing a breath, Ursula smoothed her hands over her short plaid skirt. She and Gabe had a lot more in common than she'd imagined seven short days ago.

It was uncanny, except it felt more like preordained. As if they were meant to meet.

When had she ever experienced such an instant connection with a guy?

The more they got to know each other, the more she realized she was drawn to the very essence of who Gabe was. He *got* her, because he understood life was precious and they shouldn't waste a second. He didn't need to state that they shared the same values. His compassion and empathy shone in his eyes.

She fine-tuned Curly's stance, busy work so she wouldn't choke up. "Grandma's employer relocated, and she lost her job. Her PD progressed to the point where she couldn't work for two years. Once she was able to go back to work, she got caught in a nightmare with her new employer's health insurance. State premiums for someone in her position were huge."

"The Parkinson's would have been considered a preexisting condition," Gabe commented, stepping closer.

"Exactly. It's complicated, but Grandma decided..." How to explain the situation? "Well, rather than shelling out piles of cash for premiums that didn't cover experimental procedures, she would pay *for* the emerging new treatments of her choice instead. She couldn't have foreseen her stroke, which is where insurance could have helped."

"That's lousy, Ursula." Gabe's hand settled on her shoulder. His thumb brushed her collarbone in a soothing, back-and-forth motion. "She sounds very brave."

"She was." Ursula's voice quavered. She gazed into his kind green eyes, pausing now and then as the story of her grandma's struggle flowed. Something about his quiet strength and inherent consideration appealed to her deep inside, enabling her to express herself in a way she hadn't experienced with any man she wasn't related to by blood. "Grandma was fifty-six when the first stroke hit, and it was bad. Like you said about your dad, it's a long story, involving expensive rehab and residential home care. She had to sell her house and car. She died too young for Medicare to kick in, and my mom wasn't happy with the nursing homes Medicaid covered."

Both Gabe's hands caressed either side of her collarbone now, his touch tender and comforting, yet also oddly arousing. They stood close enough to kiss.

She clasped his arms above his elbows. He pressed his forehead to hers.

"How did your parents deal with the stress?"

"Like all Scotts do," she whispered, curving her arms around his waist. "They carried on." His hands swept her neck and jaw, tingles rippling in their wake. "They took it upon themselves to place her in a high-end care facility. They felt it was their choice, so the debt is their responsibility."

He kissed her cheek. "They sound like amazing people."

The backs of his fingers brushed her face, and their gazes linked. "They are." That was something else they shared in common—their parents seemed cut from the same cloth. "They won't touch the money Grandma invested for my brother and me years before her first stroke." Ursula and Owen had offered, but their dad refused. Ursula had argued with her parents for three days, pacing the kitchen, tossing up her hands in frustration. "Owen received enough to cover a year's books and tuition at U-Dub. Living at home and maintaining his grades for scholarships will help with the rest."

"What about you?"

"My inheritance will provide the down payment for this place. Once I'm earning a profit, my dad says I can lend a hand with their debt. *That's* my goal."

Gabe smiled. "I'm impressed."

"My parents have led hard lives. I would do anything to help them, including putting up with Mackie. You and I aren't so different in that regard."

"You just had to mention my uncle…"

"Who would've thought it, huh? But it's karma. If I didn't work here, would you and I have met?"

She kissed him. Tender and gentle, a sweet brushing of lips.

Her heart chugged like a runaway train.

Tonight was *theirs*.

She didn't want it to end.

Fourteen

Seconds of exquisite tension passed as Gabe's eyes darkened, super-charging her pulse.

"Do you see us going somewhere?" he asked, tone languid.

Ursula shrugged with what she hoped translated as sassy confidence. "Maybe." A bit affected, but she'd laid it out there. "For a little while. As long as we're having fun." She smiled. She could do this good-time stuff. "But first I'm teaching you to take portraits." She stepped away, her fingertips trailing oh-so-carefree along his.

"I confess something else popped to mind," he drawled.

Same as her, but… "I'm not letting another day go by without living up to my side of the deal." Photography was her passion. She wanted to share every bit of herself with Gabe. Stooping, she fished in the case for her vintage Pentax and a roll of the black-and-white film she bought in bulk online.

"You're teaching me on an old-fashioned camera?"

"There's nothing like handling a manual SLR to get your creative juices flowing." She opened the camera back and loaded the film. "Only photography fanatics appreciate the beauty of film cameras these days, but taking pictures with one feels different. More permanent, less messing around snapping everything in sight because the photographer figures they'll delete surplus files. With film, every frame means something." She had learned that lesson from her grandmother, and she intended to impart her knowledge to her children. She held up the camera. "It's not like you can plug a baby like this into a computer and zip photos onto the internet. It takes a lot more time and consideration, which makes a person think long and hard about which pictures they share on social media."

Gabe flashed a devilish smile. "That's a plus. Sounds much more…private." He spoke the last word like a sensual promise.

Skin buzzing, she held her breath. "Check this out, Romeo." Changing the camera settings, she stepped to the tripod. "I've adjusted the aperture. All you have to do is zoom in and out and focus." She attached the camera to the stand.

"In and out, huh?" He bent to squint through the viewfinder, his shoulder grazing her arm. "Digital cameras have big screens," he grumbled.

"An ape can take good pictures with an LCD panel. Look *through* the lens, Gabe. *Feel* your subject." She flourished a hand toward the three-foot doll positioned beside the child's table.

"I'm not feeling up Curly."

Ursula batted his shoulder. "Pull on the lens to zoom in, push back to zoom out. Try it. Excellent," she said as he followed her instructions. "Adjust focus by matching the lines in the viewfinder. Experiment with different focal lengths and where you want to place Curly within the camera's eye. Alter the composition to suit your vision."

"Sounds intricate."

"I'm getting too technical. Sorry. Just play with it. We have thirty-six frames."

"Gotcha." Gabe shot two frames before detaching the camera from the tripod. "I feel constricted. I want to move around the doll, like you do with the guys on location."

"Go for it." He was a natural. Hands on hips, she monitored his progress, providing tips when necessary. "You're getting it!" Maybe sometime she could teach him to develop film.

"Thanks, but I'm tired of Curly. I'll take pictures of you." He aimed the camera. The shutter clicked.

Ursula lifted a hand. "You're not focusing! I'll be all fuzzy."

"I like you fuzzy."

Laughing, she wrestled the camera from his grasp. His arms slid around her waist, and he hugged her from behind. She twisted her neck, looking at him over her shoulder. His gaze softened, and he kissed her.

Yearning panged in her chest. *Gabe.* How had she gotten so lucky? Who could have predicted she'd fall for a McKenzie? That someone like this man existed?

Gripping the camera, she turned in his arms. "While I appreciate your enthusiasm, your lesson has only begun," she murmured.

His gaze held hers. "What should I do next?"

Make love to me all night. "Move Curly."

"Uh, what?" He glanced around. "Move him where?"

Ursula's heart banged her ribs. "Anywhere. It doesn't matter. Out of the way. I want you to pose for me, Gabe." She paused. "A good photographer needs to feel as comfortable in front of the camera as he does behind it. Staring into the cold eye of the lens creates empathy for your subjects."

Gabe caressed her back, and her skin warmed under her knit top. "Did my camera eye feel cold to you?"

"Not a bit." She kissed him. "I'm the instructor though. What I say goes."

His eyes glimmered. "Okay. But only if I get a turn. You do me, and then…" his voice lowered "…I'll do you."

She licked suddenly dry lips. *Ursula, I hope you realize what you're getting into.*

Gabe returned the doll and table to the corner while she selected an ivory background and a floor drop designed to look like worn wooden planks.

"Let's try a casual look," she said when they'd arranged the floor drop. "Remove your shoes and socks and…um, unbutton your shirt." Only the top two were open.

Moments later, he stood on the section of worn planks in bare feet, hands shoved in jeans pockets. "How's this?"

"Perfect." In every way. His open shirt revealed a hint of chiseled pecs dusted with dark hair, and the photography lights captured the rugged planes of his face. "Turn left a tad." She snapped several frames, suggesting various poses until he sat on the floor drop, his shirt heaped beside his denim-clad hip. His naked chest, tight abs, and compelling gaze were a photographer's—and a woman's—dream.

"Ever work as a model in Los Angeles?" she asked. *Click. Click. Click.* "You're very photogenic." His powerful chest and strong biceps suggested most of his jobs had involved physical labor. She visualized him on construction sites. Or fighting fires, although that didn't make sense. First responders required specialized training, which he had never mentioned.

"I did a calendar once. One of those man-of-the-month things."

She surveyed his pose through the viewfinder. "How'd you grab that gig?"

"Charity event." Scratching his jaw, he rose. "Now you."

"Wait. I'm at the end of the roll."

He pulled on his shirt while she shot the final frames. Buttons undone, he reached for the camera.

Nerves accosted her from head to toe. Belly tightening, she stepped back. "I've changed my mind."

"No, you haven't." Gabe snapped his fingers. "Hand it over."

"The film needs changing."

"Then change *it*—not your mind. We're doing this, Ursula."

How could she argue with his authoritative tone? "Okay, okay. You're one persistent dude." She retrieved a second roll of 35 millimeter film from the camera bag. At the prop table, she removed the roll of Curly and Gabe from the Pentax and slipped the film canister into her purse. "This roll has another thirty-six frames," she said as she loaded fresh film.

"Sounds like plenty."

"Don't feel pressured to take them all." She passed him the Pentax. Their hands grazed, and her tummy swooped. She wanted to look as good to him through the camera's eye as he had to her.

He examined the camera settings. "Can I use props?"

"Like Curly?"

He shook his head. "Sit on the fancy purple couch near the trunks."

She glanced at the crushed velvet chaise lounge. *Kill me now.*

"Um, that's for lingerie catalogue shoots."

A wicked grin slanted his mouth. "If you insist."

"No, no. I can sit on it fully dressed."

Grinning, he attached the camera to the tripod then picked up the floor drop and placed it aside. "Not so easy when *I'm* in control, is it?"

Ursula narrowed her gaze. He'd tossed down the gauntlet. She would show him.

She helped him drag the chaise in front of the ivory background. He returned to the prop corner and searched the trunks, ultimately choosing a white faux-fur throw. Her pulse bounced around in her veins like popping corn, but she remained quiet while he arranged the fur on the chaise.

Rubbing his chin, he surveyed the scene. "*Now* I'm ready."

"Who are you, Rembrandt?"

"If I had you naked and wrapped in that fur…" He gazed at her until she blushed.

"We don't have a paintbrush."

His eyes twinkled. "Too bad."

Beneath her bra and top, her nipples peaked. She risked a glance to the bulge in his jeans.

He possessed…the whole package. *Oh, my.*

"On the couch, my subject," he commanded.

Trembling with anticipation, she sat. Her shoes scuffed the floor. Fingers sinking into the soft faux fur, she gripped the painted edge of the chaise and crossed her legs below her knees. Her gaze caught on a snag in her charcoal tights. Crap, had that happened while they'd changed the tire?

She tugged down the hem of her gray-and-cream-checkered skirt two inches above her knees, concealing the embarrassing imper-fection.

Gabe gestured at the camera bag. "I need practice with a remote shutter release. Do you mind?"

She cleared her throat. "Of course not." She'd demonstrated the ways of the remote on her DSLR during today's Real Men sessions. "The principle is the same as the digital camera we used earlier. Do you need help?"

"I'll manage."

While Gabe dug the remote out of the Pentax bag, Ursula fidgeted with her ponytail, smoothing her hair over one shoulder before removing the elastic and finger-combing the strands.

He attached the remote shutter release and stepped to one side. Equipment ready, he snapped a frame.

"Did you focus?" Ursula asked, fluffing her hair.

"Sorry. I forgot." Moving behind the camera, Gabe zoomed and focused. He returned to his former position and squeezed the remote.

"I'm not sure the lighting works. Why not try—"

"*Ursula*. You're beautiful."

Electric vibrations shot to her core. *He likes what he sees. Relax.*

Easier said than done.

The shutter snapped again. Mouth dry, she uncrossed her legs. "Music might help me unwind." She pointed to Mackie's antiquated CD player on a shelf behind the prop table. "An instrumental disc is usually loaded."

Gabe strode to the shelf. "This better be the last thing. You're less cooperative than Curly."

"I'll improve. I promise." She fussed with the short sleeves of her top. Why couldn't she let go? She *wanted* to play seductive games with Gabe. To act flirtatious and sexy, confident and carefree.

Like him.

He pressed buttons on the CD player, and soft jazz filled the high-ceilinged room. The sound of tinkling piano keys and sultry saxophone notes floated in the air.

Slowly—*thank you!*—her jitters eased.

"Rest against the fur," Gabe murmured. "Turn your upper body. Beautiful. Chin low on your shoulder...eyes soft and sexy. Yes. Oh, baby, you're gorgeous."

He offered direction effortlessly. Within minutes, he snapped several frames.

The bulge in his jeans persisted, his gaze all-consuming.

Desire bloomed, hot and molten. Ursula slipped her top off one shoulder, exposing a burgundy bra strap.

"How about this?" she half-whispered.

He groaned. "You're so pretty, Sula. You slay me."

Her heart skipped a beat. Never in her life had someone called her Sula. Ursula, Urs, or when her family wanted to bug her, Ursie. But Gabe had chosen a unique nickname just for her.

Sula.

She liked it.

He stepped behind the camera and stooped to peer through the viewfinder. His big fingers rotated the lens. "The focus is beautiful...just a little out. The lack of sharpness is sexy, a real soft touch."

Oh, how she yearned for *his* touch. While the jazz worked its magic and his deep, coaxing voice rippled through her body, her excitement grew. Emboldened, she extended a leg and flipped her skirt, flashing her thighs.

He stepped out from behind the camera. "I keep looking *at* you and forgetting to take pictures."

"You can set the shutter to release once a second." She described the procedure. "I'll demonstrate."

"Stay right there. I've got it." His tongue swept out to moisten his lips. "Remove your nylons, or whatever they're called. I want to see some skin."

Goosebumps speckling her arms, she nodded. She hadn't shown any guy so much as an inch of skin for nearly a year, so what the heck was she doing? She *never* stripped off her clothes after only one week of knowing a man.

She drew in a breath. Ursula might not. *But Sula does.*

As if aware she battled a fresh bevy of nerves, Gabe fiddled with the camera and looked through the viewfinder. He adjusted the settings again.

She tugged off her shoes and stood. Sliding her hands beneath her skirt, she peeled down her tights. Her panties rolled with them.

Gabe appeared absorbed in the camera, but the tiny smile quirking his mouth told her he'd noticed.

In case he hadn't—this was *his* photo shoot, after all, and a professional model, especially one named Sula, followed precise instructions—she shoved the panties beneath the fur.

When he glanced up from the camera, she held only her tights. The concrete floor chilled the bare soles of her feet.

"Drape the pantyhose over the back of the couch," he said.

"It's a chaise lounge." She arranged them. "And they're tights."

A slow, sexy smile spread over his face. "Call them what you like. I want the pictures to look like you're undressing for your lover."

"*Am* I undressing for my lover, Gabe?" she whispered.

His gaze heated. "You tell me."

Her heart thundered in her ears. "Yes," she replied, hearing the huskiness in her voice below the melodic tones of the instrumental CD. Her body ached to join with Gabe's. She would be his lover for as long as he wanted, as long as the magic between them continued.

"Thank God. I'm dying over here." He clicked the camera button to initiate the continuous film advance.

As he met her in front of the chaise, the first picture clicked. They were both standing as he cupped her face and bestowed a tender kiss on her mouth.

Within seconds, their tongues tangled, and her arousal mounted. Not wearing panties increased the sensations. Her center moistened with slick heat.

Breathless, she pushed off his shirt, and he removed her top. The garments landed on the floor. Her nipples stiffened in her bra, straining for his touch.

"You're beautiful," he murmured, easing down the straps.

She allowed her head to drop back. Her long hair tickled her spine as Gabe uncovered half of one breast and tugged a nipple into his mouth.

She groaned at the onslaught of incredible vibrations.

Vaguely, she realized the camera had reached the end of the roll. Only then did Gabe unhook her bra and fully reveal her breasts. His hand slipped beneath her skirt, finding her wet cleft.

With a moan, he lifted her skirt and bared her thighs.

Wearing just his jeans, he snugged her against him. Her skirt bunched at her waist, and his pelvis rocked. The knot of desire between her legs bloomed.

Ursula's breath hitched. With previous guys, she'd been guarded, wanting a relationship like her parents shared but wary of choosing the wrong man. She needed to learn it was okay to feel vulnerable, even if she and Gabe were only temporary.

But why over-think things? Why not enjoy the moment for what it was?

He backed them up two paces, and her legs bumped the wood

trim of the chaise. She sank with him onto the faux fur, feathery and sensuous beneath her bare bottom.

Reaching behind her waist, she inched down her zipper. Her rear lifted off the fur as he removed her skirt and tossed it aside.

Her fingers itched to unzip his jeans, but he swung her legs and positioned her reclining on the fur. The replica of a Victorian lounge featured a sloping padded arm and decorative back that ended several inches shy of the plush cushion, allowing her to stretch out in sumptuous comfort.

He slid a hand up her leg, onto her hip, his thumb brushing the crease where her thigh and hip joined. His fingertips skittered over her tidy triangle of curls, and her hot button pulsed.

Supporting his weight, he lowered himself over her, one knee on the chaise, the opposite foot on the floor. As they kissed, she ran her hands over his chiseled abs and broad chest. His nipples contracted beneath her touch. He was the most beautiful man…

He grunted. A sound of pain, not lust.

She broke the kiss. "Get off me. Gabe, your leg is killing you."

"Not being inside you is killing me." He licked her nipple. Sensation arced.

"You can't get inside me wearing those jeans. Take them off, and we'll lie on our sides. That will keep the weight off your leg."

He chuckled. "You're bossy."

She smiled. "Do you have condoms?"

"Does a ship have sailors?" He kissed her before heading to the prop table and rummaging in an inside pocket of his leather jacket.

The heat of the photography lights shone upon her as she relaxed against the ticklish faux fur. The silky strands caressed her bottom. An erotic tingling centered at her core as Gabe returned with the condom tucked in a jeans pocket. His erection bulged beneath the denim, and her pulse quickened.

"Get up," he commanded.

Completely naked while he remained in his jeans, she rose. He sat on the fur and tugged her to sit on top of him, spreading her thighs until they hugged the outer sides of his legs.

She straddled him, the position opening her body and tugging at her heart.

He sucked one nipple then kissed her deeply while his hand wandered south. His finger nudged her moist heat.

Oh.

She lifted her hips, and his finger glided in and out. His mouth latched onto her breast again. He tongued her breast and nibbled the tip. Sparks shot everywhere. She panted.

"Gabe…" She rode his hand. "I don't want to come until you're inside me."

"Oh, no?" He stroked her swollen hot button.

"Oooh. You're not playing fair." It had been too long. Her body was on fire.

"I'm not playing at all," he whispered. "Let go for me, Sula."

Who was she, his submissive?

He stroked again. Gasping, she shattered against his hand.

"Typical man," she mumbled against his naked shoulder. "You never listen." Omigod, he smelled *incredible*. Like spice and musk and a dark, mysterious forest—all at once.

"I bet you're glad I didn't." A smug note laced his voice.

She heaved an exaggerated sigh. "It was passable."

"Passable?" He caressed her hip.

Lifting her head, she smiled into his dazzling eyes. "It was amazing. But I still want you inside me." Joined. Flesh to flesh.

As one.

She popped open the button of his jeans. Getting up, she clasped his hand and tugged him to standing. A flash of discomfort twisted his mouth.

"Gabe, did I hurt you? I'm sorry. I shouldn't have sat on your lap."

"It was my idea." He dug out the condom packet and tossed it on the chaise.

Drawing in a swift breath, she unzipped his jeans. As she pushed the denim and his boxer-briefs down his hips, his erection stood stiff and long against his stomach. She couldn't help staring. He was so sexy and blatantly aroused.

He stepped out of the jeans. Turning, he booted their clothes beneath the chaise. Her gaze caught on a pink scar puckering his right butt cheek.

His injury! She grabbed his arm. "What happened?" So much for her vow not to pry.

He gestured a hand. "I got shot."

Like his dad. She gasped. No wonder he didn't like talking about the ordeal.

"In Los Angeles?" she asked.

He nodded.

Oh, my God! "When?"

"This August."

Three months ago. Which explained his limp and need for physical therapy. Would the damage improve over time?

"How did it happen?" She brushed light fingertips over the scar tissue. "Does it hurt?" Anguish for the similarities to his father's tragedy flooded her. His mom must have worried like crazy. What were the odds both father and son would suffer gunshot wounds?

Gabe shrugged as if the injury was no big deal. "Sometimes it's sore. The bullet damaged my hip joint, but it'll get better. At the moment, my range of motion and flexibility sucks." He kissed her. "You know, I'm hard as hell for you and you're fixated on my ass. A guy could develop a complex."

"Aw." She smiled. "We can't have that." Stroking his erection, she whispered, "Tell me how it happened."

His eyes closed. "I walked in on a convenience store holdup. Stupid, I know. But I only had three or four hours sleep the night before. When I shouted at the first guy, his buddy fired." Gazing at her, he moaned. "Ursula, that feels so good."

She firmed her grip and continued stroking. "Why were you there?"

"Buying milk." He moved her hand off his erection. "Let's get busy. I want inside you."

"Tell me if anything hurts, and we'll stop."

"Yeah, that's likely." He retrieved the condom packet, ripped it open, and sheathed himself.

Reclining on the chaise, she reached for him. He lay on his left facing her, his long legs hanging over the backless end of the cushion.

The faux fur pillowed their bodies as they kissed. He caressed her nipples, and electricity speared her center.

Avoiding applying unnecessary pressure, she hooked her leg over his injured hip. Their mouths fused, and he entered her. Then began to move.

They rocked back and forth in a tempo as slow and seductive as the jazz sprinkling the room. The fur and lights deflected the cool night air. Their bodies sparked and heated, moving faster. His fingers targeted her swollen nub, slowly stroking while she pumped and contracted her inner muscles to increase the delicious tension.

Mouth slipping off hers, he whispered, "Sula."

A languid sensation warmed her limbs, and she opened her eyes. His gaze devoured hers, his expression serious and intense.

Heart beating wildly, she nodded. He didn't speak again, and neither did she. The mood was too intimate.

Did he sense it too? The possibilities? The opportunity?

This didn't feel like casual hookup sex. It felt like two souls connecting and merging. Powerful and explosive. Tender and enduring.

As if a lifetime awaited them. Memories and passion. Impulsive lust and dynamic love.

But that was absurd. She couldn't fall in love with a man in the space of one tumultuous week.

Yet, as her second orgasm swept her, spurring Gabe's vigorous climax, she only knew she'd never felt this way before.

In this moment, she was his and he was hers.

And they were all.

They were everything.

Fifteen

GABE SAT beside Ursula sleeping on the purple couch. After they'd made love, he'd killed the photography lights and she'd drifted off wrapped in his arms beneath the furry blanket. He had dozed as well, but the narrow lounge couldn't accommodate two for long. His over-exerted glute woke him several minutes ago.

Hand under the fur, he caressed her naked hip. He liked watching her sleep. He'd switched on a lamp near the prop table to dress, and a pale glow bathed the shadows of the vast room. He'd expected her to stir by now, but she appeared down for the count. With her dark hair streaming over her shoulders and her mouth parted, he glimpsed hints of what she must have looked like as a little girl. He smiled.

"You've surprised me, Sula," he whispered. She wore a kick-butt front, but the woman he'd made love with tonight was affectionate and tender, caring and compassionate. Within a few hours, they had shared more about each other's lives than he and Tiff Collingsworth had in a month.

That was definitely unlike him. His relationship with Tiff had worked because *he* had never stayed with any woman for long, forget her neuroses. If Ursula wanted more than a few fun weeks, how long could it last? Did he have the balls to allow himself to fall for her?

Jaw tensing, he slid his hand out from under the blanket. He

185

had no business becoming involved with a suspect during the course of an investigation, but he hadn't been able to resist the urgency this woman stirred inside him.

And didn't that feel like the worst sort of excuse? Getting caught up in the moment was unprofessional to the extreme. If only to put his mother's mind at rest, he needed to concentrate on the case.

Kneading his neck, he refocused on earlier events. As if the flat tire hadn't been enough to deal with, now it appeared the missing wheel chocks coinciding with the trailer tire showing up in place of the spare added yet another component to the mysterious goings-on surrounding his uncle's place of business. He couldn't dismiss the possibility that the person responsible for the missing coffeemaker and microwave fire was to blame. But why would his suspect mess with wheel chocks and a spare tire? To be a pain in the ass? Or because the suspect had arranged the flat somehow?

The questions warranted further examination.

With a last glance to Ursula, Gabe slipped on his shoes and quietly collected the van keys. Nature called, and hunger burrowed in his belly. The leftover apple pie from the fast food joint would hit the spot.

On the other side of the business, he visited the can before entering the alley. The motion-detector lights blinked on, brightening the parking spaces and glinting off a nail on the pavement.

Damaged thigh tingling, Gabe crouched. *Three* galvanized roofing nails pointed up beside the van's front left tire.

He scrubbed his hands over his forehead. How long had the nails sat there? Neither he nor Ursula had noticed them this morning. Mackie had arrived late for the vehicle swap, and Gabe and Ursula had immediately left to meet the day's first Real Men model. Considering Sunday's microwave incident, Gabe should have paid closer attention to their surroundings.

He limped to the patched rear right tire. Two more nails identical to the one that caused their flat rested horizontally on the ground. Gabe checked the remaining tires. The treads appeared nail-free. But if Ursula had parked two inches *to the left* this evening, the three nails might have pierced the front tire.

Massaging the bridge of his nose, he backtracked over this

morning. When he and his uncle swapped keys, Mackie insisted the van occupy this specific space, closest to the alley door. Whoever placed the nails must have familiarized themselves with Mackie's habits, intending the nails for Mackie rather than Ursula and Gabe.

Except Stacy had known Ursula planned to drive the van today. Had *Stacy* positioned the nails to do the most damage? If so, she could use a housekeeping lesson, because she'd neglected to clean up the remaining nails.

Gabe needed his compact camera, an evidence bag, and tweezers.

He returned to the backroom. Ursula still dozed. He donned his jacket, leaving it unzipped.

In the staffroom, he found a new, plastic, zippered freezer bag and tiny ice tongs to double as tweezers. He disinfected the tongs in the sink. In the alley again, he snapped pictures with both his smartphone and the new compact camera he carried in an inside coat pocket. The security lights glared, decreasing the need for the camera's superior flash, but the memory card provided additional backup.

He tucked the camera into his chest shirt pocket, bagged the nails, and dialed Ray's home phone number on his personal cell.

"Ray? Hi, it's Gabe. Sorry to call so late." Ten-thirty was midnight by Ray's standards. "Did you toss out that nail from the flat?" he asked.

The alley door creaked open. "Gabe?"

Ursula's voice, sleepy and soft.

"Ray, I'll call you tomorrow," Gabe mumbled. Stuffing his phone, the evidence bag, and tongs in his jacket pocket, he pasted on an innocent look and turned.

"Why are you out in the cold?" Shivering, she hugged her arms. A frothy pink dressing robe hung to her bare knees, and furry high-heeled slippers shod her feet.

Aw, baby. Had she scoured the prop trunks for the sexy outfit to entice him?

"I was talking to Ray," he said, pressing his elbow against his jacket pocket to conceal the bag.

But she was too clever. "What's that?" She brushed hair out of her face.

"The apple pie." The dessert remained in the van. "I was hungry."

She chuckled. "You just crushed it."

"Oops." His stomach muscles tightened. The next few minutes *were not* going to go well.

"Gabe, what is it?" Heels tapping pavement, she stepped closer. Her glance darted to his shirt pocket. "You have a camera? Is it one of mine? Doesn't look familiar."

He ignored her second question. "I wanted to take pictures of you sleeping." The idea *had* occurred.

She smiled. "Did you? Without me waking?"

"Ursula…" He didn't want to out-and-out lie. Not after they'd made love.

She plucked the camera out of his pocket and thumbed the review button. Gabe sucked in air through his teeth. *Double-damn.*

She glanced up from the screen. "Pictures of nails and the van? Where did you take them? Here?"

"Sula—"

"That wasn't an accidental flat?" She examined the screen again. "Somebody planned it?"

He paused. "Could be."

Her eyes widened. "Did they also screw with the new spare, tossing in that puny trailer tire instead? What about the missing wheel chocks?"

He scratched his chin. She was no dummy.

"Give me the bag. I can *see* it's a bag, Gabe." She stuck out her other hand.

"Sula, I don't think—"

"Give me the bag. Damn it, Gabe, we just made love. I deserve to know what's going on."

"I hear you, but it's not that simple."

Lowering her hand, she shook her head. "Why won't you let me see the bag?"

He shifted his feet on the asphalt. "It's evidence."

"This isn't about the botched ad again, is it? And everything else that's happened?" She gripped his camera by the strap. The small piece of equipment bumped her lingerie-covered thigh. "Wait. Your uncle doesn't believe *I'm* pulling these stunts?" She squinted. "Let me guess. He thinks I'm trying to devalue the business so I can get a better price. Trust Mackie to dream up such a loony scenario."

"Actually, it's pretty good motivation." Gabe should know. He had attributed it to her.

She gasped. "Are you a cop?" The cold night breeze flapped the flimsy robe at her knees, exposing her naked thighs.

He cupped her elbow. "You're freezing. Let's go indoors."

She snatched the nail bag from his jacket pocket. His phone and the tongs clattered to the pavement.

"Crap! You *are* a cop! Just like your dad. That makes total sense."

"No, I'm—"

"Don't deny it, Gabe! I'm not stupid. You show up after everything starts going wrong, and Mackie asks you to help with the Real Men shoot? I can't believe I fell for that shtick. Either you're a cop or some kind of hired gun, or you're responsible for this mess. Which is it?"

"*I'm* not sabotaging my uncle."

"Neither am I." She slammed the camera and evidence bag against his chest. "But you'd better tell me who you are and what you *are* doing, or I'll scream so loud the real police will come running."

"Scream then. Or get inside. I'm not talking out here."

Face hot, Ursula stomped down the main corridor and pivoted into Reception. Gabe's footsteps slapped linoleum behind her.

"Sula, wait."

"Don't call me that." The frilly dressing robe she'd selected *for him* fluttered around her naked legs, and the feather-laden mules pinched her feet. "I slept with you, and I don't even know who you are!" Humiliation seared every inch of her body, propelling her into the second hall leading toward the studio proper.

"Damn it, it wasn't like that."

"Wasn't like what?" Whirling to face him, she clomped backward at a pace that would do an Olympic sprinter proud. "Wasn't like you pretended you needed photography lessons?" For all she knew, he was a secret agent geared up to the rafters with night vision goggles and spotting scopes. "That you're *interested* in me? That you rented an apartment you said you couldn't afford?"

Limping slightly, he clenched the camera in one hand. The nail bag and phone dangled from the other. "You know about my apartment?"

"Your mother spilled the news." She lifted her chin.

"When?"

"Yesterday, when she called. What does it matter?" *Notice he hasn't denied a word. He's just peeved I found out.*

Shoving open the backroom door, she flipped on the light and arrowed for her clothes scattered around and below the chaise.

Gabe stuffed the camera and nail bag into his jacket pocket. "It matters because I wanted to tell you," he said in an irritatingly reasonable voice. "I couldn't."

"Uh-huh." Hands shaking, she snatched her panties out from under the fur. The dressing robe covering her butt, she presented Mystery Man with a rear view as she kicked off the preposterous mules and yanked on her underwear. "You know, ever since you showed up, I knew something wasn't right." She should have heeded her instincts. He *had* been hiding something. "If you won't answer my questions, I'll ask Mackie. And warn Stacy." She threw off the ridiculous robe, seized her bra, and caged her breasts.

Gabe stepped in front of her. "Okay, you're right. I was a cop. That's *was*, Sula."

"Don't"—her fingers splayed—"call me that." Sula, her ass. She'd thought she meant something to him, that he felt something for her. For all she knew, he nicknamed every woman who fell into his bed. Or wherever!

"I'm sorry. *Ursula.* I'm not a cop anymore. That bullet would have stuck me behind a desk for ages." His voice croaked.

A cold pit of fear dropped in her stomach. "You were shot on the job?"

"No. I was buying milk at a convenience store like I said, following several hours in court and another late-night shift. My brain was buried in a lousy situation at work. A shitty reason for not falling back on my training, but there you go. When I realized a robbery was in progress, instead of assessing the situation and calling for help, I jumped into action like some schmuck off the street. I'm lucky my stupidity didn't get me or the clerk killed."

She pulled on her top. "If you're lying to me now, I'll have your butt in a sling." *Don't think about his injury. Don't.*

"And you wonder why I thought you might have it in for my uncle? The day we met, you were a damn fireball. I would've been three kinds of dense not to deem you a person of interest."

Her eyes popped wide open as the full implications of his words sunk home. "Are you saying all the weird stuff happening around here is related? And I was—I *am*—a suspect?" Her pulse rocketed. "How far back does your spying go?"

His gaze shifted to somewhere above her right shoulder. "I'm working on clearing you of the broken window."

"From the middle of October?" Her hand flew to her throat. "That's why you were in my bedroom Saturday. Why you asked about Tom Haskell."

A ruddy hue stained Gabe's face. "I've initiated contact."

"Did you peek into my phone while I was asleep?" She glanced at the chaise. "In *this* room, *after* we made love?"

"No. I messaged him on social media last night."

"Waiting to hear back, huh?" Might as well gallivant with the nearest female in the meanwhile!

He drew in a breath. "I could have asked Deni—"

"But she might have said something to me. The smart choice was Tom." Ursula choked back a sob. Wasn't she the fool? Falling for Gabe's sexy moves and handsome face. He was so much more than she had imagined. Intelligent, resourceful, devoted to his mother, and obviously committed to his work. All were qualities she normally admired.

Normally.

She peered at him. "You weren't jealous Saturday. You kissed me to soften me up." Outside her apartment door. A real humdinger. "Let's call Tommy, shall we?" Skirt-less and barefoot, she stamped to the prop table and whipped her cell out of her purse. She swiped through her contacts. The concrete froze her feet.

"Ursula, that's not necessary."

"Quiet." Terse, sharp, and brittle. Exactly how she felt. "It's ringing." She held the phone three inches from her ear. "He doesn't know you. He might ignore your messages." Especially taking into account that Gabe-the-blow-her-mind-former-cop had contacted Tommy two nights before Turkey Day. Hadn't her brother mentioned that Tommy's family lived out of state? The guy was probably traveling. "Did you use your real name?" she asked Gabe. "I need to know how to approach Tom."

He shook his head. "Matt Bennett."

"Well, then, I'm doing you a favor." She wanted any shred of suspicion wiped from whatever-he-wanted-to-call-himself's brain.

Tommy answered. After a quick exchange, Ursula thrust the phone into Gabe's hands. "Go ahead. Ask him."

"I don't—"

"*Ask him.*"

He pressed the cell to his ear. While he interrogated Tom, Ursula finished dressing.

Gabe disconnected.

"Satisfied?" She snatched back her phone.

Tiredness lining his features, he nodded.

"Good. Explain yourself."

He sighed. "I moved home to become a private investigator. I'm applying for my license in January."

"Why wait?"

"My mom wants to enjoy the holidays as a family first." He glanced at the floor. "She went through hell when I got shot. She deserves some peace of mind. The vandalism in October upset her, so I offered to look into it."

Oh, sure, bring up his mom—and family loyalty. "What about Mackie? What does he think?"

"I told him to keep you out of the loop." His gaze lifted. "I had to clear you, Ursula. Even if you're innocent, I couldn't risk you interfering in the investigation. If you got hurt—"

"So you kept me in the dark instead. How noble." Their voices echoed above the soft strains of the CD. She wished the music would stop, but the infernal machine continued playing. "And what's with this *if* I'm innocent stuff? Either you believe I am or you don't."

"I believe you. But I couldn't rely on my gut. I needed facts to support what I was feeling." Adjusting the stance of his injured leg, he set his hands on his hips. "As of tonight, you possess alibis for every incident that occurred before I returned to town. I haven't cleared you of the shredded note, but my uncle destroyed the evidence."

The edges of her phone bit into her palm. "What shredded note?" News to her!

A beat elapsed. He released another sigh. "The Friday before you and I met, my uncle received a potential death threat in the mail. It's impossible to decipher the writer's intent without reading the note or hiring an expert to analyze the contents. But it scared him."

A death threat? Ursula's pulse pinged around behind her breastbone. Why hadn't she or Stacy seen the note? Had Mackie shielded them from an unknown menace?

Nah.

"Too bad he shredded it. My clever efforts to disguise my handwriting were in vain." She returned to the prop table, wedged her phone into her purse, and jabbed the OFF button on the dratted CD player. The music fizzled to silence. "Seriously, Gabe, how many incidents are we talking about? The crap with the windows, the mysterious note, and the botched ad?"

He stepped toward her. "Add on the rash of phone calls and the sales associates arriving for appointments Stacy says she didn't schedule."

Ursula shook her head. "That's nuisance stuff. It's been frantic around here lately, but it's not like we're discovering dead bodies in the walls."

"You watch too much TV." His thumb jerked. "The missing coffeemaker? Somebody stole it. The wrecked microwave? Sabotaged to spark a fire when my uncle heated his lunch."

She laughed. "What's next? Smearing jam on the phones?"

"It's not funny. The bomb squad wasn't laughing when they arrived to check out the inert grenade that busted the front window, were they?"

"They didn't find anything. The police said it was likely kids. A prank."

His moss-green gaze drilled into her. "Taken one at a time, the incidents *sound* like pranks. Add them together, particularly when events fall on top of each other like they have this week, and it seems someone is sabotaging the studio. Or worse, stalking Mackie. With the note, the microwave, and the coffeemaker, it appears they want him to realize it." His voice softened. Hand on her arm, he murmured, "Ursula, even if I hadn't needed to clear you, telling you before now might have placed you in danger. Telling you tonight still does."

She flinched. "Don't give me that." She'd bought his wacky job-hopper story, she'd offered him her body, and, although she hated to admit it, she'd even surrendered a piece of her heart.

For what? A man she couldn't trust?

She had to go home. Get away from here.

Away from him.

"I signed a contract to buy this place," she snapped. "I have a stake in how the case evolves."

A grimace twisted his lips. "Haven't you heard a word I said? If you stick your nose where it doesn't belong, you could get hurt. Is that what you want?"

"Of course not. But I won't fall for your macho BS either. Buying this studio is *my dream*. If someone is out to ruin *my* business, I need to find out who."

Steel glinted in his eyes. "I *can't* have you snooping around."

She snatched up her purse and jacket. "Gabe McKenzie, you're a hard-ass. A know-it-all former cop with something to prove."

He grunted. "If you can't accept that I'm trying to protect you, what was tonight about?"

"Gee, I don't know. Sex with a stranger? Not anything more. I can't trust you, Gabe."

"You *can* trust that I have experience in how these situations can develop. I need you to play along with my cover."

"Up yours. Why?"

"Because Stacy might be guilty."

Ursula snorted. "She's not!"

"I don't have proof to clear her."

"Then take what you *have* found to the cops."

"I don't have enough evidence. If you cooperate, I could get it."

Purse swinging from hand to hand, she jammed her arms into

her jacket. "I'm leaving. I refuse to talk about this anymore." She headed for the door.

"Sula, I need to know you'll cooperate."

The nickname grated like cats clawing wallpaper. "Oh, that's priceless." She turned. "I can't help or look into things even though I have a stake in this business, but *you* need *me* to do whatever you say."

"If you want to buy this place, your best course of action is to follow my lead. You're a smart woman. Act like one."

She glared. A smart woman wouldn't have allowed herself to become mired in this mess. To let Gabe McKenzie's fabricated charm seduce her.

She grabbed her cell phone out of her purse.

"What are you doing?" he asked.

"Getting a rideshare. There's no way I'm letting you drive me home now."

"Ursula, be reasonable."

"*You* be reasonable. *You* act smart. I'll go on my incompetent, irrational way. And don't you dare follow me, Gabe. I'm done."

Sixteen

EVE FELT like a human ping-pong ball bouncing between determined opponents. She sat at the head of the dining table, Gabe on her left and Victor on her right in the chair Hal had occupied last year. Today would have marked their third Thanksgiving as a couple. Divorced and with a geologist son who worked overseas, until they'd met Hal had grown accustomed to spending holidays alone. They'd dated for a few weeks prior to Thanksgiving that first year, so she'd invited him over—her only boyfriend since Doug died to enjoy her roast turkey and savory stuffing.

Gabe, visiting from California, had taken to Hal straight away, but Victor had disliked him on sight. Eve had spent the evening expending copious amounts of energy helping the two men discover common interests.

Tonight reminded her of that initial awkward holiday with Hal and Vic, except now her son and his uncle exchanged uncomfortable looks while she struggled to divide her attention between them. She would ask what was eating the men in her life, but she preferred not to chase her meal with a jigger of indigestion. They could settle their differences on their own.

"More turkey?" she asked, lifting the platter as her son finished the helping on his plate.

Gabe paddled his stomach. "Thanks, but I'm stuffed. Let's break out another bottle of wine to enjoy with dessert. Sound good, Uncle Vic?"

Eve slipped a glance to her brother-in-law. Vic's guzzling of the first bottle lent a bleary cast to his eyes and a slur to his voice. Why would Gabe encourage his uncle to overindulge? But then, she and her son had barely drunk a glass each.

"Um." *Clever response, Eve.* She lowered the platter.

Vic twirled a finger. "I'll fetch the wine from the basement."

"No, I will." Gabe pushed back his chair. "The rack is inside the door to my suite."

"Wait a minute." Eve shook her head. "How will Vic get home?" He damn sure couldn't drive with that much alcohol sloshing around in his system.

Her brother-in-law winked. "I'll sleep over. In Gabe's old bedroom."

Located beside *her* room. "No, no. Aren't you meeting your girl-friend at your apartment later?" She wouldn't encourage bad habits. Tardiness, drinking and driving. Sharing her feminine bathroom come morning.

Vic pinched his nostrils. "Shinola. Forgot about that."

Gabe stood. "I'll spring for a cab."

"That's generous," Eve stammered. "But then your uncle won't have a vehicle."

"It's a holiday," Vic boomed, arms spreading wide. "I'll worry about my wheels later. Family bonding is more important."

"True." Eve's mind spun. Gabe's cell phone, charging on her vintage secretary desk, rang. "Go ahead, honey. See who it is." She pressed fingertips to her left eyebrow. She needed a moment of peace.

Gabe limped to the desk and checked the display. "It's Ray Hill-son. I promised to call him."

One of Doug's old friends. "How nice. Say hi for me."

Nodding, Gabe unplugged his cell from the charger. "Ray and I can talk while I get the wine." Swiping to accept the call, he headed for the kitchen. The basement door clicked shut, and his footsteps resounded on the staircase.

Eve fidgeted with her napkin. "I suppose we can arrange the return of your van tomorrow," she said to Victor.

"It'll work out." He downed his wine and smacked his lips. "That was an excellent meal, Evie. You're an incredible cook."

"Thank you. Hal thought so too." She crumpled the napkin in her fist. Not Hal *again*. Memories of the good times had bombarded her all day.

"You've always taken wonderful care of your men."

"My *family*." The distinction felt important.

"Henshaw wasn't family."

"No, you're right." Hal had started feeling like family though. Almost like a husband who'd lived in a different house.

She exhaled gustily. What was wrong with her? She and her friends had discussed the breakup over dinner last night. The conversation must be weighing on her mind. Her newest friend, Sheila, thought *Eve* was being too insensitive with Hal, not the other way around. Sheila had said she understood why Hal hadn't wanted to see Eve when Eve brought his things to his office. Then Gwen and Teri defended the split, and Sheila had backed down.

Now, considering Sheila's counseling job, Eve wondered if the woman might have provided insights into her dumping of Hal that Gwen and Teri couldn't.

Certainly, Hal's proposal in August had unsettled her. No, more than that. It had plain irked her. Gabe had just been shot. As if her son's ordeal weren't horrible enough, memories of Doug's death had resurfaced, crushing her soul and narrowing her perspective. Several times during her trip to Los Angeles to visit her son in the hospital, she had feared the onslaught of darkness would swallow her whole.

Upon returning to Seattle, she'd craved Hal's compassion, and, at first, he'd supplied it in droves. But his sudden marriage proposal had felt more like an attempt to refocus her attention on him rather than a sincere desire to spend their lives together.

Three months had passed. In retrospect, maybe she *had* used Gabe's shooting as an excuse to cling to memories of Doug. Her boyfriends before Hal had complained as much.

With Hal, she'd deliberately avoided repeating the pattern. And then Gabe got shot.

Heat bathed her face. She had hurt Hal deeply.

"Penny for your thoughts?" Victor asked.

"I miss your brother," she replied in a shaky voice. Yes, she missed Doug. She always would. But tonight she yearned for Hal.

Vic's expression sobered. "So do I."

Tears pricked her eyes. She was being unfair, exploiting memories of Doug to avoid discussing her poor treatment of Hal with Vic.

What was taking Gabe so long?

Rising, she collected plates. "We'll have dessert in the living room, relaxing on the couch." Earlier, realizing Doug's police memorabilia would upset Vic, she'd placed the items inside the buffet. She would return the mementoes to the mantel and tables after Victor left. She needed to have them out just a few more days. By Christmas, she would store them away for good.

As she picked up Vic's plate, his big hand covered hers. "I'll help."

Standing, he hefted the platter and a casserole dish. In the kitchen, he hung back while she deposited plates in the sink. A funny sensation skittered up her spine. She wore pants that had never failed to elicit compliments from Hal. Was Vic checking her out?

A second later, he stepped beside her and placed his load on the counter. "I'm sorry you're missing Doug tonight." He patted her shoulder, not like an interested male, but her brother-in-law once more.

Her chest squeezed. Vic stood barely an inch taller than her, sorrow etching his intense expression. Their shared grief bonded them in a way her friends couldn't understand. And she'd doubted his sincerity.

For shame.

Gazing at him, she whispered, "The way he died..." Bleeding on the warehouse floor, without his wife or son near to offer a tiny scrap of comfort. "It was horrible, Vic."

"He should've woken you up before he left for work. Skipping out on you without a word was wrong."

"Oh, Vic." *He* was wrong. As a police detective's wife, she'd realized the dangers of Doug's job. Even so, waking to Doug's partner Bill knocking on the door in the middle of the night to deliver the awful news that Doug had been killed would haunt her for the rest of her days. "We've been through this. I had a bad headache and asked him not to disturb me. I remember him kissing my forehead while I dozed. I just never thought it would be our last kiss."

Vic's hand lowered to her waist. "Evie, my sweet Evie, if I could bring Dougie back for you, I would."

A lump lodged in her throat. She nodded.

"I know you miss him and Henshaw. On a day like today, it's natural to miss Hal. He was in your life a long time."

Tears welled, threatening to spill over her lower lashes. "More than two years."

Vic's dark eyes gleamed. "You did the right thing leaving him. You gotta know that. You weren't ready to get married again, and he pressured you."

"Y-yes." At the time, that was how it had felt.

"I would never rush you, Evie," Victor said. "Miss Hal if you need to, but set a time limit, get it over with. Another week or two. A month at most. Don't feel guilty ditching a guy who didn't understand you. Don't go crawling back to Hal because you're hurt and lonely and thinking about Doug. You never have to feel alone again, Evie. I'm here for you." His hand inched onto her hip.

Skin twitching, she stepped away. "Victor, I cherish our friendship. You'll always be family to me." *Nothing more.*

Gaze serious, he nodded. "That's what I want too. For us to stay family."

He didn't seek physical contact again. She had imagined an intimate nature to his touch he hadn't intended.

"Good," she murmured. "I don't want to lose you, Vic."

His gruff voice deepened. "You won't."

Gabe entered the kitchen, carrying a wine bottle. "What's going on?"

Vic spun toward her son. "Your mother is upset. Like any decent brother-in-law, I'm comforting her. You should try it sometime."

Gabe's eyes flashed. From behind Victor, Eve shook her head, silently imploring her son to ignore his uncle's rudeness. She couldn't handle a booze-driven Thanksgiving argument between the last two living members of her family. She wanted only pleasant memories. Easy times. Minimal conflict.

From here on in.

The cops were gaining on him. Shoes slamming pavement, sirens screaming. Flashlights slashed the inky night as hyenas cackled and steel bars rammed the soft earth, caging him.

Mackie tossed in bed, half-aware he was dreaming but unable to force himself awake. The night Dougie died consumed him.

The bars lifted. Mackie stepped into a familiar alley, scouting locations for a magazine shoot requiring a grungy, moonlit look to backdrop an upstart designer's punk jeans. The anxiety of the cop-chase receded, and pride coursed in his veins. The art director's face swam, filling his vision, her glossy lips plumping as she praised him. He was her number-one choice, at the height of his career, the top of his game. Ready to fly.

He examined the staging possibilities around a banged-up dumpster, when loud voices filtered from a warehouse a few feet away. His nostrils flared at the scent of opportunity in the night air. He should check out the warehouse. His wheels were close by. If the situation proved newsworthy, he would grab a camera from the trunk, sneak back in, and snap photos to sell to the highest bidder.

He skulked into the building—and froze.

"Doug?" Mackie blinked in the shadowy space, but there was no mistaking the larger-than-life presence of Doug McKenzie. Mackie's mind felt like he walked in heavy mud. Why was Doug in the empty warehouse?

At the sound of Mackie's voice, Dougie pivoted. Cop gun in hand, surprise plastering his face.

A shot blasted from the loft. Dougie's body bucked.

"Fuck!" Mackie shit himself.

"Call for backup!" Dougie whirled on his foe.

Shots plugging the night, Mackie tore for his car. Drove and drove and drove, stink and sweat and guilt smearing his skin.

He should go back. He had to go back. He had to help Doug. He couldn't help Doug.

Panic lanced him like the bullets hitting Doug, slugs propelling from the loft over and over, never-ending. For Chrissake, if Evie learned he'd crapped his pants when the first bullet pierced Dougie's back, that he'd humiliated himself and caused Dougie's shooting, not only would she never forgive him, she would never look at him the same again.

He would never be her man, just a big, diaper-wearing baby.

Wasn't what she thought of him more important than her freaking hero husband? Was this Mackie's chance?

In the blurry fog ahead, a phone booth loomed. Driving past, Mackie stared at the phone, saw himself standing inside the stall, gripping the receiver. Heard the quarter plunk, but didn't stop. He drove and drove and—

Mackie jolted awake, sweat drenching his chest. He swore. Heart hammering, he wiped his hands over his scorching face.

"Mackie?" Jasmine's sleepy voice drifted from the next pillow. "Are you okay?" Her hand snaked across his naked stomach.

"I had a nightmare." A freaking guilt-mare. That he hadn't done anything to help his adoptive brother. That he hadn't even called 9-1-1 with an anonymous tip.

"Poor Mackie," Jasmine soothed. Sliding close, she kissed his nipple. "Jas will make it better." She gripped his limp pecker, massaged and stroked.

He grunted. "Yeah." *Dazzle me, baby.* He needed to drown out the inconvenient reminders of allowing his brother to die. So he'd panicked that night. He'd been freaked. So he'd saved his own skin. Who wouldn't?

If he'd stayed in the area, calling for backup like Dougie had asked, more thugs might've arrived along with the cops. Wonder if the bad guy's crew had been hiding nearby? Next thing he knew, it would've been like the freaking Alamo or O.K. Corral or some shit.

The point was, *Mackie* might've kissed a bullet too.

After all, he couldn't have called the pigs and *then* run. Couldn't have risked Dougie reporting the freakish coincidence of him being in the warehouse to his boner cop pals and the bastards somehow learning Mackie had soiled himself. No freaking way. He'd chosen life and pride—at his brother's expense. And he'd battled guilt ever since.

"Mackie, Mackie," Jasmine crooned to his uncooperative dick.

Agh. He tried to concentrate on her touch, but the memories wouldn't leave him alone. As stressful as that night had been, Evie had relied on *him* afterward. For months, rolling into years. Now, he was days, maybe weeks, from winning her heart.

During their talk in the kitchen tonight, it was obvious she'd wanted him but, of course, had felt like she'd needed to act a lady about it. With a bit of coaxing, he could've had her—if not for Gabe. When Mackie arrived to swap vehicle keys with his nephew before dinner, the kid took him aside while Evie worked in the kitchen. Gabe had blathered on about nails, disappearing wheel chocks, and the dumbass trailer tire. A whole lot of what-the-flippery happening at once.

No, Mackie didn't know who'd filched his new spare. *No*, he hadn't moved the wheel chocks. Tens-to-the-zero clue who might have done any of it!

Clearly, someone with access to his van keys or a nameless face who might've made copies. If not Ursula, then Stacy.

Twit-face Stacy! What was her problem?

Despite Golden Gabe's assurances that he would get to the bottom of whatever was going on, the news had messed with Mackie's head throughout dinner, affecting his game with Evie. Worse, Gabe's social life blew, so the kid refused to leave his mother and Mackie alone for more than five minutes.

Crap on a carp! If not for his nephew butting in and derailing his focus, Mackie might be in bed with Evie right now instead of Jasmine.

"What was your dream about?" Jas worked his flaccid johnson.

"My brother. And how sad it was when he died."

Jas didn't know the details of Mackie's role in Dougie's death. No one did. And people wondered why he got a little tense at times! Keeping a secret like that was rough.

"Again?" she asked, girly-girl pouty.

Nodding, he shut his eyes and visualized her skillful hands.

"It's not your fault he died," she whispered.

It sure the hell was. If Mackie had called for help, maybe his brother wouldn't have choked on his gurgling blood on the warehouse floor.

Jasmine stroked his pecker until it puffed half-up. A sultry sigh slipped from her mouth. "That's the problem with Thanksgiving," she murmured, kissing his cheek. "We eat too much, and it pays us back later."

"Huh?" Mackie opened one eye.

"Your nightmare. Probably caused by indigestion."

"Hunh." She might have something there. Gas rumbled in his

belly. A good fart would release it, but the scent might distract Jasmine.

"Mackie," she whispered in his ear. "Grow hard for me."

"I'm doing my best, babe." *Blow a bighorn sheep!* With her perfect tits and bountiful ass, Jas was one hot piece of tail. And he couldn't get it up. *Work for it, you randy SOB.*

He experimented with a couple of fantasies before latching onto one of him and Evie starring in a home porno movie. The camera hidden in the wall, Evie as oblivious to its existence as the women he'd secretly videotaped and blackmailed years ago.

His pecker stiffened. *Ahhh.*

"Oh, Mackie," Jasmine whispered.

"Suck me."

"Honey, I always give you head. I want to make love." She straddled him.

He groaned as she impaled herself on his monster erection. As long as he didn't have to move a muscle until he climaxed, he was happy.

With Evie, sex would be different. Spiritual. He wouldn't require porno fantasies of her or Jas or any bimbos from his past. Tonight with Jas, well, this was different, because Evie wasn't *here.*

Making love with the woman of his dreams would banish his moronic guilt about Doug forever. Because then Evie would finally be where she'd belonged all along.

With him.

Jas's swaying boobs bumped his nose. Opening his eyes, Mackie gripped her tits. Hard.

"Ouch. Mackie!"

He leered. "Watcha gonna do about it, slut?"

Hurt flitted across her face. Then she grinned. "We're going there, are we?" Reaching behind their joined bodies, she squeezed his nuts until they burned.

He soared.

❦

The morning after Thanksgiving, Gabe braved Black Friday traffic to visit the tire shop and recover the nail that had caused Wednesday's flat. At Ray's, he confirmed the galvanized roofing nail matched the five from his uncle's parking spot. Unfortunately, not only had Ray's handling of the nail contaminated it for evidence purposes, the rough texture of the others left the police an extremely low chance of lifting even a partial print. For now, Gabe would add the nails to his growing findings.

He turned his pickup toward the studio, where he would continue snooping around. Specifically, in his uncle's office. When he'd first dropped in amid the chaos of the Real Men test shots, his uncle said the janitor didn't touch the space, which seemed peculiar for a business. What if a client required a private consultation? Mackie obviously didn't tidy the room himself, aside from emptying the wastebasket now and then. Hardly a boon for attracting discerning clientele.

Was Gabe's uncle hiding something in the clutter?

Driving downtown, Gabe called Todd Greenly at the *Clarion* via a hands-free device. As he had suspected, none of the newspaper employees involved in the retirement party had coughed up responsibility for the botched ad.

At this point, going behind his uncle's back and requesting his father's former partner, Bill Cruikshank's, assistance obtaining cell phone provider records for the newspaper's expired call logs wasn't an option. Gabe didn't have authority in Seattle's jurisdiction. He would need to uncover a life-or-death situation for Bill to action the warrants. Unless the situation escalated, he couldn't ask Bill to stick out his neck like that.

Arriving in the studio's neighborhood around eleven, Gabe parked two streets away and stretched his bad leg. He proceeded to the alley. The business wouldn't reopen until Monday. No one should be around, including Ursula or Mackie. Last night, Gabe encouraged his uncle to drink enough wine to embalm a horse before stuffing the man in a cab and instructing the driver to drop him at home. With any luck, a massive hangover currently bashed Mackie's skull, decreasing the chances he would leave his bed, much less his apartment.

In the alley, Gabe checked the parking spaces for more nails. None remained.

Quietly, he unlocked the back door and entered the building on light feet.

Lights off, he checked the empty staffroom and pressed his ear to his uncle's office door. Silence.

He might be here for hours. A quick scan of the building was in order.

He headed to the front, giving the waiting room a cursory glance before continuing to the studio proper. Stepping into the big room unleashed memories of making love with Ursula Wednesday night, and a knot formed in his chest as he pictured her storming out, hurt and angry. Without her knowledge, he'd tailed her until she'd safely met her rideshare. Back at the studio, he'd stashed away the remnants of their sexy photography session then headed home.

He should have explored his uncle's office before he'd left that night, but his argument with Ursula had muddied his thoughts, further underlining the gravity of becoming intimate with a suspect.

No matter that he cared for and had now cleared her, he knew better, damn it. He had every intention of honoring his promise to his mother to unearth the source of the snafus and threats against Mackie, but if Ursula's distrust inspired her to play amateur sleuth and she wound up hurt—

He shook his head. *Mind on the facts, Gabe. Mind on the facts.*

Grimacing, he returned to the hall outside his uncle's office and tested the door. *Unlocked.* Shuffling noises he hadn't heard earlier carried from inside.

He cocked an ear. Had Mackie stopped by while Gabe was checking the other rooms?

The door swung inward. Stacy jumped, screeching. "Gabe! You scared me."

He lifted his hands. "Sorry."

Yanking out ear buds, she jammed her phone into a jeans pocket. "What are you doing here?"

"Why are you?" he replied, deflecting her attention.

She pushed up her glasses. "Mackie left his door unlocked. I guess he's not used to having a deadbolt. Heh-heh." Nervous laughter trickled from her mouth. "I needed a fresh ink roller for the printing calculator. When I saw the doorknob move, I thought you were Mackie, so I shoved the package back in his desk."

"Why?" Gabe strode past her into the office. A gooseneck lamp shone on the desktop.

"I'm studying in Reception."

He had meant her stashing of the ink packet. But he would follow up on her comment, keep her flustered. Hopefully, it wouldn't dawn on her that he hadn't explained *his* presence.

"Your night school requires a printing calculator?" He narrowed his gaze. "I thought you were learning computer programs."

"I am." She wrung her hands. "Plenty of businesses use paper rolls for daily work. I need to become as employable as possible. You know, in case I...don't stay here." Pink tinted her face. "Please don't say anything to Mackie."

"I won't." Encouraging her to feel indebted to him might come in handy. Gabe smiled. "Studying without proper lights must be hard on the eyes." He flicked the office switch. Harsh fluorescent lighting flooded the room.

Stacy winced. "How did you know I turned off the waiting room lights?"

"I was just there." He wandered to the bookcase beneath the blind-drawn window. The shelves crammed with sample albums and old newspapers appeared untouched.

"The front lamp *was* on," Stacy said, on his heels. "When I came here, I turned it off and stashed my books on a shelf beneath the desk."

"Didn't want to be seen?" Hands in jacket pockets, Gabe surveyed the office.

"Mackie doesn't like me using the studio to study, but it's so nice and quiet when he's not around, and I don't have a printing calculator at home." She chewed her lip. "I feel more secure seeing the numbers add up on that cute little roll of paper. I'm double-checking my tallies until I'm confident with the different programs. I have an important test next week."

Gabe ambled to the desk. "Okey-doke."

"Don't!" Rushing over, she bumped the office chair. "Ow." She rubbed her hip.

Gabe slid her a glance. *Pretty twitchy there, Stace.* "Does my uncle keep all office supplies in this room?"

"No. Most are in my desk, some in the old darkroom." She

planted her hands on her hips. "You know, I don't understand him! He likes me to use the calculator but blows a gasket when I need to change the ink. I have to beg him for every single roller. He probably hides them to tick me off."

That's it, Stacy, keep chattering. Gabe opened the top desk drawer.

The girl shrieked. *"What are you doing?"*

"No ink rollers here." Gabe opened the first drawer on the left. "Or here."

"Stop looking!" Stacy leapt up and down.

He slid open the left middle drawer. "What were you really doing here when you're not supposed to *be* here, Stacy?"

Her hands fluttered like scattering geese. "Please don't tell Mackie. I couldn't stand it if he knew."

Gabe opened the bottom drawer. "About what?"

She slammed shut the drawer, pinching her fingers. "Ow, ow." Tears flooded her eyes.

"Damn it, Stacy, are you hurt?"

"Yes!" Wailing, she lifted her hand. A purple welt marked her left fingers, and blood seeped from a nail.

Gently, Gabe clasped her wrist. "Hold still." He examined her fingers, and she cringed. "Nothing's broken. What's in that drawer that you don't want me to see?"

Perspiration glistened on her face beneath the bottom rim of her glasses.

"Stacy..." He injected a stern note into his voice, releasing her hand.

Her eyes widened. "His girlie magazines," she whispered. "I discovered them by accident. Honest."

Gabe laughed. "A lot of men buy skin mags." He opened the bottom drawer to confirm her story. The light from the lamp spangled off the magazines.

"His favorite one is disgusting." Stacy's lips curled. "It's sickening imagining him looking at them while I might be working..." her fingers flicked "...out there."

Gabe read the name of the top magazine and tapped the glossy cover. "This one?"

She wriggled. "Yes."

"What makes you think it's his favorite?"

"Because there are so many. And the stories—"

"Did you read them?" Gabe closed the drawer and switched off the lamp.

"I didn't mean to." Her glasses wobbled. "I wanted to see what the fuss was about, so I only read one story. Then one more. They made me feel lightheaded."

Gabe glanced at her flushed face and glittering eyes. More like the stories had turned Stacy on.

Did stalking her boss while feigning innocence *also* turn her on?

"Let's bandage your finger." He would search the office after she left. Until he uncovered enough evidence to contact the Seattle police, he needed her to believe he was on her side.

"I still need the ink rollers." She tittered nervously. "Middle drawer on the right."

He smiled. "You could have saved us both a lot of trouble if you'd said that from the start."

"I was too worked up."

She had that right.

He located a tiny package of ink rollers and handed it over. As they crossed the office, the hall light snapped on.

"Shoot," Stacy whispered, clasping the packet against her bleeding finger.

Ursula walked in. "Why are you two here?" She frowned.

Gabe held back a curse. She was plenty mad at him, and he couldn't say he blamed her. Sleeping with her had been a crummy move.

"Stacy needed somewhere quiet to study—"

"Because Shelly won't stop bugging me," the girl interrupted. "Sisters. What a pain in the neck. She's having boyfriend problems, and it's all she wants to talk about. *My* life, what *I* need, doesn't mean a thing."

Ursula nodded as if familiar with Stacy's complaints. "Why are *you* here?" she asked Gabe.

"I came to clean up."

Stacy's head perked like a puppy's. "Clean up what?" she asked.

"Ursula and I had dinner in the backroom Wednesday after closing," Gabe fibbed. "We were too tired to clear our things then, and yesterday was a holiday." True enough. "I thought I'd deal with it now." Another fib. He'd left the room spotless Wednesday night.

Ursula glared. "That's what *I* came to do."

He shrugged. "Now you don't have to."

Rolling her eyes, Ursula faced Stacy. "Omigod, you're bleeding."

"I caught my fingers in a drawer. Gabe and I were looking for a bandage."

"You poor thing. The bandages are in the restroom. I'll get one."

"I'll go with you," Gabe said to her retreating back. "Stacy, run your finger under the breakroom tap. We'll meet you there." He accompanied the girl to the employee room and tore off a chunk of paper towel to staunch the bleeding. Leaving her with the water running, he popped into the restroom two doors down and closed the door.

Ursula, retrieving a box of bandages from the cabinet, ignored him.

He extracted a canister of 35 millimeter film from his jeans pocket. "You forgot this Wednesday night." He set the cartridge on the counter, beside her purse.

She picked a bandage out of the box. "You know how to wind film. Interesting, considering what a newbie you are."

"My dad had an old camera hanging around. I helped him handle film a time or two."

"Isn't that special?" She tucked the canister into her purse.

Gabe puffed out a breath. "Ursula, I'm sorry. I shouldn't have let things get out of hand."

"*We* shouldn't have. What was I thinking?"

"But I don't regret making love," he whispered. "Do you?"

She blinked.

"Sula." He touched her arm.

"Don't—"

"Call you that. I know." Man, he'd screwed up big time. Would she ever trust him again?

A knock banged on the door. Shouldering past him, Ursula opened it. The sweet scent of her shampoo lifted from her hair, tickling his nostrils.

Stacy stood in the hall, eyes wide behind her glasses. "What's going on?"

"Nothing," Ursula bit out, bandaging the girl's finger.

"Sounds like something. Are you and Gabe fighting?"

"I'm an idiot, so now she hates me," Gabe mumbled.

"Two for two." Hurt threaded Ursula's sarcasm. She sealed the bandage with a gentle swipe. "Stace, I have an idea. You have the weekend to study. Let's hit the sales, share dinner and drinks. Enjoy a girls' night out."

"I'd love to, but I'm behind in class and short on money. I do need to buy some things for Christmas…"

"I'm a whiz with numbers," Ursula said, tossing the bandage litter in the bathroom trashcan. "I'll buy dinner then tomorrow I can help you catch up." She directed a saccharine smile at Gabe. "I like assisting young people with their studies."

An auger of remorse bored deep in his chest. Yes, he'd needed to clear her, but he hadn't counted on hurting her.

He definitely hadn't expected to fall for her.

But here he was, falling all the same.

"Fantastic," Stacy chimed. "I'll grab my stuff." She hustled toward the waiting room.

Crossing his arms, Gabe looked at Ursula. "Girl's night out? What are you up to?"

Reaching around him, she snatched her purse off the counter. "She's my friend, Gabe."

"I've worked here over a week. This is the first time I've heard you two arrange to meet outside of the studio."

"So?"

"You can't expose me, Ursula."

"Don't worry, Sherlock. Your secret's safe." She stepped into the hall.

"I should tag along."

Her eyebrows snapped together. "Not on your life. Stacy needs a break, and so do I." With a glance toward the waiting room, she whispered, "I said I wouldn't blow your silly cover, and I won't."

"How can I make sure of that?"

"Gee, because *I'm* not in the habit of lying?"

His neck stiffened. "I explained that. If you tell Stacy—" He broke off. The receptionist headed toward them again, her jacket on and her study gear and voluminous purse overflowing her arms.

"Tell me what?" Stacy asked, reaching them.

"About our relationship." Gabe's lips barely moved. He was an ass, but they needed a cover story. Bearing in mind that they each regularly dealt with Stacy, as close to the truth as possible was best.

Stacy grinned. "I knew it! You're dating."

"Not anymore." Ursula leveled him a dirty glance.

"Ooh, the plot thickens." Stacy's eyes twinkled.

"I parked out front." Ursula relieved the girl of a textbook. "Let's go." Striding toward the reception area, she tossed back, "Clean the place to your heart's content, handyman. Don't forget to lock up."

Seventeen

GABE HUNG around Reception until the women piled into Ursula's car and puttered down the street. He monitored their departure through the picture window before he reentered the studio proper. There, he donned latex gloves and searched for evidence that might link Stacy to the sabotage and threats. In case the women changed their minds and returned, he'd rather pretend like he'd just finished tidying his and Ursula's fictional Wednesday-night dinner mess than risk the receptionist catch him digging through her desk.

An exploration of the vast room revealed boxes of old photography magazines and client negatives from pre-digital days blocking a scuffed door. The location of the door—in the rear right corner—indicated a possible old passage to the staffroom.

Gabe headed to the employee room and peeked behind the refrigerator. Yup, he glimpsed the other side of the door. His uncle, the building owner, or a previous tenant must have decided the convenience of the fridge outweighed another fire exit.

Was Stacy or another suspect aware of the door? Was Ursula? He imagined her rectifying the blocked exit once she owned the business, even if doing so required renovations. It was a safety issue, and if he had learned anything since meeting her, it was that his passionate Sula wore responsibility like gang members wore tattoos.

He stepped to the sink. Stacy had forgotten the ink packet for the printing calculator on the counter. He picked up the small box and turned it over. The girl had made a big deal out of needing the machine for her studies. Had retrieving the ink provided an excuse for her to poke around or otherwise do damage in Mackie's office?

Did clues to Stacy's motives for possibly hassling or even stalking his uncle exist *in* the office? The same evidence Mackie didn't want the janitor discovering?

Carrying the packet, Gabe sped to the reception area and inspected Stacy's desk. No calculator in sight. Either she'd borrowed the machine for the weekend, shoving it in her monster-sized purse, or she hadn't wanted to risk the studio's new handyman—*him*—checking the ink pad and discovering holes in her story.

Returning to the office, he placed the packet in his uncle's desk. Rummaging through the drawers produced nothing of interest other than a small key.

Bad leg aching, he pocketed the key, booted up Mackie's old computer, and tested passwords. After guessing words, he keyed in dates. His uncle's birthday, his mom's birthday—

Bingo.

The computer files offered zip. Spreadsheets indicated a boost in business since his uncle hired Ursula, but Mackie had already admitted as much.

Gabe saved several files to a flash drive to examine later. While the computer shut down, he rifled through the bookcase then moved a heavy box between the shelves and filing cabinet.

Hello.

The box concealed a locked cupboard in the wall above the base-boards. He tested the small key. A perfect fit.

He opened the cupboard. The compartment vomited ropes, a leather flogger, a feather switch, two black vinyl masks, and a red ball gag. Plus, *lookee here*, a how-to manual for S&M neophytes.

He snorted. Mackie must get off on the discovery fantasy of conducting bondage games in his office. Or were the toys refuse from a previous relationship, locked in the office to decrease the chances of Jasmine stumbling across them in his apartment?

Using his phone, Gabe snapped pictures of the cupboard. The

familiar rumbling of the van engine carried through the alley window. Standing, he peeked through the blinds. Mackie and a redhead played tonsil hockey inside the vehicle. Was the woman in question Jasmine wearing a wig...or someone else?

He couldn't waste time finding out.

He locked the cupboard, tucked the key in the drawer, and moved the box to its prior location. Leaving the office, he raced toward Reception. As he turned the hall corner into the front of the business, the slamming of the alley door echoed through the building. Gabe heard Mackie talking trash about "Red" tying him up. He couldn't make out the woman's response, but her voice sounded nothing like Jasmine's. Seemed his uncle had picked up a side dish.

He hurried out the front door. Despite his efforts at plying his uncle with wine last night with the intention to leave the guy incapacitated for much of the day, Mackie had retrieved the van. There would be hell to pay if the goon had hassled Gabe's mom with the arrangements.

Removing the latex gloves, Gabe hustled toward his pickup. Three days ago, while going through the motions of buying the new coffeemaker, he'd initiated investigating his uncle's list of ex-girlfriends. A woman named Lori Keller, who Mackie said worked in the coffee shop, had quit two weeks ago. Gabe had sweet-talked her replacement into revealing her new employer.

He checked his watch. *One p.m.*

He would try connecting with Lori Keller again now.

Ursula sipped her vodka-cranberry without really tasting the tangy flavor of the juice. Across from her in the noisy pub, Stacy munched from their shared plate of nachos.

"Are you thinking about Gabe?" the girl asked as football players pummeled each other on the huge TV above the homey fireplace. Loud cheers erupted from the male-dominated crowd.

Ursula set down her glass. "That, my friend, is a loaded question." She hadn't *stopped* thinking about Gabe since discovering him bagging nails in the studio parking lot two nights ago. They'd made love, and then, in one massive, surreal shift to her world, every-thing that had felt so good and right between them had fallen apart.

Her shoulders sagged. She had noticed tidbits of Gabe's story not fitting the man she knew. She'd contemplated contradictory aspects to his personality. Yet she hadn't pieced together the clues.

She *had* visualized him in a proactive career. Suggested he explore a field that involved helping others.

That was rich. Protecting the public was in his blood.

"What do you mean, it's a loaded question?" Stacy asked.

Ursula chose a nacho covered in melted cheddar. She and Stacy had shopped their buns off, breaking at three for a late lunch, after which more shopping had ensued. Now, at nearly seven, Ursula hadn't come any closer to determining if she could trust the girl.

The irony wasn't lost on her. Gabe had needed to ensure *she* was on the up-and-up, and over the day she had developed the same concerns about Stacy.

Gabe's suspicions must have wormed into her mind. For exam-ple, what if Stacy's crush on him and willingness to play hooky from her studies today were tricks to encourage Ursula to spill her guts? If Ursula mistakenly told Stacy something she shouldn't, would she compromise Gabe's case?

"I don't know," Ursula bemoaned in an attempt to evade committing herself one way or the other. "Sometimes I swear he's as aggravating as his uncle."

Stacy slurped her strawberry margarita, which she'd ordered along with their snacks while Ursula visited the ladies room. "He could annoy me all he wanted. I can't imagine saying that about Mackie." Giggling, Stacy reached for the last hot wing.

Show some spunk, Urs. "I hope not. Blech." She dunked her chip in sour cream. "You wouldn't think so highly of Gabe if I explained why he's not God's gift to women."

"Explain away." Stacy licked hot wing sauce off the thumb of her unhurt hand.

Ursula's lungs constricted. "I can't."

"Because you promised you wouldn't say anything?"

Go with it. Nodding, she ate her chip.

"That's one of the things I admire about you, Urs. You're loyal."

"You are too, Stace." Like *she* knew. When it came right down to it, she didn't.

Brown eyes clouding, Stacy nibbled the chicken wing and deposited the bones on the plate. "Sometimes I'm too loyal. My sister drives me around the bend." Avoiding her bandaged finger, she cleaned her hands in the hot water bowl.

"I know what you mean. I love my roommates. They feel like sisters. That doesn't stop me from getting upset with them." Kim, especially. Upbeat Deni remained focused on her approaching wedding, but Kim too often prodded Ursula to peek around the corners of her carefully constructed comfort zone.

Hence, the mess she now found herself mired in with Gabe.

Stacy dried her hands on a napkin. "Shelly and I are half-sisters. We have different dads. Our mom divorced them both." She slathered a nacho with salsa. "Shelly's ten years older than me. Maybe if we'd grown up together or shared a bedroom, I wouldn't mind how she tries to control my life or the wild things she does." She crunched the chip between her teeth.

"Like what?"

"Sister things." The girl stared glumly into her margarita. "You're lucky to have a normal family with parents who don't hate each other." She looked up. "Do you know how rare that is?"

"You're right, I am lucky." But no family came without issues. Every set of parents influenced their children's behavior in some fashion. Stacy didn't know about the house fire or about the Scott family's financial woes, just that Ursula's mom and dad were each other's best friends and the Scotts faced challenges as a team.

On paper, Ursula's parents sounded perfect, but at times she wondered if their relationship bore a weird responsibility for her failure to choose a guy capable of offering emotional stability. Like a reverse psychology syndrome.

She *wanted* a reliable, trustworthy man like her father, but every time she dated Dependable Guy, she wound up bored as a brick. As if she didn't believe sweet love existed outside her parents' marriage. So, without realizing the pattern, back she ricocheted to a good-time dude.

After she'd wised up and ditched her last boyfriend, she'd managed wonderfully as a single woman building her career and helping her family. Then along came Gabe. On the surface, a good-time guy she'd foolishly thought she could enjoy in the short term.

In reality, who was Gabe McKenzie, really?

A first-rate son willing to help an uncle he didn't like.

A former cop recovering from an injury while reprioritizing his life.

A dependable guy…who lied.

She was so confused.

Stacy scowled. "I've had enough!"

Ursula snapped her attention back to her new friend's—and potential saboteur's—problems. "Sorry, I missed what you were saying. What has Shelly done now?"

"Nothing. Yet. But if she knew…"

"Come on, Stacy, you can tell me."

The girl snatched a nacho. Several tomato bits tumbled onto the table. "Last week a friend from night school said I could move in with her. I would be stupid not to accept her offer. I'd be even stupider to tell Shelly about it first. She'd probably lock me in my apartment."

Ursula swallowed a smile. "You live above her garage, right?" On a street near the pub, the reason they'd selected the location for their "I-survived-Black-Friday" wrap-up.

Stacy nodded. "She got the house in her divorce. She's obsessed with it, micro-manages *everything*. She won't even let me paint *my* kitchen the color I want." Her deafening voice competed with the cheers of the TV crowd.

"Uh, okay." Ursula glanced around at the staring patrons. "Stacy, not so loud."

"*Sorry,*" the girl grated as she shoved the chip into her mouth.

Goosebumps sprouted on the back of Ursula's neck. This wasn't *her* Stacy.

A blonde in jeans and a dark jacket turned from the bar. The woman gazed at Stacy, then Ursula. After speaking to the bartender, the woman strolled toward their table, fingers waving hello.

Ursula tapped Stacy's hand. "Look. The person I bumped into Monday is here. She walked in a few moments ago, but I didn't recognize her until now. I was such a klutz. I knocked coffee onto her coat."

Stacy looked over her shoulder. "That's not a person. It's Shelly!" She plunged her forehead onto the table and covered her scalp with both hands. "Pretend I'm not here."

Ursula chuckled. "How many ounces of tequila went into that margarita?"

Stacy groaned, lifting her head.

Shelly reached their table. "Hey, little sister." She smiled at Ursula. "I remember you. How are you?"

"Great." Not exactly true, but Shelly was only being polite. Ursula shook the woman's hand. "I'm Ursula Scott. Stacy and I work together." She never would have identified the two women as sisters. Stacy was dark and petite, Shelly tall and curvy with expressive blue eyes. Up close, a resemblance traced their chins and noses.

"Ursula, this is Shelly," Stacy introduced in a robotic voice.

"I'm so sorry about your coat, Shelly." Ursula returned the woman's smile. "Promise you'll send me the dry-cleaning bill."

Shelly waved a hand. "That's okay. It was an accident. I'd just dropped Stacy at work, and I had my head in the clouds."

Stacy cut her sister a glance. "You were in the coffee shop on Monday? I thought you were having breakfast with Kyle." She informed Ursula, "Her new boyfriend works in a nearby sandwich shop."

Shelly sighed. "Our date fell through. *We're* through."

"You broke up?" Stacy asked. "That was fast."

Shelly's smile grew brittle at the corners. "Kyle's a boy, not a man. I see that now."

Ursula studied her manicure, feigning she couldn't hear every word.

"We'll talk later." Shelly brushed a hand through her long, shiny hair. "I came by to give Lenny—the bartender here, they're friends —a message for Kyle to stop calling me from his friends' phones. I'm blocking numbers all over the place." She shook her head. "Good to see you again, Ursula." She headed for the exit.

Ursula sipped her drink. "She seems nice."

"Yeah, when she isn't loony tunes. She's thirty, Kyle is twenty-three. *I* liked him. Next thing I know, they're together. She stole him from me."

"I don't understand. Did you and he go out?"

"No. I kept eating at the sandwich place, hoping he'd ask." Stacy slouched in her seat. "Shelly said she met him through Lenny and didn't realize he was the same Kyle. I can't compete with her, Ursula. She puts out like that." She snapped her fingers.

"You mean sex?"

"What else? She's rarely without a guy. She doesn't even have to be in love to sleep with someone. That's how she wound up with Kyle."

Dum-de-dum. Too much information, Stacy.

Ursula sipped her drink again. The girl needed space from her older, pretty, "easy" sister. Rooming with a night-school pal sounded perfect.

"We didn't finish our conversation," she said. "Are you moving in with your friend?"

Stacy's chin jutted. "You bet I am. Next week. I'm moving and I have an exam. That's why I need to cram this weekend. Shelly can knock on my door and find out I've left after the fact, for all I care."

"Do you have a lot of stuff?"

Stacy shoved another chip into her mouth. Shaking her head, she chewed and swallowed.

"I can help you move," Ursula offered. "We'll use my car. We'll pack when Shelly isn't home."

Stacy perked up. "Really?"

"Get some boxes and packing tape then tell me a time."

Stacy's face glowed. "Thanks, Ursula. You're a good friend."

Ursula's smile wavered. She hadn't volunteered out of friendship. She wanted to learn more about Stacy, with any luck find an overt clue in the girl's apartment to solidly indicate her blame or innocence for the studio sabotage. Then she would deliver her findings to Gabe, and he could cross Stacy off his suspect list.

Stacy continued beaming. Ursula's stomach swam.

Was this how Gabe had felt questioning *her*? A little sick but determined to push through?

"I need to hit the restroom." She rose. "Can you order me cranberry juice without vodka, seeing as I'm driving? Thanks." She escaped to the ladies'. She didn't require the facilities. She just needed to get away from Stacy and this damn guilt.

She pretended to wait for a stall, fixing her hair and applying fresh lip gloss. After washing her hands, she left. She dodged a crowd at the air hockey table—then saw him. Gabe Sherlock McKenzie sitting with Stacy, his big, sexy hands wrapped around a beer.

She fumed. Was he following her? Making sure she didn't blow his cover?

Thanks for the vote of confidence, Sherlock.

She marched toward them.

"Hi, Ursula." He tipped his beer to his lips.

She propped the knuckles of one hand on her hip. "What the hell?"

Stacy giggled. "I texted him when we arrived. You were in the can then too."

He asked, "Did you know Stacy crochets and collects pottery cows? Sometimes my uncle pisses her off so much she wants to club him with one."

Ursula blinked. Gabe talked to Stacy about crocheting and pottery? Had she ever known a man other than her dad willing to discuss a woman's hobbies?

Would Gabe talk with *her* like that one day? No. She'd ended the possibility when she'd stormed out of the studio Wednesday night, refusing to listen to his explanations.

Her shoulders tensed. *Wait a minute.* Gabe was undercover. He considered asking personal questions and gaining a person's trust part of his job. Like when he showed up at her apartment bearing pizza and a gazillion-dollar smile.

Or when he asked her to go apartment hunting.

When he kissed her.

When he stripped off her panties.

Or had *she* peeled them off?

What difference did it make? He'd seduced her under false pretenses.

And she'd let him!

What was it about the man that made her super-like him one second and see straight through his plans the next? Because his comment about Stacy clubbing Mackie with a pottery cow made it pretty clear he was here to grill the girl.

"Aren't you sitting down?" Stacy asked, pulling Ursula from her turbulent thoughts.

"I can't," she lied. "When I saw you at the studio earlier, I forgot I didn't only go there to clean up. I meant to print contact sheets from the magazine shoot to look over this weekend."

Gabe's gaze reflected sturdy focus. "Contact sheets?"

"Rows of thumbnail JPEGs on photo paper," Ursula explained.

"Can't you view those on your laptop or phone?"

Her face felt chiseled from ice. "Sometimes I see more details on hard copy."

"Thumbnails sound tiny for checking details."

"It's a *feeling*, Gabe. I'm checking for a *feeling*. Sheesh."

He smirked. "Like checking for a pulse?"

"No. For *emotion*." Was he purposely trying to irritate her, referencing the disaster of their short-lived relationship in some sort of photographic code?

She fished a lump of cash out of her purse to cover the snacks, drinks, and tip. "Here you go, Stace." She dumped the wad on the table.

Stacy glanced at the money. "But—"

"I'm bushed. I'm heading home."

"No more looking at contact sheets?" Gabe's mouth curved.

"Oh, for—" *Ignore him.* "You two have fun."

She rushed toward the exit. The crowd swallowed her along with Stacy's objections.

The girl should thank her. Ursula had handed her alone time with Gabe. Even better, he had no choice but to remain with Stacy until she required a ride to her apartment.

Digging in her purse for her car keys, Ursula swept into the chilly November night.

Stacy wasn't guilty of anything.

And she'd prove it.

&

"Stacy, sit down," Gabe said in his relaxed handyman tone, tilting back his beer as the girl fumbled with her purse and coat. "Ursula flew out of here so fast, she's probably halfway home." By every indication, Sula couldn't stand to remain in the same building as him, much less share a table in a neighborhood pub.

He understood that. He really did. The main thing was, at her place, she'd be out of harm's way.

Eyes frantic, Stacy glanced around the chairs. "She has my Christmas presents and study stuff! She forgot her jacket!"

"What about the calculator? You forgot the ink rollers in the breakroom. I went to replace the old pad but couldn't find the machine."

"Crud. She has that too!" The girl plopped onto her seat and moaned.

"You took Mackie's calculator?" Gabe quizzed.

"Only for the weekend. I shoved it in my purse. Sorry, I should have said something. I bought new ink at the mall and installed the pad while we were in Ursula's car. The calculator is sitting on the back seat."

Gabe nodded. A quick text message to Sula would verify the story. The question was, when to send it? She wasn't too keen on him at the moment.

"Isn't Ursula helping you study tomorrow?" he asked, lounging in his chair.

Stacy's head bobbled like a dashboard hula doll's. "Ten a.m. at her place."

Acting unconcerned, Gabe reached for a nacho. He'd entered the pub five minutes ago, ordered the beer, and stayed out of sight until Ursula disappeared into the restroom, providing an opening for him to speak to Stacy. After spending the afternoon interviewing Lori Keller and two others from Mackie's list of exes, he'd scratched all three women off his suspect list. He had posed as a PI looking into past relationships for a current girlfriend concerned about cheating. Each ex had relayed a similar tale. Mackie began his relationships oozing compliments and bestowing gifts. As weeks passed, Gabe's uncle grew obnoxious and demanding. Depending on the woman's emotional makeup, she either booted Mackie out of her life or tolerated his behavior until he tired of her.

From what Gabe could tell, Jasmine followed the second pattern. Would the woman named Red become her replacement?

In any case, with the ex-girlfriends a dead end, Gabe had wanted time with Stacy before his dagger-eyed Amazon warrior princess returned. He hadn't expected Ursula to flee on the spot. Later, she would kick herself for leaving Stacy in his evil clutches.

Unless...

What was that bit about printing contact sheets? What had Ursula really meant to accomplish on a Friday night at his uncle's business?

Stacy resettled, arranging her coat and Ursula's on an empty chair. Gabe leisurely chewed the nacho and selected another. Last he knew, Mackie was at home—without Red. He'd called his uncle's after dinner, and Jasmine answered.

"Stacy, don't worry about Ursula." He took another slow pull of his beer. "She probably realizes she has your stuff. In fact," he added in a hearty voice, "maybe text her and touch base." Ursula would respond to Stacy over him. "Ask her to take the packages indoors. Tomorrow you can exchange her jacket for the calculator."

"You think that's the best solution?"

He nodded, lifting a finger as if he'd had a brainwave. "Ask her to message pictures of your shopping expedition and the calculator sitting on her coffee table or couch." Furniture he would recognize as belonging in Ursula's apartment. "Then you'll know every-thing's safe." A little sweet talking and Stacy might show him the photos, confirming the calculator story—and Ursula's whereabouts.

Stay safe, Sula.

Stacy's eyes brightened. "Good idea." She whipped out her cell. Her thumbs flew across the tiny screen as a female server arrived with a margarita and a ruby-colored drink.

Gabe paid cash, and the server left.

"Darn." Stacy stared at her phone. "No answer."

"It's not safe to text when she's driving. Give her time to get home."

"I'll feel better if I leave a voicemail. Like insurance."

"Knock yourself out." While she called Ursula's cell, Gabe inched the margarita toward her side of the table. *Drink up, Stacy. You can trust me. I'm your buddy, I'm your pal. Confession is good for the soul.*

Pocketing the phone, Stacy wiped the damp bowl of her fancy

glass with a paper napkin. "What's going on with you and Ursula anyway?"

Gut hollow, Gabe sipped his beer. "What did she say?"

"Aside from that you're not God's gift to women?" She giggled. Then her eyes widened. "Forget I said that." She gulped the fruity margarita. "Ursula and I are becoming friends. If she gets mad at me, I don't know what I'll do. I don't have a lot of friends, Gabe." *Slurp, slurp.*

"A cute little thing like you? Who wouldn't want to be your buddy?"

Stacy shook her head. "My sister Shelly is controlling. She monitors my guests, embarrasses them asking questions. No one wants to hang at my place. I can't afford a car, so I need to take the bus to work or rely on her to drop me off. Sometimes she changes her mind, and I need to pay for an Uber."

"Sounds like Shelly needs to get a life."

Stacy was on a roll. "She has one!" The girl sucked back her drink. "Shelly says because she's ten years older than I am and our mom moved to Arizona with some loser, she has to watch out for me. But I'm not twelve."

"Your sister is over-protective. Work on proving your maturity, and she'll slacken the reins."

Stacy smiled. "Aw. Nothing against Ursula, but *I* think you're amazing."

He ate another nacho. "To tell you the truth, I really like her, but I blew it. I lied by omission. Know what I mean?"

Nodding, Stacy drained her margarita and reached for the second cocktail. Nose wrinkling, she sipped.

"Ever do that?" Gabe pressed. "Ever want to confide in someone, but you're afraid you'll get yourself or someone else in trouble?"

"I hear you. The stories I could tell."

He smiled. "Stacy, whatever it is, I won't judge you."

"Not even if I describe how mush-*much* I detesth your uncle?"

"Especially not then." Gabe detected the slur in her voice. The alcohol was acting fast on her system. Tequila packed a punch on tiny women like Stacy. How many margaritas had she guzzled before he arrived?

Hunching over the table, she confided, "He's an *asth*. He grabbed my butt my first week of work."

Gabe ground his teeth. "He deserves a whipping." The jerk.

Stacy giggled. "I think I heard him getting one once. In his office." She belched. Burst out laughing. Waved her hand in front of her face. "Phew. Nachos. Sorry."

Gabe straightened in his chair. "When was this?"

"Can't 'member. Few weeks after I started. He didn't know I was there." She slurped the ruby-colored drink.

Well, well. A touch of voyeurism dovetailed nicely with Stacy's interest in Mackie's skin mags.

"How did you feel, hearing him?" he asked quietly.

"*Dishgusted.* If any guy tried that with me, I'd—"

"You'd what, Stace?"

"Break ups with him!"

"Good start. Anything else?"

"Yeah." Glancing around, she whispered, "Punch him in the gut."

"Beat him with a frying pan?"

"Or one of my pottery cows." Flopping back in her chair, she wagged a finger. "No, no, no. His thick skull might bust it. Not worsh it."

She must really love those cows. Elbow on the table, Gabe crooked a finger. Mimicking his posture, Stacy leaned forward.

He asked, "What if you could hurt him in a non-physical way?"

She adjusted her glasses. "Like following him or sticking sugar in his gas tank?"

Gabe shrugged. "Defacing his property. Toilet-papering his apartment. Breaking a window."

Stacy snickered. "That's whath happened to Mackie. Someone chucked one of those old grenades frew the studio window. Y'know, from the army thurplush store."

"I dunno." Gabe picked at the nachos. "I heard that was a prank. The way Mackie acts sometimes, he deserved it."

She shook her head. "He's a dick, but can he help it if he'th dumb? Bethsides, I had to sweep up the mess, and *I* didn't deserve that." She poked her chest.

Gabe ventured, "So were you there when the grenade busted the window?"

"Nope. It was at night. I 'member, 'cuz Shelly was teaching me a cool board game."

He yearned to ask about the painted window at Halloween, but didn't want to risk Stacy suspecting their conversation represented more than two coworkers growing chummy.

"We should go." He stood. "You're studying tomorrow."

She giggled. "I need a ride home."

"No problem. Did Ursula respond to your text?"

"Don't think so. It woulda dinged."

He held her jacket.

Wobbling, Stacy stuffed her arms into the sleeves. When she faced him, pink dusted her cheeks.

"Thanks," she said, slinging her purse over a shoulder.

"Ursula's coat, remember?" But Stacy already wove toward the exit.

Folding Ursula's leather jacket over his arm, Gabe bolted after the girl. He needed to catch her before she walked into a wall.

The server intercepted him, carrying a full tray of drinks. "I've been so busy I forgot to bring back your money," she said.

"Keep the tip." Stacy was on the move.

"Sorry. Let me clarify. Your friend paid in advance for the cran juice and margarita mix. There was no need for you to pay again."

Gabe frowned. "Mix?"

The woman nodded. "Both drinks were virgins. No alcohol. I didn't realize your group paid twice until I reached the bar."

"Do you mean the short girl with glasses?" Gabe clarified.

"Yes. She was with the pretty brunette earlier."

Sula. "What was the short girl drinking then?"

"A virgin strawberry margarita. She's had two tonight."

Damn it. "Keep the cash as a holiday gift. My friend will understand."

"Thank you!" Smiling, the server continued to a noisy group.

Dragging in a breath, Gabe butted through the crowd to find Stacy. Either someone had slipped a drug into her drink or she'd faked getting bombed.

If the former, she needed his help.

If the latter—what was her game?

Eighteen

"DON'T BOTHER CALLING BACK. Just text when you're home." Stacy's cheerful voicemail resounded in Ursula's ear as, checking her messages, she selected a candy bar from the rack at a convenience store six blocks from the pub. Bumping into Gabe for a second time today had sent her over the edge. Pigging out on chocolate was the only cure. How many times must she relive the painful memory of waking up on the purple chaise and carefully selecting a sexy outfit before going to find him, only to discover he was undercover?

This afternoon at the studio, he'd said he didn't regret making love. Well, *she* did. Her heart felt frayed, her emotions in a turmoil. She couldn't pretend his deception didn't matter because his investigation might appease his worried mom. Gabe had crossed a line. This wasn't make-believe, and she wasn't a spunky character in a TV dramedy. This was *her life*. She wasn't the sort of person who rebounded from "I really like you, let's get it on, and by the way…"

If she hadn't discovered him bagging evidence, how much longer would he have maintained his cover? Until he solved his case?

Would he have slept with her again?

"We'll swap stuff tomorrow," Stacy's message finished. "See you then."

Ursula accessed her texts and scanned the girl's lengthy instructions. Mongo details!

She peered at the display askance. Had Gabe convinced Stacy to send the message? Did he believe the girl was trying to thieve the cumbersome studio calculator? *Sounds like him.*

Rolling her eyes, she tucked her cell in her purse and went to the counter.

"Will that be everything?" the bored-looking clerk asked.

"Uh, no. I'll get this too." Ursula plucked a giant Hershey bar off the display. "On second thought, I should only buy one treat."

"Make up your mind. A line's forming."

Ursula zapped the woman a death-glare. "I'll take both."

A half-hour later, chocolate smearing her mouth, she parked Reba in the studio lot and trolled in the glove compartment for tissues. Her fingers grazed the roll of film Gabe had deposited on the restroom counter earlier, and she groaned. The first roll, featuring Gabe with Curly, was buried in her dresser at home. However, this one, forgotten in the vintage Pentax, contained the seductive images of her and Gabe kissing and caressing, undressing each other. Not wanting the memento in her purse throughout the day, she'd stashed the film in the nearest handy spot.

Now, the canister burned her palm as if cursed. She shouldn't have instigated the sexy photography session. Using film, no less. Had she subconsciously hoped the traditional format symbolized permanence?

God help me.

She tossed the cylinder onto the passenger seat and cleaned her face in the rearview mirror. She hadn't returned to the studio solely to print contact sheets. In Mackie's office this morning, she hadn't swallowed Gabe's story that he'd dropped by to tidy the backroom. Oh, that was his rationalization, or a half-truth, perhaps an out-and-out lie. But he must have been snooping around, conducting his case, searching for clues to clear or implicate Stacy of the most bizarre criminal activity Ursula had ever heard of.

Don't worry, Stace. I've got your back.

She could snoop around too.

Her gaze drifted to the film again. Damn it, she couldn't throw it out. Call her a sucker for punishment, but maybe if she developed the roll and forced herself to face the images of her folly, she could put Wednesday night behind her. Whenever she found herself softening toward Gabe, one glance at the negatives would steel her resolve.

Plan in place, she tucked the film into a front jeans pocket. Inside the breakroom, lights on and the alley door locked, she hooked her purse on the back of a chair. The old darkroom was located next door, between this employee room and the restroom. Mackie's office occupied the opposite side of the hall. The wall to the right of his door, decorated with a shadow box and framed client portraits, stretched down the main corridor to Reception.

A weird sensation settled on Ursula's shoulders, almost as if she were being watched. She checked the reception area and the studio proper, but the business remained silent as a tomb.

She returned to the main hall. In the narrow darkroom, she moved the studio toolbox before locating the old processing tank and developing bins. Mackie hadn't used the darkroom for business in years. The space housed mainly office supplies, although sometimes he tinkered around in here, dreaming about the good old days and mourning the artistic quality of film. Or so he claimed.

As long as she checked with him first, he allowed her to print personal films after-hours, so she kept the place stocked. She hadn't requested permission to use the room tonight, but after this chaotic week she couldn't care less.

She peeked inside the photography cupboard. Strange. The timers, thermometers, and squeegees were missing. She checked the drawer usually containing negative envelopes and scissors. There were the timers and squeegees. But where were the envelopes?

Another drawer held paper clips, staples, a bag of elastics, and some rulers. Crouching, she unlocked the chemical cupboard and stared. Two, three—no *five* small paint cans huddled behind the chemicals.

She frowned. Since when did Mackie store paint in the darkroom?

Pulling out the first tin, she blinked at the dried red enamel on the sides. She retrieved the other cans. Orange, blue, black, and— *crap!*—a creepy peachy-beige, almost a white person's skin tone.

Shivers raced up her spine. The tins matched the colors of the threatening words and raunchy images marring the studio window the morning after Halloween. What did the cans mean? Had *Mackie* painted the window? Granted, he didn't always play with a full bag of marbles, but why would her boss vandalize his business and hide the evidence in the old darkroom when Ursula, Stacy, and Gabe possessed keys?

Were Gabe's suspicions of Stacy justified? Had *Stacy* defaced the window then stored the paint cans where Mackie might find them? For what purpose? To freak him out?

Biting her lip, Ursula replaced the tins. She should call Gabe. He'd know what to do.

She shut the cupboard. Scraping noises whispered along the wall adjoining the breakroom.

Her skin crawled. Someone was inside the building!

That asshole Vic's worthless business was a stinking anthill of activity today. First, the new guy had interrupted the blissful silence this morning. Then the Ursula chick had showed up, stealing opportunities, throwing off plans. The skinny twit.

Endless hours of waiting had occurred, necessitating delays. And now, after sacrificing precious time rushing all over town to maintain appearances while accommodating an increasingly tight schedule, another setback. Ursula had returned. Turning on lights, mucking about in the ancient darkroom, possibly spoiling Victor's next surprise. Presents left for *him* to discover. Like the paint.

Oh, the anticipation of Victor realizing someone had spied on him while he'd vandalized the window. And then that same remarkably witty someone had rescued the paint tins he'd chucked into a dumpster. That pleasure had been ripped away. *Shit.*

Breathe. In and out. Through the nostrils. Calm and even. Again. Again. *That's it.*

Allow serenity to emerge. Try a smile. Now a grin.

Hold it. Longer. *Good.*

Let Ursula suspect a presence, then. Tease her, lure her in. Visualize her panic, absorb it, relish the rapid beating of her heart, fear clogging her veins. *Ha!*

But don't get caught. Creep out on quiet feet. Lay low for a day, a week, or at least an hour.

Then escalate the timetable. No more kid games. Enough of Victor McKenzie's lackeys and groupies getting in the way.

Soon, it would be done. Vic soaked in blood, screaming in agony, composing an opera of *Victor*-y and pain. *Ha-ha!*

Ending in blackness. Shrunken in death.

No less than he deserved.

Joy crested.

Yesss.

Soon.

☙

Adrenaline spiking, Ursula locked the darkroom from inside and killed the light. Who was out there? Mackie? Stacy? Gabe?

Please let it be Gabe. She didn't care if she was pissed with him. Or that he'd tracked her to the pub. If Mackie or Stacy learned she'd discovered the paint tins—

If *Stacy* had planted the paint to scare their boss and the receptionist lurked in the hallway now and she realized Ursula cowered *in* the suddenly claustrophobic darkroom—

Crap, if Stacy was unbalanced or stalking Mackie—

Was this how horror-movie victims felt?

Ursula tried in vain to control her galloping pulse. She felt helpless to do anything but await her fate.

Several minutes passed. Hand over her thumping heart, she only breathed when she feared she might faint. Her cell phone sat useless in her purse. Idiot that she was, she'd left her only link to the outside world in her purse on the breakroom table.

She remained still. Silence cloaked the darkroom.

Holding her breath, she pressed the backlight button on her watch.

Seventeen minutes had elapsed since she'd heard the scraping. She couldn't hide until morning. She had to pee! For real this time.

Think, Ursula. Her purse with her ID and phone lay on the table.

If someone was here—or they *had* been—they would have checked her bag by now. They would know her name. If whoever she'd thought she'd heard wanted to chop her up into too-stupid-to-live pieces, they would have scoured the studio to find her.

But she hadn't heard a thing. Not a peep or a step. Sooner or later, she'd have to take action.

"Hello?" she croaked into the inky darkness shrouding the tiny room.

No reply.

A bit louder, she repeated, "Hello?"

Nada.

She turned on the light. "Hello?"

Unlocked the door. "Hello."

Peered up and down the hall. "Hello!"

No one.

Ursula, you nitwit.

Not *too* stupid to live, she tiptoed to the breakroom. The door remained open to the exact width she'd left it. Her purse slouched untouched on the table.

Nothing had changed.

Scritch. Scritch.

The scraping! Coming from behind her!

She whirled.

And screamed.

❦

"Hey, Mom," Gabe said toward the blue-tooth in his pickup. "I'm on my way home. Do you need milk or anything?"

"You're near a supermarket?"

He sensed her unspoken question: *Just not a convenience store, all right, son?*

"Heading for Safeway. I'll be there in five minutes." His headlights cut a swath through the night as he steered around a corner.

"In that case, we need bacon. I thought I'd make us a nice big breakfast tomorrow, like I used to on long weekends when your dad was alive."

"Bacon and pancakes? Sounds great. Do you have sausages?"

"Yes. And pancake syrup. We can squeeze fresh orange juice."

"Eggs sunny side up?"

His mom chuckled. "I'll make the pancakes, bacon, and sausages. You can fry the eggs and squeeze the oranges."

"No way. I'm making it all. See you soon." Smiling, he disconnected. Man, it was great hearing the happiness in her voice. Last night, before his uncle arrived for turkey dinner, she'd confided that she missed his dad so much she couldn't bear to talk about him.

Gabe missed Dad too, but he wasn't the one who had to deal with Mackie "comforting her like any decent brother-in-law," which was starting to feel vulgar, if he told the truth.

His smile curled into a frown. Was Mackie becoming too familiar with his mom?

When Gabe entered the kitchen with the corked wine bottle last night, a certain tension charged the air. He hadn't clued in to changes in his uncle's behavior during his infrequent visits from California, but now he'd moved home and Hal was out of the picture...

Something felt off.

Mackie had Jasmine in his pocket—and apparently also the woman he'd called Red. Didn't the numbskull realize Gabe's mom wouldn't be romantically interested in a man who treated women like dirt, sponged loans, and borrowed tools from his dead brother's shed, never to return them? Mom only tolerated Mackie out of respect for Dad and empathy for Mackie's years in foster care.

Ahead, the yellow traffic light flashed red. Gabe stomped on the brakes, thoughts whirling. Damn it, his mother had explained time and again that she thought of Mackie as a younger brother. She was a grown woman who could take care of herself. Gabe needed to allow her to handle his uncle how she saw fit, not steamroll over her decisions. But after the crap with Stacy tonight, he must have entered the Suspect Everyone Zone, because he didn't buy *her* act either.

When he caught up to her in the pub parking lot, she continued playing the tipsy game. Genuinely concerned someone might have spiked her drink, he mentioned his conversation with their server. Once Stacy knew *he* knew her drinks were virgins, she magically lost the slur and chattered about biting her tongue while eating nachos. Oh, and she was also battling a sugar high from gulping margarita mix. But goodness, how nice it was of Gabe to drive her home. She planned to hit the sack early and rush to Ursula's in the morning to study.

At her sister's house, Gabe offered to escort her up the stairs to her apartment above a three-car garage. She'd declined. Citing safety, he'd waited in his truck until her lights flickered on. She stood in a window talking on her cell before appearing to go to bed.

After the apartment darkened, Gabe stayed parked another ten minutes before driving a block away and sneaking back on foot to conduct a mini-stakeout. Stacy hadn't emerged again.

Her strange behavior inspired more questions. She'd downed two virgin drinks, pretended to be drunk, then hustled him out of the pub and blabbed an obviously bogus story about the perils of sugar.

What *hadn't* she wanted to discuss? What had she feared he might bring up? Or had she worried she might slip and reveal a secret?

What are you hiding, Stacy?

He would make it his mission to find out.

"A mouse!" Ursula laughed. That was all she'd heard.

She inhaled a ragged breath. *Nothing sinister happening here.* Just her overactive imagination and a frightened rodent, which had scurried beneath the breakroom table when she'd screamed.

Bending, she shut Mackie's cereal cupboard. The stupid thing came unlatched with annoying frequency. More than once, she had suggested he store his cereal boxes on top of the fridge, especially with winter bearing down. As usual, he hadn't listened.

If she mentioned the mouse, he would set a kill trap. She didn't like mice, but the thought of intentionally harming the little creature raised prickling sensations along her arms. She would return over the weekend with cheese or peanut butter and a humane, self-closing container, then empty the tiny mouse into the alley.

The film canister bulged in her jeans pocket as she dug her phone out of her purse. After finding the paint cans, she wanted to continue sleuthing, but not without contacting her roommates and letting them know where she was. She needed to hear a familiar voice. *Too stupid to live, goodbye.*

She tapped Kim's cell icon. The call jumped to voicemail.

Crap. She tried Deni.

Her friend answered, breathless and laughing. "Hi, Ursula. What's up?" More laughter. "Sorry, James and I are going over wedding details, but he keeps kissing my neck, and it tickles. James, honey, stop it."

Well, now, didn't *she* have great timing?

"Are you at home?" she asked.

"In the living room. Why?"

"Is Kim around?" She would rather not bother Deni and James.

"Not anymore. She left an hour ago. Very mysterious. Didn't say where she was going."

"I'll try her cell again."

"She— James, wait. Sorry, Urs. James, in a minute, baby. Ursula? She was in a bad mood. Said she might shut off her phone for the night."

A frown tugged Ursula's eyebrows together. "I wonder what happened?" Kim was addicted to her phone.

"Don't know." Deni giggled as James's voice murmured endearments in the background. "We were in my bedroom. She yelled through the door on her way out. You know how she gets."

Yep. Cranky.

"Okay, well, this might sound strange, but if I don't show up within two hours, could you and James—uh—come find me at the studio?"

"I guess so. Where's your car?"

"I have it. Call or text before you come, okay? Listen, Deni, say you'll check up on me."

"Ooh, James. Sorry, Urs. Definitely. I'll set the stove timer. It's so loud, I can't miss it."

"Thanks." Slipping her cell into a back pocket, Ursula visited the bathroom and splashed cool water on her hot face. Dabbing her skin with a paper towel, she studied her reflection in the medicine-cabinet mirror.

Gabe's suspicions of Stacy *were* wrong. They had to be. Even if he'd driven the girl home right after Ursula left the pub, Stacy didn't have a car. Barring the utter ridiculousness of the idea, Stacy wouldn't have had time to whip to the studio and pretend to be a mouse to scare Ursula. Especially when a real mouse existed.

Although…Stacy *could* have planted the paint before tonight.

Except she lacked a motive.

Ursula chucked the paper towel in the trash. Why would a twenty-year-old night-school student play creepy mind games on Mackie?

Think. If I were intent on scaring Mackie, where would I conduct my handiwork?

With no signs of a break-in, it stood to reason that her bad guy or girl possessed studio keys. Other than busted glass, the police hadn't found evidence of a break-in the night the grenade hit the waiting room window.

No wonder Gabe suspected Stacy.

Stop obsessing about Stacy. If I wanted to hassle Mackie, where would I strike next?

Her eyes widened. In his office! His sanctuary.

She returned to the darkroom and located her keys, then unlocked Mackie's office. It felt like days had passed since she'd surprised Stacy and Gabe in the room this morning. During the shopping safari, Stacy had panicked about needing replacement ink pads for the printing calculator, but why had Gabe been here? Ursula and Stacy had split, leaving him alone.

Had he searched the room?

She pored over the desk, careful to leave Mackie's things in their usual messy state. Her rummaging produced a collection of girlie magazines. Gagging, she wiped her hands on her butt and moved to the middle of the room.

Hands on hips, she surveyed the office. She had no idea what she was looking for. She should have read her mom's old Nancy Drew collection before their house burned down.

Glancing toward the door, she studied the wall opposite his desk. From this vantage point, a Victor McKenzie self-portrait hung above the side table to the left of the door. For someone entering the room, the table sat on the right.

While client photographs decorated the halls and reception area, only Mackie's gigantic half-body portrait plagued his office. Was it possible he or the crook had stashed something behind the picture?

Noooo. Much too obvious.

Twirling her pinky ring, she crossed the room and peered at the gilt-framed enlargement.

What the hell? She peered closer.

Gross! A tiny, screened hole lurked in the shadows of Mackie's crotch.

Shuddering, she removed the heavy picture and leaned it against the guest chair.

In the wall, a small door with an unscreened hole beckoned. A dusty camera lens glinted behind the hole.

Bile tinged her mouth. Had Mackie recorded or photographed himself? Or another person?

Memories of walking in on him and Jasmine nine days ago crowded her mind. Her stomach lurched. Omigod, had he secretly recorded Jasmine going down on him?

Ursula pressed a hand to her mouth. *Keep it together, girl. Do you want to find out what's going on or not?*

Steeling herself, she opened the thin wood panel. An ancient video camera hulked inside the cavity created by two-by-four-inch wall studs. Except the cavity appeared deeper than four inches, and another little door sat behind the camera. This had to be a custom job.

She squinted at the second door a full three seconds. Suddenly, possibility struck like a smack to the skull. The shadow box displaying an antique camera occupied *this exact spot* in the main hallway—on the other side of the wall.

Ursula had stupidly assumed Mackie believed in preserving photographic history, but now, it looked like the wall cavity extended *into* the shadow box, and the second door concealed the rear of the video camera.

She scratched her scalp. Super-light-bulb moment! The *contents* of the shadow box and the shadow box itself disguised the second door in the corridor while the portrait of Mackie camouflaged the lens on *this* side.

An awful lot of thought had gone into creating the cavity. The concept was disturbing on a million levels.

Breathing deeply, she withdrew the dusty camera and opened the videotape compartment. A wrinkled notepad lay inside.

She extracted the tiny pad and perched the camera on the internal wall shelf. Flipping the pages, she recognized Mackie's slanted handwriting listing women's names, dates at least two years old, and dollar figures.

Cash payments?

Had he secretly videotaped and blackmailed these women?

Ursula examined the notepad a second time. Jasmine's name wasn't listed. Either Mackie had stopped his sleazy habit or upgraded his equipment along with making a venue change.

Nausea swelled in her stomach. She needed to talk to Gabe.

Hands jittery, she set the notepad on the table to slip into her purse. She should take the camera to show Gabe. If Mackie hadn't used the camera in years, he wouldn't miss it.

Unless the *baddie* knew about the video camera...

Might he or she miss the ancient piece of equipment?

Ursula didn't know what to do!

Until she devised a plan, she needed to leave the camera in its hiding place.

She lifted the unit off the shelf again. Footsteps sounded in the alley corridor.

She froze.

Nineteen

GABE STRODE into his uncle's open office. "Ursula?"

There she was! Red-faced and gripping a battered video camera that looked like a relic from the last century.

"Don't you answer your phone?" he asked.

Her eyebrows rose. Her mouth opened. "It was in my purse," she stuttered.

He stared at her butt. "It's in your jeans pocket."

"Now it is. I didn't review new messages before calling Deni." She winced. "That was dumb of me."

The knot in his stomach loosened. "You're safe. That's the main thing." From what she'd said, she'd also checked in with one of her roommates. *Good.*

He released a breath. He had intended to resume searching the studio tomorrow while Ursula helped Stacy study, but his idea to pin down Ursula's location via Stacy's text message had failed. After visiting the supermarket, he'd called Sula on his hands-free, but she hadn't answered. Her earlier comment about the contact sheets suggested she might have come here before returning home, so he'd called back his mom saying a friend had contacted him for a beer.

He jabbed a thumb toward the banged-up video camera. "Where'd you get that? Is it VHS?" The acronym for Video Home System. Flipping old-school. As a kid, Gabe had owned several animated movies on the large cassettes while his dad had collected seasons of *Columbo*, a TV series about a bumbling detective who trapped suspects into confessing crimes. Many a pleasant McKenzie family evening had been spent chuckling over the lead actor's comedic performance.

Ursula nodded. "It was hidden behind Mackie's portrait." She opened the videotape compartment. "The notepad on the table was in here." She closed the slot again. "I think Mackie might be black-mailing women with sex tapes he secretly recorded. Or he *was* blackmailing them. If he still is, he's hiding the evidence some-where else."

Gabe held up his hands. "Stop. You're slathering prints all over the evidence." He yanked latex gloves from an inside jacket pocket and pulled them on. "I'll take that." He grabbed the camera.

"Hey!" Ursula reached for the notepad. "I'm just trying to help."

"I know you are," he said before her fingertips contacted the cover. "But don't touch anything." He retrieved another pair of gloves. "Put these on."

Rosy color burned high on her cheeks. "I deserve to wear the great Sherlock's gloves?"

"We don't want more fingerprints contaminating evidence, do we, Nancy?" He could reference literary detectives with the best of them.

"Look, I'm sorry. I suppose we can't wipe off my prints without destroying your uncle's."

"Or someone else's. Put on the gloves, do what I say, and tell me everything you know."

She snapped on the gloves with a pout. "Why are you so snotty?"

He gazed at her injured expression. He hadn't meant to ream her out. He just wanted her safe. Softening his tone, he said, "Ursula, I told you. I don't want you getting hurt. Who knows where these bizarre incidents might lead?"

Her chin raised. "I found the camera. That has to be worth something." She picked up the notepad between three latex-clad fingertips.

A smile quirked his lips. She was cute in sleuth-mode. "I would have located it eventually. Mackie showed up after you and Stacy left this morning. I slipped out front before he saw me."

"But you didn't find the camera," she reiterated. "I did."

"All right, you done good. Happy?" Gingerly holding the old video camera in gloved hands to prevent further destruction of latent prints, he peered into the wall cavity. "Find any tapes?"

She shook her head.

"I'll search after we put back this stuff." He set the camera in the cavity. "Was it like this?"

"Yes."

"Thanks." He snapped his fingers. "Pass me the notepad."

"The most recent date is over two years old," she said, handing it over. "I didn't notice Jasmine's name or the names of Mackie's other ex-girlfriends."

"Gotcha." Gabe glanced at the wall cavity. "I wonder why he used VHS and not a smaller camera?" Or a digital recording device.

Ursula shrugged. "He's weird."

That was an understatement. "How many of my uncle's girl-friends have you met?"

"Including Jasmine? Four or five in six months, I guess."

"Any redheads?"

"No. Mostly blondes. Why?"

"Just clarifying." Gabe opened the notepad. He wouldn't mention Red. "How about brunettes?"

Her lips pursed. "One. She didn't last long."

Nodding, he scrutinized the names: Lisa Sanders. Lynette Lafleur. Kathy Martin. Miki Timmins. Desiree Lewis. Mary Bliss.

Most sounded like strippers. They probably were.

"Without the tapes, I can't be sure, but it looks like blackmail," Gabe said. Even if his hypothesis was correct and some of the women listed in the notepad worked in the sex trade, that didn't mean they wanted family members or other people in their lives exposed to the tapes. A peeler might have elderly parents living in another state or teens who thought their mom brought in colossal tips as a cocktail waitress. A woman's occupation didn't preclude her right to privacy.

Ursula sneaked a peek around his arm. "What should we do about it, Sherlock?"

"Well, Nancy, we have a disturbed scene of a possible crime featuring a dusty video camera, a mangled notepad, and, so far, no tapes. The alleged blackmail appears like it's no longer occurring."

Her forehead puckered. "So your uncle will get away with it?"

"Not necessarily." He tapped the pad. "I can vouch this is his handwriting."

"Me too. Let's call the cops."

He shook his head. "We can't prove anything without the tapes, and I doubt they're in the building. I went through Mackie's desk, the bookshelves, the backroom." He didn't bring up the S&M cupboard. She might barf all over his shoes.

"He has this hiding place. He must have others."

Gabe inhaled roughly. The person responsible for the vandalism and threats might return tonight to stage another dirty trick and his sexy version of Nancy Drew wanted to argue?

"I realize that," he stated. "I'll conduct a thorough search after you leave."

"I'm not going anywhere."

His neck stiffened. "You shouldn't be here in the first place. You said you were going home."

"I changed my mind."

"Obviously. Why?"

She glanced at the floor, mumbling something about Stacy.

His fingers dug into the notepad. "Ursula, at the minimum, you have to concede something about her isn't right. Did you know her margaritas tonight didn't contain alcohol?"

Sula's eyes rounded. "No."

"According to the server, both drinks were virgins. After you left, Stacy pretended to get drunk on booze-less cocktails. Before I knew it, I was driving her home."

"Did you ask her about the drinks?"

"Yeah. In the parking lot. I was worried someone spiked them, but she spouted a story about sugar highs and biting her tongue."

A smile curved Ursula's mouth.

"What's funny? The point is, other than needing transportation, she didn't want to be alone with me. She might suspect I'm onto her."

Ursula perched a hand on her hip. "Gabe," she admonished in a manner a mother might use with a clueless teenager. "Stacy doesn't have a lot of experience with men. You make her nervous. She's crushing on you. Except she thinks you want me."

He did want Sula. But her safety trumped his needs.

"Is Mackie's calculator in your car?" A muscle in his jaw flexed.

"Yes, Stacy texted me about it." Ursula's dark blue eyes narrowed. "Were you behind that idea for her to take pictures of it once I was home?"

"I felt you were more likely to respond to her than me," he admitted.

"Hmm. Pretty accurate." She inspected her fingernails. "Stacy bought a new ink pad at the mall. She tossed out the old one there."

"Damn it." He rubbed his whiskered cheek. "I wanted to check the ink. If the pad didn't need replacing, her reasons for messing around in my uncle's office this morning become more suspicious."

Ursula smoothed a fingertip over the middle nail on one hand. "Isn't that a stretch?"

He puffed out a breath. "I thought I asked you to go home."

"And I thought I said I wouldn't."

"Fine," he grumbled. "Stay for now." If they continued arguing, they would be rehashing the issue until the sun rose. "Find a pen and paper."

Excitement gleamed in her eyes. "What are we doing?" Moving to his uncle's desk, she tore a page from a large yellow pad.

"Putting everything back like you found it. Photocopying the notepad might damage the pages. I'll take pictures as backup, but first I need you to write down the information as I read it to you."

Remarkably, she complied, transferring the details to the yellow sheet within a couple of minutes.

"Now what?" she asked.

"The pictures. Using camera *and* phone."

"You're meticulous."

"If the phone or camera fails for some unforeseen reason, I'll have the other." He set the sheet on the table and retrieved his compact digital. Ursula held the notepad while he snapped. They repeated the process with his phone. Finished, he lifted the video camera off the shelf and slipped the notepad into the tape compartment. "Is this how it was?"

She shook her head. "That's upside down."

"You do it." He handed her the pad and video camera. "Handle them gently."

"Aw, you trust me." She adjusted the pad then positioned the camera within the wall cavity.

"You're positive that's how you found it?" Gabe asked.

"Yes."

He snapped more pictures. On the yellow paper, he sketched out the scene of the secret cavity and folded the sheet and slid it into a pocket in his jacket.

Ursula shut the wall panel. "I don't get it. Why aren't we calling the cops?"

"Not enough evidence. As private citizens, we're not obligated to report our findings. Until I learn if what we uncovered tonight is connected to the vandalism and threats, I'm keeping it under wraps." He stepped around her and hefted the huge portrait.

"*My* findings," she insisted.

Shoulders rigid, he hung the picture. None of the women listed in the notepad matched the ex-girlfriend names Mackie had provided, which, in itself, wasn't surprising. The man's relationships appeared to last as long as a guppy in a shark tank. But tonight's possible evidence of illegal activity added another potentially dangerous layer to the case.

"Don't fight me on this," he told Ursula. "If I learn one of the women in the notepad is behind the shit that's been happening around here, I'll call the Seattle police. Otherwise, I want the old blackmail undisturbed. I can't have my uncle getting suspicious."

"Good plan. I like it."

He didn't require her approval. "Your part in my investigation ends here."

She crossed her arms over her sweater. "You might want to reconsider that, Sherlock."

"I doubt it, Nancy."

"Too bad. I could help you. Oh, well," she said in an unconcerned tone. "You'll see things my way sooner or later. For the sake of *our* case, preferably sooner."

He cut her a glance. "What aren't you telling me?"

She smiled like a cardsharp holding trump. "I know more."

"What more?" He ground his molars. Why couldn't she understand he was trying to *protect* her? He needed every shred of information she'd uncovered.

"Tut-tut, Sherlock. You'll have to work on your communication skills, or we'll never get anywhere." She gestured at the portrait. "Don't forget to take a picture of the picture. The hole for the video camera is hidden in your uncle's, um, lap."

Gabe studied the portrait. So it was. *Uncle Vic, you have an inflated opinion of yourself.*

"That's your more?" He snapped the portrait with his smartphone.

Smile gleeful, she shook her head. "There's something in the darkroom too. Or have you searched it?"

"Not yet." Mackie and Red had interrupted him before he'd had the chance. "What did you find?"

"Are we partners?" she asked.

He stared her in the eyes. "No."

One of her shoulders flounced. "Then why should I show you?"

"Forget it. I'll find whatever *you* found myself." He marched into the hall, bad leg bitching.

"Don't you want more pictures of the picture?" Ursula called. "Your camera has the memory card—excellent backup."

"You take them." He'd left his tiny digital camera on the side table. "And *stay there.*" Out of trouble.

Entering the unlocked darkroom, he flipped the first switch his fingers encountered. A red glow illuminated the confined space. He located a second switch on the door's other side. A low-wattage bulb shone. He turned off the red light.

Ursula breezed into the darkroom. "Partner, I know you said to stay behind, but I'm too efficient. Also, as you're about to learn, extremely helpful." She lifted a hand. "Before you begin shouting orders, don't worry, I took additional pictures of the picture. I took pictures of the shadow box in the hallway too. You were right. It was best I take them. I am the professional, after all."

Gabe itched to smack a palm against his forehead. To clutch his skull between both hands and give it a good shake. She drove him crazy, and her flippant tone didn't help. He couldn't concentrate when she screwed around, trying to prove her point. Moments ago, he'd strode straight past the display case his uncle must have modified to cover the back of the secret wall cavity.

"My camera?" He held out his hand, accepting the device and jamming it into a jacket pocket. "Thanks. You were in the darkroom tonight?"

She nodded. "Looking for processing supplies."

"Ah." He absorbed that nugget of information. "So, after leaving me at the pub with Stacy, you decided to develop film." He hadn't intended to mention the mysterious lump in her front jeans pocket, but now he directed his gaze to the two-inch bulge. "Is that the film in question, or are you happy to see me?"

A blush splashed her face. "Ha-ha."

"The pictures on that film wouldn't happen to involve me, would they?"

She glowered. "I haven't developed *either* film from that night."

Which, rough and dirty, occurred forty-eight hours ago. Considering yesterday was Thanksgiving, she'd hardly had the time.

"But you thought about developing *this* film." Otherwise, why carry around the canister instead of leaving it in her purse? He hadn't noticed the lump at the pub. He grazed a finger over her jeans pocket, and she shivered as if the light caress tickled or aroused her. "Nancy, I'm flattered. Should we develop the film now? Could get kinky."

She stepped back, hands fisting at her sides. "I *planned* to process the roll so I could burn the negatives afterward. I can't tell you how much satisfaction that would bring me."

He stifled a smile. "There's only one film in your pocket. Where's the other?"

She ignored his question. "When I looked for the processing supplies, they were out of place. Now I'm wondering if someone moved them on purpose, to irritate me or Mackie, or whoever checked first."

Gabe paused. "Sounds like something the suspect would do." He glanced around the room. "Does my uncle develop film anymore?"

"I don't know. I don't think so, but sometimes he comes in here."

"Okay. If one of the women listed in the notepad moved the supplies as part of an overall scheme to harass my uncle, maybe she has reason to believe he still uses film from time to time."

"It's possible. But there's more." Sidestepping him, Ursula crouched in front of the lower cupboards and curved her long hair behind one ear. A tiny ruby earring adorned the lobe. "This is the chemical cupboard." She looked up. "When I opened it, I discovered paint tins in the same colors used to deface the window the morning after Halloween." Hands clad in latex, she opened the cupboard. "The tins are behind the supplies. Each can matches colors from the words and paintings." She pointed.

Gabe hunkered beside her, butt aching. He spied the paint. *Well, well.*

They remained crouched. "Did you take pictures of the painted window we could use to prove the connection?" he asked. "My uncle says he didn't take any."

"No, it didn't occur to me, and it should have." She shook her head as if aggravated with her lack of foresight. "Mackie was incredibly rude that day, ordering me to scrape off the paint when I had a full roster of appointments booked. I barely spoke to him the rest of the day." She moistened her lips. "Stacy wound up cleaning off the paint, and she kept her distance from him too. But, Gabe, the T-shirt shop next door only opened in July. Mackie had words with loitering teenagers over the summer and even as late as the end of September. We thought the window-painting was related."

He couldn't fault her logic. "Did you touch the cans when you found them tonight?"

"Before you gave me the gloves? Yes. Sorry."

"So, your fingerprints are on the cans. Unless the suspect—or suspects—wore gloves, we can assume their prints are on them as well. Not to mention prints from the clerks, stockers, and customers at the store where the paint was bought."

"I guess, but here's another thing. I used the darkroom the Saturday after Halloween to develop pictures of Kim from the party she didn't want me leaving at an in-store place. Gabe, the tins *weren't* here then."

He swore. "Halloween was on a Wednesday, correct?"

She nodded.

"There must have been cell phones all over that party. Why would Kim care if her picture got taken?"

"Like a lot of people who attended, because of her job. The host had a no-social-media rule in case the party got a little wild, which it did. Anyone who brought a phone checked it at the door. I had a disposable camera with built-in film. Those and instant cameras without Wi-Fi interfaces were allowed."

He nodded, glute clenching. "My leg is killing me." He pushed himself up. "Leave the cupboard open." He removed his gloves.

Standing, Ursula tugged the latex off her fingers and handed the gloves to him. "Let me guess. We take more pictures now."

"Yes, but don't handle anything out of the ordinary." He crammed both pairs of gloves into a jeans pocket, retrieved his camera, and snapped away. "Back to the fingerprints," he said, thinking out loud. "We also have to consider those of whoever stored the cans in this cupboard. Which might be the same person who painted the window. Or it might be someone else."

Ursula rolled her ruby earring between two fingers. "How could it be someone else?"

"Just brainstorming. What if the suspect *didn't* paint the window? Maybe kids painted it but didn't realize the suspect was watching them. Or the kids left the paint behind, the suspect came along, saw an opportunity, and seized it. Then later, after you developed your pictures, the suspect placed the tins in the cupboard, hoping they'd be discovered."

"That's a lot of maybes, Gabe."

"Maybes and coincidences rule the world."

Her gaze grew reflective. "Could Mackie have done this?"

"Defaced *his* window then stored the paint where he must have realized you'd find it? I wouldn't rule it out. But what's his motivation?"

"To scare me out of buying the place?"

"Why sign a contract then?"

"I don't know. Quite frankly, I'm baffled."

"It's a puzzler," Gabe agreed, walking around her. Their sleeves brushed, and she stepped aside again. To give him room or to gain physical distance because he'd hurt her with his cover? Before they left tonight, he needed to determine how they would proceed. As much as he regretted causing her pain, she planned to tutor Stacy tomorrow. The receptionist might ask about their relationship. What would Ursula say?

"I suppose the paint isn't enough evidence to take to the police," she murmured, toying with her rings.

"Not without proof linking it to the painted window, which my uncle didn't report, by the way." Gabe returned his camera to his jacket. "If we like the one-person scenario, whoever painted the window has access to these locked cupboards and most likely wanted the cans discovered."

"If it wasn't me and it wasn't Mackie, then it must be—" Ursula rubbed her temple. "I don't want it to be Stacy."

"I know you don't." He touched her shoulder. "I'm not pinning this on Stacy. I'll also follow up on the blackmail names. Those women have excellent motivation to pester my uncle. Maybe the suspect is a locksmith." He grinned.

She did not smile. "Why wait two or three years to get back at him?"

"I have no idea. But I plan to find out." He tipped up her chin with his knuckles. "Hey," he said gently, gazing into her thickly-lashed eyes. "I'll need your cooperation."

"Not to stick my nose into the case?" She retrieved her keys from the counter and locked the chemical cupboard. "I hear you, Gabe. I just don't agree."

He trailed her into the hall.

Locking the darkroom, she said over her shoulder, "I found the paint and camera, and I have a stake in this business. You know how important it is to me, what it might mean for my family. I will not bow out."

"You don't have to bow out." Gabe accompanied her to Mackie's office. She locked it.

"Yeah, but your definition of not bowing out is playing along with your cover, doing whatever you ask, and *only* what you ask."

Crossing the hall, she strode into the staffroom and screamed. "Omigod! It's the mouse again! It ran under the table." Keys clattering onto linoleum, she tented her hands over her nose. Her breasts and knees jiggled as she bounced up and down. "It must have come in from the alley. It's been living in Mackie's cereal cupboard. Poor thing, I'll leave a saucer of puffed rice until I can return with a live trap." She inched open the cupboard, and four mice scampered out. "Gross!" She scrambled onto a chair.

Chuckling, Gabe closed the staffroom door so the scattering rodents wouldn't race into the hall. "Women. You can run a country, but you can't stand the sight of a few mice."

Ursula squealed. "How did they get inside without Mackie or Stacy or me noticing?"

"Maybe the momma and daddy had babies."

"In the two days since I've been in this room? They're huge."

Kneeling, he peered into the cupboard. At least ten remarkably tame mice—none babies—gorged on cereal leaking from a ripped box. Tiny rodent turds littered the area.

"When did you see the first mouse?" He shut the cupboard to prevent further escapees.

"Tonight." She squealed again as the fugitive mice scurried around under the table. "I was in the darkroom when I heard them scratching. I thought someone was here."

"You may be right." Gabe stood. "I hate to say this, but I don't see how more than a dozen mice miraculously found their way inside the studio. Someone must have placed them in this cupboard. Yes, maybe even *while* you were in the darkroom."

Her fingers splayed. "That's creepy."

To put it mildly. "Buying mice to simulate an infestation fits with defacing the window." He wasn't convinced the mice were tied to the inert grenade or threatening note, but he wouldn't share those thoughts. She was too freaked out. "I'll call exterminators tomorrow morning for a rush weekend job. My uncle will have to shut up and pay."

"I don't want the little mice killed!"

His mouth kicked up at one corner. "I'll ask the exterminator if he can make alternate arrangements. *No* promises. We can't have customers arriving Monday morning and discovering mice swarming the place. What if the suspect returns over the weekend and lets them out of this room?" Picking her keys off the floor and tossing them on the table beside her purse, he advanced toward her chair. "Come down from there."

Her fingers whisked to her face. "I can't!"

He grasped her hips. "Don't be afraid. I've got you." The chair positioned her a foot above him, her breasts about level with his nose. He looked up at her gorgeous face and sexy, mussed hair.

The spark between them hadn't died. He saw it in the midnight-blue depths of her eyes, heard it in her intake of breath. They'd shared passion Wednesday night, but she meant so much more to him. She represented more. A future, putting down roots. *Returning* to his roots.

A sense of finally capturing the elusive *something* he'd longed for his entire life.

He didn't know why Ursula, of all women, made him feel these things. He only knew she did.

"Gabe..." Her hips squirmed as their gazes locked. "I need to find out who's behind this."

"Sweetheart, you're afraid of a few mice."

Her eyes flashed. "I'm afraid of nothing." She peeled his fingers off her jeans. "I watched my house burn to the ground when I was ten. I might startle, but I don't scare. I want to help with *our* case. If you don't agree, I'll investigate on my own. Don't think I won't."

He groaned. "Is this all we're going to talk about until the case is solved?"

"Agree to work *with* me and I'll dazzle you with my conversational repertoire." She climbed off the chair. As she gathered her keys and purse, a mouse ripped past her shoes. She didn't flinch. "The sooner we learn who's responsible, the sooner I can return to concentrating on building the studio's reputation so it won't become an albatross around my neck when I buy it."

Gabe raked a hand through his hair. If he refused to allow her to work with him, she *would* snoop on her own, like she had tonight. He'd only known her nine days, but he recognized an unstoppable force of nature when he encountered one.

What if the suspect had realized she was in the darkroom tonight? If the culprit had confronted her? Hurt her? He never would have forgiven himself.

He needed to protect her, but it was becoming glaringly

apparent that she needed to feel like she was contributing to the case. Any other option could place her in greater danger.

"All right," he said gruffly. "You win. You can help."

"So we're partners?"

"You're my trainee. We'll see how it goes from there."

"Yes! You won't regret this."

He doubted that. But he felt backed against a wall. At least this way he could keep an eye on her, guarding her safety as much as possible while, hopefully, regaining her trust.

It wasn't a guarantee, by any means, but it was a start.

Twenty

STACY'S KNEE brushed Ursula's as the girl tidied her study gear on the coffee table then relaxed against the sofa cushions. "Ursula, you were a fantastic help." Stacy glanced at Kim occupying the easy chair. "You too, Kim. Thanks to you both, I'm gonna kill this exam."

"No problem," Kim said.

"You're welcome," Ursula responded, skin twitching. As far as Stacy knew, the girl's visit to the apartment this morning related solely to their blossoming "friendship." However, as Ursula and Gabe discussed before parting ways last night, Ursula needed to monitor Stacy's habits for reasons that had zilch to do with becoming her buddy. In the end, learning whether Stacy was hassling Mackie was worth a little deception, which struck Ursula as disturbingly similar to Gabe not telling *her* about his cop background.

Her face warmed. Gabe hadn't mentioned the discrepancy, but she'd obsessed about it throughout her muddled sleep—when she wasn't dreaming of his hands on her hips or the intensity of his gaze when their eyes had met. He had called her *sweetheart* yesterday, and she hadn't objected. She should have said something, insisted he not dub her Sula or sweetheart or honey, or anything resembling an endearment. She couldn't allow herself to get swept up in him again.

When it came down to it, he was a great guy. They both cared for their families. They each worked hard. And, wow, every time their bodies grazed, a sizzle zapped from point of contact straight to her toes…and other regions.

But none of that mattered now. Jumping into bed with him had reinforced a lesson she'd thought she'd learned long ago. She wasn't built for impulsive choices. It wasn't in her Scott DNA. Unlike her last two slacker boyfriends, Gabe was a stand-up guy. But the fact remained, she operated best when she remained focused. And that, first and foremost, entailed solving the case so she could move forward with her plans to buy the studio and help her family. Any other decisions, especially those involving her heart, needed to wait.

Kim pushed out of the easy chair. "Let's break out refreshments. Green tea all around?"

"Since when do you drink green tea?" Ursula asked her friend. Or any tea. She and Kim were latte aficionados.

"Since last night." An enigmatic smile flirted on Kim's lips.

Stacy stood. "I love green tea. Can I help?"

Ursula shook her head. "Stay here. I need to speak to Kim about the, uh, internet bill."

"Oh, roommate issues." Stacy plopped back onto the couch. "I can't wait to experience those." She plucked a magazine off the side table.

Ursula accompanied Kim to the kitchen. "You're chipper today," she murmured, leaning close to her roomie.

"Why wouldn't I be?" Kim fetched the teapot from a cupboard.

"For one thing, you shut off your phone last night. Not like you. When I called Deni, she said you were in a bad mood." She smiled. "Okay, that's sorta like you."

Kim sighed. "Can you blame me for being a bit grouchy?" She whispered, "It's noon, and the happy couple is still asleep. I swear, the sounds coming from Deni's room last night…" She filled the kettle with water and plugged it in. "I know she's in love"—Kim rolled her eyes—"but I can only stand so much of those two making whoopee, especially now that I'm giving up smokes. My nerves are shot."

"You're really trying to quit?" This morning while Kim was in the shower, Ursula noticed the utter absence of cigarette butts in the makeshift ashtray on the sundeck.

She nodded. "Like Deni said, if I want clean lungs by her wedding, I need to get serious now. I went cold turkey."

"That's great. How long has it been?"

Kim glanced at her watch. "Thirty hours."

Ursula chuckled. "You're in pretty good spirits for someone going through nicotine withdrawal."

"Wellll, I might have purchased an e-cig kit. All right, I did. The idea is to wean myself off the flavor of tobacco. Then I'll work on kicking the dreaded nicotine."

"Kim, that's wonderful. I'm proud of you." Ursula located the cups and a new box of green tea.

"I'll need a lot of support."

"You've got it."

Kim closed the cupboards. "My friend Amy wants to move in after Deni leaves, but she's a raving anti-nicotine banshee. If I don't quit, we'll have to find another roommate willing to take her chances with the master bedroom." She chose a teabag from the box. "Then I realized if I'm stopping smoking, why not experiment with other positive lifestyle choices? I bought the tea on my way to the movies with Amy last night." Her gaze darted to behind Ursula's left shoulder. "We have company," she whispered.

Ursula glanced around to see Stacy standing by the communal desk. When had the girl left the living room?

"Are these pictures of the Halloween party you guys went to?" Stacy asked, wiggling the envelope Ursula had placed on the desktop earlier. As part of her agreement with Gabe to double-check Stacy's Halloween alibi, she'd positioned two pictures peeking from the envelope as bait. All well and good, but she'd hoped to manipulate the party into their conversation without upsetting Kim.

No such luck. Her roommate charged to the desk, scowling.

"Urs, we agreed to store these," Kim practically shouted.

"I thought we'd do more culling first. Don't worry. I shredded the shots showing you at your worst." Kim had over-imbibed.

"Can I look?" Stacy asked.

Kim muttered, "I suppose."

Stacy rifled through the photos while Kim supervised. Ursula stepped to the whistling kettle, explaining, "Stace, remember I told you Kim, her friend Amy, and I went as the three witches from *Macbeth*? Kim's nose melted off when she dunked for apples in a hot tub."

Stacy laughed.

"I thought it was a cauldron," Kim said, touching a photo. "And that mountain-of-makeup witch nose was covering a zit, I'll have you know."

"You look cute, Kim." Stacy examined the pictures, sounding wistful. "I wish I'd had a fun Halloween. I just handed out candy with my sister then went to bed."

Eavesdropping from the kitchen counter, Ursula prepared the tea. Stacy had related the same tale of lonely woe at work the day following the party, before she'd cleaned the painted window. If Gabe required further confirmation Stacy hadn't left her sister's house during Halloween night, Ursula would have to formulate a way to verify the alibi with Shelly. If nothing else, Ursula could mention the woman's dry-cleaning bill again, ask for her cell number, and proceed from there.

The tea steeped and piping hot, they resettled in the living room. Their phones lined the coffee table like soldiers at the ready. Ursula blew on her hot mug of tea. Her phone rang.

Closest to the devices, Kim glanced at the display. "It's Gabe. Want to answer?"

Stalling, Ursula sipped her tea. Stacy operated under the mistaken assumption that she still possessed a mad-on for the guy. Meanwhile, her roommates had no idea their relationship had progressed to a personal level—then back down again.

"I don't know," she mumbled. "After last night..." How to complete that sentence?

"Talk to him," Stacy urged, hands curled around her mug. "You and Gabe work together. What did he do that was so awful anyway?"

"Yeah, Urs, what did he do?" Kim asked, curiosity gleaming in her eyes.

"I don't want to talk about it." Ursula gulped her tea, scorching her mouth. Now she had to devise a reason?

"I see." Kim nodded knowingly. "We need to have a chat, Ursie-Boo."

No doubt Kim would grill her about the Three Gets Plan: Get Gabe, Get Laid, Get Out.

In a way, Ursula had succeeded. Except the Getting Out part was proving a challenge. She hadn't expected to like him so damn much.

Regardless of his deception, she did like him.

A lot.

She flipped a hand in the air. "Let it go to voicemail."

"Not a chance," Kim replied. "He hurt you somehow. I can tell by your face. *I'll* deal with the hot, jerky knob-brain. Has your passcode change?"

Ursula shook her head.

"All righty then." Putting down her mug, she picked up Ursula's cell. "Gabe, it's Kim," she answered in a snooty tone. "Yeah, she's here…Stacy is too. Just finished tutoring…No, you can't…Because I said so…Okay, wait…I said, hang on." She reported to Ursula, "Some guy named Norm called the studio. Gabe is there borrowing a toolbox for his mom. He heard Norm leaving a message on the machine and picked up. Says it's important."

Stacy straightened. "Norm is from the Real Men shoot," she informed Kim. "He's a model."

Ursula set down her mug. Norm had her cell phone number. Why would he leave a message on the studio answering machine during a holiday weekend?

Kim passed her the phone. Standing and placing the cell to her ear, Ursula affected aggravation as she spoke to Gabe. "What's going on?"

"Good morning." His deep voice swirled ribbons of awareness in her veins. "I take it Stacy is close by."

"Yeah," she grumbled, turning and walking to the desk. "Norm called?"

"A few minutes ago. Sounded frazzled. Said he mixed up his cell phone contacts, thought he was calling you and reached the studio instead."

"Okay." There was one mystery solved.

Gabe continued, "Looks like Melissa left town with Juno this morning."

"Wasn't she going tomorrow?" Doing her best to ignore the butterflies fluttering inside her as his voice caressed her ear, Ursula paced back and forth between the desk and small dining table, arm across her middle.

"They had a fight," Gabe said. The connection crackled. "Norm wanted to pull out of the shoot, and I guess she hit the roof. She'd already told a couple of friends and her mom about it."

Ursula slapped a hand to her chest. "He can't pull out." Norm's indecision was becoming a serious issue. Her deadline was next Friday. *Six days.*

"Not to worry. He isn't. I talked him down."

"Omigosh, you had me worried for a minute there. I don't have time to pass another model by the editor." Committing her personal hours to developing her detective skills had resulted in a major crunch.

Voice sensual and husky in her ear, Gabe murmured, "He asked if there's any way we can do the hot tub photos today instead of Monday night. He hopes moving up the session will calm Melissa when she calls him later. I know we have a lot to accomplish this weekend, but can we squeeze him in?"

Ursula couldn't see where they had a choice. What if Norm wavered again? She needed his images on her camera card ASAP.

"Sounds manageable," she replied, slipping a glance to Kim and Stacy. The women were thumbing through a magazine Stacy had picked up earlier and debating the merits of a sex quiz. Ursula asked Gabe, "Is there anything else?"

"Yeah. When Kim answered your phone, I heard her explain why I'm at the studio," he said quietly. "I'm not here to borrow the toolbox. The exterminator arrives at two."

Ursula maintained her "peeved with men" attitude. "I don't want to hear about it." The innocent mice!

Gabe chuckled. "I fabricated the excuse in case Stacy tried listening in. How did she react to the news about Norm? Say 'yes' if she said or did something unusual. Say 'no' if she didn't."

Clever, Gabe. Mackie stored the toolbox in the old darkroom. If Stacy was their culprit and had stockpiled the paint, wouldn't she have flinched or recoiled or something when Kim said Gabe was at the studio getting the tools?

"*No.*" Ursula emphasized the word. Stacy had perked up when Kim mentioned Norm's name, but the girl coordinated studio appointments, so the behavior fit.

"Good," Gabe responded. "Unless she's an amazing actress, minimal reaction works in her favor. You'll be happy to hear I searched the reception desk, but couldn't find evidence linking her to the vandalism and threats."

Ursula darted a glance at Stacy, who smiled from the sofa. Feigning frustration, Ursula snapped into her cell, "That's too bad for you, isn't it, Gabe?"

Humor lacing his voice, he continued, "I staked out the studio until four a.m. No one showed."

"That's a relief." Ursula paced to the desk.

"Not really. If someone had come along, at least we'd know who to tail."

Ah. So sue her, she was new to sleuthing. "Right."

"Do you want to book a time with Norm for tonight, or shall I?"

"*I'll* do it," she said with an extra dose of bogus irritation.

"Make it around six, if that's okay. We'll leave at five. I need to look into some names on our list before and after the mouse guy comes."

"If you want to rehash *that*, we'll do so tonight." Disconnecting, she slammed her cell onto the desk and returned to her tea.

Stacy adjusted her glasses on her pert nose. "Are you giving him another chance?"

Kim, chewing a fingernail, peered up from the magazine.

Ursula sliced a hand across her neck, terminating the subject. "It's work stuff. Nothing else."

❧

Following the evening hot tub session at Norm's, Gabe packed the photography equipment in the Dobson family room while his new sleuthing partner nuked hot chocolate in the microwave for their reluctant model.

Norm shuffled into the room as Gabe zipped the duffel bag. The man had changed out of his wet trunks into pajamas, slippers, and a bathrobe—snug as a toddler at seven p.m. Gabe glanced away, hiding a smile. His gaze caught on Ursula exiting the kitchen.

"Here you go," she said, handing Norm a mug topped with miniature marshmallows. "This will warm you right up."

"Thanks," Norm replied in a monotone. He sat on the couch and sipped the hot beverage.

"Norm, you did great." Gabe stuffed lenses into camera bags. "What made you think you couldn't go through with the shoot?" A drizzle had fallen throughout the appointment on the Dobsons' covered deck. Norm had worried the shower would ruin the pictures, but Ursula convinced him the photography lights glinting off glistening raindrops enhanced the atmosphere.

Norm sighed. "Auditioning was Melissa's idea, as you know. I didn't want to do it at all. But she told my sister-in-law, and then my brother found out. The ribbing I've suffered..." He looked at Ursula. "You really think she'll like the pictures?"

"Absolutely. In fact, after your brother sees how good you look in the magazine, he'll wish *he* had auditioned. So will his wife."

"As long as Melissa is happy, I don't care what my brother thinks anymore."

A fat gray cat strutted out from behind the couch and twined between Norm's legs. While Gabe finished packing, Norm bent to stroke the furbag. Pictures of the Dobsons with Juno or the big cat littered the tables and upright piano. Countless dog and cat toys, sleeping baskets, and a six-level cat perch dominated the family room.

"All set." Gabe hoisted the duffel bag.

Ursula collected her jacket and purse from a chair. "Norm, can I use your bathroom before we leave? I'd like to fix my hair."

The man nodded.

"Which door is it?" she asked, starting down the hall.

"On the right."

Setting down the equipment sack again, Gabe sank onto an overstuffed armchair. Ursula sashayed toward the bathroom, jacket and purse in hand. She wore the same dark blue jeans and white blouse as the day they'd met, and, man, her sassy behind filled out the snug denim to perfection.

Her positive outlook throughout the last couple of hours gave him hope their temporary PI arrangement might work. During the drive to Norm's, he'd told her about the S&M cupboard. Now that they were working together, he needed to keep her informed, and he expected the same respect from her.

He glanced at Norm. The man gazed into his mug.

"What's the cat's name?" Gabe asked to foster conversation.

"Hmm? Lillian."

Gabe's top lip twitched. "Isn't that sort of human for a cat?"

"I named her after my mom."

Ookay. Gabe drummed his fingers on the armrest. A moment later, Ursula returned, mouth puckered as if she'd swallowed a lemon.

"You said the door on the right?" she asked Norm, zipping Gabe an unreadable glance. "I assumed you meant the first door. Sorry, Norm. I entered the wrong room."

The man's face glared red. "My fault. I should have been more clear." He stood with his mug. "*I'm* sorry you had to see that mess. When Melissa is angry, she can get unruly."

Gabe lifted his eyebrows. What had Ursula seen?

She slipped on her coat. "Let's go."

"You don't want to use the bathroom?" Norm asked.

"I can wait." She lifted her jacket hood over her head.

Gabe collected his coat and the equipment bags. They said goodbye and hurried into the rainy night.

At the curb, Gabe stashed the bags in Reba's back seat while Ursula unlocked the passenger door and climbed in behind the wheel. Cold rain splattering his scalp, Gabe squeezed into the compact automobile.

"Melissa can get unruly?" he asked. "What was that about?"

She started the engine. "Remember Norm wrote on his forms that he makes his own fishing lures? I opened his hobby room by mistake." She shook her head. "What a mess. Supplies and tackle boxes strewn everywhere. I think Melissa trashed his stuff."

"You're kidding. She doesn't look the type."

Gabe's detective trainee flipped off her wet hood and switched on the headlights. "Appearances can be deceiving. We both know that." The car chugged down the narrow residential street.

"Still, I wouldn't have pegged her as the sort. Getting upset is one thing, but trashing your spouse's possessions takes things to another level." The cop in him wondered, could someone associated with the Real Men shoot be their culprit? Someone like…Melissa? Was it possible she had a past her husband didn't know about? Did that past include Mackie?

He shifted on his seat. This case had the potential to spin off in countless directions.

"What's your take on her?" he asked Ursula.

Her eyes widened. "You're not suggesting we add *Melissa* to our suspect list?"

"If the notepad names don't lead anywhere, I wouldn't dismiss the possibility. It's a long shot, but—"

"Wow." Ursula returned her attention to the road. "Come to think of it, we don't actually know where she's gone."

"Precisely. Is she visiting her sister or just pretending to?"

Ursula checked her side mirrors. "She pestered Norm into responding to the perverted-sounding ad, and he tried backing out." Her fingertips fluttered on the steering wheel. "But why leave town—or pretend to—without tidying the fishing lures? She knew about the hot tub session. The only change was moving it to tonight."

Gabe shrugged. "Maybe she destroys stuff during their fights, and Norm cleans up. Who would guess you or I would mistakenly enter that room?" He waved a hand. "Don't mind me. Sometimes I can't help myself. They've been married fourteen years and where would she get studio keys?"

Ursula nodded. "Also, they don't have kids. She might have too much time on her hands or maybe unresolved issues stemming from possible fertility issues come to light when things get rough. Some marriages are mired in power struggles."

"To hear the guys from my old precinct talk, more often than not."

"Yes, on TV they say all the time that cops are lousy at marriage."

Gabe chuckled. "My parents managed nicely, thanks."

"Mine get along like salad and dressing."

"Mine were like baskets and balls."

"Mine like cheese and burgers."

"I'm sensing a food theme in your case."

They both laughed.

She drove past a school. Soon, modest homes and playgrounds surrendered space to strip malls and service stations decorated for Christmas. November boasted five Thursdays this year, which had created an early Thanksgiving, but that didn't prevent the average Seattleite from heralding in the holiday season with neon-glaring gusto.

As they continued toward the studio, traffic grew congested. Ursula stopped her car behind several vehicles at a red light. The windshield wipers slashed at rain falling from a moonless sky, a rhythmic *fwap-fwap-fwap*. The heating vents puffed warm air. Her slim hands, adorned with white-tipped fingernails and simple rings, firmly gripped the steering wheel.

While the old engine rumbled, Gabe allowed his gaze to journey over her pink lips and porcelain profile. She was, quite simply, beautiful. The most striking woman he had ever met.

"You said you're twenty-five, right?" he asked.

"Yes." She glanced at him. "Why?"

"You're pretty goal-oriented for someone so young."

Her lips pursed. "And you're how old?"

"Twenty-nine."

"Also goal-oriented, from what I can tell."

"Yeah, but I've had an extra four years to decide what I want. It's the maturity. Drives women wild."

She snorted. The light turned green, and her car lurched forward. She trailed crossovers and SUVs through the busy intersection. "I'm determined," she said, shoulder-checking blind spots before changing lanes. "Is that a crime?"

"It's nice to leave yourself open to possibilities." *Like me.*

"I've left myself open plenty. I didn't finish college, but my brother will." Pride shone in her voice. "Owen wants to be a doctor. The family backs him one hundred percent." Her right hand lifted off the steering wheel. "My parents insisted I try a semester, but I quickly learned studying courses I had no interest in was a waste of time and money."

"I can relate. I have a criminology degree. It was interesting, but I itched to get on the street."

"College graduate, huh?" Her lips quirked. "I'll bet your degree helped your application to police academy."

"Yep. There's a minimum age requirement, so they look at your schooling and life experience, personal conduct, and so forth." But he wanted to talk about her, not himself. "Are your photography skills self-taught or learned from your grandmother?"

"Grandma B encouraged me, but she was more familiar with point-and-shoot cameras." Concentrating on the traffic, Ursula checked the rearview mirror. "After my college experiment, I took a few art school courses, worked, tried to figure things out while helping my parents, traveled a bit, then worked more."

"Where did you travel?" She had an advantage over him there. Aside from a family vacation to British Columbia when he was twelve, he hadn't ventured beyond the United States. Travel was on his "someday" list.

"New Zealand," she said as they approached another light. She wiggled her right thumb, indicating her hammered-silver ring. "I bought this on the south island as a memento. An art school friend and I picked up serving jobs as we explored. I earned enough to finance backpacking both islands. My friend met a guy in Auckland and stayed." She spared him a glance. "The scenery is amazing."

"The guys or the islands?"

She laughed. "Kiwi dudes can be seriously hot, but yes, the countryside. When I came home with my camera glued around my neck, I knew I wanted to become a photographer. I'm not into free-lancing though."

He nodded. She needed security. Not difficult to guess, considering the pain she'd suffered as a child, losing everything, even her cat, in a scary house fire. He understood the pain of loss, the uncertainty of the future, but she had experienced both at a much younger age.

"Do you think not being drawn to freelance work is related to your house burning down?" he asked, intrigued.

"Probing into my psyche now, Mr. College Grad?" Her voice softened. "It's more than that. It's my family. My mom and dad are solid, dependable, sweet. I want that cocoon of safety in my life. I don't want to continually search for it. I just want it *there*."

A dull ache suffusing his glute, Gabe rearranged his position on the passenger seat. "Do you prefer safety in personal relationships too?" The question suddenly felt infused with importance.

"Optimally," she murmured.

Propping his chin on his knuckles, he stared out his window. Sweet, safe, dependable—did she want a man or a cocker spaniel?

What had he expected? That she'd forget the turmoil of the last few days and take a chance on a banged-up former cop? Build a future with him?

Silence settled between them. The car motored along. Eventually, she turned on the radio. Music floated from the speakers. The rain poured harder, and she squinted against the oncoming headlights.

"I can drive," he offered.

She shook her head. "It's okay."

He massaged his thigh. They'd met at the studio before leaving for Norm's. Gabe parked his truck behind the building with the idea that if the suspect returned, he or she would assume someone was inside and not enter—a perfectly rational suggestion on Ursula's part. But now it occurred to him that every time they drove somewhere, she wanted to take the wheel. With her car and with the studio van.

If the interior of his pickup had enough room for the photography equipment, she would probably commandeer it too.

Either she craved control or she didn't trust him.

Or both.

URSULA STEERED Reba into the dimly lit alley and pulled in beside Gabe's beige pickup. The studio's security lights flared on but, otherwise, the area appeared as deserted as it had more than three hours ago, before they'd left for Norm's. After their discussion about their college years, swollen silences and attempts at conversation had filled the return trip while heavy rain and traffic demanded her attention. Ultimately, she'd realized she couldn't concentrate on driving and continue a balanced dialogue, especially when Gabe's proximity played fast and loose with her emotions.

In the cozy confines of her car, his deep voice had sounded as smooth as aged whiskey, as intimate as a caress. Add on that his chiseled jaw sported two or three days' growth of beard, and the Ultra Sexy Gabe Combo proved most drool-worthy. Not to mention a distraction. In the interests of not accidentally rear-ending another vehicle in the crowded intersections, her responses to his anecdotes about his life in LA had shrunk to a series of noncommittal "uh-huhs."

Shifting Reba into park, she asked, "Are you phoning more pet shops tomorrow?" On the way to Norm's, he had mentioned calling several stores today while the exterminator dealt with the mice. So far, no luck tracking down their baddie.

He nodded. "I don't know if it will help. Smart suspects

wouldn't buy all the mice from the same store or restrict themselves to stores within city limits."

"Did you make a list?" Ursula asked over the quiet tones of the radio. "We can split it in half."

"Thanks, but you have your own assignment tomorrow. I need you to get your nails done."

"Excuse me?" Her lips tugged into a smile. "A manicure? Deni usually does mine." Until the studio brought in a profit—under *her* ownership—she couldn't afford the luxury of a salon.

"Then this will be a treat. Desiree Lewis, one of the women in Mackie's notepad, works at a place called Just Nailed. I googled Seattle and her name, found a local spa-and-salon review site. Several entries for Just Nailed mentioned her."

"How do we know she's the same Desiree Lewis?" Ursula asked as Reba idled and the windshield wipers swished back and forth.

Gabe smiled back at her, and her pulse leapt. "Welcome to PI work. We *don't* know for sure yet. But the salon receptionist said *this* Desiree has a cancellation tomorrow. The salon stays open seven days a week during the holidays. I booked an appointment on my credit card pretending it's an early Christmas gift for my girlfriend."

"Sheesh, what a rip. This mythical girlfriend doesn't get a gift *on* Christmas?"

He chuckled. "I'm in the doghouse. I'm bribing my way out. What do you think? Can you handle the interview?"

"Am I the girlfriend?" Ursula's face heated. "I mean, as Ursula Scott? Or what name did you book me under?" She stumbled over her words like a nervous ninth-grader waiting for the cute new boy to ask her to dance.

"Megan Fleming." Gabe's green eyes twinkled. "You work in a supermarket deli."

Ursula studied Reba's RPM dial. *Concentrate on the case, not the color of his eyes.* Blue, green, brown. It made no difference. She was *his* assistant now. She needed to prove her worth.

She looked at him again. "Cool. A fake identity." *Ursula Scott, Super Sleuth, at your service.* For *her* future—and her family's. "But if she's the same Desiree, assuming she's our baddie and has been lurking around the studio, won't she recognize me?"

"That's a risk," he responded. "We can't be certain if the suspect has seen you up close or from a distance, or if they've seen you at all. Maybe he or she only visits the studio at night, when you're usually not around. Maybe they saw you enter the darkroom before they planted the mice. Or you were in there already, and they thought they were alone. A number of variables could apply. You don't have to interview her, Ursula. It's your choice."

To say no and chance him shutting her out of the case? *Nope.*

Hands resting on the bottom curve of the steering wheel, she said, "I want to help."

"All right. But be aware. If this Desiree *is* our suspect and she recognizes you, she might confront you at the salon. Or she might try masking her body language so you won't realize she knows you're using a false name. Keep an eye on her but act as normal as possible. If you have any reason to believe she recognizes you, make an excuse and leave, then call or text me once you're out of sight. In between phoning more pet stores tomorrow, I'm surprising my uncle with a visit. I'll see if I can sniff around his apartment for the old blackmail tapes. He doesn't live far from the salon. If you need me, I can run over."

"Not literally, I hope." His leg!

He chuckled. "Mackie doesn't live around the corner. It's four or five blocks. I'll drive."

"Okay." But it wouldn't happen. She didn't *want* Gabe to have to rush to her rescue. She could do this. She *would.*

"Good," he replied in a husky voice. "Conduct the interview as well as you can without arousing her suspicions. Even if she doesn't seem to recognize you, she still might be our suspect. Keep her talking—about anything. The subject doesn't matter so much as where it might lead. If you don't contact me, we'll meet here after your appointment and reevaluate. Understood?"

"Got it, Sherlock. What about the studio? Should we stake it out tonight?"

"I can't. I have my own deal."

Oh? "Can I help?"

His dark eyebrows bobbed. "I doubt Tasha Manning wants you on our date."

"You have a date with Tasha?" She wasn't jealous. Not in the least.

"I only asked her because of the investigation."

Uh-huh. Their contact at the *Clarion* possessed cheekbones that put most actresses to shame. "How did you know she'd say yes?"

His mouth curved in a too-tempting half-smile. "She hinted she was interested when I spoke to her about the ruined ad. After everything that's happened, I thought I should follow up."

"You'll interrogate her during your date? Now that takes skill," Ursula said lightly, although she disapproved of the approach. A week ago, he'd practiced similar techniques on *her.*

"I'll work the ad into our conversation. After all, talking to her about the error was how she and I met." He nudged Ursula's thigh. "You okay with the plan?"

She sniffed like an aristocrat. She was above judging his investigative techniques. "You can date whoever you want."

"What if I want to do more than date?"

She scowled. "You want to sleep with Tasha?"

"It's a hypothetical question. Can I sleep with whoever I want?"

The gall! "Go ahead."

"Excellent," he murmured. "Too bad the only person I want to sleep with is you. Have dinner with you. Spend time with you. Really get to know each other. What do you say?"

I wish… "Bad idea. We need to keep our heads in the case."

"How about after it's solved?"

Ursula's stomach muscles tightened. "Gabe, I can't think beyond finding an end to the sabotage and meeting my deadline. There's too much riding on both outcomes."

"Okey-doke," he said, as if her response didn't affect him one way or the other. "So I'll see Tasha tonight and you'll interview Desiree tomorrow. Your appointment is at noon. Need the address?"

"I'll find it on my phone." A hollow sensation carved inside her as Reba continued idling, wipers swiping the glass and headlights brightening the old brick building now that the security lights had dimmed.

Gabe placed a hand on the passenger-door handle. "Remember, after your appointment, we meet back here and compare notes."

"Who'll watch the studio tonight?"

"I will, after my date."

"I can do it."

"Not on your own."

"But I'm already here."

His expression darkened. "Ursula, I'm not saying no because I think you're incapable. I don't want you getting hurt."

Same old, same old. Sighing, she shifted the car into reverse. "Well, thanks for letting me work with you today."

His gaze moved over her face. "We need to take in the equipment."

"I'd rather not while we're working the case. The bad guy might steal something. I'll store the cameras at home."

He nodded. "I'm checking the premises before you leave." He opened the car door, and cold air swept in as he climbed out. "Lock up and leave your car idling. If someone comes, honk long and hard. I'll hear you."

"I'll just text."

"Honk first, text second."

Ursula saluted. "Yes, Master Detective, sir."

Shaking his head, Gabe turned toward the building. The security lights flashed on again as he unlocked the alley door and disappeared inside.

Ursula shifted Reba back into park and locked both doors. The mechanical glitch in the passenger door only applied to unlocking. Reba was temperamental that way.

While rain drummed the roof and the old engine contributed to global warming, Ursula inspected her surroundings. Three businesses to her right, traffic crawled past the alley entrance. On her left, beyond the bright beam pooling over Gabe's truck and the tiny parking lot, a narrow lane behind more buildings stretched into rain-swathed darkness.

The reflection of the army-green dumpster hulked in her rearview mirror as the music on the radio segued into the eight-thirty news. The announcer reported a shooting in Auburn. A teenage boy had died, poor kid.

Leaning back against her seat, Ursula inhaled deeply. Despite her efforts to remain calm, an uneasy sensation crawled over her skin. Last night, while she'd visited the darkroom, their suspect had planted the mice. He or she had *sneaked into* the studio, and Super Sleuth Scott hadn't suspected a thing until the scratching noises had reached her ears.

She shivered in her raincoat. Had the baddie *wanted* her to hear the mice? Once the creep noticed her purse in the breakroom, had he or she gotten their jollies at the thought of Ursula hiding in the darkroom, worrying someone was there?

Had the suspect hung around—maybe even *in* the alley—long enough to watch her and Gabe leave the building?

A chill pierced her bones. *Hurry up, Master Detective, sir.*

She fiddled with her jacket zipper. She should go find him.

No. Stay here. Prove you can follow instructions.

Right. If he didn't return in two seconds—

A fist pounded on her window. Yelping, she glanced toward a wrinkled face peeking at her from beneath a soggy, dark wool cap.

"Spare change?" the homeless man asked through the closed car window. A drenched black garbage bag served as his raincoat.

"Sorry, you startled me." She rolled down the glass a sliver. The musty scent of the man's wet clothes streamed into the car.

"Didn't mean to. Ya' shouldn't be out here all alone, friend."

"My coworker will be back any minute." She opened Reba's ashtray for loose coins.

"Hey!" Gabe's voice bellowed.

The homeless man ran off.

Gabe hunkered at her side of the car. "Are you okay?"

She rolled down the window halfway. "He just needed money."

"You don't know that." Rain flattened his thick, wavy hair. "The coast is clear inside. You can leave."

"Gabe, that old guy was soaked through. It's cold tonight. Did you see what he was wearing? He must be freezing."

Gabe's fingers gripped the window edge. "You need to watch out for yourself."

Ursula leveled him a look. "It's bad enough I'm melting the polar ice caps idling Reba for eighty thousand minutes, now you're suggesting I ignore a harmless homeless man? Maybe he's seen our baddie hanging around. Instead of scaring him away, we should have talked to him."

One of Gabe's eyes closed against the dripping rain. "You're right." He wiped back his hair.

"I'm right about a lot of things. Get used to it."

He grinned. "Tell you what. If I see him again, I'll talk to him. *I will, Ursula.* For all we know, he's the suspect in disguise. For that reason, I don't want you near him."

She groaned. "He looked at least seventy."

"I don't care if he looked one hundred and three." Rain trickled down Gabe's face. "Listen, if it makes you feel better, my mom stores old blankets and clothes in her basement. I'll talk to her about donating them to the nearest shelter. Your fellow might benefit."

Ursula smiled. "Great idea. Maybe we should canvas surrounding businesses, start an annual coat and blanket drive. Stacy can print flyers. What do you think?"

"That my uncle won't go for it. Sounds like an Ursula Scott Photography act of charity though." He patted the window edge, which she interpreted as her signal to leave.

"Damn straight." She shifted into reverse. "Once I own the place, nothing can stop me."

Grunting, Mackie jabbed Evie's doorbell. "Open up, darlin'. I got a surprise." What a pain in the icy arse, untying the Christmas tree from his van roof while rain sluiced from the dark sky like Noah was building a second ark. The soggy branches pressed into his wet coat, and the rough bark bit his palm, and needles pricked his chapped hands. He should've worn gloves.

Only for Evie. No other woman could inspire him to trudge through a crowded tree lot in the cold rain, searching for *The One*. A perfect seven-foot Noble fir, greener and fuller than any tree Hal Henshaw had ever carted to her door.

"Evie!" He punched the bell again before adjusting the Santa hat he'd pulled from his jacket pocket upon reaching her covered stoop.

"Victor?" Her pleasant voice carried from inside. "Why are you here on a Saturday night?" she asked as the door opened. Her pretty eyes widened. "You brought me a tree?"

"Paid for and delivered." Mackie squared his shoulders. "With Hal out of the picture, I figured you could use the help."

Her face fell. "Oh, Vic. I don't know how to tell you this, but Hal called me today. We agreed to go tree-hunting next weekend."

Mackie's gut churned. "You always get your tree the first Saturday after Thanksgiving."

"Yes, but the holiday fell early this year."

"That don't matter. It's a tradition!" He flung his free hand toward the multi-colored Christmas lights trimming her roof and picture window. "Did he put up your lights while he was at it?" The handy hindquarters!

"No." Her eyebrows bunched. "Gabe strung them this morning, before he left to take care of the mice. It wasn't raining then."

"*What mice?*" No one in this frack-forsaken family communicated with him!

"Gabe said you had mice at the studio." Evie's tone sharpened. "I assumed you knew, Victor. He's not here, or you could ask him."

Mackie swallowed. Now he'd done it. He placed his hand on his wet coat, over his heart. "Evie, I apologize. What can I do? I have the tree now, and it's too big for my apartment."

"Give it to Jasmine. Your girlfriend." Evie crossed her arms.

The two women had never met, although, in a weak attempt to rouse Evie's jealousy about a month ago, Mackie had shown her a photo of Jas on his phone.

He injected a note of holiday misery into his voice. "Her living room is smaller than mine, and she does this sort of stuff with her folks. They're getting on, you know." He had no clue if Jas's parents were alive, but the story would appeal to Evie's kind heart. Like he would offer the giant Christmas tree to Jas these days, anyhow. She'd interpret the gift as a sign that he wanted to "make love" again, and he'd had it with that bullshit. Just when he'd thought he could restrict himself to one woman, Jas's whining had forced him to look up good ol' Glory Rhodes. That redheaded broad could suck the chrome off ten fenders and still want more.

Evie's gaze took in his Santa hat and cold hands. "I'll disappoint Hal if I cancel."

Who cares? Mackie plastered on a smile. "Do you want the tree, Evie? Whatever you need. I can take it back."

"No, no, that's all right. You went to so much trouble picking it out and driving it here. I appreciate the thought, Victor. I do usually buy my tree this weekend. I'll explain the mix-up to Hal. He'll understand...I hope."

Mackie couldn't give a flying flute if Hal accepted the situation or not. He planned to provide Evie with her Christmas trees from now on. This time next year, it would be *their* tree, and Henshaw nothing more than a dusty memory.

She opened the door wider. "Come in. It's freezing. I'll find towels to protect the carpet." She headed for the hallway, her shapely rear wiggling in her jeans. The TV droned in the living room. *Their* living room once they became husband and wife.

Returning, she arranged the towels on the entry floor. "Lean the tree against the wall," she said. "I'll put it up tomorrow after it dries."

Mackie lugged in the tree, puffing as a branch wedged in the doorframe. "I'll come back in the morning to help with the stand and stuff. You have a little saw, right? I'll make a new cut tomorrow. Makes for better water absorption, according to the guy at the lot." The fir dropped needles as he propped the huge Noble against the wall. He glanced at the mess. "Gabe can clean those with a shop vac." Glancing around Evie's warm, cozy home, he gestured at two boxes sitting behind the couch. "Those your ornaments?"

She nodded. "Gabe brought them out of storage along with the outdoor lights."

Well! Mackie puffed out his chest. "Then me coming tonight is a sign." He gave a thumbs-up. "I was meant to bring your tree this year, not Hal."

"I suppose." Her smile wobbled. "Thank you, Vic."

"You bet." He stuffed the Santa hat into his pocket and shrugged out of his soaked coat. "You closing the door, or should I?"

She cleared her throat. "Where are my manners? Yes, please close it." She hung his coat in the closet. "Would you like rum and eggnog?"

"Now you're talking." He toed off his wet shoes.

Evie flipped off the TV, rustled two fancy tumblers from the dining room cabinet, and wiggled her sweet ass into the kitchen.

Mackie hankered to plop onto the couch and rest his feet on the coffee table, let her serve him like a good future wife should.

But women these days! He needed to ease her into her role, not dump demands on her.

Lowering to one knee, he dragged three sets of tangled tree lights out of one of the boxes. His thick fingers fumbled with the wiry nest.

"Fucking things," he muttered.

"Victor!" Laughing, Evie appeared at his side. She extended his glass.

"Pardon my French. I didn't hear you come back." He lifted the lights in both hands. "Kinda busy here. Set my drink on the coffee table, will you?"

She carried the glasses around the couch. Seconds later, cheery carols floated from her sound system, and the scent of vanilla-flavored Christmas cookies flooded his nostrils. His belly warmed.

"You baked for me, Evie?" He straightened the strings of lights on the carpet.

"It's a candle. I have fruit cake, if you'd like."

"Naw." He hated the crap. The candied fruit and almond paste. Next year, to please him, Evie would bake loads of shortbread. He couldn't wait. "You can help me with these lights."

Coming around the couch again, she knelt beside him. As they untangled the strings, their hands grazed, but she didn't move away like she had two days ago in her kitchen.

After a moment, she asked, "Why aren't you with Jasmine on a Saturday night?"

Mackie rolled his lips. Because Jas wanted to "make love" all the time now, and he wanted to fuck. Get his need for beaver out of his system, so when he and Evie got hitched he could remain faithful. He never wanted to let down his lovely future wife.

"She, uh, had a family thing." He fixed his gaze on the tiny lights.

"You should have gone along. Don't you want to meet her folks?"

"It's a bit soon in the scheme of things." The day would never freaking come. "I'd rather be with you this year, after everything that's happened with Hal and Gabe."

"Thank you, Vic," she murmured.

Her soft voice slid around his pecker. The holiday smells of the candle and tree, combined with the magic of her light perfume, swarmed his bones. In an instant, he was hard.

Not now, he commanded his prick. Face hot, he couldn't look at her. His dead adoptive brother's widow. *His* Evie.

Shame prickled his skin. Damn it, banging Glory yesterday had been a mistake. And cheating on Jasmine with the redhead was a crappy move. Jas was supposed to have been his last bimbo before he committed himself to Evie.

Now, tonight, with Evie close enough to kiss if he dared, cheating on Jas sort of felt like cheating on *her*.

No more.

No more sluts or bonus BJs. Not even if Glory appeared on his doorstep with five of her randy girlfriends. Just Jas, *one woman*, until he weaned himself completely.

Focusing on the lights, he pushed everything out of his mind except the simple pleasure of enjoying tonight with Evie. They continued to work together. Like a team. Man and wife. Mackie's knees ached by the time they finished untangling the strings, but when she crawled a couple of feet away and plugged the joined strands into an outlet, not one bulb required replacing.

That seemed symbolic, yet another sign his shitty life was sliding back on track.

The lights would look beautiful on the tree. As beautiful as Evie did now, her face radiant with womanly satisfaction, her attention on him while they remain crouched beside the glowing strings.

Quietly, he asked, "Do you remember the night before your wedding?"

Her gaze flickered. "Yes."

"I was a kid, Evie. I didn't know what I was saying."

"Vic..." She adjusted her legs on the carpet, sitting sideways and plucking the hem of a pants leg. "We've never talked about that night. I'm not sure we should."

"I understand, and I wouldn't blame you if we never talked about it again. I was an idiot." He paused. "I felt like a jackass afterward. You were marrying my brother." But now she was free. And he was free to pursue her.

She wet her lips. "Did you mean what you said then? About you and me?"

That she was meant for him? That marrying Doug was the worst mistake of her life?

If the moon grew moss and the stars fizzled and sparked like busted Vegas signs, he would never forget their conversation—or how his dreams of Evie falling into his arms, realizing with stunning clarity that he was her man, had shattered.

Tonight, here and now, the importance of his reply weighed on his chest. He selected his next words carefully.

"I should've kept my mouth shut. You've always been kind to me, and I treasure you for it."

Her mouth tipped up at the corners, and optimism flared in his chest. He had hit his mark. Ladies adored gushy language.

"I misread your kindness," Mackie said. "That night was on me." He clasped her hand and gazed into her sincere eyes. "The next time I tell a woman I love her, I'll know to choose the right time and do it like a gentleman. That's what you taught me. Watching you with Doug years ago, growing to understand how you felt about him... Evie, you've shown me what true love is. That's what I want. And I mean to have it."

"Victor, thank you," she said, voice tender. "That's the nicest thing you've ever said to me." She kissed his cheek, and his crusty heart swelled.

"Any time, darlin'."

For the rest of his life.

URSULA STROVE TO remain calm and treat her expedition to Just Nailed like she would any normal weekend activity. She sprang for breakfast with her brother at his favorite pancake house Sunday morning before arriving at the salon ten minutes early for her noon appointment. The salon featured six pedicure chairs and three rows of white-lacquered manicure stations, each affording space for clients to walk between.

"Megan, you have lovely fingers," Desiree Lewis said as she massaged Ursula's right hand with fragrant lotion. "Long and slim, like an artist's."

"Thanks." Ursula battled the urge to chomp her stick of spearmint chewing gum like a horse eating apples. Despite her efforts to feel composed, her nerves threatened to pop free of her skin, and if not for the gum, her mouth would have dried shut by now. When Gabe texted her at the pancake house an hour ago to ensure she felt comfortable taking the appointment, he'd reinforced that the best way to interrogate Desiree was to keep the woman talking.

Unfortunately, Ursula's interview skills sucked. While Desiree removed her old polish, shaped her nails, allowed her hands to soak for several minutes, then pushed back her cuticles, they'd discussed the weather, movies, music, and men—to no result.

In her guise as Megan Fleming, which Desiree appeared to have accepted, Ursula had gushed over the French manicure gift without mentioning Gabe's name. In turn, Desiree dished about her current guy, a church pastor who didn't mind Desiree working Sundays as long as she attended his nine a.m. service first.

Ursula couldn't fathom a woman who had been involved with Mackie dating a pastor, but if the Desiree doing her nails was the woman from the notepad, maybe the blackmail experience had motivated the manicurist to change her life. In particular, Ursula yearned to ask who Desiree had dated before Pastor Pat. But if she snooped too much and Desiree *was* their baddie, wouldn't the woman grow suspicious?

How did Gabe encourage complete strangers to spill their guts?

"It's too bad you have to spend your days sinking these beautiful nails into trays of cold meat," Desiree said, pushing up Ursula's left sweater sleeve and massaging her other hand.

As Megan, Ursula shrugged. "A job is a job. It's temporary."

"Oh?" Desiree's blue gaze lifted from her task. The woman was knocking on forty's door, but her large eyes, although caked with too much black liner, were mesmerizing. A cloud of honey-blond hair framed her face, but excess blusher stained her cheeks and her leopard-print blouse barely restrained her large breasts. Aside from the gold crucifix nestled in her cleavage, she looked like Mackie's type. "What are your plans?" Desiree asked.

"That's the thing," Ursula responded. "I don't know yet. Until I decide, I might as well work at the deli. They treat me well."

"Hon, I know all about trying to find yourself," Desiree murmured above the feminine chatter floating throughout the busy salon. "It took ages to commit myself to beauty."

Ursula's pulse kicked. Had she stumbled upon a line of questioning that might lead somewhere?

"You haven't been doing this long? I wouldn't have guessed. You're so talented."

Desiree massaged the skin between Ursula's twitching fingers. "I've had my license five years. What I meant was I would have enrolled in beauty school earlier, but my daddy was against it."

Ursula practically wriggled on her seat. *How about a yippee and a ki and a yay?* Between their conversation about Pastor Pat and now Desiree's comment about the woman's father, Ursula's curiosity popped. Did Desiree kowtow to every man in her life? Mackie would have exploited the trait, for sure.

As Megan, she said, "My dad wants me to join his accounting practice, but I'd rather paint."

"I knew you were an artist." Desiree increased the pressure on Ursula's hand. "Don't let him push you, hon. I tried joining my daddy's business, but my heart wasn't in it."

"What does your dad do?" *Ouch, that hurts.*

"He was a locksmith. He's no longer of this earth, praise God." Desiree touched her cross.

Ursula almost swallowed her gum. Gabe had joked about their suspect knowing his or her way around locks. And had Desiree just said a prayer because her father was dead?

What did that mean? Had Desiree hated her father? Or was "praise God" shorthand for safeguarding the man's soul?

"He wanted me to take over the business because he didn't have sons," Desiree continued. The tortuous massage finished, she toweled off Ursula's nails.

"Do you know how to pick locks?" Ursula tried a smile. "That would be cool. I'm forever locking myself out."

"I can pick them, change them, cut replacements for lost keys. Comes in handy." The woman winked. "I didn't enjoy working with Daddy though. I felt creatively repressed. You understand, seeing as we're both artists." She swiped polish remover over Ursula's nails, eradicating the last traces of lotion. The strong scent tinged the air. "When he died, I sold the business. Now I'm living my dream."

"That's wonderful. Do you manage the salon?"

A grimace pulled down Desiree's mouth. "No. I felt so free after Daddy died that I wasted his money on fast times and bad men."

Ursula's ears hummed. "Bad men?"

"Guys who treat women like trash." Desiree ground a cotton ball soaked with polish remover into Ursula's thumb. The cuticle stung. "Not like your sweetie, treating you to a manicure. That's so thoughtful. And not anything like my precious Pat." Desiree tossed aside the cotton ball and snatched a bottle of white tip polish, knocking over the forgotten container of base coat. She unscrewed the tip polish. "Men that need a swift kick in the family jewels, know what I mean? Shoot, forget a kick! They need those suckers crushed in a vice grip." Her hand jerked. White polish flew off the tiny brush and splattered her cross.

"Fuck!" Desiree's eyes widened. "Damn—*darn* it, sorry. Pat doesn't like cursing."

"Don't worry about it." Ursula plucked a tissue from the box and pressed the flimsy paper into Desiree's hands. "Quick, clean the tip polish before it dries on your necklace."

Desiree dabbed at the crucifix, anguish brimming in her gaze. "I try! Lord knows I do. No one understands how hard it is. I *need* to be good."

❧

Clenching the puny disposable cell phone, Mackie paced his crummy apartment. "Enough excuses, Bloomfield! You didn't make the drop this morning. The payment's late." Mackie had watched that stupid garbage can in the cold rain for ninety minutes, making *him* too late for trimming Evie's Christmas tree. When he'd finally arrived at her place, his nephew had already put up the tree and strung the lights. Gabe had jumped right in there and done his mother a solid after Mackie and Evie spent last night untangling the strings and checking for duds.

St. Pecker!

Mackie had tried sticking around to decorate the heavy branches with ornaments, but it wasn't the same with Gabe loitering about the house. The sooner the kid moved into his own digs, the better for everyone.

Paul Bloomfield's meek voice whispered over the cell. "I know I missed the drop, and I'm sorry. You asked for more money this time. Christine has access to my accounts. If she sees a large withdrawal on the next statement, she'll question me."

"Don't let her see the statements then. Or switch to online. This ain't the 1970s!"

"That's not as easy as it sounds," Bloomfield whispered. "We have joint everything now, and she insists on paper. If I don't intercept the mail—"

"What, she'll think you're spending the cash on a tasty slice of lasagna?"

Bloomfield didn't respond.

Mackie yanked the phone off his ear and positioned the speaker in front of his mouth. "I don't care if the twit thinks you're bumping uglies with a flock of sheep. *I want that payment!*"

"Then give me more time," Bloomfield pleaded. "Only a day or two."

Mackie slapped his palm on the newspaper spread on his kitchen counter, stinging his skin. Bloomfield's smiling mug and his rich wife's snooty expression splashed an article about a midweek charity event.

Deepening his tone for added menace, Mackie pressed the cell phone to his ear again. "Maybe you shouldn't have let the media get wind of your party time with that blabbermouth hooker four years ago, hey, Paul? Then you wouldn't have to worry about Chrissie learning you were up to your old tricks again this year in California."

"I didn't do anything in California!" Paul's cry-baby voice blasted his eardrum.

"Says *you*, you pecker-less pip." Mackie grinned. "I have evidence proving otherwise."

"*Fake* evidence."

Mackie spun on his heel and trundled toward the recliner. "You think Chrissie will care how the pictures came about? She'll only care that there's another scandal. Paulie, you're an ambitious man. And smart." He laid it on thick. "Or you were, before I happened along. You don't need another scandal in your political life, do you, Paul?" Mackie slackened his imaginary fishing line. He'd done this before, and not only with women. There had been another man or two over the years. He knew how to capitalize on Paul's fears.

Nervousness flooded Bloomfield's voice. "I *will* pay, Mr. McKenzie. You have my word. Give me two more days. Until Tuesday. I'm begging you."

Strolling to the counter again, Mackie scratched a nostril. *That's it, Paulie. Come to Daddy.* He had suckered the fear of public humiliation into the uptight prick. Time to allow a tiny inch of leeway.

"Okay," he grumbled like a character from a mob movie. "But don't let me down."

"Th-thank you," Bloomfield replied. "When will this nightmare end?"

"Like we agreed, after two more payments. First *this* payment, now happening Tuesday. Same place. No screw-ups. Set your effing watch. And the last drop is two weeks from *today*, not two weeks from freaking Tuesday. *Capiche?* I'm a man of my word every bit as much as you claim you are. More so. If I say our arrangement ends in two weeks, it will." He could hardly propose to Evie Christmas morning with a shroud of dishonesty weighing him down. That she and Hal had made plans to shop for a Christmas tree clanged in his ears loud and clear. He needed to propose before she went soft on her ex.

Once Mackie slipped a ring on her finger, Henshaw would be toast. Evie honored her promises. She was a real sweetheart.

Buuuutttt, to be safe, Mackie would spring for tickets for a quickie New Year's Eve trip to Vegas. He and Evie could get hitched before the year was out. An Elvis-impersonator officiant sounded perfect, the guy crooning "Love Me Tender" while they signed the papers!

He needed Bloomfield's money first.

"I believe you," Paul said, relief shuddering in his wimpy voice.

"It's not like you have a choice, is it?" Mackie ended the call and buried the secret cell phone in a canister packed with tea bags. Christ. Dealing with morons was exhausting.

Shaking his head, he shuffled to his laptop on a small desk banking the far side of his home filing cabinet. Sitting on the chair, he typed in his password and opened his photo editing software to the artwork that had Paul Bloomfield panicking on the phone just now. Mackie cackled as the image blossomed on the screen.

For his farewell blackmailing gig, the doctored photos of Bloomfield necking with a bimbo on a California beach were unadulterated genius. Accustomed to waiting for what he wanted, Mackie had done his homework, selecting a target with utmost care and biding time until opportunity arose. The municipal conference in California in early September had felt like a gift from heaven, arriving on the heels of Gabe's shooting and Evie's breakup with Henshaw.

Using the brush tool, Mackie drew a thick red bull's eye around the image of Paul's head, which he'd expertly transplanted onto some nameless guy's body.

Aiming an imaginary gun at the head, he muttered, "Bang-bang, fart-face."

Chortling, he closed the program without saving changes. Opening a web browser, he cruised to his favorite big-titty site.

Just because he wasn't banging women other than Jas anymore didn't mean he couldn't *look*. Winky-wink.

He unzipped his fly.

A knock rapped on the door.

"Go away," he snarled.

"Uncle Vic, it's Gabe. I have something for you from Mom."

"What is it?" Hurriedly, Mackie shut down the laptop and zipped his pants.

"Let me in, and you'll see."

Plastic food container in hand, Gabe checked messages on his phone in the hall outside his uncle's apartment door. No news from Ursula. Her appointment with Desiree Lewis must be going well. Good for her.

Stay safe, Sula. His new mantra.

Pocketing the cell, he asked against the door, "Everything okay in there?" A full minute had elapsed since he'd knocked.

"Just tidying up." Mackie's gravelly voice carried into the hall. A moment later, the door swung open. A phony-looking smile stretched across the boor's face as he grabbed the container and peeled off the lid.

"Rice cereal squares," Gabe described. "Mom said they're one of your favorites."

"Yes, they are. She's a dear, our Evie. Come in, come in." He ushered Gabe inside. "She didn't need to go to all this trouble."

"She wanted to apologize for putting up the tree without you." Gabe's mom had actually made the cereal bars for him, but he'd needed a reason to poke around his uncle's apartment. "Have coffee?" he asked. "I wouldn't mind a square." His uncle was already chomping down.

"I'll fix you some instant. Me, I'm having a beer." Mackie gobbled his square and chucked the container onto the counter. As he retrieved the kettle, his gaze zipped to the Sunday paper. He whacked it shut. The page number marking his spot peeked from a corner.

"Thanks," Gabe said. "I think I *will* have a square."

"Help yourself." Turning to the sink, Mackie filled the kettle.

Gabe flipped the paper back to the Social and Community Events page. A photograph of a smiling couple dominated the newsprint. The caption read, *Seattle Council President Paul Bloomfield and wife Christine attending the Annual Thanksgiving Fundraiser for the Homeless Ball November 21st.*

"Uncle Vic, do you know this Bloomfield guy?"

Glancing over his shoulder, Mackie stopped the faucet. "Never heard of him." He plugged in the kettle. "Why?"

"I thought you hated reading newspapers. You were always more of a TV guy. And the community events section? I'm surprised you subscribe to a daily paper when you can find most of this information free on the Web."

"I don't subscribe to no papers." Mackie twisted the end of his nose. "Sometimes I borrow Old Lady Chadwick's. She don't mind. She's half-blind anyway. You want the paper? Take it. I'll run out and buy the gal another." He scratched his stomach. "Yeah, that's what I'll do."

"I'll take you up on that offer." Gabe folded the newspaper section into the pocket of his wet jacket, removed the coat, and tossed it on a chair.

Mackie's dark eyes darted back and forth. "That the only part you need?"

"Mom likes the Social pages," Gabe said, choosing a cereal square and stepping into the living room. Aside from the over-stuffed recliner facing a cracker-thin, wide-screen TV, ancient furniture populated the messy space. "Nice place." *For trolls.* He bit into his square.

Mackie pulled a beer from the battered fridge. "I do all right."

"Is the TV new?" Gabe nodded at the wide-screen perched atop a shiny black entertainment unit.

"Yep. The latest technology." Walking over to join Gabe, Mackie swigged his brew.

"A digital recorder too, I see. Plus a DVD player. Yet you still have an old VCR." Out of the corner of his eye, Gabe glimpsed an extensive porn collection littering a bottom shelf of the stand. Jasmine mustn't mind Mackie leaving out the discs where anyone could see them. Who knew, she might enjoy them. Gabe's mom, on the other hand, would advise her brother-in-law to store them out of sight. Luckily, Mom rarely visited the apartment—if she ever had. As long as Gabe remembered, his uncle came to the house.

Pretending he hadn't noticed the porn, he glanced around the room.

"I'll trash the VCR sooner or later," his uncle said, hospitable for once.

"Uh-huh." Before or after Mackie transferred possible blackmail tapes of the women in the notepad to DVD or another media?

Or had he already transferred them?

Gabe squinted. If the tapes existed, they or DVD copies or digital versions must be stashed in this dive somewhere. A packrat like Victor McKenzie wouldn't toss them out.

"Did Mom tell you about the mice?" he asked conversationally. Eating his square, he sauntered to a new-looking laptop on an old phone desk.

"Yeah." Mackie drank his beer. "What's going on with those stupid rodents anyway?"

Gabe placed a palm on the closed laptop. *Warm.*

"What're you doing?" his uncle asked, hustling over.

"I need a computer for my PI firm. I was thinking laptop. Do you like this brand?"

"Meh. It works."

Finishing his square, Gabe lifted the screen. "Can I check it out?"

"It's got a virus."

And he was Bill Gates. "Boot it up. I'll debug it for you." What did his uncle not want him to see?

"It needs a virus protection program." Mackie passed his beer can to his other hand.

"Haven't you installed one? How long have you had the machine?"

"Why all the questions? I bought it a month ago." The kettle whistled. Running a palm over his stubby ponytail, Mackie returned to the kitchen. "I'll make your coffee, and we'll discuss the mice. Nothing else, you hear? I have a date with Jas."

&

"I can't believe Mackie is splurging on new studio locks," Ursula said to Gabe as she squirmed on the passenger seat of his pickup. Cripes, her butt *ached*. They had been watching Desiree Lewis's brightly decorated duplex in the light rain for nearly two hours, after waiting for the woman's shift to end and then tailing her home.

As planned, Ursula had met Gabe at the studio following her visit to Just Nailed. In the breakroom, she'd relayed her conversation with Desiree. Gabe had agreed that conducting surveillance on the manicurist took precedence over investigating other leads. In the event their efforts led to a dead end, Ursula had parked Reba in the alley as a deterrent to their baddie vandalizing the business again. To further the ruse that she was inside the building, they'd also turned on lights and left Mackie's old transistor radio playing.

The rain pattered the roof of Gabe's truck. He'd cracked his window to prevent the windshield from fogging, and cold air snaked into the cab. Not wanting to attract attention, he'd cut the engine, rendering the wipers immobile, but had raised the center console to create extra seating space. A family-sized bag of ripple chips perched between them.

"Once I explained that the suspect might have planted the mice, my uncle realized he was out of options," he said. "It's clear *someone* is messing with him. He'd have to be pretty dense not to agree to changing the front and back door locks. He should probably change every lock in the place, but I can only push a tank so far."

Ursula sipped her bottled water. "Like I said, I'm in utter shock."

Gabe chuckled. His gaze tracked Desiree's movements through

the living room window while the woman trimmed her Christmas tree and the shower tapered to a drizzle.

"Are you doing the work again?" Ursula asked. He'd fixed his uncle's office door the day after they'd met.

He shook his head. "I need to stay on top of the case. Mackie is hiring a professional."

"He's paying someone?" The surprises kept coming. "Did you arrange that?"

"Yep. I called Brinley's, the hardware place, from the studio yesterday after contacting the exterminator." His glance darted her direction before returning to Desiree's rain-splattered window. "The locksmith arrives tomorrow at eleven. Tightwad that my uncle is, he wasn't happy I hired both guys without asking him first."

"He must understand we can't allow our suspect free run of the studio." Tucking her water bottle between her legs, Ursula dug two ripple chips out of the bag and munched.

"He didn't like incurring the expense, but he agreed."

Glory be. "Does he know I'm working with you?"

"No. And let's not tell him, if you don't mind." Gabe rustled in the bag for a handful of chips. "As far as he's concerned, I'm under-cover as your assistant while sniffing around on his behalf. If he finds out you're involved in the case, it complicates things. I can't risk him interfering. He'd only get in the way."

Ursula studied Desiree hanging an ornament. Gabe had put forth the same rationalization about her participation in the case, after she'd discovered him bagging the nails. In a way, tonight, she was interfering. Well, not interfering, exactly, but she didn't *have* to be here. She'd wanted to tag along, and he hadn't argued. Last night, similar to Friday, he'd staked out the studio alone. Today, after her successful interview with Desiree, he'd permitted her to step deeper into his world. Maybe he'd accepted that she had too much at stake, too much to lose, and wouldn't back down. However he'd arrived at his decision, she wanted to prove herself a valuable ally.

Gaze on the residence, she asked, "If Stacy winds up being our suspect, won't changing the locks alert her we're on to her? As the receptionist, she'll receive a copy of the new keys."

Gabe snacked his way through his handful of chips while they spoke. "We'll fabricate a reason for the change, like my uncle's insurance requires new locks installed every couple of years or something. Then we'll tell her we don't have enough spares. As the owner, Mackie needs a set. As his assistant, so do you. Stacy, not so much. She was only part-time until the *Seattle Lights* job, right?"

"Yes, but she locks up sometimes." As had prior receptionists. For that reason, Ursula had insisted Mackie provide each woman with keys to the building. Now, she realized he hadn't changed locks between any of those employees. After the receptionist prior to Stacy, when the high staff turnover became apparent, Ursula recommended installing new hardware but he'd pooh-poohed the idea.

Given everything he had to hide—the S&M cupboard, the video camera, the notepad—he was naïve, stupid, or overconfident.

Or a mix of all three.

She nibbled another chip. "I'm not sure Stacy will understand why she doesn't need a set. You and I are busy with the shoot. It's natural she would want one."

Gabe wiped his hands on his jeans. "My uncle will say she has to wait a few days until he can get more copies cut. If you and I aren't around at closing, he'll stay every evening until she leaves, then lock up himself."

"That's good. If she is our baddie, not giving her keys might prevent her from doing more damage inside the building."

"Correct. And if waiting for new keys upsets her, that tells us something."

Ursula looked at him. "Seeing as you're acting as my trainee, you shouldn't receive a set."

"Nope, I shouldn't. I *will* have keys, but Stacy won't know. Kind of like *you* not needing to know how the exterminator dealt with the mice." He grinned.

Ursula swatted his knee. Her water bottle wobbled between her legs. "You promised not to say anything." At the studio, she'd curtailed his report of the exterminator's methods.

"Nancy, I believe you're a soft touch."

He should know. He'd touched her in all her soft places. "If the mice entered the building under their own steam, I might feel differently. But if someone *planted* them—"

"It wasn't their fault. They were forced into lives of crime."

They both smiled.

He resumed watching the duplex. "You did an excellent job interviewing Desiree," he said after a moment. "It's hard to believe the first woman we checked out from the notepad has experience picking locks."

"It was dumb luck," Ursula replied, idiotically delighted with the compliment.

"Don't sell yourself short. Whatever happens from this point, you asked questions under the pretext of conversation until you hit the right ones. That's half the battle."

"If you say so." Desiree's accident with the tip polish had resulted in a reprimand from the salon manager. The manicurist had settled down, but her resolute concentration throughout the remainder of the appointment had seemed a bit strange. Like the woman might explode again any minute.

"I do say so," Gabe said. "I'm proud of you." He patted her thigh.

Ursula's skin warmed. "Thanks." Picking up the chip bag, she held it toward him. "Want more?"

Hand on her leg, he shook his head. Oh, his touch felt so good. Not sexual, just comforting and supportive, although, dear God, their attraction couldn't be denied.

But right here and now, in the coziness of his pickup while the shower outside abated, the light pressure of his hand on her leg mirrored a sudden ache in her chest. A sweet, sweet yearning blossoming with heat and tugging at her heart.

She held her breath, and he glanced at her leg.

"Sorry." His hand moved onto his lap.

It's okay. She longed to speak the words, but they remained lodged in her throat. Four nights ago, in the studio proper, she'd cut him out of her life. Granted, she'd had grounds, having discovered his deception not ten minutes earlier. But until he'd agreed to work with her, she hadn't wanted to hear another word come out of his mouth.

Then last night, when he asked about seeing her after they solved the mystery, she couldn't offer him *anything.* He was sticking around, building a life in Seattle. A great guy with the best intentions. What was holding her back? Her plans to buy the studio and assist her parents were evident. But there was something else. Something underneath.

She needed to figure it out later, when she was alone. *No, after the Real Men shoot.* Her professional reputation held the key to her future. No navel-gazing until she met her deadline.

"Gabe?" She uncapped her water. "What you said about being forced into a life of crime... Did you meet anyone like that as a cop?"

"Yeah. Usually kids." Retrieving his bottle from a cup holder, he drained the remaining contents. "In certain areas of LA, the pressure to join a gang is intense. People like you and me who grew up in safe neighborhoods can't understand the overwhelming need for protection."

"What do you mean?"

"Refusing to join a gang can result in becoming a victim of one. You might get beaten to within an inch of your life. Your family could be targeted. Gangs are like a brotherhood. They not only protect their members, they provide a sense of belonging. A lot of teens feel like there's no way out. Their gang is their security and family."

Aww. How sad. "Isn't the brotherhood thing prevalent with cops as well?"

He nodded. "We're a tight bunch. In Los Angeles, my best friends were with the Department."

"Do you miss them?"

"Of course. Being a cop fills you with purpose, and seven years is a long time to build friendships and trust." A tinge of irony curved his mouth. "After my shooting, my last girlfriend missed the perks my career offered."

Ursula coughed. She hadn't expected the conversation to veer into ex territory. "Perks?"

His left shoulder lifted. "She had a uniform fetish. She only dated cops and firefighters. Once she realized my injury might end my career, she was out of there."

"Why would you date someone like that?"

He wedged his empty bottle beneath his seat. "I know this doesn't sound very mature, but when I moved to California, I wasn't looking for anything more. I was young, into my job, and wanted a good time on my days off. Women like Tiff fit the bill."

Ursula directed her gaze to the thin rivulets of rainwater staining the passenger window of his truck. *Don't ask more questions about his ex.* He might reveal that *Ursula* was only a good time too. That he didn't want more from a relationship.

Her pulse tripped. Did *she?*

Abruptly, he grabbed her bottle and jammed it into a cup holder. "Desiree is leaving."

Ursula swiveled her head to the residence.

"Don't look. She might recognize you."

"We're across the street, and it's dark."

"We can't take the chance. Get down." He grasped her shoulder, applying pressure. Her head plopped onto his lap. Scrunched chips spewed out of the bag.

"This might not be the best arrangement," she mumbled. "I'm down, but you're up." In more ways than one. The bulge in his jeans hardened beneath her face.

"Sorry." He grunted and shifted his leg. "Again." Slouching in his seat, he wrapped an arm around her. Her head moved up, hair flying everywhere as her cheek squashed against his leather-jacket-clad chest. "Desiree is unlocking her car," he murmured, slapping on a baseball cap. The scents of old leather and hot PI filled her nostrils. "We can't risk her identifying either of us a few hours after your appointment. Stay low."

"For how long?" Her lips moved against his jacket.

"A few seconds. She's climbing in her car." His arm unfurled from her shoulders. "She's heading down the street. Let's go."

Ursula sat up, buckling her seatbelt as Gabe revved the engine and steered the truck onto the road. Five minutes later, they remained about a block behind Desiree's car when the woman parked at a convenience store and disappeared inside.

"Stay here," he advised. "I'll get close enough to visually esti-mate her frame of mind."

"Be careful."

"Always." The pickup door shut behind him.

Ursula slumped in her seat. She needed a baseball cap.

Two minutes later, he climbed behind the wheel again.

"How did she look?" Ursula asked.

"Happy. Smiling. Cheerful."

"Did you see what she bought?"

"Tinsel and tape."

Ordinary holiday paraphernalia. "She can't be our saboteur then."

"Unless she plans to plug the studio plumbing with five pounds of glitter." He started the truck. "She's leaving." Reaching over, he opened the glove compartment. "Wear this." He passed her a navy-blue cap with a low profile.

"Sherlock, you read my mind."

They motored after their suspect again.

Twenty-Three

GABE PRECEDED Ursula into her kitchen. Looking cuter than hell in the long-billed cap she'd donned in his truck, she hung their jackets in the entryway closet. "Deni? Kim?" she called toward the living room.

"We're on our own," he said, glimpsing two notes on the fridge.

"It's after ten. They might be in their rooms."

"Nope." Tapping the appliance, he directed her attention to the slips of paper tacked beneath magnets.

"What do they say?"

Hands in jeans pockets, he read the first note aloud. *"Staying at James's. Be good."*

"Obviously Deni."

"And this one says, *'Out all night. Don't call.'* 'Don't' is underlined."

Chuckling, she set her purse on the counter. "Kim."

"She seems different. Not as cheerful as Deni."

"Kim's going through a cynical phase. Remember her secrecy with her laptop a week ago? Maybe she *is* online dating. She might think I wouldn't approve."

"Why not?"

"It's too risky." She plucked the notes off the fridge and crumpled them into a recycling bin beside the communal desk. "Do you know how many players are out there, pretending to be someone they're not? It's tough on a girl looking for love these days."

Gabe arched his eyebrows. "Are you?" he asked. "Looking for love?"

"I plead the Fifth." She removed the cap. "Here you go."

"Keep it. For our next stakeout." He tossed the hat onto the desk.

"I will." The corners of her mouth wavered as she smiled. During the drive from their last surveillance stint, she had told him to expect at least one of her roommates home while they conducted their debriefing. Would she have invited him for a late-night meal if she'd realized they would be alone?

"Hey, I can leave. Get something at a drive-through." Anything to ease her misgivings.

"No." She flapped a hand, pulling a face. "We have a lot of ground to cover. I promised you bacon and eggs. It's no problem."

"I'll help."

"Great. Start with the eggs. Be right back."

She headed toward the bedrooms and bathroom. Gabe washed his hands in the double sink and rummaged in the fridge for the eggs, stomach grumbling. He had subsisted on snacks since lunch.

He located a bowl and pan. As he broke six eggs and whisked them, she returned.

"Be right back," he parroted with a grin. His bad leg ached from sitting in the truck for hours, and he cursed the slight limp impeding his short visit to the bathroom.

In the kitchen again, he found her at the counter arranging bacon strips on a paper-towel-covered plate.

"I'm sorry we wasted so much time following Desiree," she said, layering more paper towels on top of the meat. She placed the plate in the microwave and pressed the timer.

"It wasn't a waste." He poured the whisked eggs into a hot pan on the stove. "We needed to determine if she's the same Desiree listed in the notepad."

"But we still don't know if she is."

"We do know she has lock-picking skills and has dated jerks. We also know she becomes easily agitated." The welcome scent of sizzling bacon permeated the kitchen as Gabe scrambled the frying eggs. "She might wind up being my uncle's Desiree or she might not. Either way, we're narrowing down names."

On the surface, he agreed with Ursula. Despite Desiree's background and outburst at the salon, the woman's activity throughout the evening suggested revenge against a former lover was the last thing on her mind. After she left the convenience store, they tailed her to a bungalow near a nondenominational church. A man kissed and hugged her at the door. The rain had stopped, increasing visibility from Gabe's pickup but upping the chances Desiree or her gentleman friend might spot them. The longer the truck appeared parked, the better. After thirty minutes, Gabe crept to the driveway and inspected the name on the mailbox: *P. Willard.*

A quick address search on Ursula's phone had confirmed Mr. Willard was indeed Pastor Pat. Gabe and Ursula staked out the bungalow from across the street. A multi-paned window with sheer drapes revealed Desiree and her boyfriend cooking dinner, trimming a tree, then snuggling in front of a fire watching TV.

At nine-fifteen, Desiree left, and they tailed her home. Her duplex quickly darkened. At that point, Ursula had conceded that if *they* didn't eat some real food and catch a good night's sleep, tomorrow's location shoots might suffer.

"Maybe she's laying low for a while," Gabe said, stirring the eggs. "We haven't discovered more incidents in two days." Since the mice on Friday.

"It's frustrating." She gathered plates and cutlery while the microwave droned. "Desiree looks like a dead end, calling pet stores didn't provide us with a single lead, last night Tasha Manning gave you the same song and dance as the first time you talked to her, nothing happened when you staked out the studio two nights in a row, and I have *no* idea why Mackie might be interested in a news story about Paul Bloomfield."

"Welcome to my life." The microwave beeped. Stepping around Ursula in the narrow kitchen, Gabe removed the plate and sponged the bacon with a clean paper towel. Their shoulders grazed, and an electric hum vibrated in his chest like it did every time they touched.

He had never experienced such an intense attraction with a

woman. Every inch of him wanted, needed, to connect with her in a way he couldn't explain.

He swung his gaze to glimpse her expression, but she turned, lifting the pan off the stove.

"Why are we still investigating women?" She cast him a glance. "Tasha insists a man changed the ad."

"She doesn't insist. It's what she recalls. I didn't interview her, remember. Just made small talk as part of our date."

Ursula's nose scrunched, and he stifled a smile. Her body language spoke volumes whenever the subject of Tasha arose. If he wasn't mistaken, his Amazon warrior princess harbored a wee streak of jealousy.

"Her memory stinks." Ursula scooped a large portion of scrambled eggs onto one plate and a smaller portion onto the other. "What Tasha remembers doesn't make sense, unless a man *and* a woman are involved in this mess." She doled out bacon in similar portions.

"Or a woman wrecked the ad using a handheld voice changer or spoof service."

"What's a spoof service?" She carried their meals to the small table butted against the living room wall.

"An online way of disguising caller ID. Spoof sites and apps let you input a phone number of your choosing to display on another person's phone. Our suspect could have used the phone number for the studio. If the suspect is a woman from the notepad, she also could have used a spoof site's voice transformer to sound like a man. In real time, while speaking to Tasha."

"I've never heard of that." Ursula returned to the kitchen for two glasses of orange juice. "Is it legal?"

"If used for legitimate purposes, like having fun with friends or conducting PI work," Gabe said as he sat. "Not if used with criminal intent to deceive."

Joining him at the table, Ursula seasoned her eggs. "Why didn't you tell me this earlier?"

"Your head was on my lap."

Her gaze shot up, and she laughed. "Okay, Romeo, concentrate. Tomorrow we're busy with the Real Men shoot. Give me the goods, and we'll plan our week." She pushed her fork into her eggs. "That's why you're here."

&

What was she going to do about Gabe? And the way she felt around him?

It was unlike anything she'd ever felt before. Stronger. Deeper. Why him? Why now?

Gazing at him from beneath lowered lashes, she dipped her last rasher of bacon in the ketchup puddle on her plate and chewed the tasty meat. She'd asked Gabe to allow her into the case, and he had. She should have anticipated spending extra time together would wreak havoc with her emotions—but she hadn't.

His engaging smile and quick wit were impossible to resist. She was only human. As Grandma B would have said, Gabe was "a fine catch."

The man was incredibly fine. In every way.

Ursula finished her bacon. Tasha Manning from the *Clarion* was probably checking her phone every thirty seconds, hoping Gabe would text or call. In another few days, if Gabe didn't contact Tasha, would the newspaper clerk message him?

It wasn't Ursula's business if Tasha and Gabe wound up dating for real. At least Tasha was a nice person. She semi-deserved Gabe. But his ex-girlfriend in LA—Tiff or Tat or Twit or whoever— dumping him for getting shot? What a piece of work.

"That hit the spot." He patted his trim stomach. "Thanks."

"You're welcome." Suppressing a shimmy of heat, she pushed back her chair and picked up their plates. While eating, they'd discussed the merits of investigating the women in the notepad ahead of the list of ex-girlfriends Gabe had cajoled from his uncle. Gabe had already spoken to an ex named Lori Keller with no results, and it stood to reason a blackmail victim would harbor a greater grudge against Mackie than a woman the oaf had volunteered.

The redhead Gabe spotted entering the studio with his uncle early Friday afternoon remained a mystery. Was Red a new addition to the Vic McKenzie fan club? Did Jasmine know about her?

Ursula stepped toward the kitchen. "You should take me to get Reba now." She dumped the plates into the sink.

"We might want to leave your car in the studio lot overnight," Gabe suggested, carrying the condiments.

"No one will believe I'm staying there all night."

"Until the new locks are installed, it can't hurt." He ambled back to the table for the empty juice glasses. "I'll pick you up in the morning so you don't have to ride the bus."

"Thanks, but I'm used to taking it most days. Besides, we decided Mackie shouldn't know I'm helping you. Theoretically, I don't know about the mice or the case. So what reason would I have to leave my car at the studio?"

He reentered the kitchen. "Afraid we'll give the wrong impression if we arrive together?"

"What do you mean?" Except she had a feeling she knew exactly what he meant. "Are you talking about Stacy?" She accepted the juice glasses and rinsed them.

He nodded. "For the sake of argument, let's say Stacy is our suspect. If we purposely arrive at the studio after she does, she might think we've grown close again." Ursula's skin tingled as he asked, "Isn't it to our benefit if she believes we're a couple rather than her guessing we're snooping around?"

"I suppose." Him and his indisputable logic.

He retrieved a stainless steel canister by the sink. "What's this?"

Ursula closed her eyes. She should have stowed away the piece of equipment as soon as they'd walked in the door, but she'd totally forgotten her plan to process the films from Wednesday night in order to—what was it again? Oh, yeah. Force herself to face the images of her folly, which would miraculously verify that she and Gabe had shared hot sex and nothing else.

Certainly nothing resembling deep, strong, and, the scariest of all, possibly true love.

"A processing tank," she replied, aiming for a casual air.

"For what?"

She dried her hands on a dishtowel. "Developing film."

"Don't you need a darkroom?" He rolled the cylinder in his hands.

"Not if you have a changing bag." Her heart pounded. She *knew* him. He would hound her with questions until she confessed.

"What's a changing bag? I'm your apprentice. Teach me." His eyebrows wiggled.

Ursula crossed her arms over her chest. *Act like it's no big deal, and he'll lose interest.*

She explained, "The bag is shaped like a T-shirt. You stuff what you need into it, then shove your hands into the sleeves, open the films, and feed them onto the reels. The 'darkroom' is the inside of the bag."

"What sort of stuff?"

"Films, the processing tank, reels, scissors, a bottle opener."

"Really?" Curiosity sparked in his tone, damn it. "Is it hard to learn?"

"It's tricky, but I'm used to it. After the films are on the reels, you cap the tank and remove everything from the bag. Then you pour developing chemicals into the tank." She tucked her hair behind her ears. "About your idea to drive in together…"

Gaze on the processing tank, he spun it in his hands again. "I gather you have film to develop?" Looking up, he grinned.

"I considered it." *No big deal. No big deal. Not any sort of a deal.*

"Isn't it ethically irresponsible to develop film without my permission, especially when I'm the star of the photos?"

She snorted. "Get over yourself. I'm on them too."

"Ah, you planned to develop *both* films. The one of me with Curly and the one of…*us.*"

Her face burned. "I won't process either film now."

"Then why is the tank in the kitchen?" He placed it on the counter.

"I'm sure you can add two plus two. I was *thinking* of developing them. But I see your point. I'll toss them out." Turning, she arrowed for her bedroom.

"Where are they?" Gabe asked, close behind.

"In my dresser." She yanked open the top drawer. The two films from Wednesday night nestled on her panties. Grabbing the rolls, she shut the drawer.

"Wait. I like the red pair."

Uh-huh. "Out of my way, Gabe."

He stood a foot from the doorway, his broad shoulders crowding her path. "Why are you angry? I'm not the one crossing a line."

She huffed out a breath. "I'm not angry with *you*. I'm ticked at myself." For believing she could rationalize the freefall sensations he'd unleashed inside her the night they'd made love. For trying to convince herself he was no different from the guys of her past. For her utter lack of foresight. "You're bang on the money. I have no right processing these films without your permission. I would blow a gasket if a guy did that to me, so where do I get off doing it to you?"

He touched her wrist. "Sula, slow down. If I had the films and the knowledge to develop them, I admit, I'd be tempted."

"But you don't know how."

"I've never developed film in my life."

"And you *wouldn't* dream of taking them to a photo lab."

"And violate your trust again? Not a chance."

"Good." She shoved the rolls into his hands. "You keep them. Or throw them away. Clearly, I can't be trusted."

His gaze lowered to the films. "I want to develop them," he half-whispered.

Pulse racing, she snatched them back. "You said—"

"I *don't* know how to do it, Ursula. I want to develop them *with* you. Show me how it's done."

No, her personal Emergency Broadcast System screamed. She hadn't marked the films during their late-night photo session. She had no way of telling which contained the images of Gabe with the prop doll and which might reveal his sensual kisses as they'd undressed.

Developing the films alone would have felt hazardous enough. Developing them *with* Gabe would bare her soul.

He smiled. "If you can trust me not to develop them behind your back, you can trust me not to go crazy with lust when I see the images forming."

Why did that sound like a bad thing?

"Ursula, we're alone," he said, tone quiet and coaxing, sexy and smoky. "No roommates, no coworkers, no one with a vendetta against my uncle barging in. When will we have this chance again?"

She pressed her lips together. There was the gist of it. They wouldn't. Not if she remained firm in her conviction to go their separate ways after they concluded the investigation. By this coming Friday, she would have delivered the Real Men photos to *Seattle Lights*. With luck, Gabe would quickly solve the case. Their baddie had to trip up sooner or later, and then this whole ordeal would reach a rapid close.

Her heart ached as it thumped. "We can't print them here, only process them. We'd see tiny images on negatives, not black-and-white enlargements."

"Even better. Less temptation." His gaze honed in on hers, capturing her, holding her in his spell.

Her lungs squeezed.

Oh, boy.

She was in a mountain of trouble.

"It *does* look like a T-shirt." Gabe leaned forward on his chair. Across the table, Ursula's hands moved inside the changing bag, creating bumps in the black fabric.

"Shh. I'm concentrating." Her head tipped, and her raven hair shifted on her shoulders. "I'm guiding the second film onto the reel. Almost...*there*. Scissors next." She'd described the procedure in her alluring voice while feeding the first film. Now, her scissors snipped within the bag as she cut the tape fastening the film to the spool inside the roll. Basically, she operated sightless.

"Is the film on the reel yet?" Gabe asked, fascinated by the dexterity of her fingers.

"Yeah." She glanced at him. "I could have talked you through this part."

"I didn't want to botch it." Even with her expert tips guiding his progress, he hadn't wanted to chance accidentally destroying the reminders of the closeness they'd shared Wednesday night. Nope and nope and triple not-happening.

Their steamy photography session hadn't only been about sex for him. It had never been about lust with this woman, although making love with Sula had felt fantastic. No matter what happened after he wrapped the case, regardless of whether she changed her mind about pursuing a relationship, she had left her mark on him for life.

Because now he understood at least a tiny bit of the love his parents had shared, and he and Sula had barely scratched the surface of their potential. Chaotic though his world was right now, these last nine days had solidified what he was looking for, what he hadn't had a clue was missing in LA. Something strong, solid, and incredible. He had wasted years keeping women at an emotional distance, choosing uncomplicated badge bunnies like Tiff who hadn't wanted anything more than a fun time in bed.

Who or what had he been trying to protect? The heart of a good woman—or himself?

The bumps of fabric covering Ursula's hands moved again, claiming his attention. "I'm loading the reels into the tank." Her teeth sunk into her lower lip. "The cap is on." Her hands slipped out of the changing bag's sleeves. She unzipped the bag and placed the contents on the table.

Gabe straightened in his chair. "Amazing." Film ends, the bottle opener and scissors, spools, the film rolls and tops surrounded the processing tank. "The stuff reproduced."

A smile curved her mouth. "The chemicals come next." Rising, she strolled to the organized kitchen. Earlier, they'd cleaned their dinner mess and arranged developing paraphernalia on the counter. "Bring the tank." She glanced over her shoulder. "You're definitely doing this part. No chickening out."

"Aye, aye, Nancy." He met her at the sink. Their hips and arms brushed as she coached him through mixing the developer to the optimum temperature in a measuring jug. So far, no mess-ups. As per her instructions, he poured developer into the baffled top of the light-tight tank, recapped the tank, and shook it to distribute the solution. "Thanks for sharing this part of your life with me."

"You're welcome. Keep shaking the tank, ten seconds at the minimum. Then tap the bottom against the sink so bubbles don't stick to the films. Every thirty seconds, you shake another ten seconds then tap the bottom again. Over and over, for about five minutes."

He agitated the hell out of the tank. "I feel like I'm playing percussion."

She mixed another solution with an eye on the stopwatch. "You were a band geek in high school?"

He hadn't intended to reveal that secret. "I also played football. Linebacker."

"Don't worry, Sherlock. I won't blab about your band years. Which instrument?"

He should say drums. Something bad-boy and rock-star. Instead, he answered honestly, "Cymbals. Smashing them together helped release my teenage frustration." He paused. "Especially after my dad died." When he'd been furious at the universe and out for blood.

"Oh, Gabe." Empathy filled her voice. "You were only eighteen."

"Kind of old to get a kick out of crashing cymbals, huh?"

"Not at all." She placed her hand on his shoulder. "What time of year did your father die?"

"March. Two months after my birthday, to the day."

Her mouth dropped open. "That's horrible." She reached for the tank. "Here, let me do that."

He shook his head. "It helps." Continuing the shaking-and-tapping process dulled the throbbing in his solar plexus. "When an officer is murdered, the Department calls it the End of Watch. But it's not the end. The spirit of a fallen officer guides his brothers throughout the years."

Tears welled in her eyes. "What a lovely sentiment. Was there a public service?"

"Yeah. It was huge." Hearing the gruffness in his voice, Gabe agitated the tank. "A twenty-one gun salute, everything. Afterward, Dad's partner Bill and Bill's wife came back to the house with my mom and me. So did Ray from the tire shop. I ducked into my bedroom, saying I needed time alone. But I didn't want time. I wanted to memorialize my dad *my* way. I stood in the middle of the room with those damn cymbals and smashed and smashed and smashed. Twenty-one times."

A tear rolled down her cheek.

"Honey, please don't cry." Gabe tapped the tank in the sink. Leaving it there, he covered her hand with his on the counter. He had never admitted his twenty-one cymbal salute to anyone. Not his friends or his cheerleader girlfriend. Back then, no one knew aside from his mom, Bill, Darlene, and Ray.

But telling Ursula just now felt like second nature.

"Gabe, my heart breaks." She wiped away more tears. "What did your mom do?"

"She realized what was happening and let me get it out. After the twenty-first crash, I bowed my head and blubbered like a baby. Without a word, she slipped inside my room and hugged me. Darlene came in and hugged us both. Then Bill and Ray showed up. One big group hug while I bawled. Later, Bill and I talked. Ray and I talked. Over the weeks and months and years, we've had a lot of support."

Ursula whispered, "I'm glad you and your mom had good friends to help you through. When Grandma B passed, Kim and Deni were fabulous. And my family... We leaned on each other." Extending her right hand with the glossy new manicure, she spread her fingers to display the slim, gold, pinky ring. "This was her wedding ring. It's been nearly a year since she died, and I haven't taken it off." Her smile trembled. "The anniversary is coming quick now. December eighth."

"Sula..." He grazed her jaw with his thumb. He yearned to be there for her on that day. To offer the support they both knew was so important.

She glanced at the stopwatch. "Time's up. I don't want to lose the highlights. We'll use water to stop the developing."

Gabe nodded. He wouldn't push his luck. Whether she liked it or not, they grew closer with every passing hour. And he wanted to see those negatives.

Under her supervision, he drained the tank and proceeded to the stop bath and fixer steps.

"You must have loved chemistry," he said while tap water washed over the reels.

"Not my style. I worked on the yearbooks. My school had a small darkroom. Our teacher taught me both the correct and the slapdash ways to process film. This way is slapdash."

"Will it still work?"

She nodded. "Do you like it?"

"I like you."

A pretty rose suffused her face.

"We work well together," he added. "Not only today tailing Desiree, but cooking and cleaning up. And now." He wished they felt this ease and comfort with each other all the time.

Vulnerability shone in her eyes and on her face, but she forged ahead with more instructions. "Last step. A wetting agent to protect the negatives." She prepared another jug in the sink. "Lower the reels into the jug."

While he stacked the reels, she tucked two clothespins into her front jeans pocket. Seconds later, she towed the first reel out of the jug, her hair hanging over the front of her sweater. Unable to help himself, Gabe pushed back the dark strands.

Grasping the reel, she looked at him.

"You're beautiful," he whispered.

Her gaze lowered. "Gabe, you have a way of wearing me down."

"Sounds ominous."

"It's not. I enjoy spending time with you."

"I enjoy spending time with you too."

She smiled. "Okay, but we're not finished yet. Open the second reel, like this."

She twisted her reel, removing the top half. Gabe mimicked her actions, clipping a clothespin onto the end of his roll. Gripping the peg so he wouldn't touch the exposures, he let his film unwind and skimmed off excess liquid between two fingers.

He yearned to sneak a peek at the images, but imitating her efforts without ruining his exposures required every ounce of his focus.

"Now we hang them," Ursula said. "The shower is a perfect spot, but if Kim decides to come home…"

"Not a good idea." He didn't want either of her roommates spotting the negatives of their private moments.

"We'll use my closet."

He accompanied her down the hall. In her bedroom, she elbowed clothes out of the way and clipped both rolls onto empty hangers. Clothespins tagged the bottoms of each film to prevent curling.

"How long until they're dry?"

"Several hours. Even if we wanted to, we couldn't make prints until morning. And I'm not going near Mackie's darkroom until we catch this creep. We can look but not touch."

Hands on thighs, Gabe bent beside her to study the thirty-six exposure film of the prop doll and table. He'd mucked the first shots, but others showed improvement.

The exposures segued to out-of-focus frames of Ursula laughing, her hand partially covering her face. The remainder of the roll looked perfect...because she'd snapped them.

"Not bad." She pointed out a picture of him in jeans, his shirt unbuttoned. "You could be one of my Real Men models. Or maybe I'll ask Curly."

He grinned. They studied the second roll. The first frames presented Gabe's handiwork. This time, his subject looked as incredible as he'd felt that night—Ursula in soft focus, reclining on the purple lounge. Her tights draped the back of the chaise, and the white fur cushioned her bare legs in her short skirt.

The next exposures showcased them kissing and stripping above the waist while the shutter clicked at timed intervals. The final frame would have revealed her breasts as he'd unclasped her bra, but the camera angles were off.

Arousal barreled through him. He stepped back from the negatives.

"Time to go." Before his need for her chewed him up and spit him out.

She grasped his arm. "Please don't leave."

"If I stay any longer, you know where this will lead. In bed," he clarified, in case she thought he hankered for more scrambled eggs.

"I know." Her soft voice skittered along his skin. "But I want you. I want tonight."

"Sula, we've talked about a lot of personal stuff today. Don't let that influence your choices. Don't do something you'll regret later."

Her blue eyes grew hazy. "I want to let go with you, Gabe. For once in my life. To go with what I'm feeling and worry about the consequences later."

A pang squeezed in his chest. Falling in love with her was a freaking huge consequence.

Gently, he clasped her upper arms. "Honey, I care about you. This isn't fun and games for me. I've never felt this way before."

She lifted her fingertips to his mouth, the fluttering of her warm skin against his lips intimate and sensual.

"Let's not dissect it." She guided his hands to her hips. "Let's just... Oh, Gabe."

She kissed him, tugging him close. His erection pulsed beneath his jeans. He backed them toward her bed, lifting her sweater as she grappled with his shirt buttons.

Their mouths parted, and he pulled off her sweater. Her dark hair crackled with static before resettling on her shoulders.

Urgency driving him, he ripped off his shirt and unsnapped her bra. They tumbled onto the bed, mouths joined.

His injury protested, but he blocked the discomfort from his mind. The only ache he wanted to feel, the only hurt that meant anything, was the overwhelming need to drive deep inside her.

Over and over, for as long as she would have him.

In her bed.

In her life.

And, if he was lucky, in her heart.

Twenty-Four

Sunshine streamed through Ursula's bedroom window. Eyes drifting open, she wriggled her spine against Gabe's beneath the rumpled sheets. Last night, before they'd made love a second time, she'd flicked off the lights but hadn't closed the blinds. The hope of a clear day beckoned, perfect for their mid-morning photo session with horse trainer Tyson Cummings. Her heart felt lighter too. Light, yet full. Happy. Content.

For how long?

Closing her eyes again, she drew in a long breath. She didn't want to analyze last night—or fixate on the future. A bubble of bliss had enveloped her as she'd slept. She longed to luxuriate in it.

To luxuriate in Gabe.

Rolling over, she kissed his shoulder. They'd put his injury through the paces last night. Would he suffer additional discomfort today?

She caressed the scar on his butt. *Poor baby.*

A deep groan of pleasure lifted from his pillow. "Trying to seduce me, Nancy?"

"Only if you want me to, Sherlock."

"Oh, yeah." Shifting to face her in the bed, he pulled her close. His morning arousal prodded her leg as he brushed a kiss across her mouth and swept back the hair at her temple. "Hello." His husky voice spiraled through her, and her tummy swooped.

"Hi." *Her* voice sounded soft and adoring, darn it. She curled a hand around his hard length.

He moaned, eyes drifting shut. "I like your thinking, but the clock is on this side of the bed. We have the Woodinville shoot before too long."

Propping up, she peeked over his shoulder. "Ten after nine!" She vaulted out of bed. She'd planned to snap Tyson in cowboy gear astride a stallion outdoors and save the skin shots for pitching hay inside the barn. The weather was cooperating, but they needed to *move*. "Mackie wants us to drive his van again. He'll be ticked I parked in his spot all night." She jammed her arms into her bathrobe. *Shower, here I come.*

"We'll say you had car trouble." Gabe reached for his boxer-briefs. Tugging them on, he winced.

Her heart wrenched. "How's your leg?"

"Stiff, like other body parts. Not that I'm complaining." He grinned. "I need more physical therapy. Can you spare me for an appointment tomorrow?"

"Try to book one for today. You shouldn't suffer on my behalf."

"Thanks." Jeans in hand, he walked toward her. "Meet me in the shower?" Slipping an arm around her waist, he placed a tender kiss on her mouth.

"Yes, but no funny business." His arousal strained his underwear.

A knock banged on the door. "Ursula, you left a mess in the kitchen!"

"Ugh." Just what she needed—a roommate interrogation. "Kim is home." Finger-combing her messy hair, she cut a glance to the film negatives hanging in her open closet.

"I saw your purse on the counter," Kim shouted outside the bedroom door. "I know you're here. I hate it when you leave your photography junk out! We discussed this."

"She's cheerful," Gabe murmured, kissing Ursula's temple.

The door flew open. Kim gaped at them. "You have company!" The door whacked shut.

Ursula's hand whipped to her mouth. "Gabe, I'm sorry." Her face blazed, but a laugh tumbled from her lips. The look on Kim's face—shocked, aghast, embarrassed. Priceless.

Hugging her, he chuckled. "It's okay." He kissed her again. "Lend me toothpaste?"

"On the vanity. New toothbrushes are under the sink."

Carrying his clothes, he left the room. "Good morning to you too, Kim," he called toward the living room before disappearing into the can.

For the space of three heartbeats, Ursula stood in her room, arms crossed over her robe.

Game face applied, she strode to the kitchen. Kim organized the developing equipment, jeans and top wrinkled like she'd slept in them.

"Urs, I'm *sorry*." Kim's cheeks went chalk-white, and she staggered back against the counter.

"Forget that." An alcohol odor hovered around her friend. "Were you drinking?" Obviously, Kim had been. "When did you get home?"

"None of your business."

"Oh, and barging into my room is yours?"

"How was I to know? You've never had a guy here overnight." Kim gripped her skull. "Ow, I have the world's worst hangover."

"Where were you?" They usually kept track of each other. And Kim was right. Gabe was the first and only man Ursula had ever allowed to share her bed until morning.

A trickle of unease wormed into her veins.

"I had a date," Kim said. "It didn't turn out well."

"With who?" Ursula clasped Kim's arm. A hint of cigarette smoke clung to her friend's clothes. *Oh, no.* "Are you smoking again?"

"No, I swear." Kim clutched her stomach. "Pass me a bucket. I'm calling in sick." She dry-heaved.

Ursula fetched a large mixing bowl from a cupboard. "I'm worried about you."

"You're also late for work. We'll talk later. Go." Grabbing the bowl, Kim scurried to her room.

❧

Patting the handle of his cash-filled briefcase, Paul entered his office, a spring in his step. His lack of preparation for the Transportation Committee meeting an hour ago had soured his stomach, but his visit to the bank afterward made up for it. Tomorrow's pay drop for the vile Victor McKenzie was secure.

In thirteen days, Paul would deliver the final payment and close the chapter on McKenzie for good.

He allowed himself a small smile. With the slime-ball soon out of his life, he looked forward to refocusing on politics and his future with Christine. City Hall buzzed with the news that Mayor Smithson wouldn't seek reelection. A council president boasting an impressive track record and a child on the way was an ideal replacement for the aging Smithson.

Closing his office door, he turned to the coat rack. Behind him, a desk drawer squeaked.

Paul's neck hairs bristled. Jacket still on, he swiveled on his calf-skin wingtips. "Who's there?"

A blond head popped up behind his desk. "Paul!" The woman of his nightmares beamed, smile dazzling against pink lipstick.

"How did you get in here?" Sweat dampened his armpits. He couldn't bring himself to speak—or even think—his former lover's name.

She rose from her knees. "I can't find my address book. Did I forget it here?" She held one hand behind the waist of her blue dress.

"Address book? I've never seen it. Why would I have it?" Didn't she store that sort of information in her phone?

She giggled. "It's tiny and red. I've had it forever."

Paul gulped. She was lying. He could see it in the artful lift of her eyebrows and the cunning glint in her eyes.

Wary of alerting her to the contents of his briefcase, he set the case on the carpet at the base of the coat tree.

"You shouldn't be here." He strode to the desk. "I'm calling Security." He plucked up the phone, a ploy to hasten her departure.

Her free hand clamped his, sharp fingernails scraping his knuckles. "Paulll," she drawled in the sex-kitten voice that had lured him into an affair last spring. "There's no need. I'll go." Her right hand whipped out from behind her back. She stuffed something into her bra.

Alarm pelted him. "What did you take?"

"Wanna frisk me?" She cupped her boobs and jiggled her cleavage. Her necklace of fake stones bounced on her ivory skin.

He stepped back, raising a palm. "You can't *be* here. If Christine finds out—"

"Your stupid wife doesn't know I'm alive."

"Because we broke it off." Two months ago! McKenzie's repugnant blackmail scheme with the fictional California woman had taught Paul when to cut his losses. McKenzie had zero inkling he could have squeezed triple the money out of Paul—if McKenzie had realized *this* woman existed.

She sashayed over. "Paul, sweetie-buns, we only stopped seeing each other as a precaution."

His mouth dried. He'd made up the precaution thing in an attempt to soften the emotional blow. He'd thought she would have latched onto another man by now. Someone *available*.

He firmed his tone. "Christine can't learn about you."

She loosened his tie. "Would it really be so terrible if she did?" She unlatched the top two buttons of his shirt.

"She's pregnant," he blurted.

Eyes slitting, she yanked the tie. "*What?*"

"P-p-pregnant." Perspiration dotted his upper lip.

"*How did that happen?*"

"An accident," he lied.

Her anger dissolved. "Oh, that's different." A saccharine smile touched her lips. "Boil her in the hot tub for me, won't you, baby? What's a little miscarriage between man and wife?"

He choked on his saliva. Good Lord, she was certifiable.

"Don't say that," he hissed. "She's carrying my child."

She laughed. "Lighten up, Bunsy. I was joking." She gazed coyly at him through her lashes. "Paullll, I didn't appreciate you not responding to my text last night. It was one tiny message."

More like ten! While he was out for dinner with his in-laws. "We agreed you were not to email or text me. Not even once." He'd needed to shut off his phone.

"I know, but"—she wriggled her fingers—"it's time to agree to something else. I've been soooo patient. I need to have you again, baby." Reaching down, she massaged him through his trousers. A sigh trickled from her mouth as he hardened. "Uh-huh, there we go."

Paul's heart pounded. "We can't."

She smiled. "You said can't, not won't. You still want me, Bunsy." An odd light glittered in her eyes. Was she high?

He thought fast. "S-sweetie, you know we can't be together right now." Never, if he had his way. For now, he needed her gone from the building before someone recognized her. He'd devise a plan of action later. He couldn't think while she pawed him.

She pouted. "The Oval Office has seen plenty of action. Why not us?"

"I'm not in the Oval Office yet. If you keep this up, I'll—I mean, *we'll* never get there."

"Oooh, I like the sound of that 'we.'" She licked his lips, her tongue tasting of the cigarettes he'd asked her to give up more than once.

Stomach lurching, he lied, "I'm meeting Smithson in ten minutes. Please leave. It can only work between us again if you wait for *me* to contact you. No matter how long it takes." An eternity would pass before that happened.

Her forehead furrowed. "Because of the baby?"

Stacking lie upon lie, he nodded. "I can't abandon a pregnant wife. But once I'm mayor..." He'd hire a hitman to deal with this unpredictable woman, if necessary.

"Aww." Misreading him as he'd intended, she tapped a fingernail against his lips. "See? All I needed was a little reassurance." Grabbing her purse, she sauntered to the door. "Later, lover."

She left. Shaking, Paul wiped his face. Sweet Lord, two months ago, when he'd explained the California fiasco that had placed him within McKenzie's sights, she had seemed stable and poised, accepting of the situation. And now this. He'd miscalculated her attachment to him by a massive margin.

Forget McKenzie's blackmail scheme with the doctored conference pictures. If Christine learned Paul had indulged in a full-blown affair after her public humiliation following the hooker incident, she would leave him, baby or not.

Without his wealthy wife's support, his political dreams would go up in smoke.

Swearing, he stepped to his desk and rifled through the drawers. He had risked everything because he couldn't keep his dick in his pants. He was a walking cliché—and the world's biggest fool.

He peeked into the drawers, shaking his head. Everything appeared in place.

What had she taken?

❧

Eve curled trembling hands around her latte cup, pulse racing as she waited at the small table for Hal. They hadn't seen each other in three months. Now, he stood in line for his mid-morning coffee at the cafe equidistant from their employers, where they had first noticed each other.

A convenient location—one she had avoided since their breakup—but she questioned her choice to meet him here today. Memories surged, tugging at her heart: Hal's warm smile when someone jostled her in line and she'd bumped his back, his charming acceptance of her apology and invitation to share a table. Electricity had sparked as they'd discussed innocuous subjects like the weather, their jobs, and the wonder that they hadn't run across each other before.

Four days later, she'd stumbled upon him a second time, on the street near a menswear shop where she had often shopped for Doug. After a short conversation, Hal invited her to the symphony, and their relationship blossomed from there, the closest thing she'd experienced to the kismet of meeting Gabe's father.

Across the cafe, the barista placed a cup on the counter. Hal grasped his coffee and scanned the crowd. Eve raised a hand, gesturing him over. Nodding, he shoved his gloves into a coat pocket and dodged customers until he reached her table. His mouth curved, crinkling his brown eyes.

"Eve. Nice to hear from you." Sitting on the empty chair, he sipped his coffee. "What did you want to talk about? I didn't expect to see you until Saturday."

Their tree-hunting date this coming weekend. "I didn't want to text this, Hal. I can't go."

Hurt tinged his gaze. "I messed up so badly you can't accept my help getting your Christmas tree?"

She shook her head. "No, no, Victor surprised me with a tree two days ago. It's trimmed already. I couldn't turn away the gift. Hal, he found the tree in the pouring rain."

Hal's shoulders heaved as he sighed. Voice weary, he asked, "When I called about the tree-hunting, why didn't you just explain that you and McKenzie are together now?"

Eve clenched her cup. Why did Hal believe they were? "I don't know how you got that impression. Vic's a friend. Like a brother."

Hal grunted. "I highly doubt that's how he feels about you."

A chill sliced her bones. "Vic and I *aren't* together." Oh, God. Did *Vic* think they were?

Hal's gazed remained steady. "Eve, I want you to be happy. Deny it all you want, but you don't run away from him. With me..." He inhaled. "Every time I tried to take our relationship to the next level, you'd shut down. You don't do that with McKenzie."

Because she didn't love Victor. Not how she loved this man.

Her heart thundered in her ears. She still loved Hal.

"It's not the same thing at all," she tried to explain, extending a hand across the table. Her fingertips fluttered, but Hal didn't touch them. She withdrew her hand. "Hal, I miss you. We always laughed, and...and I could talk to you about anything." Except Doug. She had failed him there. "I—"

"Eve," he interrupted in a gentle tone. "Why did you agree to go tree-hunting with me?"

She ran a thumb along her cup. "You sounded alone when you called." A direct correlation to how she felt. Despite having Gabe home, despite her friends and colleagues and brother-in-law supporting her, a huge chunk was missing from her life. A significant other.

A man like Hal.

"Yes, I'm alone. Please look at me, Eve."

She lifted her gaze. Pain shone in his kind brown eyes.

"I'm willing to remain alone until I find a woman who isn't afraid to love again," he said, voice breaking. "I know I'm not Doug.

I never will be. But Doug died eleven years ago, and the only man in your life other than your son is your dead husband's brother. I don't know how that plays out in your mind, but it doesn't sound like a healthy situation to me." Leaving his coffee, he stood.

Eve grabbed his hand. "Wait." Vibrant energy shot up her arm, and she gasped, uncertain how to react, what to say, what to do. Hal had hit the nail on the head, pinpointing her emotional failures with astonishing clarity. She needed to stare down her past before she could hope to brave a future with anyone, much less this man whom she'd already hurt with her selfishness.

He shook off her grip. "I've waited months, Eve. I had some hope with the holidays upon us, but after this tree thing, I just don't know what to say." Turning, he pushed through the crowd.

Hot tears burned her eyes as the weight of a million stones clogged her throat.

At this rate, *she* was guaranteed to remain alone.

Forever.

&

By the time Ursula arrived at the equestrian center with Gabe to meet Tyson and Carla Cummings, the sun had slunk behind low-hanging clouds. The scent of approaching rain mingled in the midmorning air with the smells of horses, hay, and damp earth. If good fortune sided with her, she would capture the photos of Tyson straddling his horse before the rain busted through and they returned to the barn for the shirts-off shots.

Carla, dressed like her husband in jeans, a sheepskin jacket, cowboy boots, and hat, led Tyson's chestnut stallion along Ursula's left. A few steps ahead, Gabe and Tyson carted the photography equipment and a thick blanket to protect the gear from the ground. The men had traded war stories since shaking hands and thumping backs. Gabe's limp had piqued Tyson's curiosity and spurred tales about the cowboy's wild days on the rodeo circuit. Gabe, playing Ursula's assistant, attributed his bad leg to a motorcycle accident.

As the guys strolled toward an outdoor arena banking a thick growth of evergreens, Carla leaned toward Ursula. "Listen to them, trying to impress us with their studly ways."

Was that what the men were doing? Tyson's stories, while entertaining, reminded Ursula of Gabe's shooting. Even though she hadn't known him in the summer, thinking about the pain he must have endured filled her chest with a dull ache.

She asked Carla, "How did you handle all those times Tyson got hurt?"

"I didn't know him then. A rodeo clown isn't for me. They're adrenaline junkies."

"I heard that," Tyson called.

"You were meant to," Carla called back. The horse nickered, and she stroked the animal's muzzle as they strolled. "Tyson and I met after he got gored."

"*Gored?*" Ursula's eyes popped. She hadn't noticed scarring above the waist during Tyson's test shots. Had the bull speared him in the leg?

She shivered. *An awful lot like Gabe's injury.*

Carla nodded. "Yep, and the reality is every bit as grisly as it sounds. Rodeo performers distract the bull when the rider dismounts or gets bucked off. It looks funny, but it's dangerous work. The performers are like bull fighters, but the public sees them as clowns."

"Omigod, I would freak. Was he rescuing someone?"

"Yeah. A novice rider. The guy slipped on mud. That's all it takes. The bull caught Tyson in the thigh and flung him against the fence. Tys was lucky he survived."

So was Gabe. What if the convenience store thug had shot him in the chest instead of his glute? His mom might be dealing with the loss of her son right now. And Ursula would have never met him.

Emptiness drilled a hole inside her. She shook off the encroaching feeling of dread that had been shadowing her since Kim burst into her bedroom, interrupting her moment with Gabe, then topped off their conversation in the kitchen with the observation that last night was the first time Ursula had allowed a man to share her bed throughout the night.

Granted, Ursula hadn't *expected* to wake up with Gabe. The warmth of a soul-deep afterglow had swirled inside her as they'd cuddled after making love a second time last night. She'd drifted off, and, evidently, so had he.

Did the emotional significance of staying overnight count if it wasn't planned but just happened?

A question to consider another time. She needed to work.

She glanced ahead to Gabe and Tyson, who had stopped at the arena. Ursula and Carla caught up to the men as Tyson arranged the blanket on the ground. Gabe set down the photography bags and crouched to retrieve the cameras.

Opening the arena gate, Tyson continued his story. "After I recovered, I accepted a job here, with Carla's uncle. I wasn't much use to him at first, but he kept me on and I learned from the best. When I wasn't trying to catch the attention of his hard-working niece, that is." Tyson grinned at his wife.

Carla smiled. "My Uncle John rode bulls back in the day. He respected Tyson a great deal. When Uncle John got sick…" Her eyes glistened with unshed tears. "He lost his wife and son in a car accident when I was a child. I've loved horses my whole life and worked here since I was sixteen, so he left the place to me. I was honored he trusted me with his legacy. Over the last ten years, the business has taken off. Tyson's participation in your article is free advertising. That can't hurt."

Pulling on gloves, Tyson nodded. "Why does she think I auditioned for the shoot? As long as the business thrives, my job is safe." He accepted the reins from his wife.

Carla laughed, turning her attention to Gabe. "Do you like working for family?" she asked Ursula's faux assistant while Tyson guided the whinnying stallion into the arena. Carla latched the gate, and her husband mounted the horse. With a tip of his black Stetson, Tyson trotted the stallion around the ring.

Gabe pushed off the ground. "Let's just say my uncle isn't likely to mention me in his will." He handed Ursula a camera body and large zoom lens.

"Gabe is helping me temporarily," she explained.

"A few more days, and we'll be done, I hope." Gabe's steady gaze met hers, and her pulse leapt. "With me working for my uncle, at any rate."

Carla glanced between them. "So *that's* how it is." Her voice brimmed with innuendo.

Hands shaky, Ursula looked down at the camera to attach the lens. Did Gabe mean what he'd said? Did he want more time with her?

Did *she* want more time with him after they solved the case?

How much time? A week? A month?

Years?

Nerves jumping, she snapped the lens into place. What had she been thinking, making love with him last night? She'd wanted to say to hell with the consequences and now look where she was, confused as all get-out again. Because every moment they spent alone, whether in bed or sharing details of their lives over a processing tank, brought them closer and closer, scaring her silly.

Their relationship had evolved so rapidly. And it felt too real. She craved stability. Despite Gabe's abundance of amazing qualities, wouldn't he always hunger to bring down bad guys, even if as a PI instead of a cop? Could she live with the uncertainty? Waiting each night for his safe return, like his mom had waited for his dad, until, ultimately, bad news came—

Her throat clamped shut. She couldn't even bear to think about it.

She didn't yearn for an adrenaline junkie any more than Carla had.

She did *not* want to fall in love with Gabe.

Twenty-Five

THEY RETURNED to the studio at two. Gabe gazed at Ursula as she steered the van into the alley. Puddles from yesterday's rain stained the asphalt, but the leaden skies had yet to release the downpour she'd worried about at the equestrian center.

Hundreds of photos packed her camera card of Tyson riding his horse and leading the stallion around the ring. Afterward, the cowboy had doffed his shirt and flexed his muscles for shots of pitching hay and mucking out stalls. The *Seattle Lights* editor would flip over his fit body. Carla certainly had, Gabe remembered, lips quirking. Ursula should be overjoyed with Tyson's session and the positive impact the photo spread would have on her career, but she hadn't uttered more than five sentences during the drive back downtown. Was she concerned about the case? Or was it something else?

"You've been quiet," he broached.

"Traffic is a nightmare." Angling him a glance, she pulled the van into Mackie's space. Gabe had left his pickup in a parking garage, and her car occupied the second spot.

"That's not it." Last night had been incredible. Not only the best sex of his life but also the most intimate lovemaking he had ever experienced. Then Kim raced into the bedroom this morning, disrupting their privacy.

When Ursula joined him in the shower, it became abundantly

clear something had changed. Damned if he knew what. She'd still responded to his touch, but subdued didn't begin to describe her mood while they'd picked up the van and established his motivation for changing the locks before driving to the Woodinville shoot.

"I'm a big boy," he said. "I can take it. Do you regret sleeping with me last night?"

"No," she replied after a beat. "I'm just tired. We didn't actually do a lot of sleeping." She grinned, but the expression didn't reach her eyes.

"Okay." He tapped the armrest.

She cut the engine. "Gabe, I *don't* regret it. I wanted to be with you again." A pale pink dusted her face. "I still do."

She didn't sound convinced, but he'd take it. "Great. You free tonight?"

"Sorry, I'm visiting my parents. My mom boxed old jackets to donate to a shelter."

"I spoke to my mom about the idea too. She put together a couple of bags. I can drop them at your place after you visit your folks. We can google shelters."

Lashes lowering, Ursula cleared her throat. "Maybe bring them to work in the morning instead. We should let your leg recover."

"Not necessarily." He hadn't managed to book a physical therapy appointment today, but tomorrow's slot would suffice. "I need to maintain the treatments and my exercises, not stop living." His recuperation had suffered since he'd returned to Seattle. He could blame his uncle's troubles for disrupting his schedule but prioritizing his time fell on him. Besides, if not for Mackie's problems, he wouldn't have met Ursula. He would accept that trade any day. She'd softened the blow of his reentry into civilian life. She challenged him and made him laugh. While holding her in bed this morning, a deep sense of contentment had tunneled into his bones. A longing to return to her again and again.

There was an emotion he hadn't experienced before. With any other woman. Ever.

It should scare the hell out of him.

It didn't.

But maybe, if she felt the same, it might scare her.

"I'm not making excuses," she whispered, looking at her keys. "Can I ask you something?"

"Go ahead."

"Did you really hurt your leg in a motorcycle accident?"

He angled his head. "Yes. Three years ago. Same damn leg."

"Do you still ride?" Concern shone in her dark blue eyes.

"Not since the shooting. I sold my bike to a friend in LA. I might take it up again after a year or two."

"I see." She pocketed the keys.

"Hey." He stroked his fingertips along her jacket sleeve. "Are you all right?"

"Yeah. I just don't know how to tell when you're making something up. I realize it's because of the case. You need to maintain your cover."

"How about when we have a private moment, you ask." Like she had now. "I won't lie to you, Ursula."

"But you have."

"Before you discovered me bagging the nails."

Face flushing, she nodded.

"Have previous boyfriends lied to you?"

Her gaze turned toward the windshield. "They basically told me what I needed to hear then did whatever they wanted."

"Did any of them cheat?"

"Not that I know." Her troubled gaze moved back to him. "I have a bit of a track record of falling for, um, good-time guys."

Leaning against the passenger seat, he shook his head. "What do you mean?"

"Unreliable. Out for fun." Her lips pursed. "Cads."

He laughed. "Cads?"

"Scoundrels."

"Ne'er-do-wells?"

Her mouth curved. "That's one of the reasons I promised myself I wouldn't date again until after I bought the studio and built up the business. I'm finished with men who treat women like gum sticking to the soles of their shoes."

He nudged her shoulder. "So your plan was to take a vow of celibacy for the next five years?"

Her smile broadened, brightening her beautiful face. "It sounds ridiculous, but, yes, more or less."

"Then I showed up."

"You sure did."

"A cad, a scoundrel, a ne'er-do-well."

"Or so it seemed."

"It doesn't anymore?"

Her gaze cast downward. "No."

"Good." If not for the van's awkward center console, he would pull her onto his lap and wrap her in a big hug. Instead, he clasped her hand on the small storage compartment separating their seats. Their fingers interlocked, her grandmother's wedding ring resting cool against his skin. "I wish I could have told you about the case earlier," he said in a low, quiet voice. "I don't regret making love with you last week. I will never regret sharing that time with you." But neither would he forget the hurt slashing her face when she'd stomped off in that frilly dressing robe and feather-swathed shoes. "I don't regret it, but as a professional I should have known better. I *do* know better. Does that make sense?"

"Yes. You were undercover. It was part of your job."

He shook his head. "Concealing my identity until I cleared you of the studio sabotage was my job. Getting so lost in us that I couldn't resist becoming too friendly before I verified your alibis wasn't. I, the man Gabe McKenzie, made love with you last week and last night. Not Gabe the former cop and future PI."

Her voice softened. "I get it."

Did she?

He laced and unlaced their fingers. "Sula... Can I call you that?"

Nodding, she smiled at him through a dark sweep of lashes.

"I know we happened quickly, but I don't consider us a one-time thing."

"I think we've established we're a two- or three-time thing."

She was trying to make light of the rapid development of their relationship, so he would follow suit.

"Four, five, six." Or ten thousand, if he was lucky. "Who's counting?"

She smiled shyly up again, and the truth walloped him in the chest. He wasn't falling anymore. He'd fallen. Totally and completely in love with Ursula Scott.

This was it. She was it. She was the one.

Don't tell her yet.

His gut was rarely wrong, and instinct warned she wasn't ready to hear those words from him. And maybe not from any man.

Her pleasant voice broke into his thoughts. "Can I ask something else?"

"Yep." Anything she wanted. "And you don't have to ask *if* you can ask first."

"Okay." She paused. "Why did you move to Los Angeles? Why didn't you join the local police?"

The million dollar question. "My mom didn't want me to apply to the academy at all after my dad was killed on the job," he said, allowing her fingers to slip back and forth through his, over the console. "What mother would want her only child entering the same line of work?"

"Why did you?" she half-whispered.

"I needed to be my own man. I grew up wanting to be a cop. It's not unusual when your father is one. I've met entire families in law enforcement. Brothers, sisters, fathers, mothers." The warmth of her palm slid against his. "After my dad died, the idea of me following in his footsteps upset my mother so much that I forced it out of my mind. I wasn't only marking time at U-Dub until I was old enough to write the academy exam. I planned to use my criminology degree to springboard to grad school or law."

She gazed at him, her lustrous raven hair begging for his touch. "I could see you as a trial lawyer, but not an academic," she said as he caressed a silky tress.

"Tell me about it. I felt useless sitting in class. During those first two years, I told myself the despondency would pass, that it was part of working through my grief. By junior year, I'd talked enough with Bill and Ray and my buddies to realize I was holding myself back out of a need to protect my mom. I didn't want to study the slime of the earth, I wanted to collar them. I moved to LA to distance her from my everyday life."

Ursula wet her full, kissable lips. "Did it work?"

"Not a lick. She was pretty pissed at first. Bill was like my second father at that point, and she held him responsible for influencing me. She didn't speak to him or Ray for a month."

Ursula's gaze melted. "Your poor mom. She wasn't mad, Gabe. She was terrified for her child. Any mother would be."

"I understand that now. At twenty-two, I didn't. As time passed, she accepted my choices. Then I got shot, and her emotional roller coaster began all over again. I couldn't stand the idea of feeling chained to a desk while my buddies worked the streets without a limp slowing them down. And I couldn't put my mom through something like that again. Moving home to become a PI seemed the next logical move."

"PIs still find themselves in danger."

"Despite what TV and movies portray, it's not the same thing." Unable to deny himself any longer, he leaned across the console and kissed her, caressing the curve of her cheek, savoring her soft lips. He would love to sit in the studio van and kiss her for hours. But the *Seattle Lights* shoot beckoned. And so did the case.

"Ready to put on a show for Stacy?" he whispered, easing away from Sula's succulent mouth. This morning the receptionist had noticed them entering the studio together. In their haste to meet Tyson Cummings, they hadn't determined if the girl bought them as a couple again or not.

Ursula nodded. "As I ever will be."

"You hate deceiving her." She saw so much good in others.

"I'll deal with it."

Gabe got out and met her on the driver's side of the van. Standing between the vehicles and cupping her face while the cold air buffeted their jackets, he kissed her again, and tenderness swelled in his chest, the need to tell her how he felt battling to burst free.

For years, he'd denied himself his childhood dream of becoming a cop. Only now did he fully realize that all those years he'd spent in Los Angeles hadn't been solely about protecting his mom from the harsh realities of his job. He'd hidden away in California because he hadn't felt ready to find love, to risk placing his heart and soul in the care of another human being only to have every moment of joy and happiness ripped away in a violent instant.

It was all so clear to him. His heart, his family, and his future—the past seven years had led him home.

To this woman. His Sula. His love.

"OMG, you *are* back together!" Stacy's excited voice pierced the air.

Gabe turned, slipping an arm around Ursula's waist. "Hi, Stacy."

Dark circles shadowed the girl's eyes behind her glasses, but her wide grin lit the gloomy lane. "I told you the sparks hadn't died with him, Urs."

"Why aren't you inside?" Ursula asked. "It's cold."

Stacy held up a deli bag. "Mackie took pictures of the high school kids through lunch. He wanted a sub, so I bought one for myself on his dime. It's the least he can do, considering I didn't receive a key for the new locks."

Gabe shrugged. "He said neither you nor I would until he receives the entire set." The locksmith had been scheduled to arrive after Gabe and Ursula left for the equestrian center. Mackie was to have informed Stacy about a fictional mugging Saturday night resulting in the loss of his wallet and keys. Gabe had suggested the story to his uncle while Stacy made coffee in the staffroom.

"But you get to help Urs," Stacy complained. "I have to stand around and wait in the rain if Mackie is late. Why bother changing locks anyway? If the mugger with his old keys finds the studio address in his wallet and tries to sneak into the building, wouldn't they get frustrated by the new locks and smash the front window like whoever threw that dumb grenade? Muggers want money. Mackie's keys are probably at the bottom of a garbage can by now."

Eyeing Stacy, Gabe asked, "Why make it easy on a criminal by *not* changing the locks?" *Unless you're the culprit, and you resent the extra work.* "Most businesses keep petty cash hanging around. The goon who attacked my uncle might decide the studio is an uncomplicated score."

Stacy switched the deli bag to her other hand. "You're right. I'm sorry. I'm so bagged. My exam is tonight, and tomorrow I move. Ursula, can you still help? It's a total stress."

Sula nodded. "After work? We'll leave from here."

Gabe squeezed her waist, indicating approval of her plans. Tonight, before staking out the studio, he would tail Stacy and confirm the girl really had an exam. Then, if more sabotage occurred while Ursula helped Stacy move, he'd cross the younger woman off his suspect list.

Changing the locks sent the saboteur a vital message: *Continue this mischief and you will get caught.*

If the updated security didn't work, Gabe would *live* in the studio until he caught the suspect. He needed to close this case and move on with his life.

Hopefully, with Ursula by his side.

Jasmine giggled as Mackie hauled her into his apartment, hands squeezing her shapely rear. Two doors down, Old Lady Chadwick flashed a disapproving glare. Mackie snarled at the wrinkled hag, and she ducked back inside. The nosy crone.

"Aren't we going for dinner?" Jas placed her purse on the counter and straightened her denim jacket.

"You bet." Closing the door, Mackie pushed her onto her knees. "First, I need some of this." When her hands didn't graze his zipper, he glanced down. "Hurry, darlin'. I'm famished."

She glowered at him. "No."

"Playing hard to get?" He unzipped.

"Mackie, no! I'm not a pro. I can't blow you five times a day. My lips will turn to rubber."

"Yeah, yeah." He guided his johnson into her mouth, and she licked the tip with the enthusiasm of a five-dollar whore.

Damn it. Mackie grabbed the limp base and rammed his dick deeper into her mouth.

Jas toppled onto her rear. "Guess he doesn't want me tonight," she griped, yanking down her hiked skirt, her long legs sprawled on the floor.

Mackie stuffed his useless prick into his pants. "It's the stress at work." Changing the locks, photographing teenagers, delivering the Windermere pamphlet—he'd had enough.

"Can I get up?" Jasmine rubbed her mouth.

"What the hell? You never wipe me off you."

She scrambled to her feet. "We're going to a nice restaurant!"

"Not no more." He strode into the living room and grabbed the remote. Flipping on the TV, he sank onto the recliner.

"What?" Hands on hips, she strutted over and blocked his view of the game. "I can't do you through no fault of my own, so you won't take me out to eat?"

He peered around her hip at the blaring TV. "Sit down. I need to relax. Then you'll do your business, and we can leave."

"*No*. I'm not some trick you can call whenever you want. I work in a fancy store downtown. I help ladies choose their high-class lingerie. It takes talent, Mackie!"

He stared coldly at her. "That's exactly what you are to me. A slut, like all the rest."

She gasped, tears spilling over her heavy mascara. "Vic McKenzie, you're an asshole." She flung out a hand. "You think I don't know what this is about? You've been dreaming about your sister-in-law for weeks. You call her name in your sleep, you crud." She bawled, knuckles grinding her eyes like an inconsolable four-year-old. A hiccup popped from her mouth. "I thought if I was patient—"

"Jesus, woman, pipe down. The quarterback caught the ball." He waved her out of his line of sight.

She stomped a foot. "No! You used to care. You were a gentleman. When's the last time you bought me something special? Chocolates? Flowers? Jewelry? I'm cutting you off until you learn to romance me again."

Shit on a stick, his ears hurt. He pushed her out of the way. "That's not gonna happen." He'd diddled her a hundred times already. There was no point wasting his money on silly gifts.

"Then what am *I* getting out of this relationship?" she screeched.

He grabbed his crotch. "This."

"Is sex all you think about?" She blubbered. "I care about you, Mackie, but I'm tired of waiting for you to appreciate me! To think about our future."

"I broke it off with my other girls. What else do ya' want?"

Tears streamed down her face. "A man who loves me for more than what's between my legs—"

"Or below your nose." He snickered.

"That's not you, is it?" She hiccupped.

"Give me a break. No, it's not. Happy?" He peered at the TV.

She snatched the remote out of his hand. "Look at me. Look at *me*, Mackie!"

"For fuck's sake, find some other schmuck to look at you. I'm sick of it already."

Her eyes snapped. "Screw you." She chucked the remote against a kitchen cabinet. It clattered in pieces to the floor.

He leapt from the chair. "You broke my new remote!"

She filched her purse from the counter.

"I want my keys back!" Mackie lunged for the purse, but she dodged away on her four-inch heels, swift as an acrobat.

"You just gave them to me. Twenty minutes ago!" Her makeup bled black streaks on her splotchy cheeks, creating ugly raccoon eyes. "*My own key* for this apartment. And one for your office. You said they were symbols of your trust!"

For the freaking love of Michael Bublé, she was so easy to dupe. "I only said that to stop your whining," he spat out. "'Make love to me, Mackie. Romance me, Mackie.' Boo-flibberty-hoo. I gave you keys to shut you up."

"It didn't work! I'm gonna tell every woman I know what a creep you are."

"Like hell." He charged at her again. She bashed his skull with her rock-hard purse and raced out of his apartment.

He ran to the open door. "Those keys are fakes!" he called after her. A lie that would leave her a blithering wreck like she deserved.

The keys were real, but Jasmine needed to believe otherwise, or who knew what the emotional basket case would do. *He* needed to start thinking things through. Yeah, Jas had shut up but not for near long enough. Twenty minutes of less nagging? Get real. She was to have been his sole source of sexual release until a few days before Christmas, when he proposed to Evie. But now, because Jas's pouty mouth was impossible to resist, copies of the new keys to his office—*his refuge*—sat in her cement lump of a purse.

He yelled down the hall, "You have forty-eight hours to return those fakes and any property of mine at your place, or I'm coming after you! It won't be pretty, I promise. And then I never want to see you again! *Do you hear me, Jasmine Jones?*" He slammed the door, head throbbing.

Crap-apple, she packed a punch.

He didn't have to be thumped on the noggin twice to learn his lesson. It was way past time to cut Jas loose.

To cut them *all* loose.

He stamped to the filing cabinet and opened the false back in the bottom drawer. Tugging out the old videotapes, he yanked tape from one, crushed a couple of cassettes beneath his shoes, and tossed the rest in the garbage can by his laptop desk.

Screw Jasmine. Screw the women on the grainy tapes. They were distant memories anyway.

He didn't need those sluts anymore.

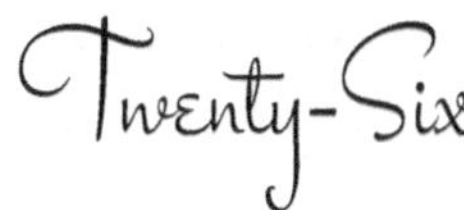

"HOW ABOUT THIS ONE?" Ursula's mom asked, choosing a photo from a packet on the kitchen table of her parents' rented house. "You're cute as a button in it."

"I remember you taking that." Ursula stroked a finger over the snapshot of herself at ten wrapped in the orange-and-brown afghan Grandma Betty knitted for her after the fire. "Gosh, I miss her. This is definitely going in the new scrapbook." She placed the photo on the stack dedicated to her next project, which would accompany the album of Grandma Betty she'd given her mom at Thanksgiving. The tinkling piano and saxophone strains of Billy Joel's "Just the Way You Are," a favorite from her parents' garage-sale CD collection, drifted from a player on an open shelf. Downstairs, Dad and Owen watched a football game, their favorite after-family-dinner pastime.

"I can't believe I found this box of pictures behind those bags of too-small clothes." Mom rubbed her wrist. She'd removed her carpal tunnel brace before stirring her famous zesty spaghetti sauce in case the sauce splashed and stained it. "I worried I'd lost them in one of our moves."

"I know. Isn't it exciting? It's nice having tangible evidence of my memories." Ursula touched her mom's hand. "Do you need ibuprofen or your brace?"

Her mom shook her head. "It's a minor flare-up. I refuse to

allow this injury to run my life. I'll ice the spot later and wear the splint to bed."

"You should cut your hours." Her mom's job as a supermarket cashier wreaked havoc with her wrist.

"Not an option. We need the money."

"Mom—"

"Sweetie." Her mom's gaze held steady. "I don't want to mope about my aches and pains. Let's sort pictures." She wagged a finger. "No arguments."

Ursula sighed. Her parents were proud but not unreasonable. "Just so you understand, I intend to help out you and Dad as soon as I can."

"Buy that business and make it a success. Then we'll talk."

"I'm serious."

"I know you are. You and Owen are as determined as your father. I love that about all three of you." Her mom sipped her glass of chardonnay. "Remember, honey, we Scotts might splinter, but we don't break. Your grandma's illness kicked us in the pocketbook"— a fine sheen of tears glazed her eyes as she spoke about Grandma B —"but we'll climb back up, like we pulled together to rebuild after the fire."

Ursula squeezed her mom's hand. "Yes, that fire changed our lives forever."

"We survived, and that's what counts."

Ursula smiled. Her family had endured disasters and financial setbacks, but they remained intact, a solid unit, perhaps stronger than they would have been otherwise. Gabe hadn't been as fortunate, losing his father and then getting shot himself.

She gave her head a small shake. *Stop obsessing about Gabe.* As the days passed, he consumed her thoughts with alarming frequency. If she kept this up, their attraction would spiral out of control, and soon she'd find herself focusing on *him* to the detriment of her plans. When he'd caressed her hand in the van this afternoon, her feelings of "I really, really like this guy" hovered dangerously close to toppling into love—in under two weeks.

That was fast. *Too* fast.

Could she trust what she was feeling? Or was she only caught up in the moment?

Pulse careening, she swallowed a mouthful of wine.

"There are hundreds of pictures I wish I could have saved from the fire," her mom said in a reflective tone. "Your and Owen's baby pictures, your first birthdays, your first teeth." She opened another packet. "All those firsts, gone forever."

"Except for the copies you gave Grandma B," Ursula said.

"And those I gave other extended family. It's not the same as having my children's original baby books. You'll understand when you have kids." She drew in a breath. "You know what? There's no sense dwelling on the past. We're creating new memories now with these scrapbooks. Let's theme this one, *Moments To Treasure.*"

Ursula's heart melted. "I love it. And Mom? Maybe around Christmas"—after the first anniversary of her grandmother's death was behind them—"we can go through Grandma's albums and compile new baby books for me and Owen. They won't be the originals with our tiny tufts of hair and those little ink-pad handprints, but at least it's something."

"Sweetie, that's perfect."

Happiness bubbled inside Ursula. For several minutes, she and her mom drank chardonnay while sorting through and laughing at the old pictures of Ursula and Owen. As Bruce Springsteen sang "Glory Days," Ursula flipped through an assortment of the family working in the backyard of the house her parents owned upon first moving to Seattle.

"Look." She showed a picture to her mom. "You and I building Owen's tree fort." Both females wielded hammers, and green paint splattered Ursula's torn girlhood jeans.

"I was frustrated with your dad that day." Her mom pointed at the picture. "See my sourpuss look?"

"What happened?"

"He probably criticized my handyman skills. It's not important." Her mom searched another packet. "Remember your cousin's wedding?" She held up a snapshot. "You were in charge of the guestbook."

"Yuck. That's not going in the pile." At fourteen, Ursula's limbs were as skinny as a crane fly's.

"It certainly is." Her mom thumped the picture onto the scrapbook stack.

"Please, Mom, no."

"Sweetie, cut me some slack. I don't have any pictures of my wedding to your dad."

"There must be some in Grandma B's albums."

Her mom's gaze skittered to the fridge.

"What?" Had Ursula upset her? "Okay, okay." She caved on the crane-fly imitation. "The picture stays. It's not like you'll have pictures of my wedding any time soon."

"If you're talking about it, you're thinking about it." Her mom grinned.

Ursula blinked. She wasn't thinking about it!

"I'm only twenty-five. There's plenty of time."

"I was twenty-one."

"No, you weren't. You were twenty-two."

"More wine?" Her mother topped up their glasses.

"Mom? You always said you got married at twenty-two."

"I did." Mom cleared her throat. "The second time."

Ursula's eyes nearly bugged out of her head. "You were married before Dad?" Shock and bleeping awe!

"No, sweetie. I married him twice."

"What? Why? Did Grandma Betty know?"

"Nope." Her mom chuckled. Eyes aglow, she relayed, "Your grandparents wanted me to finish college first, but your dad and I couldn't wait. We were so in love. It was pure fireworks, Ursie." A wide smile spread across her face. "What fun we had, being secretly married for months while I lived at home. It was so romantic. Removing my rings around your grandma so she wouldn't guess. Sneaking out to see him when she thought I was studying. Oh, the things we did in his car."

"I don't want to hear about what you did in his car!" Giggling, Ursula clamped a hand to her mouth.

"The elopement was for us," her mom said, "and the church service was for my family. We planned to eventually spill the beans, but when your dad and I realized how badly your grandma wanted to play mother-of-the-bride, we decided to keep our first wedding a secret. All these years, we've celebrated two anniversaries. Your father loves to celebrate his anniversaries." A coy glint entered her eyes.

"Mom!" Too much information.

Her mother pshawed. "Just because your dad and I rarely fight doesn't mean we don't have passion. We definitely did. And there are plenty of nights we still do."

Oh, my God. Note to Self: Do not ply Mother with wine ever again.

"I don't know where I got the idea you and Dad were best friends who married."

"Of course we're best friends." Her mom picked up her wineglass. "Show me a woman who can't share her innermost thoughts with her husband, and I'll show you a marriage in danger of crumbling." Her mom's voice saddened. "I really miss not having pictures of our elopement."

"No one was there? Who stood up for you?"

"The officiant in Portland provided the witnesses. We had a few snapshots hidden in the back of my lingerie drawer, but they were destroyed in the fire. Your grandma only had pictures of our church wedding taken several months later."

Ursula glanced over the old photos stacked neatly on the table-top. "Mom, why don't you and Dad renew your vows on the date of your elopement? You could wear vintage outfits. I'll take the pictures."

Her mom squealed, fisting her hands. "Yes! You're full of wonderful ideas tonight. It would be April first, Ursie, because we were fools in love."

Ursula's dad strolled into the kitchen, rubbing his stomach. "Do we have chips?"

Her mom's eyebrows lifted. "There's my fool now."

He stopped at the table. "What's going on?"

"We're getting married, Bob. Ursula suggested it. Third time's a charm."

"You told her about the elopement?" He rubbed Mom's shoulder, and she clasped his hand. Bending, he kissed her cheek. "I'd marry you a thousand times, Lizzie."

Ursula guzzled her wine. *Okay, universe. Message received. No need to clobber me over the head.*

If her parents' experience was anything to go by, evidently not all relationships beginning with vibrant fireworks exploded in the participants' faces. That didn't mean a trip down the aisle awaited her and Gabe.

If you're talking about it, you're thinking about it, her mother's voice resounded in her head.

If you're thinking about it—

Then what?

Ursula swallowed the lump of panic in her throat.

Her life was becoming way too complex.

Tuesday morning, Gabe stepped off the elevator in Ursula's building with two capped lattes and a bag of freshly baked muffins. Kim, head down as she rustled in her purse, plowed into him.

"Kim, watch it." He held the cups high, but his muffins and her cigarettes flew to the floor.

Dropping to her knees in a dressy raincoat, pants, and heels, she returned the cellophane-wrapped package to her purse. "Sorry, Gabe. What are you doing here?"

She stood, passing him the coffeehouse bag. He gripped it against one cup.

"I brought Ursula breakfast," he replied as the elevator doors whisked shut without Kim inside.

"Is she expecting you?"

"No, it's a surprise. Am I too late?" When he'd arrived at the studio with the muffins and lattes, Stacy said Ursula was driving Reba today. He'd hopped into his truck and raced over.

"No, the building boiler broke down, and hot water was scarce. We're all running behind." Kim chewed a fingernail. "Don't tell Urs about the smokes, okay? I'm trying to quit, but it's harder than I thought, even with the vapes. Carrying around an unopened pack reminds me what's at stake."

"Which is?"

"My lungs. If I crave the real thing, I stare at the warning label until my eyeballs bleed. It's simple, cheap, and effective." She punched the elevator button, and the doors swooped open again. Entering the compartment, she faced him. "Do you care about her?"

"Yes." A hell of a lot.

"Good. Because if you break her heart, I'll bust your balls. Understood?" The elevator doors swished closed.

Chuckling, Gabe strolled to the apartment door. Deni exited, tugging on a jacket and her warm brown cheeks glowing. Her eyes lit up.

"Hi, Gabe." She left the door open. "Ursula is dressing. We had a problem with the boiler."

"I saw Kim. She told me."

"If she was grouchy, ignore her. Turns out she was dating some guy she met online. All he wanted to do was party, and it was wearing her out. I'm glad she wised up and broke it off. She's facing horrendous deadlines at work."

He shrugged. "She was nice." Although protective of Ursula, like any good friend should be.

"Good to hear," Deni called, glancing around as she hurried down the hall. "You're welcome to wait in the kitchen. You'll score points if you shake cinnamon onto one of those lattes."

"Already accomplished at the coffee shop." He added, "You shouldn't allow a guy you barely know free run of the place."

"Ursula trusts you, so I do too. Bye!" Curls bouncing, Deni disappeared into the elevator.

Gabe elbowed open the apartment door. "Ursula?"

No answer. He stepped into the living room as she exited her bedroom, towel-drying her hair. Dark jeans and a knit turtleneck the rich green of a forest hugged her curves.

His heart warmed. "Good morning, Nancy."

She jumped in sock-clad feet. "Gabe!"

"Deni let me in. I brought breakfast." He extended a latte. "Cinnamon on top, just how you like it."

"Thanks." Holding the towel, she accepted the cup. "I'm driving Reba today. I didn't expect to see you. Did you text? I didn't receive anything."

"Nope." His physical therapy appointment bumped into her first location shoot of the day, so they had agreed he wouldn't tag along. Driving over for a quick visit, he'd thought she would be happy to see him, but something was off.

He longed to kiss or hug her but now wasn't the time. Yesterday, while they'd sat in the van in the studio parking lot, she had as much as admitted, without outright stating it, that the quick onset of their relationship concerned her. She put a lot of stock in her carefully laid-out plans to buy the studio and help her parents. Did she worry that allowing time for a personal life would interfere with her goals?

"I stopped at the studio to give you a recap of last night," he said. "My uncle said he needed his van, and Stacy confirmed you weren't coming in for a trade, so here I am." He hesitated. "I missed you."

"I missed you too." Voice soft, she eyed her cup.

He checked his watch. "Should we sit?" Plenty of time remained until her morning Real Men session at Pike Place Market, where their next model worked as a vendor. Whatever was bugging her, unless her schedule had changed, it wasn't work.

Nodding, she went to the table and hung her towel on the end chair. Gabe sat across from her. The damp strands of her hair shone in the morning light. The strawberry scent of her shampoo teased his nostrils as he extracted muffins and napkins from the bag.

"Banana-nut or blueberry?" He spread two napkins on the Formica table.

"Blueberry, thanks." Lifting her latte lid, she blew on the cinnamon-laced foam. "Smells wonderful." She sipped. "I needed that." Her smile stretched tight.

Unnatural.

Forced.

Gabe placed the blueberry muffin on her napkin. "Was my coming here a mistake?"

"No, sorry. I have a lot on my mind."

"Like what?" He was in love with the girl. If she needed help, he was there.

"Family stuff. Something came up with my mom last night." Setting down her latte, she twisted her thumb ring.

Now *he* was worried. "Is she okay?"

"Yes, she's—" Sula shook her head. "Everything's fine. I'm mulling over something she said. I had a restless night."

Interpreting her woman-speak, he figured she didn't want to talk about whatever she and her mom had discussed. He should have texted or called instead of dropping by unannounced. But he was here now, and they had a lot of ground to cover.

"Well, you'll be happy to hear I tailed Stacy last night, and she really did write an exam. I hung around the halls then followed her home. By all accounts, she hit the sack early."

Sula inhaled. "That's a relief."

"It's a step in the right direction." Gabe drank his milky espresso. "Keep your eyes and ears open when you help her move tonight. If you notice anything out of the ordinary, call or text."

Nodding, she broke off a muffin chunk. "Did you stake out the studio?"

"Yes. I got there after Stacy's apartment was dark for an hour. From what I can tell, no one's tried to break in since Friday." Four days. "Maybe they located what they were after or decided it's no longer worth the effort."

"Or the new locks are keeping them out."

"Or they're waiting before striking again."

"I hope not. I want this to be over, Gabe."

"So do I." They needed to move on with their lives. As a couple, if he had his way. He bit into his muffin. "I spoke to the homeless guy. He hasn't noticed anything suspicious around the neighborhood."

Her forehead crinkled. "Do you think he's telling the truth?"

"It's hard to say, but I mentioned the blankets and clothes, and he seemed grateful."

"I'll take my bags to the shelter later. My mom located one near the studio."

"We can do it together, following the afternoon photo session. My boxes are in my truck."

Glancing down, she picked at her muffin. "I can manage the Real Men stuff on my own this week. We don't need to keep pretending you're my assistant."

"That's a negative, Nancy. I don't want Stacy learning we duped her until we catch this creep."

"I haven't duped her, Gabe. I played along because I felt like I had no choice."

Narrowing his gaze, he studied Ursula's perfect posture and

composed features. "What's happened in the last twenty-four hours?"

"Nothing. I shouldn't have said that." Avoiding eye contact, she sipped her latte.

"Sweetheart, give me some credit. We spent all Sunday night together. Holding you in my arms while you slept felt fantastic, one of the best experiences of my life." *The* best, but he didn't want to overstate and make her even more skittish. "Yesterday in the van, I suspected you were nervous about us. I could feel it. But now you're flat out pulling away. What did I do?"

"It's not you, it's me." Wincing, she clutched his hand for a second. "That came out wrong. I didn't mean it that way. Gabe, you didn't do anything. I'd like you to work the case today, that's all."

"Without you?" That was a switch. On Friday, when they'd discovered the mice, she'd insisted on becoming involved. Had threatened to snoop on her own if he didn't agree.

What had changed between then and now, other than he'd fallen hard?

What was she *really* trying to say?

Stop thinking like a cop and listen to her.

"It makes sense to separate at this point," she said before taking a drink of her latte. "For the day, if not the week. We're close to eliminating Stacy as a suspect." She counted out one on her right pinky finger. "We put aside Mackie's list of old girlfriend names in favor of investigating Desiree Lewis, which didn't lead anywhere that I can tell." Down went her fourth finger, counting off two. "What about the other women listed in the notepad?" Tap to the middle digit. "Five are left to look into, right?" Tap to the index.

Gabe nodded. "I made some calls during the stakeout. Mary Bliss and Lynette Lafleur both work at The Dirty Kitty Show Lounge, a strip club. Mary is assistant manager there now."

"Have you talked to them?" Ursula asked, the tension receding from her face now that they spoke about the cold, hard facts of the case.

"Not yet." He ate more of his muffin. "I spoke to the manager and found out Mary is working this morning. I'll interview her after my PT appointment. I'm also considering booking a meeting with Paul Bloomfield."

"The councilmember you saw in the daily paper at Mackie's? Why?"

"He's council president. Acts as mayor when Smithson isn't available."

"Council president then." Sula smiled, and Gabe relaxed.

"While Stacy was writing her exam last night, I had an interesting phone call with Tasha Manning from the *Clarion*." As he'd learned during his charade of a date with Tasha, the twenty-six-year-old had been employed by the community rag for ages. Tasha might work in Classifieds, but she kept her ear to the ground. "Were you aware Mr. Bloomfield had an encounter with a prostitute four years ago?" At Ursula's puzzled look, he elaborated, "It made the news. I scoured internet archives this morning. Bloomfield hired the hooker then backed out. Looks like the woman wanted her fifteen minutes of fame, because when she learned his identity, she contacted the media. According to one gossip forum, the experience humiliated Paul's rich wife, who contemplated divorce."

Ursula chewed and swallowed a bite of muffin. "I must have heard something at the time, but it didn't stick." She cleaned crumbs off her hands. "Why would old gossip about a Seattle politician concern your uncle? Mackie and the Bloomfields don't run in the same social circles. Does your uncle even vote?"

"I don't know, but when I visited his place Sunday not only did he act strange when I asked about Bloomfield's picture in the paper, he has a pricy new laptop, a state-of-the-art TV, wireless sound-surround speakers—"

"What? I asked about updating the studio computers last month. He said the business couldn't afford it."

"He claimed he bought the laptop a month ago."

"Using studio money or personal funds?"

"That's the burning question. If the studio isn't doing well, where's he getting the cash?"

She leaned back in her chair, rubbing her neck. "Business has improved, but it's not fantastic."

"I have a theory."

But she'd already caught up to him. "He has something new on the council president!" She gaped. "Gabe, is it possible Mackie remembered the hooker incident, and when an opportunity arose to exploit Paul Bloomfield, he pounced?"

"My thoughts exactly. Problem is, I haven't unearthed more dirt on Bloomfield." On top of his research, he'd checked with Bill Cruikshank and the seasoned cop hadn't heard a thing. "Paul's record was squeaky clean before the hooker thing and ever since. He and his wife support a number of charities, and he's well respected at City Hall."

Twirling her thumb ring, Ursula leaned forward. "There's a portrait of the Bloomfields in one of Mackie's sample albums. I paged through them when he hired me." She glanced up. "Paul has status in the community, so Mackie labeled and dated the page. If I remember correctly, the portrait was taken a year before the hooker incident. Gabe, Mackie has blackmailed women from his past. Maybe now he's blackmailing the council president. You said Paul's wife is rich?"

"As sin. She's a Rasmussen. Old Seattle money."

Bouncing on her chair, Ursula thumped the table with the flat of her hand. "Maybe Mackie has had his eye on Paul Bloomfield the last four years. Maybe he's been tracking any number of wealthy Seattleites, waiting for his chance. He must know something Paul can't risk getting exposed. Bloomfield has weathered one scandal, but would the public or his rich wife forgive another?"

"Bingo." Gabe grinned. "You're a natural, Nancy."

She leapt off her chair. "You have to talk to Paul. Do whatever you can to speak to him this week. Tomorrow. Today! Have you called his office?"

"No, but I will." Gabe stood, bad leg aching. He massaged his hip, palm grinding his jeans.

"Do it before your physical therapy appointment. Do it now." She reached toward his jacket pocket. "Where's your phone?"

He touched her wrist, stilling her abrupt flurry of activity. "Slow down, sweetheart. I need a reason to request a meeting with the president of the Seattle Council."

"Make one up. Is your phone in your truck? Use mine." She strode to the desk and plucked her cell out of her purse. "I'll google City Hall." She swiped the screen.

"Not so fast. Let's think this through."

Selecting a browser app, she shook her head. "I need my real life back again."

"Will that life include me?" The question popped out. *Shit*. His face prickled.

Ursula's gaze flew from her cell. "Life? Include?"

Gabe shifted his weight from one foot to the other. He'd kicked the damn elephant into the middle of the room. "We've circled the issue for days, Sula. I care about you. I want to be with you."

Her cheeks reddened. "Gabe, I—I have to put the business first right now."

"Ouch." He flinched.

"You know what I mean. It's my family." Her voice squeaked. "The anniversary of Grandma Betty's passing is around the corner, and I can't think beyond helping my mom and Owen through that or—or getting my plans for buying the studio back on track. My inheritance is the down payment. It's like Grandma's legacy."

"I realize that, honey." Gabe peeled her cell phone out of her hands. "I understand your grief for your grandma. If anyone can help you through the first-year mark, it's me. You can help your family, and I'll help you." He set her phone on the table. "I want to be there for you."

"Gabe." Her eyes glistened with moisture. "I know you understand. How can you not after losing your dad?" Raw emotion scraped her voice. "But there's other stuff. We've only known each other ten days."

"Two weeks tomorrow." He knew what she was driving at. They were like a bolt from the blue. Cupid's arrow. All that cheesy stuff.

Except loving her didn't feel cheesy in the slightest.

"I don't usually become involved with a guy so quickly," she said.

"I don't become involved at all. Which means we're special."

Panic shone in her gaze. "We have separate life plans."

"So, we'll make plans together."

She pressed her fingertips to her temple. "Why are we doing this now? I have to go to work. The magazine deadline is this Friday. You just moved home. Your uncle is my boss. You haven't moved into your apartment."

"I signed the lease for February." What was her point?

"You're opening your agency. You need to take the state licensing course." Her hands somersaulted over and over each other, level with her breasts. "You're in therapy to heal your leg. You have old friends you haven't seen. And you and I—we're all tangled up." She sucked in air. "Don't you want to give yourself some breathing room?"

"That's the last thing I need." But she obviously did. "I had seven years of freaking space in LA. And you know what? It sucked. I *want* to be tangled up with you, honey. To be tangled up in life. I don't want to hide anymore. You're it for me, Sula. I am in this thing with you so deep, I can't tell you."

"I'm in there with you. But I can't process this. It's slamming into me, Gabe. It's—" Her shoulders heaved.

He swore. "Come here." He gathered her into his arms. Fingers threading in her drying hair, he cupped her head against the indentation of his shoulder.

Big, wrenching sobs spilled out of her. Hot tears drenched his shirt beneath his open jacket, her body shuddering.

"Shh. Shh." He stroked her head, and his chest pinched. Damn it, what had he done? *McKenzie, you idiot.* Ursula liked order. It helped her cope. Just because he had found the love of his life didn't mean she was ready to be found, to become part of an insta-couple or consider a future beyond establishing a safety net for the very thing that drove her, the essence of who she was, the people *she* loved—her family.

In less than two weeks, he'd blown into her life and complicated the hell out of it. The studio sabotage, her grandmother's swiftly advancing first deathiversary...

Who was he to barge in on her pain, to grab at her heart and shove his feelings onto her when she carried the struggles of her parents and the hopes of her deceased grandmother on one wobbly plate?

He consoled her with quiet sounds and gentle hugs. When her gaze met his again, her blotchy cheeks and tear-stained face hammered a railroad spike into his heart.

"I want to figure us out," she whispered. "I don't know if I can."

"It doesn't matter. Tell me what you need." He cupped her face, thumbs stroking her jaw. "Tell me, Sula."

"The case." She gulped, grasping his wrists. "Solved. Over with. Done. My deadline is in three days. I can't handle everything happening at once. I'm sorry. It's too much."

Was *he* too much?

He brushed at her tears. "Don't say another word, and don't you dare apologize. I've got it." *I've got you.*

Except he didn't have her. And maybe he never would.

Being alone throughout most of his twenties had sucked, although he hadn't realized it while he was buried in police work, spinning his wheels with badge bunnies like Tiff.

Now he knew what he wanted. A home, a future, family. It all began with Ursula.

Look at the mess he'd made. He thought being alone in California had sucked? He needed lessons in the most cherished of human emotions. Love. He'd left his mother on her own for years. He'd bungled today with Ursula. The evidence of his ineptitude lay strewn around him.

"You finish the shoot, and I'll wrap the case." Lowering his head, he gazed into her crystalline eyes. "All right?"

"I…I'm still helping Stacy move tonight," she whispered.

"Agreed. As her friend. I'll take care of everything else. I need to know that if I leave now, you'll be okay."

With a tiny intake of breath, she nodded.

He kissed her forehead and strode to the door, glancing over his shoulder at the soft sound of her footfalls. He stepped into the corridor.

She stood alone in the entryway beside the kitchen, hugging her arms. Gaze glued to the carpet, she rubbed a knuckle below one eye. His heart shredded at the sight.

The door clicked shut, closing her in, cutting him off.

He pivoted on his bad leg and headed for the elevator. From this point forward, he would direct every ounce of his energy toward catching the scumbag threatening the studio and destroying Ursula's dreams.

They might not have a future. She might not be ready.

But this was something he could do.

Something he could do for her.

This woman he loved.

GABE KNOCKED on the manager's door at The Dirty Kitty Show Lounge. Ursula needed the case solved, and he would solve it. As quickly as possible, without placing her in danger. Her wellbeing remained his top priority. He hadn't wanted her jeopardizing her safety playing detective in the first place.

"Come in," a woman's voice filtered through the panel.

He entered the office, sore glute cramping. Upon leaving Ursula's, he'd canceled his physical therapy appointment and pushed up his meeting with Mary Bliss, now known as Mary Bismarck, assistant manager of The Dirty Kitty. A busty brunette in her early forties, Mary flicked her gaze his way as her multi-ringed fingers tapped the computer keys.

"One moment," she said. "I'm pressed for time." Hitting the Enter key, she rose and smoothed the waist of her snakeskin-print dress. "Gabriel, is it? You spoke to Curt on the phone last night. He and I share this office."

Nodding, Gabe shook her hand over the big desk. "He said I could talk to you about security work. Sorry for rescheduling at the last minute. The young woman who took my call a little while ago said it was fine."

Mary's dark eyebrows rose. "It was. Then. But that's all right. Things change on a dime around here. Your card?" She extended a hand.

Gabe passed her one of the fake McKenzie Security business cards he'd printed on his mom's desktop computer this morning. Glancing around the office, he noted an abundance of twentieth-century collectibles and movie paraphernalia. Pinups of curvy sex symbols vied for wall space with a decade of nudie calendars and several unlit Dirty Kitty neon signs.

He gestured to the Marilyn Monroe poster behind Mary's desk. "My granddad had that poster in his garage," he fibbed in an amiable tone.

A wry smile tipped her mouth. "She never loses her appeal, unlike some of us." Gesturing for Gabe to take the guest chair, she sat down again. "Twenty years ago, I bleached my hair and worked the stage to songs from her movies. The customers loved it."

"I'm sure they did. You have a beautiful figure."

"Flattery will get you everywhere, Mr. Kent."

Spying his opening, Gabe asked, "Excuse me?"

"Mr. Kent," she repeated, then glanced at the card. "Gabe McKenzie?" she read, brow wrinkling. "Curt scribbles, but I can usually decipher his handwriting. The sticky note on my computer screen this morning said your name was Gabriel Kent."

Gabe offered a polite smile. "He must have misheard me. There was a lot of background noise when we spoke, and my cell reception had a lot of static." He'd used a phony surname with The Dirty Kitty to decrease the chances of Mary canceling today's meeting based on the McKenzie name alone.

Gaze shrewd, she rubbed the card. "McKenzie, huh? Any relation to Victor McKenzie?"

Here we go. "Matter of fact, he's my uncle."

Her lips thinned. "Get out of my club," she said, voice seething.

Feigning alarm, Gabe repositioned himself in his chair. "Why?"

She shot to her feet. "I don't need you McKenzie jackassess hanging around."

He lifted his hands. "You know my uncle?"

"You bet I do. And I want no part of his sleazy schemes—or yours."

Gabe stood. "Ms. Bismarck, I'll leave if you want, but please don't judge me by my uncle. I just returned to town. He and I don't talk, and he's definitely not my buddy. If you have to know, I hate the turd."

"Well, goddamn good for you."

"Damn it. I've been gone seven years. He must have pissed off half of Seattle during that time, because you're the second person in thirty minutes to kick me out of their office because of his lousy name. I'm just trying to start a business."

Mouth softening, she sighed. "Mr. McKenzie, I'm sorry, but your uncle is the worst sort of scum. If you want your security firm to succeed, steer clear of him."

"I don't get it. What did he do to you?"

"Oh, no, you don't. For all I know, he sent you here to find out if he can scam me again."

Gabe gentled his voice. "Whatever he did, it must have been awful. I'm sorry."

She inhaled a shaky breath. A second later, the phone by her boss's name plate rang.

While she talked to the person on the other end of the line, Gabe scrubbed his hands over his face to disguise his examination of the desk. Legal-sized paper files stacked a corner, and a snow globe of the Space Needle perched atop a wooden box similar to the style his mother used to store recipes, except, in keeping with the flavor of The Dirty Kitty, this box featured a faded cartoon Betty Boop.

Mary hung up the phone. "You should go."

"I have references." He reached into his back jeans pocket, maintaining his eager-to-please persona.

The phone rang again. "Give me a second." She picked up.

Gabe hitched his thumb in his belt loop. His references were as fictitious as his business cards. If she googled the names in his presence, he was sunk. Considering her reaction to his uncle's identity, what were the odds she'd consider his referrals during their meeting?

Pretty much zilch. A risk he would take.

She finished her call. "I need to check a liquor shipment out back."

"I'll return later." If he had a tail, he would wag it. Anything to gain her trust and encourage her to talk.

"Wait here. I won't be long, and I have something to say."

Leaving the door open, she hurried the rear of the club. Gabe let out a quiet whistle. *That was easy.*

He inched the door closed until only a sliver of space remained. Sneaking to the desk, he eyed this evening's performance schedule on the computer screen and checked the Betty Boop box. His fingers skipped over tattered employee index cards, which, for whatever reason, hadn't been tossed out in favor of digitizing every document in the office.

Using his smartphone, he snapped photos of the index card information for Mary and also Lynette Lafleur. He itched to snoop further, but the assistant manager could return any time.

He bolted to the door and opened it wide. Remaining standing, he favored his bum leg while pretending to admire a poster of a young 1960s movie idol juxtaposed on the far wall with glossy photos of contemporary sex symbols.

Ten seconds later, Mary strode in. "Mr. McKenzie, I need to deal with a problem with the shipment."

"You asked me to wait. Should I return this afternoon? Or whenever is convenient?" Wag, wag.

She shook her head. "Please don't waste your time. I know it isn't fair to compare you to your uncle, but if I hired you, whenever we saw each other I would think about the hell he put me through. Then I might have to strangle the son of a bitch, and I'm not keen on landing in jail."

Gabe groaned. "I understand." He had what he needed anyway.

"Good luck with your business." Mary hustled him out of the office.

Ursula had a crappy day. As she went through the motions of her first Real Men session with Issaquah potter Tony Rand and his romantic partner at the Market, her thoughts circled back to her meltdown in her apartment this morning. She'd freaked out on Gabe big time. About Grandma B, about the case and magazine shoot. About everything.

Gabe had said he was "in this thing so deep" with her, which should thrill her. And, for the briefest of moments, before she'd lost her mind completely, it had. But after her confusing outburst, she wouldn't be surprised if he assumed a new identity and holed up in a safe house, far away from her riotous emotions.

Barely noticing the vibrant colors of the vendor stalls and omnipresent hum of conversations, she bade goodbye to Tony and his partner and repacked her equipment. Biting her lip, she lugged the last case to her car. Since her talk with her mom last night, she couldn't shake the feeling that she was falling, falling, falling...so deeply in love with Gabe McKenzie that she might never claw her way back out. But falling in love shouldn't feel like a panic attack, like she'd lost her defenses and was utterly exposed.

Was that normal?

She shut Reba's trunk. Her phone dinged in her purse, signaling an incoming text. Scanning Stacy's message, she frowned. Her session with Deiter Reinhold, an architect who lived on a houseboat and collected nautical antiques, had been scheduled for this afternoon. Now the poor man had caught a nasty flu.

He wants to postpone until tomorrow, Stacy texted. *But what if he's still sick?*

Ursula typed, *If that happens, I'll shoot his backup Thursday. Deiter suits the magazine's demographics. I want to give him a chance.*

Okay, Stacy replied. *Are you returning here then?*

And chance running into Gabe? She couldn't face him yet.

No, she texted. *If Mackie asks, say I'm busy.*

Doing what? Stacy messaged.

Just busy.

Stacy didn't respond, and Ursula swore. Had she been too short with the girl?

She texted, *Stace, I haven't forgotten your move. I'll pick you up after work. Is five okay? We'll head straight to your place.* She added a couple of happy-face emoticons.

A prompt reply whooshed in. *Sounds perfect!!!* Cat and heart and ecstatic-face emojis bubbled across her screen.

Feeling marginally better, Ursula delivered her bags of clothes to the homeless shelter. Afterward, sitting in Reba, she contacted the *Seattle Lights* editor and agreed on revised plans for Deiter. Cell phone powered off, she played hooky the rest of the day, gorging on movie-theater popcorn and watching the better part of two matinees back-to-back. If she thought about Gabe, she pulled up her turtleneck sleeve and pinched her wrist. By the time she cut out of the second movie to get Stacy, her skin looked like a mosquito convention had assembled on her forearm.

She met the girl on the street outside the studio. Stacy hopped into Reba and complained about Mackie throughout the drive to her sister's house. As per her directions, Ursula parked outside a detached three-car garage several yards from a large contemporary home featuring a stucco exterior, impeccable landscaping, and additional enclosed parking.

While Stacy checked the house, Ursula stood in the empty garage, arms crossed over her leather blazer. Her chest squeezed as if a vice-grip clenched her heart. Hiding in the movie complex had accomplished squat. She still felt lousy, and her mind refused to stop whirring. Gabe wasn't anything like the guys of her past who had only been out for a good time. If he was "in deep," didn't that mean he cared about her, like she cared about him? So why did her entire world feel as if it had flipped inside out?

Stacy breezed into the garage. "Coast is clear. Shelly isn't home."

"Is she at work?"

"Beats me." Stacy extracted flattened moving boxes from behind an old dresser. "She's temping, and her schedule's up in the air. Besides, *I'm* not allowed to keep tabs on her life, just the other way around." She repositioned the dresser. "Can you carry some of these?"

Taking four boxes, Ursula trudged up a narrow staircase to the garage apartment. "Your sister has a huge house. Why two parking areas?"

"Her ex-husband liked his toys." Stacy unlocked the door. "He had a speedboat and an ATV. You know the type. Always showing off."

Inside, Ursula meandered her gaze over the tiny kitchen lining one wall of the cozy apartment. Japanese screen dividers separated the bedroom from the main living space. "Why are you living out here?" Instead of with her sister in that humongous house.

Stacy set down her boxes. "Our mom wanted me to move in

with Shelly, but I thought this cute little place would give me privacy. I was wrong." She retrieved scissors and packing tape from a drawer. "That's weird." She rummaged in the drawer again. "I had two rolls of tape."

"One is enough for seven boxes, Stace." Ursula removed her coat.

"That's not the point." Returning to the living area, Stacy shook the large roll of clear packing tape. "A roll is definitely missing. Which means Shelly has been *in* here—in *my* space—going through my stuff. This is the kind of behavior that makes me pissed." Kneeling by the coffee table, she assembled a box. "We need to move fast. Shelly could be gone until morning or she might pop back within a few hours. If she sees me packing, she'll hit the roof." She held the bottom of the box while Ursula ripped a sticky swath of packing tape off the roll and secured the flaps. "One down, six to go!" The girl beamed, her irritation dissolving. "Let's build all the boxes first."

"Sounds good." Ursula reached for another box.

"Are you okay?" Stacy asked after they'd assembled four. "You seem down. Is it because Deiter Reinhold cancelled?"

Ursula shook her head. "It's not his fault he caught the flu." Deiter's illness wouldn't affect her deadline. The *Seattle Lights* editor expected delivery of her final selections first thing Friday. Okay, so maybe Ursula shouldn't have wasted precious time at the movies, but even if Deiter's poor health extended beyond twenty-four hours and she couldn't shoot him tomorrow afternoon, she would edit the files for the first seven models later tonight, leaving the morning free for her last subject and Thursday available to photograph and edit Deiter or his replacement.

If only she could manage her personal life as easily.

"Stace, can you contact Deiter's backup and pencil him in for Thursday?"

"Already done. And Urs? Don't lose heart about Deiter. Look at the bright side. Gabe didn't hang around the studio today but hopefully he'll be on hand to help you tomorrow."

"I don't know, Stace." Ursula had asked Gabe if *he* needed breathing room...but maybe she did.

Stacy constructed the fifth box. "Ursula, what is it? Something's wrong."

Ursula's heart twisted. "I don't want to burden you, Stacy. We need to pack."

"We're friends now, right? You can tell me anything."

Could she? Ursula expelled a breath. She hadn't dared confide in Kim or Deni about her rapidly developing emotions. Once she began unloading on either of her roommates, she would spill about Gabe's past, the case, her boss's sleazy blackmailing. Everything.

"Gabe and I had a fight," she blurted. Except that wasn't the right word. They'd disagreed about the timing of their relationship, and panic had hit her hard. But then he'd hugged her. Oh, how he'd hugged her, his warmth and understanding heating her deep inside. When he'd left, she'd felt empty, her soul aching from already missing him.

Stacy's brown eyes saddened behind her glasses. "You and Gabe are arguing again? You just started dating."

"It's complicated." More than Stacy realized.

"Aw, Urs, he's hot, he's nice, he's into you. What's the problem?"

"I like him too much." There, she'd admitted it. "I like him so much, Stacy, and it scares me to death."

Stacy's gaze narrowed. "Do you mean like or love?"

"I love him, all right?" Ursula's heart pounded. "It's terrifying. I've never been in love before. What if I screw up?" Her worst fear, splayed wide open. She was in love with Gabe, and she didn't have the slightest idea how to act or what to do. Everyone she knew had suffered heartbreak or ruined their relationships.

Except her parents.

And now Deni and James.

How to ensure she followed those positive role models? Aside from her family and closest friends, eventually she lost everyone and everything. Her grandmother to a debilitating disease and multiple strokes, her childhood home to a nightmarish fire which had eroded the simple security of feeling rooted to one place.

She'd tried to latch onto a concrete future with her plans for the studio. Yet each day of these past two weeks, every time she or Gabe uncovered evidence of more sabotage, even the career goals she had naively assumed she could attain by the sheer force of her determination were in jeopardy.

Was it any wonder she'd tripped out this morning? At ten years old, she couldn't protect her helpless pet from the smoke and flames. At twenty-five, she'd hung her hopes on building a commercial career in an era when anyone with a camera could cobble together a website and advertise low-cost alternatives.

She called herself a professional, but she felt like a sham. With so much doubt crowding her mind, how could she convince herself she possessed the bravery to take a leap of faith into a series of uncertain tomorrows with Gabe?

Mackie stomped down the sidewalk, hands stuffed in his pockets and head lowered against the cold wind whipping his coat. His after-work visit to his latest haunt a few blocks from the studio had ended on a bitter note. Usually an intense lap dance satisfied him between servings of emotionally insecure women like Jas, but tonight, despite riding an all-day high after collecting Bloomfield's second payment, he couldn't get his motor revving. The lap-dancer had slipped him a knowing sneer, indicating she'd noted his dismal condition. And she was one of his favorites. The humiliation would drive him from the strip club for days!

Reaching the studio, he unlocked the front door with jerky movements and chucked his wool cap onto the reception desk. What the frig was wrong with him? First, his johnson had shied away in the aftermath of the microwave fire. Then, last week, when he woke from the nightmare about Doug, another flop when Jasmine attempted to comfort him with sex.

Both times, the effects had been temporary, but c'mon! Never in his life had he failed to rise to the occasion, until recently when he'd realized declaring his love to Evie lay within reach.

His hands flung skyward. *That's it!*

He loved Evie with a frenzy. Had the message finally gotten through to his dick? After he married his darling sister-in-law, there would be no more sluts. No more lap dances or sex tapes. No more guilt-demons chasing him, taunting how he could have saved Doug.

Just Mackie and his sweetheart of a wife, living out his early-retirement dreams.

He raced to his office. Time to junk his girlie magazines, empty the S&M cupboard, even trash the battered video camera concealed in the wall to remind him of his glory days. Time to completely purify himself for his woman, his new life, his love.

He stopped, eyes peeling wide as he realized his office door stood open. In his hurry to visit the club, he must have left the thing unlocked.

Racing into the room, he flipped on the light. He skidded to a halt in front of his desk. "What the—?"

A massive lifelike vibrator perched "up" on the wood surface. Clear red syrup coated the head of the fake penis. More syrup pooled at the base, trickling to stain the blade of the breakroom butcher knife he'd used at lunch to slice his sub into portions Evie would consider appropriate.

Squinting, he lifted the sex toy. As his fingers smeared the sticky syrup, he spied black felt pen ink scrawled along a flesh-toned vein: *Love, Lorena.*

He scratched his nuts. Who the hell was Lorena?

A nugget of information in his brain twitched, and he gawked at the dildo.

Holy sheep! Lorena Bobbitt? The woman in the nineties who'd cut off her husband's pecker while he slept and threw it out a car window? She was the stuff of internet lore.

He dropped the toy. The desk phone rang, and he nearly leapt out of his skin. He snatched up the receiver. "Yeah?"

"Mackie?" Jasmine's whiny voice lacerated his ear. "Why won't you return my calls or texts? I tried your place, your cell, now work. I've been thinking about our fight. I'm sorr—"

"Stop screwing with me, bitch!" Staging a mock-up of a severed johnson? She had lost her freaking mind!

"What? What are you talking about? I'm not screwing you, Mackie. I wish we *were* screwing..." A husky note softened her tone.

But he was too smart for the likes of Jasmine Jones. "If you think tricks will get me back, you're dead wrong. We're through." He slammed down the phone.

It rang again. He grabbed it. *"I said no."*

He yanked the cord from the receiver. Clenching the butcher knife, he sliced at the soft outer covering of the vibrator until red syrup sprayed his hands and chunks of silicone pelted the air.

Jasmine must have been watching him since the business closed its doors today, waiting for him to leave long enough so she could test her studio key. Plainly, she hadn't bought his lie that the set he'd given her last night were fakes.

Tossing aside the knife, he whipped out his cell phone and blocked her number.

Jas, you imaginative dingbat. He hadn't thought she had it in her to play sick jokes. That only went to show how into him she was—and had been all along.

Evie would be into him too. Once she knew she was his. And that it was okay to love him.

The phone in the waiting room rang. He ran down the hall and ripped out the cord. *Hah.* Now Jas couldn't badger him with her pathetic apologies. At one time, he would have relished her warped fantasies. Let her tease him then reward him.

But she'd gone too far with the syrupy dildo.

No man stood for that.

Twenty-Eight

Seated at her vintage desk in the living room, Eve tugged at a lock of hair. "You'll come over tonight then?" she asked Hal over her landline. "I wouldn't have called if it weren't important."

His sad sigh whispered in her ear. "I thought we covered things yesterday at the cafe."

"You covered things," she reminded him gently. "It's my turn. I need you to hear me out."

"All right. I have to go to the office for a couple of hours. I'll come after that."

Yes. She wriggled on the chair. "Thank you, Hal. You won't regret it."

"See you soon." He hung up.

Smiling, she swept into the kitchen and filled the stovetop kettle, placed it on a burner, and turned the temperature control to high. Back in the living room, she clicked the stereo remote. Nostalgic soft rock streamed from the speakers.

Eve pressed her chin to clasped hands, more giddy than a thirteen-year-old. Two hours to kill. She'd go crazy. *Oh, Hal.* If only he would knock on her door right now.

Like an answer to a prayer, the front bell rang.

"Coming!" It couldn't be Hal. Even if he'd jumped into his car straight away, a thirty-minute drive extended between their homes. A neighborhood child likely stood on her stoop, anxious to sell candy bars for a school activity. She needed the distraction. And the chocolate.

She peered through the peephole. The light bathed her brother-in-law, and he wasn't holding chocolate. Vic shifted his feet and rubbed his nose. Dragging a hand through his thinning hair, he mussed his stumpy ponytail. The man fidgeted as if a colony of fire ants had taken up residence in his body.

Eve opened the door. "Hello, Victor. What a surprise. How are you?" The evening air chilled her skin through her blouse, and she shivered.

"Not bad," he responded in a gravelly voice. "Can I come in?"

"I guess so." She stepped back as he entered, accepting his coat and sliding it onto a hanger in the closet. Facing him, she stared. "There's a red splotch on your forehead." Like a melted lollipop.

"Huh?" He wiped off the spot. "Is it gone?"

She nodded. "To what do I owe the pleasure?"

He drew in a breath. "The pleasure is mine, Evie. That's what I came to tell you." He clasped her hand, his cold palms chafing her skin. "I dumped Jasmine. I should've done it long ago."

Eve's thumb twitched in his two-handed grip. "I'm sorry. Did you have a fight?"

He shook his head. "She's not what I want."

"It's probably for the best." Casually, so as not to offend, Eve slipped her hand free. "I'll admit I never understood your attraction to her." She chewed her lip. She wasn't being fair. She hadn't met Jasmine. However, she had seen selfies of the couple on Victor's cell phone, and, once or twice, while he'd sat in her living room as she'd prepared dinner, she'd overheard his end of Jasmine's numerous phone calls. Their relationship seemed to revolve almost entirely around sex, which was fine and dandy, but not enough in the long-term. "You need someone to take care of you." A kind-hearted woman with the patience of a saint who could encourage him to be a better man.

"I agree." His dark gaze latched onto her face, and goosebumps rippled up her arms.

"I'm boiling water for tea. Would you like a cup?"

"Nah. I'll have scotch. Pour yourself a glass of wine while you're at it."

"Good idea." She had a feeling she'd need it.

As he wandered to the couch, his gaze snapped to the seven-foot Christmas tree in the stand by the picture window. The lights were unplugged and the heavy branches bare.

"Evie, where are your decorations? When I left the other day, you and Gabe were trimming the tree with baubles. If you needed my help, I would've stayed."

"Gabe said he wouldn't mind, so I took down the ornaments last night."

Vic's nostrils flared. "Why?"

"Hal is coming over. I thought it would be nice if he and I decorated the tree together."

"Henshaw? When is he showing his ugly mug?"

"Victor, don't be rude." Hal was quite handsome, with his deep brown eyes and full head of graying hair. "He'll be here in an hour or two." She held her breath. She owed her brother-in-law the truth. "Vic, I appreciate the gift of the tree. It was very generous. But I've been thinking about Hal a lot lately. We had coffee yesterday—"

The kettle whistled from the kitchen. Grateful for the reprieve, she pasted on her hostess smile. "Make yourself comfortable. I'll fix our drinks." She hurried to the buffet for the scotch.

In the kitchen, she shut off the stove and scooped ice cubes into a lowball glass. Carrying Vic's scotch and her pinot gris, she returned to the living room. In her absence, he'd sat on the sofa. Bending over, he pawed through an open box on the floor.

Her heart plummeted to her stomach. Remaining standing, she placed the scotch on a coaster. A romantic song issued from the stereo, and flames leapt on the natural-gas hearth. She had intended the loving touches for Hal.

Vic yanked Doug's Police Department portrait out of the box. "What's with the cop crap?"

She touched the locket around her neck. "I put them on the mantel, for Gabe." And for herself. Her wineglass cooled her other hand.

"They aren't on the mantel now." The words shot from Vic's mouth. My, he was in a grim mood tonight.

"It's time I stored them away for good," she replied calmly. "If

Gabe wants, he can take his father's memorabilia when he moves." She would keep one small item.

Vic slugged back a swallow of scotch. "Where is the kid?"

She cleared her throat. She hadn't spoken to or texted her son since this morning. "Out for dinner." She really didn't know where he was, but weird vibes rolled off her brother-in-law. It wouldn't do to explain that she'd asked Gabe for privacy this evening for her talk with Hal.

"Dinner? Where?"

"I'm not sure." *Well, Eve, you could have made something up.*

"Will he be late?"

"He didn't say." She gave a mother's indulgent smile. "You know, even when he's out, he'll drop by sometimes to check on me. I couldn't ask for more in a son."

"Yeah, he's a real champ." Vic stuffed the portrait of Doug back into the box. "Sit with me, Evie." He patted the spot on the sofa next to him.

Maintaining a polite distance, she lowered herself onto the plump cushions. Vic shifted closer, his slacks skimming her thigh. Gripping the hem of her skirt, she inched away.

Downing his scotch, he gazed at her upper chest. "You've been wearing my necklace a lot these days."

She caressed the heart-shaped locket. "I treasure it." He'd surprised her with the memorial gift two weeks after Doug's funeral. His care selecting portraits of her and his brother to resize and cut into hearts had touched her deeply. "It reminds me of Doug." She would tuck the necklace into a drawer before Hal arrived. She'd just wanted to wear it one last day.

Victor rolled his lips. "Don't you think it's time you started seeing another man?"

"Funny you should mention Hal—"

"*Hal?*" Victor's glass slammed onto the coffee table. "He hurt you, Evie. He's a loser."

"No, he's not. I've been too hard on him. So have you."

"How do you figure? Henshaw proposing right after Gabe got shot was a bullshit move to hog your attention."

Eve set down her wineglass. "Please don't speak about Hal in that barroom-brawl tone."

Victor scowled. "Evie, *I'm* your man. Stop toying with me."

"Wh-what? Oh, no. Victor, no." Not a repeat of his post-wedding-rehearsal-dinner confession, after all these years! "I love Hal. I shouldn't have pushed him away in August. That's why I asked him over tonight. I need him in my life."

Vic shook his head. "You need me."

"Don't say that." Skin crawling, she leapt off the couch.

Grabbing her arm, he hauled her back down. "Don't say what? That I want you? How much *I* need you? I've waited years for you, Evie. Since before Doug died, damn it."

Oh, God. "You're not referring to our conversation after the rehearsal dinner, are you? That was booze talking, Vic."

"It was *me* talking." His blunt fingers dug into her arm. "But you married Dougie anyway. Knowing how I felt about you, you chained yourself to that schmuck. You had a kid with him. A kid who should've been mine."

Her ears rang. "What are you talking about? I adored Doug. How could you not understand? You were his little brother." Her voice broke.

"Jesus, Evie, you never got it. But you will now. You have to save me, like you saved him. With your sweet love."

He pushed her backward onto the sofa arm. Her spine pressed against the curve. Squeezing her breast so hard it hurt, he plastered his lips on hers and plunged his tongue inside her mouth.

The rubbery organ tasted like day-old meat. His pelvis crushed her thigh, his erection obvious.

Oh, God, oh, God!

Her heart bashed her ribs. Willing herself not to gag, she squeezed back tears and fixed her thoughts on another place, with warm sand and a balmy sky, where Victor's vulgar pawing didn't exist.

He relaxed, slowing the slobbery kisses until he nibbled at her lips.

She screamed.

He clamped a hand over her mouth.

She bit his finger. "Get off me!"

"Shit!" His teeth sank into her breast. Pain lanced her flesh, and he laughed. "You like it rough, huh?"

No, she didn't like it rough. She didn't like it at all! "Help!"

"I'll help myself, if you don't mind." He gripped her locket and blouse. Ramming a leg between her thighs, he bunched her skirt above her waist.

"Victor, no! Stop!"

"Shut up." He fumbled with his zipper.

Adrenaline streaking, she forced her body to slacken. Victor freed his penis.

Mustering her strength, she kneed him.

He rolled off her, yowling. Her blouse ripped, and the chain of her necklace snapped.

Doubled over, he clenched the chain in his meaty fist. "Why did you do that?"

She kicked him. His knee smashed the coffee table, and her wineglass toppled. Pinot gris splashed the carpet.

He stumbled backward, his shoe hitting the box of police memorabilia. Eve pushed his chest hard. He buckled to the floor, head whacking the side table.

She jumped aside. Mother of God, had she killed him?

The romantic music played on the stereo. The gas fire glowed. One eye on Vic, she grabbed the decorative poker. He moaned and rolled on the carpet. Eyes dazed, he pushed himself to standing. As he zipped his pants, she raised the poker. Her blouse sagged, revealing her bra.

Swaying, he flung the broken necklace at her feet. "Know why I gave this to you?"

"Because you loved me like a sister! That was what you said." Hot tears streamed down her face.

He swore. "The stupid thing probably still has the picture of Doug in it!"

"Of course it does. You put it there!" She tightened her grip on the poker.

"You're clueless," he roared. "Sooner or later, you were supposed to replace his picture with one of *me*. That's why I gave you the necklace. Evie, I've loved you since you and Doug started dating. You were so sweet. I couldn't stand the thought of him screwing you, stealing your goodness every time he shared your bed. You should've been mine. You could've saved me from the darkness that's hounded me my whole life. Then you screwed Hal for two freaking years! How long did you expect me to wait for you?"

She gasped. "I never wanted you to wait. We were family!"

"Yeah?" As if the poker presented less danger than a fly swatter, Victor spread his arms wide. "Would your loving family member let his brother die?"

"*What?*" White spots dotted her vision, and she thought she might faint. What was he saying?

"The night Dougie died—I was there."

"No, you weren't." How was that possible? "Doug died in an abandoned warehouse." She wanted to cover her ears, but her hands remained glued to the poker.

Vic jabbed his chest. "I saw him get shot."

That didn't make sense. "You wouldn't shoot your own brother!"

"I *didn't* shoot him, you silly twit. Aren't you listening, Evie? Do you ever freaking *listen* to me? I was as surprised as Dougie when the dealer plugged him in the back. But I saw it happen."

Hatred glittered in his dark eyes. Why hadn't she ever noticed their icy glint before? She sobbed. "But how? Why?"

"Fate," he said smugly. "I happened along, scouting locations for a nighttime shoot. Remember when everyone in town was humping for Victor McKenzie to snap their stuff? Their fashion ads and crap? I was hot to trot. I was on top! Doug's killing was a sign." He pointed at her. "You were supposed to be mine. All my life, I couldn't measure up to Doug. The lucky bastard. Who wouldn't want to be born the biological son of decent folks, instead of a smelly, snot-faced, orphaned three-year-old no one else would touch? *Huh?* Damn Doug. A decorated cop. The loving husband. It was sick! Goddamn Dougie Do-Right. Well, he can't do nothing now!"

"Get out!" She swung the poker. "I'm calling Bill Cruikshank."

Vic laughed. "I can't be arrested for running from a gunfight, baby. I was in shock."

"You're a coward!"

"*Then.* I'll give you that. But I'm not anymore." He thumped his chest. "This is *me*, Victor Giordano McKenzie. If you want a real man, you can have me. Prove your loyalty, slut."

She positioned the poker like a baseball bat. "Get out of my house. Get out! Get out!" Before she smashed in his skull!

"Fuck you." He spat on the carpet. "We could've had a life together." He kicked the box, denting the side. "You don't deserve to keep Doug's shit."

Hands and arms trembling, she clenched the poker. "I'm warning you."

He wiggled his fingers like a Halloween goblin. "Oooh, I'm scared. *Not*." He tramped to the door. Fist on the knob, he turned. "You'll be sorry, Evie. Who do you think you're dealing with? You fucked up my life. Now I'm gonna fuck up yours."

And then he was gone.

She raced to the door and snapped shut the deadbolt. Only then did she realize she'd dropped the poker.

She crumpled onto the entrance mat and cried.

❧

Mackie squealed the van away from Evie's house, heater blasting. His head hurt like a sonuvabitch. He touched his scalp, and his fingers came away with a tiny smear of blood. He must have really smacked his skull. What was up with women lately, shoving him around?

He jammed his wool cap on his head, covering the wound. Twitball Evie had his coat. Let her keep it. When she found it in the entryway closet, she would realize what she was missing. *Him*. In her life. In her bed.

The van swerved, and he grasped the steering wheel with both hands. For the first time in eleven years, a powerful sense of invincibility stroked his veins—and his dick.

The big guy hardened in his pants, no worse off for Evie's rejection. He cackled. Confession *was* good for the soul. He was free! Free of his guilt for distracting Doug from the drug dealer, for not calling 911, for allowing his brother to die in that godforsaken warehouse. When Evie came to her senses, would *he* want *her* anymore?

She had made him wait too long. The gleam was off her crown, and he saw her clearly. A shrill woman who didn't appreciate his risks and sacrifices. Who needed her?

Stomping on the gas, he aimed for home. His cell phone rang in the center console. He glanced at the screen. *Unknown Name.*

Carnivore crap! The damn thing would ring six or seven times before going to voicemail.

He grabbed the cell. "This better be good."

"Victor," a seductive voice whispered. "It's been ages, Stud."

His Italian stallion swelled, and the van veered, nearly hitting a parked car.

"Victor, I've missed you," the familiar voice murmured. "I'm sad we broke up."

Mackie recognized the inflections, but a haze clouded his brain, muddling his customary genius. "You still pissed your family saw the tape?" he asked, careful not to assume the caller's identity and make a mistake. He was pretty sure he had her nailed, but there had been a lot of families and a lot of tapes.

"My husband left me over it, if you can believe it. I should have made the final payment, Victor. You gave me enough chances. In hindsight, you were very generous."

His sister-in-law had said the same thing about his gift of the Christmas tree. Yeah, he was generous to a freaking fault, and the stubborn boob sucking up to him on the phone *should have* paid him. Damn Miki. The only one of his blackmail babes who hadn't forked over all the dough, she'd caused him several sleepless nights. She'd gotten off on the fantasy of bondage office sex every bit as much as the others. All insecure, gullible bimbos starved for affection.

Each had bought his "feelings" for them hook, line, and sinker.

Oh-ho, the thrill of recording raunchy sex games without a slut's knowledge had revved his fantasies for weeks. Tying up a broad and recording her in the thralls before allowing her to bind him was an erotic power-switcheroo that did it for him like he couldn't believe. The first time, featuring a chick whose name he couldn't recall for some reason, he'd intended the video as his personal prize. Then Bimbo One blabbed about how much it hurt her tender feelings when her snobby sisters judged the short length of her skirt and abundant cleavage. If she worried about silly shit like that, how would she feel if her sisters saw his secret sex tape?

Boom. His clever blackmail scheme had been born.

A strange buzzing sounded in his brain. He shook his head. "You were feisty, standing your ground," he spoke into the cell. He wouldn't quibble with an old flame over a few thousand dollars. He had Bloomfield's cash now. *Forgive and forget.*

"My ex asked too many questions. I thought if I confessed the affair, he'd forgive me."

"But he didn't." Monitoring the traffic, Mackie sneered.

"No. The ass."

"Do you miss him?" If she said yes, he'd chuck his cell out the window.

"He never quite satisfied me, if you know what I mean. He would tie me up but never let *me* bind him. Victor, you're the only man who's ever allowed me the fantasy of being in control. On your terms, of course. I miss our sexy give-and-take."

Oh, yeah. His johnson could shatter a brick wall. "Baby, that's music to my ears. I love a woman who knows what she wants." Unlike his brain-dead sister-in-law. Eventually, he'd stopped recording his bimbos—for dimwit Evie. Not that she had known about or would have understood how his secret sex tapes had helped him remain faithful. As much as he *could* remain faithful. Hey, a man had needs.

But this September, stumbling upon the news story about Paul Bloomfield attending the municipal conference in California had felt preordained. Mackie had blackmailed a few men now and again. His elderly neighbor's Peeping Tom of a brother, the baker at the local grocery who'd cheated on his wife with *Mackie's* favorite lap-dancer. But no one approaching the stature of a Council president.

Paul Fraidy-Cat Bloomfield had practically offered himself up on a platter as a last chance for Mackie to fatten his bank account in anticipation of a new life. Now the woman he'd idolized for years had ruined everything.

"I know what *I* want, Victor," Miki's voice murmured in his ear.

Triple-yeah. After all this time, the nympho lusted after him. Like Jasmine would for the rest of her life.

Like Evie would, if she knew what she was missing.

His foot jerked on the gas pedal. "What are we waiting for? Let's hook up. I'm heading for my place." Now he wouldn't have to bother satisfying his kink itch by calling Glory Rhodes. He'd do Miki tonight and save Glory for his next fix. A different broad every night of the week. That was his future.

"Oooh, I have an errand. Let's meet in our usual spot. I can't wait to strap you down, Victor. Bound and spread for my enjoyment."

Shinola, he nearly came in his pants! "Meet you at the door. Don't be long. You know how antsy I can get." Disconnecting, he shoved the cell into the console, pulled a U-turn, and zoomed in the opposite direction.

Long time, no see. He had the luck. Tonight of all nights, he needed this.

His gut gurgled, and an image of the syrup-soaked dildo wormed into his mind. He frowned. The sick joke hadn't been Miki's doing, had it?

Nah, impossible. The traffic swam in front of his eyes, and he blinked.

Frack. Concentrating was proving an effort, but he remembered without a doubt that the locksmith had changed the front and back door studio bolts yesterday, and he hadn't allowed Miki *any* of his keys. He'd been juggling two or three chicks during those months, and she'd harbored a jealous streak.

No, the dildo was on Jasmine's head. How stupid could she get?

He grunted. It didn't matter. With Miki's help, he would not only bid goodbye to Jasmine but wipe thoughts of Eve McKenzie from his mind and heart forever. His days of trying to rehabilitate himself to impress his brother's widow were over. From now on, if Evie didn't approve of his behavior, tough. She was to blame.

Because of her rejection, he would take advantage of every slut he encountered until he died.

Twenty-Nine

Night shrouded the cemetery. Although a frigid breeze pierced Eve's coat and the leaves that had yet to drop rustled eerily in the old trees, peace slipped into her bones. Looking after Doug's grave always brought her comfort, even in the aftermath of his brother's terrible ranting.

The minute Victor left the house, she'd collapsed on the entrance mat and sobbed her heart out. Then anxiety had scrambled up her throat. What if he returned, deadbolt be damned?

Mind awhirl, she'd changed her ripped blouse and escaped her home, totally forgetting her cell phone charging on the kitchen counter. She could have used the device to text Gabe or Hal or to check the cemetery's early winter closing hours. Fortunately, an office worker staying late had recognized her from previous visits. Achieving access to her husband's resting place at odd hours remained a dubious benefit of being a fallen detective's widow.

Her breath shuddered into her lungs. Never mind about her phone. She wasn't ready to speak to her son or Hal. Her thoughts scrambled around in her brain, as if absorbing Victor's hatred of his brother lay beyond her reach. Yet, through her horror and bewilderment, one overpowering certainty asserted itself. She needed to say goodbye to Doug. Regardless of how or why her husband had died, she needed to close this chapter of her life. It was the only way she could embrace a future without Doug by her side.

As she knelt, the cold earth froze her shins. She removed the wilted bouquet from the holder at the base of his headstone and replaced the dry blossoms with a single cellophane-wrapped rose.

Gazing at the inscription, she smoothed her fingertips over the dates. A lump lodged in her throat. "I'll miss you forever, Doug," she whispered hoarsely.

But should her love prevent her from living?

She wept. Hal had been right.

"You compare every man you date to a corpse," he'd accused when she'd responded to his impulsive marriage proposal as if the very idea of committing to a future with him insulted her memories of Doug. But, oh, before Hal's fateful words incited her to shrink into despair and grief, he'd spoken of possibilities and promises. Days after she'd returned from Los Angeles, he'd consoled her in the kitchen, whispering as he'd enveloped her in a hug, "Eve, I wish you'd allowed me to go to California with you. I couldn't bear picturing you alone in your hotel room each night, counting the hours until you could see Gabe again."

She'd tensed within his embrace. He had said something similar before she'd left. "I needed to be alone," she'd explained. "I needed it to be only me and Gabe." Wiping her eyes, she'd stepped away.

Hurt had filled Hal's whiskey-brown gaze. "Ah, Eve, I'm only trying to comfort you. It's been years since you lost your husband. I understand you might not feel ready. But someday soon, I hope you will be." He'd touched her shoulder. "This might not be the time or place, but I want you to know how much I love you. I want to build a future with you. Sweetheart, my greatest desire is that before too long you'll agree to marry me."

"Marry?" How had their conversation transitioned from visiting her injured son to marriage? "I can't think about marriage right now. Gabe needs me."

"That's blunt."

"You have to understand, my family is all I have. Gabe and Victor..."

"There you go, bringing up McKenzie again. Must he always come between us?"

"What do you mean? Vic is like a brother. He supports me. He doesn't pressure me or—or try to manipulate me."

"Are we talking about the same man? Because I think he manipulates the hell out of you. You refuse to see that, but to me, it's clear as day."

Her mouth had dropped open. "How dare you!"

"Eve, I know what it's like to lose someone. My wife didn't die, but she left me all the same, alone with a child to raise while she gallivanted God-knows-where. And now my adult son lives half a world away. How can you think I don't understand your heartache and loneliness? Your husband is your past. I want to be your future."

Her hackles rose then, her need to shut herself away and lick old wounds shutting out everything else. Their exchange escalated out of control, resulting in unkind barbs and a horrible argument. Eve had kicked him out of her home, out of her life, and—she had thought—out of her heart.

Foolish woman. Within days, she'd regretted her actions but hadn't known how to pick herself up and move forward, especially with Victor sniffing around, assuring her she'd done the right thing. She had felt stymied and locked in place.

And she had pierced a dagger into the heart of the only man in over a decade patient enough to tolerate her insecurities.

A breeze rustled in the cemetery trees, and her stomach twisted. Looking back, Hal had hinted at marriage for months, but she had never failed to let him know, far too subtly, that she wasn't prepared—no, she hadn't *wanted*—to move on.

She placed a hand on the gravestone. "Doug," she whispered. "I clung to Victor all these years as a way to cling to you."

She squeezed shut her eyes. Awful, just awful, Vic's story about witnessing Doug's murder, abandoning his brother, and not calling for help. Was there any truth to the tirade, or had Victor spun a wild tale to cause her pain?

Acid burned behind her breastbone. Had Doug noticed his brother in the warehouse? Was Vic the reason Doug turned his back on the shooter for a tragic split-second?

Sobs shook her body. *Please, God, don't let it be so.*

Opening her eyes, she whispered, "Doug, your mother and dad and you all loved Victor. But something inside him is broken."

Victor had assaulted her tonight. The deep scratches and bite marks stung her chest.

Had she led him on somehow? Provided any reason for him to believe she...liked him...in that way?

No. She held cold fingers to her flushed cheeks. Nothing in this world justified Victor's behavior. She was a police detective's widow. She knew the score.

Get over yourself, Eve.

As much as she hated the idea of exposing her personal life to public scrutiny, she intended to press charges. But first she ached to reconnect with Hal.

Getting up, she reached into her purse for her car keys and cast a last glance at the gravesite. She would always love Doug. Yet, she loved Hal too. Her love for Doug was a beautiful memory. Her love for Hal lived in the present. It was strong and true.

Doug had been the hero of her heart from the day they'd met. She needed to tell Hal *he* was her hero now.

And would be for the rest of her days.

Ursula sealed Stacy's second box of belongings. "That's the last of the kitchen stuff," she said. "What's next?"

"Books and knick-knacks."

"All right." Trinkets, tattered volumes, and pictures crammed shelves behind a worn couch.

Stacy chose a box. "I'll take care of the bedroom things while you stay out here. I hid newspapers under the couch. Can you wrap fragile pieces in them?"

Nodding, Ursula carried a box to the shelves. As she hunkered to pack the first row of books, Stacy disappeared behind the Japanese screens.

Ursula cushioned the bottom of the box with paperbacks. The room dividers didn't offer much solitude, but she'd take what she could get. Dodging Stacy's questions about her newfound feelings for Gabe was proving tricky.

Holy moly, she was *in love* with the man. Yes, she was scared, but she needed to make things right. Instead of discussing her colossal realization with Stacy, she needed to find alone time with Gabe and, for a start, apologize for freaking out on him this morning.

She glanced toward her purse on a table by the door. He hadn't texted or called all day. When she'd powered up her cell after her movie marathon, only a text from her mom organizing a lunch next week had appeared on her screen.

He was probably working the case. She didn't want to distract him, but one message couldn't hurt.

Twirling her pinky ring, she rose.

Stacy's head darted around a screen. "How's it going?"

Cripes. Curious kitties had nothing on Stacy Thompson. "I thought I'd check my phone. And a glass of water might be nice."

"Can you wait? I'm in a rush, remember? Shout if you need anything. Like, anything that won't take extra time." Stacy vanished behind the screen again.

"Got it." Ursula would message Gabe later in private.

Crouching, she retrieved the newspapers and wrapped Stacy's cow collection. The figurines stood two rows deep—cows lounging, cows standing, one holding an umbrella, another relaxing in a claw-foot bathtub. She wrapped the tub cow then reached for a squat cat figure. Finally, something different. The compact object weighed a ton.

Wait a minute. Ursula rolled the cat over. She'd seen this figurine before.

Stacy stepped from behind the screens. "I need some newspaper."

Rising, Ursula showed her the cat. "This is different from your cow collection. Is it a paperweight?"

A blush stained Stacy's face. "Ugh, that thing. I forgot I had it. I'm not sure I'm taking it to my new place."

"Where did you find it? It looks like one at the studio." The same color and texture of clay. The approximate mass. "Only this cat is standing and the studio cat is lying down."

Stacy huffed. "Ursula, drop it. I mean, don't drop the cat *on the floor* or anything." She extended a palm. "Hand it to me."

"Relax, Stace. It's only a paperweight. It doesn't even match your collection." Was it her imagination, or was Stacy growing a mite agitated?

"Stop calling him a paperweight!" Stacy snatched the cat. "Don't touch him. Just don't!"

۶

Eve entered the house through the kitchen and placed her purse on the counter beside her charging cell phone. She checked the screen. No messages. Hal should arrive before too long. What would he say when he saw her bruises?

She wrung her hands. Should she contact the police while she waited for him?

Yes, of course. She really needed to get it together. She should have called Bill Cruikshank as soon as Victor left the house, but a veil of disbelief had obscured her thoughts. Even now, they remained a mish-mash. She had misjudged her brother-in-law so badly.

One step at a time, Eve. Hang up your coat, then call Bill and check in with Hal.

She stepped into the front hall. Vic's jacket hulked in a lump on the floor of the open closet. It must have fallen from the hanger. *Leave it there.* Bill might want to check the pockets, and the idea of touching anything of her brother-in-law's sickened her stomach.

A tingle spread from the base of her neck, almost as if the phantom presence of Victor's attack lingered in her living room.

Steeling herself, she turned. "Oh, my God!" Her home was destroyed!

She gawked at the contents of Doug's police memorabilia box, some items strewn by the fireplace while others lay broken on the coffee table. Shattered glass marred his portrait, a jagged X slicing his face. Gouges dug into the clear plastic encasing his badge, as if the memento had been bashed against the damaged fireplace mantle.

Had Victor returned? Had he done this?

Her gaze caught on another casualty of the destruction. The flag that had draped Doug's coffin and rested in the triangular display case pooled in a torn jumble on the carpet beside his mutilated memory album.

With a cry, she dropped onto her knees and scrambled for the heart-shaped locket containing her first love's picture. *Where is it, where is it?*

Tears blurred her vision. Vic had said she'd be sorry. Was this what he'd meant?

What if he came back again to hurt her? What if—*no!*—he lurked in her house right now?

She raced to the desk and punched in 911. "I need to report a break-in. A-and attempted rape." She rattled off her address. "I'll be at a neighbor's." Hanging up, she ran into the kitchen, unplugged her cell, and plunged the device into a coat pocket.

In the carport, she glanced around her streetlamp-brightened neighborhood. Which house should she choose? Should she have specified? Shoot, had she cut off the dispatcher? Should she call them back?

Her cell rang, and she whipped it out of her coat. Hal's name shone on the screen.

Thank God. She answered. "Hal?"

His kind voice filled her ear. "I'm on my way. Eve, are you okay? You sound a little—"

"Hal, I'm scared. I called 911. I'm going to a neighbor's. I didn't tell them who." A lamp gleamed in the living room window next door. One of the Donaldsons was home.

"*911?* Eve, sweetheart, what happened?"

"Victor." Trembles shook her from head to toe. Teeth chattering, she yanked her coat tight around her middle and strode down the driveway. "He tried to rape me. I left the house. When I came back—"

"*He did what? I'll kill him!*"

Her pumps clacked asphalt. "Hal! Please, I need you. He smashed Doug's things." She hurried along the Donaldsons' walkway.

He cursed. "Where's Gabe?"

"Out. I'm calling him next." Sirens rent the air. "I think a cruiser is nearby. I can't see it yet, but I can hear the noise."

"Good. Sweetheart, are you at your neighbor's?"

"I'm knocking on the door. The brown house on the other side of my carport." She rapped her knuckles against the wood and jabbed the bell.

Carol Donaldson answered, eyes widening as the sirens wailed. "Eve!"

"Carol, I've had a break-in. I'm on the phone with Hal."

Mouth gaping, Carol gestured her into the house.

"Eve?" Hal's worried voice again. "Call Gabe."

"What about Bill Cruikshank? I mentioned his name to the dispatcher."

"I have his number from the barbecue we hosted in July. I'll contact him."

"Okay. Thank you, Hal. I love you." Steadfast, reliable Hal. She trusted him with her life and with her heart.

"I love you too, with everything in me. I'm five minutes away. Listen, sweetheart, ask your neighbor to lock the door. Lock every door and window in the place, then call back 911 and tell them where you are. Don't open to anyone other than the police, Gabe, Bill, or me. I don't care who it is. Sit tight, love. I'm coming."

Ursula stared at Stacy. "Okay, okay. Take it easy. You have him now." Whoever "he" was. She couldn't judge the girl for personalizing a cat figure. After all, she had named her car.

Stacy burst into tears. "I don't want him anymore. I hate her!" She lobbed the cat onto the couch.

Yikes. Mondo mood swings. Ursula hugged the girl. Stacy blubbered against her turtleneck sweater.

"Shh, Stacy. Who do you hate?"

"Shelly. I'm sorry, Urs. I'm so stressed out. My sister used to be my hero, but she's turned into someone I don't even know." Gulping sobs, she stepped out of their embrace. "I rescued Clive from the trash after Shelly threw him out. He's half of a bookend set. That's why he's leaning against a tiny wall. You can have him if you want." Bumping her glasses, she wiped her eyes. "Need a bag?"

Ursula's heart hammered. "Yes, please." Was she jumping to conclusions for thinking Stacy's bookend cat matched the paperweight at the studio? The cat in the backroom lacked a wall, but a flattened area behind its haunches could double as one.

Stacy had escorted the Real Men applicants into the room two weeks ago. Ursula couldn't recall the girl entering the space before that time. Was that why Stacy hadn't noticed the resemblance between the pieces?

"Where's the second half?" she asked while Stacy fetched a plastic bag, shoved the cat inside, and dumped the lot onto a side table.

Stacy rolled her eyes. "Shelly gave Clive to some jerk she dated a few years back. She cheated on her husband with the guy. When her ex learned about the affair, he left her. Shelly blamed the jerk."

Ursula shook her head. "Why blame the lover? Shelly had the affair."

"I know. But that's Shelly. Lately she's getting worse. I have to move before she drives me batty." Kneeling, she wrapped framed photographs.

"What is your sister mad about now?" Crouching alongside Stacy, Ursula packed the protected frames into the box.

"Another failed romance." Stacy handed over a frame. "But she isn't only mad this time. She's around the bend." She leaned in close. "Get this. Shelly says the guy who wrecked her marriage is responsible for the breakup of her latest affair."

"Excuse me?" Shelly sounded like the type of person who refused to admit accountability for anything. No wonder Stacy was stressed.

"Confusing, right?" Stacy whispered. "Ever hear of the council guy, Paul Bloomfield?"

Ursula nodded. "He was involved in a sex scandal once." The hooker incident Gabe had run across.

"Really? As far as I know, that had nothing to do with Shelly. But..." Stacy's voice remained hushed "...she temped at City Hall last spring. That's when she and Mr. Bloomfield started *their* affair. So she says. I never know if I can believe her."

Ursula blinked. "What happened?"

"He dumped her in September. She thinks she can win him back, the silly goose. When they were together, she swiped a key to his office. She's been stealing odds and ends to build a love pyre in her living room ever since."

"A love pyre?" This was some tale!

"Yep." Eyes huge, Stacy described, "Bizarre things. Like I've seen opera tickets, an extra toothbrush, a spare dress shirt and tie. You know how some businessmen keep an unopened shirt package in a desk drawer? In case they spill coffee on themselves or something? Like that. She also stole his sticky notes, a set of cuff links, a comb, a travel-sized bottle of mouthwash. That's only what I've noticed when I've stopped by for tea. There might be more." She glanced around the tiny apartment, as if picturing her sister eavesdropping behind the screens. "She's stuffed everything in a trashcan along with some handwritten love letters she hasn't mailed. She says..." Stacy looked around again "...when she's finished building the pyre, she'll light the can on fire, magically relighting *his* fire. I'm telling you, Ursula, she needs help. After I'm gone, I hope she'll smarten up and see a doctor. She won't listen to me now."

Ursula plastered a benign expression on her face. *Don't say anything. Poor Stacy needs to vent.*

The girl stretched on her knees and plucked a ceramic frame off the bookshelves. "Here we are seven years ago." She handed Ursula the picture. "I was thirteen and Shelly was twenty-three. Wasn't she beautiful?"

Eep! Ursula whisked her fingers to her lips as she studied the picture of the smiling teen and pretty blonde. *Oh, crappp. What the hella heck?*

She could practically feel neurons firing and synapses pinging in her brain. She and Shelly spoke at the pub Friday night, but Ursula's determination to prove Stacy innocent of the studio sabotage had closed her mind to numerous details suddenly flooding her gray matter.

She hadn't only met Shelly at the pub and bumped into the woman over a week ago, spilling coffee on Shelly's winter-white coat, but—but—during Gabe's first morning as her assistant, four days before the latte accident, Ursula had encountered him in the coffee shop. As they'd talked, she'd moved away from the condiment counter to allow a blonde access to the cream and sugar.

That woman had been Shelly. It was so obvious now.

"Your sister is still beautiful," she murmured, tummy pinching. Yes, yes, she and Gabe had bought coffee and muffins before addressing the absurdly dressed men milling on the sidewalk, waiting for the studio to open.

Wasn't that *also* the day Stacy misplaced her studio keys?

And Shelly—possibly unstable by her little sister's own admission—had been in the vicinity.

A shiver raced up Ursula's spine. Was Shelly involved in the studio sabotage? Why had the woman been in the neighborhood that chaotic Thursday? Had she dropped off Stacy at work after Gabe called in the girl to assist with the Real Men mob?

Ursula hadn't noticed or thought to ask Gabe or Stacy about the girl's mode of transportation. Sometimes Stacy received a ride from her sister and sometimes, like Ursula, she rode the bus. Ursula gulped. Shelly driving Stacy to work now and then might have provided the woman with myriad opportunities to monitor studio shenanigans—or to initiate more peculiar stunts.

Striving for a casual tone, she asked, "Where does Shelly work now?"

"She temps all over town. Usually as an office assistant or data entry clerk. Temping suits her, seeing as she can't keep a permanent job."

Yes, constructing magical love pyres would mess with a person's ability to focus.

Playing with an earring, Ursula handed back the picture. "Why are there capital M's and A's on the frame?" Curly gold lettering embellished the ivory ceramic.

A smile curved Stacy's mouth. "Our mom hand-painted them. Shelly has one like it. The A's stand for Anastasia. That's me. Shelly's formal name is Michelle. Mom named us after her favorite aunts but uses our nicknames for daily life. It's more personal that way, Mom says."

"Uh-huh." Pretending to adjust her earring, Ursula pondered the blackmail names listed in the notepad. *Darn it, no memory of a Shelly or Michelle.* "Did Shelly ever mention the name of the guy who ruined her marriage?"

"No. She loves being a woman of mystery." Looking at the photo, Stacy sighed. "I thought the world of her when this picture was taken. Whatever happens after I move, I'll always cherish my memories of my pretty older sister who paid attention to the dorky kid who worshipped and adored her." She kissed the glass before wrapping the frame in newsprint. Glancing up she said, "I'm keeping Clive after all. You'll have to check thrift shops for another cat."

"Good idea." Ursula scratched a thumbnail. *Lisa, Lynette, Desiree… Who else is named in the notepad?*

She drew a big, fat blank.

This was frustrating beyond compare!

"Um, Stacy, when you have a moment, can you snap a pic of Clive and send it to me? That'll help when I'm visiting thrift shops." Or when she told Gabe about Clive's resemblance to the studio cat.

"Not *now*, Ursula." A frown dragged Stacy's eyebrows together along the top rim of her glasses. "When we're finished packing. Or tomorrow."

"Whenever it's convenient." Ursula reached for the wrapped frame of Stacy and Shelly. *Stay cool. Don't say or do anything to alert Stacy I might suspect her older sister of criminal activity or anything, but—*

Had Mackie blackmailed Shelly, entering the woman's name in his notepad under an alias? Had Stacy's job at the studio inadvertently played a part in the craziness of the last two months?

If Shelly was harassing or stalking Mackie, would she have been on the lookout for employment opportunities which might suit her little sister, thereby affording Shelly an inside scoop, so to speak, on studio routines?

Ursula's mouth dried faster than California during a hundred-and-ten degree drought. She had placed the ad for the receptionist job on multiple websites. Had Shelly googled or happened to catch sight of "Victor McKenzie Photography" on the internet and passed the employment prospect onto Stacy?

Or had Stacy learned about the job and then informed her sister? Before or after Mackie hired the girl?

How had Shelly reacted to the news?

Ursula inhaled a rickety breath, her throat so dry she couldn't manage a simple swallow anymore. Had Shelly's obsession with

Paul Bloomfield instigated or worsened the woman's weird revenge plot against Mackie?

She dared not ask for water again. Her mind whirred with dozens of scenarios, and interrogating Stacy seemed counterproductive—even detrimental—at this point.

What if asking Stacy more questions sparked the girl's curiosity? About Ursula's feelings for Gabe, about her sudden interest in Shelly's love life, about Stacy's job or the strange occurrences at work?

What if Stacy was stalking Mackie *along with* her sister for some warped reason? And Gabe had been justified in investigating the girl from the start?

Egad, what might Stacy do if she guessed Ursula realized she might be involved in the studio sabotage?

Water. Water. She craved water!

Stacy hadn't demonstrated a whole lot of what one might describe as self-composure or levelheadedness or I-got-it-togetherness this evening. Ergo, her massive overreaction when Ursula asked about the cat bookend.

Ursula's only course of action was to play unsuspecting and continue helping the girl move.

Except some way, sometime tonight, she needed to check the notepad for clues to Shelly's potential inclusion in Mackie's probable blackmail scheme.

She needed to call Gabe. He had the names. She didn't.

But Stacy had kyboshed one phone-checking attempt already.

Agh. Ursula couldn't just twiddle her thumbs while Shelly—possibly utilizing her younger sister as a smokescreen—might be up to more nasty tricks. Her brain and fingers and feet and entire body itched with the deep, burning, relentless need to escape the garage apartment and crack this case.

Thirty

Baseball cap low on his forehead, Gabe slumped in his pickup outside an unassuming brick-and-stucco fourplex. His snooping earlier today had uncovered that Lynette Lafleur, also known as University of Washington grad student Lynne Munson, shared the rental accommodation with a pair of elementary schoolteachers. As Lynette, Lynne stripped three nights a week at The Dirty Kitty. As Lynne, at least according to what he'd witnessed during tonight's stakeout, she rarely left the apartment. Even a little dragging-the-garbage-can-to-the-curb activity would make a nice change from her sitting at her kitchen table with her gaze riveted to her tablet.

Sipping his cold coffee, he glanced at his personal cell sitting on the passenger seat. Two nights ago, Ursula had snacked on chips in the same spot during their surveillance of Desiree Lewis. Later, they'd returned to her place and spooned until daylight.

Love swelled in his chest. He'd grown accustomed to having his Amazon warrior princess around, contributing to the investigation, talking about their families...exploring each other's bodies. He yearned to fill her in on the day's activities, except he only had dead ends to report, and honoring her request to stay out of her way while she focused on her deadline trumped all.

Returning his attention to the kitchen window in Lynne Munson's apartment, Gabe mulled over his findings. Armed with social security numbers from the outdated Dirty Kitty index cards, he'd tracked down concrete addresses for Lynne and Mary Bismarck this morning. Mary had moved twice since starting at the show lounge. This afternoon, while Mary was at work, Gabe adopted his Matt Bennett persona for Quality Customer Satisfaction Surveys. Using his burner phone, he'd interviewed Mary's elderly parents, who she now lived with and cared for. His questions about their shopping preferences revealed a conservative mindset and also the belief their daughter managed a successful clothing chain. A far cry from operating The Dirty Kitty. Meanwhile, neither of Lynne's roommates appeared to realize the thirty-three-year-old woman pole-danced to finance her PhD.

On the surface, both Lynne and Mary possessed motivation for ensuring Mackie's sex tapes never came to light. But why wait years since the suspected blackmail to exact revenge?

In the fourplex, Lynne rose from the kitchen table. Leaving the tablet, she exited the residence with a backpack slung over her shoulder. The outdoor light illuminated her movements as she climbed into a gray Chevy coupe and inched the car onto the street.

Gabe swallowed the last mouthful of his coffee. He waited until the car passed through a stop sign. Starting the pickup, he tailed the Chevy at a discreet distance. Lynne drove as if distracted, accelerating and slowing down multiple times.

Five minutes later, she parked on a side road beneath a street-light. Straining his peripheral vision, Gabe motored past her. Makeup cluttered her dashboard. In his rearview, he spied her tugging on a long red wig over her loose blond curls.

Interesting. "Lynette" wasn't scheduled to perform tonight. Not at The Dirty Kitty at any rate. What was *Lynne* up to? Was she the woman his uncle called Red? Or did she don a disguise for her sociology thesis research?

He turned a corner and pulled over, tapping a thumb against the steering wheel as he monitored his suspect's car in a side mirror. His cell vibrated on the passenger seat. Glancing at the ID, he answered. "Hi, Mom."

"Gabe? Where are you?"

His spine seized at her anxious tone. "What's wrong?"

"Your uncle was here. He attacked me."

"*What?*" His voice boomed in the pickup.

"Honey, I'm okay. I'm at the Donaldsons' next door. I called 911, and Hal and Bill are on their way. Son, I trusted Victor. I was so gullible."

"Mom, don't blame yourself." What had that animal done to her? "I'm coming."

"I'm not sure I want you hearing the details—"

"Nonsense." He slammed the truck into gear. "Stay with Carol. I'll be there as quick as I can."

"I hear Hal's car outside. I—I need to see him."

"Do that. He's a good guy. He'll watch out for you."

Disconnecting, Gabe tossed aside the phone. It landed on the floorboards as he peeled down the street. Lynne Munson could suffocate Mackie with her wig tonight for all he cared. Gabe's sorry excuse for a relative had assaulted his mother.

If someone else didn't murder him first, Gabe would.

The pounding on the Donaldsons' door rattled the living room window. Eve's heart raced.

"Eve, it's Hal. Open up."

"I'll give you privacy," Carol Donaldson said.

"Thank you." Eve flipped the deadbolt as her neighbor disappeared into a bedroom. Her words were intended for Hal alone.

He burst inside, the cold breeze streaming in his wake. "Sweetheart, are you all right?" His big hands swept her arms as he crushed her against his chest.

She let out a sob. "I'm shaken up. Hal, I'm so relieved to see you. I phoned Gabe, and the police are here. Carol's husband went to my house to explain. I wanted to see you before going over there." Hal's presence would give her strength to face the destruction again.

He kissed her cheek. "I saw the cruiser. Bill should arrive soon."

"Th-thank you."

Gently grasping her shoulders, he glanced down at her open coat. His jaw clenched. His gaze narrowed. "That asshole scratched your chest," he muttered.

"And bruised my inner thighs. Hal, he bit my breast."

He swore. "You said he tried to rape you. Love, you have to tell me." Tugging her close, he whispered, "Did he succeed?"

She wept against his shoulder, her tears soaking his overcoat. "No. I fought him. I—I had to wait until he unzipped." Nausea roiled in her stomach. "Then I kneed him."

"You are so brave," Hal whispered, caressing the hair at her temple.

"I acted on instinct and…and techniques Doug described. I still can't believe it. My brother-in-law." She shuddered. "The idea sickens me."

"I know." Cupping her face, Hal gazed into her eyes. His handsome features reflected love, integrity, and compassion. "Eve, pride has kept me away from you. I haven't been able to stop thinking about what I said yesterday at the cafe. I was so wrong."

"Hal—"

"Please, let me finish." He brushed a kiss against her forehead. "I thought about everything throughout last night, and when you called and asked me over." His deep voice roughened. "I understand a part of you will never stop loving your husband, Eve, and that's okay. He was taken from you in a way I can't imagine. That you honor his memory is a treasure, not something to be thrown in your face when you're feeling vulnerable. Sweetheart, I hurt you—"

"We hurt each other," she whispered through a tight throat.

He nodded. "But I love you. I want to try again."

Her heart sang. "Oh, Hal." She glided a hand over his jaw. "That's why I asked you to my place tonight. More than anything, I wanted to tell you I want you back. I love you, and I need you in my life. When Victor showed up, I told him the same thing. That's when I learned he's carried some sort of torch for me since before Doug died." Her face heated. "I'm ashamed. All these years, I thought he looked up to me, but like an older sister. But he wanted —he tried—" She choked down a sob.

"It's okay, Eve. Let it out."

As Hal held her, she wept. When she could speak again, she explained her fear of losing Hal like she had lost Doug, like she had almost lost Gabe last summer, Victor's words of whatever he considered love the night before her wedding, how he'd planted doubts against every man she'd dated since her husband died.

But, especially, his disparaging comments about Hal.

Victor must have realized her relationship with Hal was special, different from any other man in her life, so he'd acted on a distorted version of misinterpreted feelings.

In retrospect, her brother-in-law's emotional exploitation shone clear. Vic had used her grief as a means to keep her close. If his outburst during the attack held true, he had witnessed Doug's shooting. Perhaps he had even been the cause of Doug's death in some terrible fashion.

In Hal's arms, she gasped. "How will Gabe react when he learns his uncle was in the warehouse that night? Victor did nothing while Gabe's father bled to death." Her poor son. Doug's murder had traumatized them both.

Hal rubbed her back. "Gabe is a grown man. He's brave and honorable, like you are. Whatever the police discover, he'll deal with it."

She inhaled a trembling breath. "I hope you're right."

"Eve," Hal whispered. "You couldn't have guessed how despicable McKenzie is. He pulled the wool over your eyes because you are a generous, loving, giving woman. You gave him the benefit of the doubt, because that is what you do."

"Except when it came to you. When you asked me to marry you—"

"My proposal stands. I still want to marry you, but if that sort of commitment isn't in our future, I'll be just as happy. As long as I know you're my love, you don't have to be my wife."

Heart melting, she kissed his lips. "I *want* to be your wife. I never want to let go of you. I love you so much, Hal. If you don't propose again soon, I will."

"Ah, darling." He squeezed her close. "When the moment feels right, I'll surprise you with a ring."

She smiled through her tears. No matter what happened with Victor, no matter how Gabe responded when he learned his suspicions about his uncle's vile nature had proven correct, they would get through it. The three of them. Together.

Her new family.

She was blessed.

Gabe struck the kitchen counter with a clenched fist. *"He witnessed Dad's murder?* Bill, are you kidding me?" White-hot fury roiled in his veins. He would throttle Victor McKenzie! From this point forward, they were *not* related. Not by blood and not by law. The cretin could roast on a spit for eight trillion eons and not atone for the suffering he had caused Gabe's mother these last eleven years.

"I know." Bill grasped his shoulder. "It's a lot to absorb."

"That's a gross understatement." Gabe scraped a hand over his face. Bill's supervisor remained in the living room with a CSI and the detectives assigned to the case while two uniforms canvassed the neighborhood to determine if anyone had observed a prowler entering the house through the broken primary bedroom window. Another uniform had accompanied Gabe's mom and Hal to the hospital. There, a sexual assault nurse would collect evidence to document the attempted rape.

Attempted rape!

Gabe raked both hands through his hair, forearms solid as stone. The next time he saw Victor McKenzie, the swine had better be behind bars, because Gabe would gladly wring his neck. According to his mom's account to the supervisor, Victor's presence in the warehouse had somehow distracted Gabe's father or affected his judgment, resulting in his dad getting shot.

Logically, Gabe realized Mackie witnessing the shooting wasn't the same as actually watching his brother die, but Mackie had boasted about fleeing the scene. Dad hadn't stood a chance.

"Bill, wonder if Victor was the actual killer?" Gabe asked, voice wild. "What if *he* murdered my dad?"

"Son, think rationally. The report from all those years ago concluded that the bullet came from the warehouse loft. We have the gun, slugs, and fingerprints. Unless your uncle was with the drug dealer physically forcing the guy to take a shot, he didn't murder your father."

Spinning on his heels, Gabe paced the kitchen. "I hear you. But I've always felt something about that night was off. Now I know why." Damn Mackie! "I wanted to look into the case again—"

"Which will happen as a result of your mother's report," Bill reasoned. "Buddy, take into consideration she can only relay what he said. We don't know if he told her the truth. Maybe he wanted to emotionally torture her."

"That makes it worse. For over a decade, he pretended to be her friend when all along he had *the hots* for her?" Gabe needed to break something. If he had a log, he would throw it through a wall. "There was a third set of footprints on the warehouse floor. The emergency personnel obscured them, but they were there. *They were his.*" *Victor McKenzie's!*

"We don't know that for certain."

"We can find out. If Victor confessed to Mom, he might confess to me."

"True, but tread carefully. Don't let hate obscure your judgment. Thinking about how that sleazebag might have saved your father's life makes me want to rip out his throat, but you and I both know that unless the current investigation reveals your uncle was involved in the felony resulting in your father's death, our hands are tied." Hands on hips, Bill asked, "Have you ever known Victor to use drugs? Or talk about friends who do?"

Gabe's jaw clenched. "No." Damn it.

"Your mother agrees."

"Well, as we know, he's full of surprises. You can tag him for the sexual assault. Haul him in for questioning. I haven't found evidence of drug use at the studio, but who knows what he's hiding in his apartment." Wiping his mouth, Gabe paced the kitchen again.

"The detectives will proceed through the proper channels. Have faith. Gabe, you need to compose yourself before you see your mom."

"I'm composed." Right. He wanted to choke the life out of Mackie.

"And I'm James Bond. Look, your mother wants you to meet Hal at the hospital. She'll see both of you after her exam. I can't allow you to drive in this riled-up state."

"Yeah, yeah." Gabe willed his heart rate to decelerate. Bill had done his mother a favor, responding to Hal's call off-duty. Bill was here as a friend. He didn't deserve to bear the brunt of Gabe's wrath. "Did Victor steal anything?"

"Your mother's locket with your parents' pictures inside it is missing. So is her torn blouse and a page from your father's memory album."

"Which page?"

"Your mom said it featured photos of her with your uncle after the funeral and also photos of the pair of them with you."

Their remaining family. What a joke.

Gabe's talon-stiff fingers curled and uncurled. "It's enough to justify a search warrant?"

"Given some of the shit he shouted at her, I would say so."

"Excellent." Gabe pointed to Bill. "Take it to the judge. I want that creep to pay for every charge the DA can make stick." Including the attempted rape along with the suspected former and current blackmail. Mackie was a hothead. If the toad had been involved with the warehouse crime, he would have flung the truth in Gabe's mom's face tonight.

After coveting his brother's wife for decades—since before Gabe's parents were married—Mackie couldn't have resisted the opportunity to goad her. He would have thought he had nothing to lose.

But he did.

More than he realized.

"Get your supervisor in here," Gabe said to Bill. "I'm laying a charge."

Ursula parked Reba in the studio alley, beneath the glaring security lights. Crafting a reason to leave Stacy's place without revealing her suspicions about the girl's sister had tested her wits, but desperation had finally delivered the perfect plan. Ursula would drive the full moving boxes to Stacy's new apartment while Stacy finished packing. That way, if Shelly returned, Stacy would have fewer boxes to hide.

Stacy had bought the scheme. Three crammed boxes sat in Reba's back seat. Unbeknownst to Stacy, Ursula wouldn't deliver them until after she examined Mackie's notepad.

She checked her phone. Still nothing from Gabe. Stacy hadn't sent a photo of Clive yet either.

She shifted on the seat. A block after leaving Stacy's, she'd pulled over and called Gabe's personal cell, but he hadn't answered. Was he embroiled in an aspect of the investigation that required him to use his disposable cell? She didn't have the number because the idea was to keep the burner phone as untraceable as possible.

Although, didn't he usually carry his personal cell regardless?

Her heart beat faster. He wasn't in some sort of trouble, was he? *Don't think that way.*

Before her meltdown, he had said to call or text if she encountered something suspicious at Stacy's. After she fell apart, he'd reassured her she should only help Stacy move as a friend. Now that Ursula wanted in on the action again, she should report the discovery of the cat bookend and Shelly's supposed relationship with Paul Bloomfield. To do otherwise felt dim.

She swiped her thumb over her screen. Gabe didn't pick up. She left a message. "Hi, Gabe, it's me. I'm, um, at the studio. I know when we talked this morning I said I wanted out of our partnership"—a blush washed her face—"but I need to take another look at the notepad. So I'm kind of breaking into your uncle's office. Except I have a key, so it's not illegal. I don't think." *Stop babbling.* "Also, Stacy is sending me a picture of a bookend I saw at her apartment. I'll forward it to you. Please call when you get this, and I'll explain."

She set her phone to vibrate and slipped it into her purse. Wielding a miniature flashlight, she entered the building through the alley door between the breakroom and Mackie's den of gickiquity. *Blech.*

A glint unrelated to the dancing flashlight beam caught her eye, and she squinted toward Reception. A pale glow leaked into the long, dark corridor.

Ursula cocked her head, but silence reigned. Was someone here? *No snooping until you know.*

Purse bumping her hip, she tiptoed toward the front entrance. The lamp on the reception desk burned, illuminating one of her boss's thick wool hats. The telephone cord, unplugged from the wall, coiled in a jumble on the floor.

Mackie must have worked late, his mood ultra-foul. At such

times, he claimed the mere possibility of a ringing telephone disrupted his creativity. Without the main landline plugged in, the answering machine couldn't record messages. They had missed important bookings because of his annoying quirks.

Looking out the window, she glimpsed his van parked on the street—further evidence he was working late or maybe partying downtown. She needed to make sure he wasn't lurking in the studio proper before she returned to the first hall to check the bathroom, darkroom, and breakroom. Only then would she enter his office.

Gabe would be proud of her. She was checking *everywhere* this time.

Flashlight off and stored in her jacket pocket, she crept toward the backroom in super-sleuth darkness. As she neared the room, opera music swelled from within. A vibrant soprano resonated in the high-ceilinged space. Something Italian?

Palms on the door, Ursula pressed an ear against the wood. Her nose wrinkled. Gross, if her boss and his girlfriend were getting it on in the same room where she and Gabe had made love—

Way to spoil my romantic memories, hairball.

Her purse knocked the door. The hinges creaked, and the painted slab inched open.

Gross, *gross*. How many times had she asked Mackie to lock his doors?

Cringing, she turned away.

Loud scuffling noises reached her ears. A reverberating clang crested over the opera music, as if Mackie had thrown an empty trashcan onto the concrete floor. A warped-sounding man's voice shouted lewd words about another man's privates.

Ursula gulped.

That voice isn't Mackie's!

8.

Neck stiff, Gabe drove his pickup toward the downtown hospital. Bill was bang on the money. He needed to rein in his anger before he saw his mom. Speeding over to Mackie's and squeezing the life out of the scum-sucking pervert would feel immensely satisfying, but death was too easy for the likes of Victor McKenzie. If justice prevailed, Mackie would become another prisoner's bitch in jail. Gabe would sleep well at night knowing the creep was finally getting screwed. In ways Mackie had never counted on.

Stopping at a red light, Gabe inhaled through his nostrils. His cell on the passenger floorboard buzzed.

The mobile had toppled off the seat earlier. In his hurry to see his mom, Gabe had forgotten. He answered using his bluetooth. Stacy's voice emitted from the speaker.

"What can I do for you, Stace?" Gabe studied the busy intersection. Five more blocks until he reached the hospital.

"I'm worried about Ursula. She's helping me pack tonight."

"I remember. She's there, isn't she?" He had longed to touch base with her all day.

"She *was*," Stacy said. "Then she got this idea to take the full boxes to my new place while I kept packing. I'm finished."

"She needs time to drive there and back," Gabe responded as the traffic light flashed green. He trailed a slowpoke sedan over the crosswalk. *Move it, pal.*

"Yeah, but I gave great directions, and my roommate Carrie says she hasn't arrived. The building is twenty minutes from here. It's been more than an hour."

He frowned. "Have you messaged her?"

"I'm too embarrassed. I acted weird before she left. Maybe she thinks I'm not mature enough to move out of Shelly's. Maybe she's decided not to help me. She wanted me to send her a picture of Clive, but if she's not helping me move, why should I?"

"Who's Clive?"

"A little cat statue." A beat elapsed. "Actually, half of a bookend set."

Gabe tightened his grip on the steering wheel. Why was Stacy concerned about a bookend? Why was Ursula?

He said, "It doesn't sound like Ursula not to want to help or contact you, Stacy. I'll call her and find out what's going on."

"Okay. Get back to me."

"Sure thing." He ended the call and steered into the lot for Brinley's Hardware. Parked, he retrieved his cell.

Damn it. Two "Missed Call from Ursula" notifications and one voicemail prompt displayed.

He dragged air into his lungs. He was new to being in love. After the mess he'd made with Sula this morning, jabbering about a future when the first anniversary of her grandma's death loomed, he'd thought it wise to stay out of her way, continue working the case while she focused on her deadline. Now, his cop-radar tingled.

Had he been wrong?

Thirty-One

BILE COATED URSULA'S mouth as she peeked around the door into the shadowy recesses of the studio proper. Scarlet spotlights zeroed in on a surreal vignette of Mackie sitting blindfolded on a wooden chair, wearing nothing but baggy boxers and slouchy socks. The nasty man. Barging in on Jasmine servicing him beneath his desk two weeks ago had been revolting but nothing approaching these depths of depravity. Countless loops of rope coated with clear packing tape covered his hairy legs, arms, and chest, and a messy pile of what looked like his clothes bunched between the chair legs.

Ursula squinted. Was that a blouse sleeve plugging his maw? *Why?* A ball-gag couldn't suffice?

The bulk of the ripped blouse draped his belly, and more packing tape fastened a heart-shaped locket onto his forehead.

A tickle burrowed up Ursula's nostrils. She stilled.

Gasoline?

Did she smell gas?

Stifling a squeak, she pinched her nose. Now that she'd noticed it, there was no mistaking the stench of gasoline wafting from mounds of rags, papers, blankets, and also props spilling from the studio trunks.

Why would Mackie, or whoever had tied him up, splash gasoline around the room?

Unless they intended—

Oh, no! To light the mounds and trunks on fire?

"Mph." Mackie struggled against the ropes. The chair wobbled. A width of packing tape yanked his matted chest hair. The blouse sleeve stuffing his mouth muffled his yelps of pain.

Ursula's world slowed to a crawl as a woman with her back to the door waved an electronic device. And a butcher knife?

The blonde shrieked into the gadget, her voice morphing into the scratchy baritone which, moments earlier, had drifted into the darkened hall.

"Your boner's dead now, asshole!" the woman taunted Mackie using the voice-changer. "Thanks to this little darling." She shook the electronic box. "Don't like hearing a man talk dirty to you, Victor? Too damn bad. All those three-ways you promised me, and in the end you couldn't handle screwing me with another guy in bed. Your dicks might have touched, and you might've liked it. Can't have that. Now you'll never have to worry about it, because I'm gonna hack you!"

Holy crap! Ursula's heart bashed against her ribs like a frantic monkey shaking the bars of a zoo cage. *Run*, her brain commanded, but her legs refused to cooperate. She was as useless as Stacy's bookend cat without its twin.

"All those newbie bondage games?" the woman shouted through the voice-changer. "I did them for you. What did *I* get out of the deal? A stupid, grainy videotape that ruined my life! You were even too cheap to upgrade your equipment. That's insulting!"

Mackie wriggled on the chair. "Mph. Mph."

The woman bounced around, brandishing the knife. Her profile flashed into Ursula's line of vision. Omigod, it *was* Shelly—Michelle—whoever-she-was!

Ursula ducked behind the door and wracked her brain for the names listed in the notepad, which, as far as she knew, remained in the battered video camera hidden in her boss's office.

Lynette, Desiree, Lisa, Miki—

Miki!

The list included Miki Timmins. Could Miki be a nickname for Michelle?

Ohhh, crap. This woman was Stacy's sister?

Was Timmins Shelly's married name—or an alias?

Or because Shelly and Stacy had different fathers?

Who cares?

Palms clammy, Ursula fished in her purse, fingers fumbling for her phone. The door and the shadows beyond the reach of the spotlights shielded her from Shelly's view. If she escaped down the hall prior to calling the police, might the woman follow through on her threat and cut Mackie? Leaving him helpless and bleeding, waging a losing battle as he struggled to cling to life—

Like Gabe's father in the empty warehouse.

I can't live with that.

It wasn't even a question. Mackie might be scum, but he was Gabe's uncle, his only remaining family other than his mom, his deceased dad's younger brother. Ursula wrestled with loads of guilt for deserting her childhood pet while her house burned down. She couldn't bear the thought of abandoning *any* human bound at the mercy of Stacy's sister.

She dragged her phone out of her purse. It slipped from her shaking hands, clattering to the floor and skating into the room. *Shit!*

Lungs squeezing, she crouched at the door's edge. By the grace of every deity around the globe, Shelly didn't turn. The opera music gathered speed, a male tenor joining the soprano, neither sounding happy.

Along with the darkness shrouding the door as well as the area around the prop table, the singers offered valuable cover.

"Don't whine about your sister-in-law," Shelly mocked Mackie with the voice-changer. "She wasn't home when I trashed her house. I stole stuff to make them think it was you." Her maniacal laughter competed with the soaring opera. "How sick are *you* to fall in love with your dead brother's wife? *Then* agree to sleep with me because she turned you down?" The voice-changer crackled, and Shelly swore. "Stupid thing."

Throwing the device into an open trunk, she bellowed in her natural voice, "Did you think I *wanted to hear* I was your second choice tonight? Jerk! I finally found someone new. My Paul. Now you're blackmailing *him*. That's why he dumped me. He says the public won't put up with him leaving his skinny wife, especially if you release pictures of him slobbering all over some whore in California. His political career would be ruined."

Ursula's breathing quickened. Shelly's rant didn't make sense. Was the woman angry because Paul had stopped seeing her or because another of Mackie's apparent blackmail schemes might destroy the council president's career?

Either way, Ursula's suspicions about Mackie having something on Bloomfield had proven correct. Wait until Gabe found out.

She shot a glance to her phone on the concrete floor halfway to the prop table. *What would Nancy do?*

Grab the cell, call Emergency, and record the scene for the police.

"I didn't tell Paul I knew you," Shelly harangued Mackie as he whimpered. The knife dangled from the woman's fingertips, with any luck about to fall. Or forgotten, if Ursula created a diversion. "But I had to do something! You'll never guess what happened. My little sister answered your receptionist ad and got the job. The universe threw you a curveball while doing me a huge favor. I told Stacy something better would come along, but *no*, she needed to prove her independence. I don't *want* her independent. I want her dependent on me!"

Shelly pounded her chest. "I need *someone* to love me, Victor. To stick by me. Ice water doesn't run in my veins like it does yours. Stacy kept the job anyway. Then you started vandalizing your business. Breaking and painting the window—what an idiot. Your stupidity inspired me to make you pay for what you're doing to Paul. For what you did to me. To make you pay for all the women you've screwed over."

Behind the door, Ursula tore off her shoes and jacket, thoughts tumbling. Was Shelly telling the truth? Was it possible *Mackie* tossed the inert grenade through the studio window and painted threats on the new glass on Halloween?

Had he purposely botched the Real Men ad? Or had Shelly wrecked the ad using the voice changer?

Where did Mackie's self-sabotage end and Shelly's crazy antics begin? As Stacy's landlord, Shelly would have had ample opportunity to steal and copy the keys to the studio. *Ursula's* studio in a few months. Her future. The cornerstone to helping her family.

She needed to get to the bottom of this right now.

As the tenor's voice receded and the soprano launched into a boisterous aria, she covered her nose with her turtleneck collar, clamped her purse against her waist, and raced in quiet socks to her phone.

"What I don't understand is why you screwed with your business," Shelly shouted.

Mackie choked on the blouse-sleeve gag, head lolling as he fought the gas-fumed air. Scooping up her phone, Ursula ran for the darkened safety of the prop table. She hid between the table legs, secured her makeshift nose mask, and surveyed the scene.

"I can't hear you," Shelly yelled.

Mackie retched. Vomit seeped from his gag as the opera music climbed toward a crescendo.

"No sudden movements," Shelly hissed, pressing the blade to Mackie's gut and yanking the blouse sleeve out of his mouth.

"Please, Miki!" He spit barf, shaking his head. "I didn't realize you knew Paul. I needed Evie to feel bad for me. To pay attention. That's why I did the window. B-both times."

"She'll pay attention. She'll stand over your grave and spit on it." Shelly grabbed Mackie's crotch along with a hunk of boxers, and he howled. "Admit what you did to Paul, or I'll slice off your prick. Those pictures are fakes! Paul wouldn't cheat on me."

Ursula's hands trembled. Flitting her attention between the blonde and her phone, she swiped a wobbly thumb over the screen.

The display brightened.

One bar showed.

Her pulse went ballistic.

She couldn't remember the last time she'd used her cell in this room. She hadn't considered the signal strength.

Who's the idiot now?

Anxiety swam in her stomach. *She* was.

"M-Miki." Mackie sniveled. "Yes, I faked the pictures. I needed Paul's money to build a life with Evie."

"Stop calling me Miki!" Shelly twisted his privates. He screamed. "Miki and Mackie are stupid nicknames. You said they were cute. *I* thought they sucked."

"I-I-I'm sorry. My head hurts. Mik-shell..."

"Shelly, you flea-brain. *Shelly!*" Releasing his crotch, she wrenched her pendant of multi-colored stones. "Know what this says?"

Glancing back and forth between the noisy scenario and her phone, Ursula tapped Emergency. A dialer appeared. Dare she speak to the call center? Would Shelly overhear? If she punched 911 and hung up, would Emergency call her back?

"I can't see what you're talking about." Mackie moaned. "If you remove the blindfold—"

"I'm not falling for that, Victor. The rag stays on." Shelly patted her necklace. "It spells *P.S. I Love You.* P. for Paul and S. for Shelly. P.S.! P.S.! P.S.!" She gripped his privates again. He shrieked. "Tell me about Paul!"

Ursula's fingertips hovered over her phone screen. Could she *text* 911? She wasn't up to date on the latest protocol, which services existed or if they had changed.

Make a decision. Time was of the essence. She needed to channel her inner Rambo-chick and improvise.

Twice she dialed 911 and disconnected. She did it again. Her phone vibrated. She hit Ignore.

Bzzz.

She tapped the screen. *Ignore.*

Please send help regardless. This past summer she saw a link on social media about not allowing kids to fool around with old phones because dispatch couldn't chance a call wasn't an emergency. Despite that she'd hung up, they'd trace the signal to the nearest cell tower.

They *would* send someone.

Help was near.

Saying a quick prayer, she accessed her camera and pressed Video. Popping up her head, she set the phone on the table, camera aimed at Mackie.

"I saw Paul in the newspaper," Gabe's uncle sputtered as Ursula ducked back down. "L-leaving for a municipal conference in California, it said. I recognized him from taking his portrait and—and the hooker scandal. I t-took a long weekend, flew down, and snapped pictures of a couple on the beach. People will do anything if you pay them a few bucks. I took photos of Paul at the conference without him seeing me and pasted his head on the other guy's body."

"That's kid stuff!" Shelly accused.

"I'm a professional. I do incredible work." Mackie groaned.

"You took advantage of my Paul. Your pictures are why he hasn't left his wife. It's *your* fault. He will leave her though. Once you're dead."

Mackie bawled. "Miki, please. I love you! You're the woman I want."

Ursula peered over the table, gaze scanning to the left. *Clive II!* The cat bookend she had mistaken for a paperweight perched two inches from her fingertips.

"Too late." Shelly backed away from the chair and tested her blade with her thumb. "You hurt the man I love, so I'll hurt what *you* love, Victor. That's your imaginary future with Eve McKenzie, your useless dick, and your stupid business." Humming along with the opera, she tugged a cigarette lighter out of her bra. She placed the lighter along with the knife on the floor, approximately a foot from the chair.

Ursula snatched Clive. Shelly jammed the blouse sleeve back into Mackie's mouth. His blindfold remained undisturbed. Shelly retrieved a toppled gas can and set it beside the knife and lighter.

Ursula's pulse clamored. *No, no! Gas plus lighter equals fire.*

Shelly checked her watch and smiled. Standing in front of a sobbing Mackie, she closed her eyes. As if she were meditating, she pressed her palms together.

It's now or never. Ursula gripped the pottery cat. Swinging her purse over her head, she ran toward the demented woman. Loud blasts exploded from the deepest reaches of the room, and a putrid smoke scent filled the air.

The opera music struck a dramatic pause.

Ursula's socks skidded.

One hand flung out.

Clive whacked the concrete and split in two.

Shelly whirled around. "You!"

Pouncing, Shelly grabbed Ursula's purse. They fell to the floor. Ursula's foot knocked a chunk of Clive as more blasts exploded from the direction of the breakroom.

Had this lunatic set them on a timer?

Breathing heavily, Ursula scrambled to her knees. The stink of gas filled her nostrils as the music resumed. "Shelly, think about what you're doing. Think about Stacy." The rancid scent of smoke intensified, and perspiration slickened her skin. Flashbacks of her family's house fire spiraled in her brain: waking to the smoke, trying to reach Pierre, her dad's arms around her waist, dragging her away, saving her at the expense of her cat.

Like any father would.

Shelly's mouth twisted. "I *have* thought about my sister, you wench. Ever since she started working in this hellhole, I've thought of nothing except Stacy, Victor, and my Paul." Clenching the purse, she snatched the knife off the floor. Pointing the blade at Ursula, she stood. "What do you care? Stacy says Victor is a lousy boss." The scarlet spotlights tinted her sinister smile. "I have an idea. Cooperate, and I'll let *you* de-nut Victor. I get to saw off his prick. Or we could flip for it. Got a quarter?"

An eye on the knife, Ursula glanced around the room. She smelled smoke, but no accompanying flames ensued. Shelly must have timed the explosions to induce fear, not fire.

Okay, okay, there is no fire.

But if Shelly ignited the clothes beneath Mackie's chair—

Ursula would *not* let that happen.

"In m-my purse," she said, acting the part of the accommodating victim. She refused to die here. She wanted to live. To grow old with Gabe. She didn't believe for one second that Shelly intended to spare her life. The deranged woman just wanted to torture her by forcing her to cut Mackie. "Th-there's a zippered compartment in my purse. My coins are in there."

Shelly dug into the purse, producing a small wallet. She chucked the purse onto the floor.

On the prop table, Ursula's phone vibrated and fell over.

"What do we have here?" Wielding the knife, Shelly circled to the table.

"Emergency, calling me back." Ursula's chest tightened. "I phoned 911." *Please, God, plunge the fear of the Seattle police into Shelly's soul.* The video recording might have stopped when the call came in. Until help arrived, Ursula needed to operate under the assumption that she was on her own.

"Wrong again, bean-breath. It's not 911," Shelly said, snatching the phone. "You might want me to answer this. What's the code?" Grinning demonically, she brandished the knife.

Oh, God. Was Gabe trying to call? Or one of her parents? Her brother?

She supplied the password.

Shelly put the phone to her ear. "Hello, Gabey-poo."

"Who's *this*?" Gabe's commanding voice echoed from the cell, and Ursula cried out.

"Your worst nightmare. You're too late, nephew-lips. Yep, I know who you are. I've been watching this place for weeks. Too bad, so sad, your girlfriend invited herself to Victor's roasting. How brave, but she's dug her own grave. Hah-hah!"

Ursula shouted, "Gabe, we're in the backroom!" The smoke from the blasts had thinned, but every second ticked by as slow as an hour.

"Shut up," Shelly yelled. She muttered into the phone, "Both your girlfriend and your rotten uncle are about to die." Moving away, she extracted a second lighter from her jeans pocket. Back half-turned, she ignited the gasoline-drenched trunks.

Flames licked the papers and rags Shelly must have packed on top of the clothes and props. Terror lashed Ursula as documents crinkled and sizzled into floating ash. A feather boa swayed like a hypnotized snake before sagging onto the floor. Curly's wool moptop crisped and snapped.

More contents popped with heat as smoke twisted toward the ceiling. Burning Ursula's nose, stinging her eyes. Mackie whimpered and struggled against the ropes strapping him to the chair, as powerless as Pierre huddling beneath her childhood bed.

"Gabe," she shouted toward the phone, grabbing a chunk of Clive and jumping to her feet. "She's lighting the studio on fire!"

Shelly growled. "I'll gut you first."

"Not on my watch." Ursula gritted her teeth. She *would not* become a victim of a second fire. Her family had survived disaster countless times.

She was a Scott. She could *do* this.

She hurled Clive at Shelly's head.

❧

A scream pierced Gabe's ear. He gunned his pickup through a yellow light as the connection to Ursula's phone died. She must be terrified. Whoever had answered intended to torch the place. All Sula's hard work to help her family, that comment about gutting her—

He couldn't drive fast enough.

One hand on the wheel, he swiped Recent Calls. Bill Cruikshank answered.

"Bill, I just got off the phone with a woman threatening to kill Victor and one of his employees. Send backup to Victor McKenzie Photography ASAP." Gabe barked the address.

"Backup? Son, where are you?"

"About to arrive. It seems a fire has been set. There might be old photography chemicals in the building, plastics, various toxins." And Sula was in the middle of it. "Call the fire department and EMTs." Gabe screeched to a stop across the road from the old brick structure.

"Copy that. Gabe, my supervisor says someone from the vicinity dialed 911. Help is on the way. Don't go near the place."

Like that was gonna happen. He punched Off.

Launching out of his truck, he noted his uncle's van parked on the street.

Inside the studio, smoke funneled from both corridors into the waiting room, the thick haze engulfing his face and filling his throat. Sprinklers sprayed. Alarms beeped.

"Sula?" Gabe ripped off his jacket and shielded his head with the battered leather. Bad leg screaming, he ran to the backroom. The opera music he'd heard on the phone spilled into the hall as he spied Sula's shoes and coat on a dry patch of floor.

Grabbing the coat, he elbowed the door. "Ursula!" His ribs felt splayed apart, chest gaping, every emotion he possessed laid bare. He had finally opened himself to love. No maniac was stealing her away.

Flames swallowed the trunks and prop furniture as archaic sprinklers waged an ineffectual battle from the high ceiling. A woman with blond hair laid face-up on the concrete, head bloody and a huge goose egg forming on her skull.

"Sula," he shouted, kneeling and checking the woman's pulse. *Alive.* And obviously not Sula. Where was she?

Coughing, he waved his hands to part the smoke. He loved her. *Don't let Victor's jealousy and cowardice cost the life of another person I love.* "Ursula!"

"Over here!" Her voice rang through the smoke.

"I'm coming," Gabe yelled.

Hunching, he burst through the haze to glimpse her sawing a butcher knife against several ropes strapping Victor to a chair. The man was damn near naked. A blindfold hung from one of Victor's ears, and a blouse Gabe recognized as his mom's pooled on the floor.

Wide, clear tape, blistered from the heat, sealed his mom's broken heart locket to Victor's forehead.

"Help," the animal mumbled.

Ignoring him, Gabe covered Ursula's head with her coat. "Thank God you're safe."

"Grab my cell. To your left. I videoed some of Shelly's ranting."

Gabe spied her phone with a spider web of cracks on the screen. He wedged the device into a jeans pocket. "Stacy's *sister* is Victor's stalker?"

"Looks like. He called her Miki. Her real name is Michelle."

"Miki Timmins." The next woman on Mackie's list whom Gabe had planned to investigate. Now he knew why his initial attempts to track her down had led him nowhere.

Ursula wheezed as she struggled with the knife on the ropes around Mackie's chest.

"Your hands are shaking too much." Gabe took the knife. His jacket protected him from inhaling the worst of the smoke as he sliced the cords and she retrieved clothing from under the chair.

The ropes fell away. Sula shrouded Victor's face with his shirt and yanked him up. He moaned.

"Move it," she ordered, her coat muddling her voice as she dragged him to the door.

"I got a concussion."

"You're lucky you're alive. Thank me later."

Despite the gravity of the situation, Gabe's mouth tilted at one corner. In the hour of her worst fears being realized, despite how poorly Victor had treated her, his brave Sula had saved the man's worthless hide.

Staying low, he raced to Shelly. Her head lifted, eyes fluttering open.

"Paul?" Shelly's voice wobbled. "I love you. I did this for you."

"I'm not Paul." Lifting the woman against his chest, Gabe ran after Ursula and Victor. "Stay down," he advised Sula. "Your coat will provide cover from the smoke."

She stumbled into the hall with her human cargo. "It's too thick. I can't breathe." She slipped on the wet linoleum. Victor collapsed.

A firefighter reached through the smoke, steadying her arm.

"Fire Department. Is anyone else in the building?"

"I don't think so." Her voice rasped. "Just us four."

Gabe's eyes and throat stung. "Get her out," he yelled as more firefighters strode into the hall.

He didn't care what happened to him. He needed her safe.

Thirty-Two

Ursula's lips quivered. Her arms trembled. The oxygen mask jiggled on her cold nose as she inhaled deeply from the tank a paramedic had provided.

"Here's an extra blanket," the attendant said, arranging a third layer of warmth around her shoulders and setting another bottle of water by her hip. Her sooty jacket laid bunched on the cushion at the rear of the open ambulance.

"Thank you." Hot tears leaked from her stinging eyes, and she gripped the blankets, head throbbing. Thanks to Gabe snagging her shoes after a firefighter took charge of Shelly, her feet hadn't frozen, but the smoke and the stress of the last hour had taken its toll.

Gabe had followed close behind while a firefighter carried her from the building. Fear had lashed her mind and launched an adrenalin-assault on her body as the reality of her situation had struck her full force. If not for Gabe arriving in time and the city's hardworking first responders heeding her haphazard call to 911, she and Mackie and Shelly might have roasted to death.

Ursula gazed at the crowds and reporters milling around the barricades while firefighters toiled to squash every small flare-up of the blaze. The paramedics had wanted to transport her to the hospital, but she had declined. Near the barricades, Gabe huddled in conversation with his father's old partner and other members of the Seattle police. Although he'd inhaled some smoke, he'd insisted on staying at the scene to receive treatment. Ursula's therapy required a longer duration, but she wasn't going anywhere until they talked.

Her throat choked up. He must be going through hell. When Bill Cruikshank arrived, she'd overheard bits of their conversation, and shock whipped through her anew as she recalled their words. Mackie had bragged about witnessing his brother's shooting. Eve remained at a nearby hospital with her boyfriend, because Mackie had tried to rape her.

His sister-in-law. Ursula shivered.

Eleven years ago, Mackie could have saved Gabe's dad. Instead, tonight, *she* had saved her villainous boss.

She swallowed a sob.

"I need to check your vitals again," the attendant said.

"Okay." Ursula lifted the mask. "I don't need this anymore, thanks."

The earnest young woman set aside the equipment and strapped on a blood pressure cuff. "I'll determine that."

As the examination ended, Gabe finished his conversation with the group and strode toward the ambulance. Hurt and anger tightened his features, but caring lit his gaze as it caught hers. Love expanded in her heart, spilling over to flood her chest. He was so valiant. Courageous, selfless, and everything she had desired in a man someday.

But he was here now. For her. *With* her.

"How is she?" he asked the attendant, clasping Ursula's chilly hands between his large ones.

"Alive. You're lucky, both of you." The woman looked at Ursula. "You're doing well, but a visit to the Emergency Room remains in order."

"I'll drive us to the hospital to get checked out," Gabe said. "Can we have a moment alone?"

The attendant moved to the front of the vehicle with the equipment.

"Hi," Ursula murmured, as Gabe rubbed her chapped skin and the night wind rustled her grimy hair.

"Hi." He opened the water bottle and encouraged her to drink before downing a slug and setting aside the container. "Why didn't you go to the hospital?" he asked in a gentle tone, creating warm friction with their hands again.

"I wanted to stay with you." Ursula's voice emerged thin and feeble. They were alive and together. They had survived. But his eyes were bloodshot from the smoke, and soot smudged his face. Creases lined the corners of his mouth. "How are *you*?" she asked quietly. She had lost plenty tonight, but his family would never be the same.

"I feel like shit, to tell you the truth. I let down my mom. I moved away when she needed me, and look what happened."

"Gabe, no. Please don't say that." Ursula stilled his fingers, squeezing them. "She wanted you to live your life, to grow into the man you are today. Sometimes finding ourselves includes being away from our loved ones for years. Your mom is lucky to have a son like you. *I'm* so grateful you walked into my life two weeks ago. You *have* been here, for each of us, every day."

His expression softened, and emotion thickened his voice. "You're special, you know that? When I think of you putting your life on the line to save my so-called uncle—" He inhaled. "Your life is worth ten thousand of his."

She clutched his hands, the blankets shifting on her shoulders. "Gabe, I'm incredibly sorry about what happened to your dad. What kind of man is Mackie to flee a crime scene? Even if he made up the story to hurt your mom?"

He drew in an unsteady breath. "Bill's supervisor questioned him. Vic admitted my dad noticed him at the warehouse that night. His presence distracted Dad from the drug dealer." A muscle in Gabe's cheek ticked. "He hasn't changed his story about not being involved with the shooter's gang. He cried about how bad he felt leaving Dad. He says he was a coward, nothing more."

Oh, Gabe. "Do you believe him?"

"He's definitely a coward, but my gut says he's telling the truth about the shooter's crew. If he'd had dealings with the drug gang, someone would have ratted him out. Those goons were all about saving their own hides."

"Mackie is your uncle. That sort of betrayal—"

Gabe's chin firmed. "He's a criminal. His blackmailing of the council president and the attack on my mom tonight prove that. If

Victor doesn't recover from the damage to his lungs, it will serve him right."

Ursula nodded. The first ambulances had carted off Mackie and Shelly with police escorts. In addition to Mackie's rope burns and shock, he'd probably suffered a concussion when Gabe's mom defended herself. Shelly most certainly reeled from some sort of head trauma as a result of Ursula's dead-on aim with the chunk of Clive.

Both Mackie and Shelly had inhaled more smoke than Ursula or Gabe. Following treatment, each would face charges.

Poor Stacy. Ursula didn't look forward to revealing Shelly's plan to murder their boss. Given the love pyre Stacy had described, plus her sister's other erratic behavior, Ursula wouldn't be surprised to learn Shelly suffered from an undiagnosed mental disorder.

While she wouldn't wish Shelly's plans for Mackie on anyone, she hoped guilt for abandoning his wounded brother haunted the creep to *his* grave.

She pressed her forehead to Gabe's and whispered, "It will take time for you to come to grips with what happened to your dad."

"I've always felt something about that night wasn't right," he whispered in return. "Now I know why. It also explains a lot about the changes in Victor over the years. Guilt can do a number on a man's psyche, and his life has gone to hell since Dad's shooting. If Paul Bloomfield cooperates, Victor will head to jail for blackmail."

"The council president had *better* cooperate." In this day and age, the story would likely leak to the media. From there, it wasn't even a hop-skip-and-jump to total public condemnation on social media platforms. If the politician succumbed to blackmail based on phony pictures, he might be capable of worse behavior. His career aspirations would reach a rapid halt regardless of whether he pressed charges. "What about the women from the notepad?" she asked Gabe.

He placed light kisses on her knuckles. "I spoke to Mary Bliss this morning. She had good reason for paying off Victor, but a couple of years can put a new spin on things." His thumb caressed each spot he'd kissed. "Victor victimized a lot of women. The police might discover more evidence in his apartment, perhaps individuals not listed in the notepad. Paul might not be the only man."

"If one or two victims come forward, others might feel empowered to expose what he did to them," Ursula mused.

Gabe smiled. "Exactly."

"I heard Shelly say he's responsible for some of the studio vandalism, which he admitted."

"Under duress." Gabe lifted her chin. "Don't worry. The police will pursue all avenues. Victor wasn't a favorite of the Department's, and my dad was one of their brotherhood. They'll want justice served."

Ursula looked at the building. "I need to give my statement to the detectives." Doing so would entail reliving those awful moments when she'd thought about the house fire and equated Mackie to her helpless cat.

More like a plague-infested rat.

Gabe hugged her. She rested her head on his shoulder, drawing from his quiet strength and fortitude, his resilience and honor. Her eyes hurt and her temples pounded. With the stench of smoke clinging to her skin and her dirty hair sticking to her neck, she must resemble a scarecrow, but he cradled her as if she were a priceless gem.

She flicked another glance to the studio. Tonight reinforced more than ever that her heart belonged to her family...and now this man.

Gabe.

He murmured, "Don't worry about your plans for the studio, honey. The building is intact. Fire damaged the backroom and part of one hallway. The staffroom and bathroom reek from smoke bombs, but new paint will cover the smell. The water damage won't be as severe because the firefighters got here in time." He rubbed her spine, his hand comforting over the blankets. "You can approach the owner about assuming the lease. His insurance should cover repairs to the interior."

"Okay, stop right there." Scooting back on the ambulance cushion, she looked Gabe in the eyes. "I'm not buying this place or taking over any lease. After what Mackie did to your family, I refuse to be associated with him. As far as I'm concerned, our contract is toast." She smiled. "A little fire-survivor humor."

The fine lines around his eyes wrinkled. "You counted on building the business."

"Not *this* business. Not anymore. I don't care how long it takes, I'll find another job, and this time I won't let my goal to help my parents trap me in another dicey situation. After they learn the details of what happened here, if I took over the lease they would turn down any money I earned from the place anyway." And she wouldn't blame them. "They're stubborn about doing the right thing."

He kissed her hands. "Now I know where you got it from."

There went her butterflies again, a buoyancy she only experienced in his presence. "They wanted to drive here, but I asked them to meet us at the hospital." She'd called her parents before relinquishing her phone to a detective for the video of Mackie and Shelly. "They're probably freaking out."

"I'm surprised you're not feeling more stressed. What will you do?"

"You know, I've given myself a severe case of tunnel vision these last six months. I've been so focused on helping my family, I might not have considered the bigger picture."

"Photographer humor?" Gabe's lips quirked.

Ursula smiled. "I've expanded my commercial portfolio. I'm proud of my work. It won't all be in vain. I might try freelancing." If she could risk her life to save a couple of lowlifes, she could punch through her comfort zone to strike out on her own without the safety net of buying an established business. "I'm worried about *Seattle Lights* though. The editor is depending on me."

"I doubt she'll hold you responsible for the studio burning. You backed up your digital files?"

"Yes. I'm paranoid that way."

He chuckled, and she joined in. It was true. After a couple of episodes earlier in her career, she was a trifle vigilant, triple-saving everything. Tonight's fire would destroy the flash drive in her purse. For that matter, the flames would have charred her wallet, ID, and bank card. But another flash drive hid in Reba's glove compartment. Ursula updated her online data backup regularly, and her old laptop at home harbored files.

"The work I've done so far is secure," she said. "But our model

Deiter Reinhold was sick today. Even if he feels better tomorrow, will he want to participate? *His* standby might change his mind once the fire hits the news." The editor expected delivery of Ursula's files in two days. She would *not* miss her deadline. The rest of her life might be up in the air, but her determination hadn't changed.

Gabe gestured. "If you need a substitute for Deiter, I'm game."

She nudged his arm. "You're kidding."

"Nope." He grasped her hand on her lap, and her skin tingled. "If you need me to model for the magazine, we have pictures from last Wednesday night. Your work is half-done."

Her heart melted. "Gabe, that's so nice of you to offer." A former LA street cop turned PI and son of a fallen Seattle detective... The magazine's female readership would swoon.

"Well, I'd do anything for you, Sula, because I love you." He kissed her, and her pulse kicked, joy filling her. "I'm a real man, and I have a real life. All I need is a real love." He kissed her again. "I love you with my whole heart, baby. I know it's only been two weeks. I don't care. I love you."

Tears moistened her eyes. "Gabe, I love you too. I think that's part of why I crashed and burned this morning. I was trying to process everything." She kissed him. "I understand life won't always be easy, but I've fought my feelings for days. I've never been in love before. It scared me."

"Tell me about it. I've never been in love in my life."

"It's a first for both of us." They smiled at each other. Kissed tenderly.

Certainty filled Ursula. She wanted forever with this man. She had never experienced a truer, more vibrant, or powerful emotion. Her love for brave, caring, sexy Gabe McKenzie would surmount any challenge life threw in their path.

"You do realize what you're getting into?" she whispered against his whisker-roughened jaw. "Once I commit to something, I hang on for the long-term."

"You're my first love, Ursula. If I have anything to say about it, you'll be my last."

He kissed her again. As their lips touched and his hands caressed her arms beneath the blankets, overwhelming pleasure heated her from deep within. Never again would she tease couples like Deni and James. She'd joined the romance club.

Gabe said, "My truck is a short walk from here. Let's drive you to the hospital for that checkup." He removed the blankets from her shoulders and fetched her coat and water. "The detectives can take your statement after you see a doctor and speak to your family."

"You need to see your mom. Then you're getting checked out too." She cupped his face and made him look at her.

He grinned and kissed her nose. "Later, we can check each other out."

"You have a deal, Sherlock."

"I'll hold you to it, Nancy."

He helped her off the cushioned seat and into her sooty jacket. She tugged her grungy, stinky hair out from under the singed collar.

Hand in hand, they strolled toward the rest of their lives.

Acknowledgments

Thank you to my family for putting up with my creative eccentricities and to my kids for not minding when I have conversations with the beagle in front of your peers. I also owe a debt of thanks to several writer friends who supported me emotionally and creatively throughout the writing of this book, by reading early drafts and partials, brainstorming plot points and characterization, and providing understanding shoulders during the rough patches.

The first of these goes to the now-disbanded Looney Bin, my former brainstorming group. I miss you guys! Jamie Sobrato and Brenda Jernigan, my former critique partners and friends-for-life, read partials or fulls of an earlier manuscript that eventually blossomed into this story. Laura Langston and Susan Lyons, your perceptive eyes helped me see the characters in a different light at later stages of the writing and revision process. Thank you as well to Loreth Anne White for not throwing me off that balcony in Florida when she had the chance (consider the research possibilities!) and holding my hand during the following months of the writer's curse —waiting.

But most of all, I must thank Mary J. Forbes, whose reading of this book and help with some of the extensive research brought my characters to life in a way I can't explain. Mary, thank you for once more helping me see the forest for the trees. This story is the better for it.

About the Author

Cindy Procter-King writes steamy romcoms and contemporary romances bursting with laughter and emotion. Sassy feel-good fiction!

Cindy's books are available from eBook retailers all over the world, as well as in trade paperback, some library hardcover and large print, and some foreign editions.

Cindy lives in Canada with her family, Ghost'Da Allie McBeagle, and too many grand-dogs to count!

For more books and updates, visit:
www.cindyprocter-king.com

facebook.com/cindyprocterkingauthor
instagram.com/cindyprocterking
bookbub.com/authors/cindy-procter-king